HEIGHTS
OF GREEN

LISE
MacTague

Bel
BOO

201

Bella Books, Inc.
P.O. Box 10543
Tallahassee, FL 32302

First Bella Books Edition 2015

Editor: Medora MacDougall
Cover Designer: Sandy Knowles

ISBN: 9-781-59493-458-2

Other Bella Books by Lise MacTague

Depths of Blue

Acknowledgments

As always, thank you to my crew of alpha and beta readers (in no particular order): Lynn, Christina, Fern, Shari, and my mother Penny. It's doubtful I would have gotten through the first draft without your encouragement and reassurances that the book wasn't terrible. Thank you also to Mary Lou, my writing partner. Without our weekly writing sessions, I might still be working out the drafts. Finally, a big thanks to Medora MacDougall, my editor. Your suggestions were on point, and have made this a much better story.

About the Author

Lise MacTague left Winnipeg, Canada for warmer climes before realizing those had gigantic bugs, so she settled in Milwaukee, Wisconsin instead. Now she amuses herself by telling the natives it really isn't *that* cold. When not pestering Wisconsinites about the weather, Lise writes lesbian scifi and dreams of the day when she'll be able to quit her real job to write full time. This is her second novel.

Dedication

To my mother, Penny. Thank you for being willing to proofread my books. It means more to me than I can say that you'll wade through them in their excruciatingly rough forms. I appreciate every cleaned up comma, poorly-thought out metaphor, and heaving bosom. I know I don't have to tell you this, but never stop telling it to me like it is. I love you.

CHAPTER ONE

Torrin shook her head sharply and regretted it immediately. An insistent whine bored into her skull, rousing her from a deep, dreamless sleep. She tried to burrow into its embrace for a tiny bit longer, but the noise made further sleep nearly impossible. At the edge of her memory she had the impression of warmth and arms holding her close as she rested from...something. Something really nice. Her mind snatched at the elusive memory. Her fingers closed around it, and it disappeared, pricked out of existence like a soap bubble. The whine persisted, deepening its tone until her teeth vibrated against each other.

"Torrin. Torrin. Torrin." Dimly she became aware of her name being repeated over and over. The repetition quickly became as irritating as the incessant tone. Both became impossible to ignore any longer and she pried her eyes open.

White light stabbed into her retinas, sending pain shooting like lightning through her synapses. She clamped her teeth down on a whimper and forced her eyes open again. Slowly, the room around her swam into focus.

The view from the pod looked out into a brightly lit, white room. On the underside of the pod's lid was a monitor. The Asian woman on the screen smiled at her and stopped chanting the mantra of her name.

"Hello, Torrin!" Tien said, a little too cheerfully.

"Tien," Torrin acknowledged her. She smacked dry lips and probed them with a tongue that tasted like the inside of an old boot. Her memory trickled back as cryosleep was reversed. This was her least favorite part of the process. She sneezed at the sharp smell in her nostrils and moaned quietly at the stabbing pain behind her eyes. She squeezed her eyes shut and breathed through her mouth, waiting for the chemicals to clear out of her sinuses. It almost always took her some time to recover from being frozen and the cocktail of chemicals that went with it. In her life, she'd met exactly two people who could bounce back from cryosleep without any ill effects. Sadly, she didn't have that talent, and every time she thawed out, she resented it.

She sniffed experimentally. The acrid odor was almost gone, leaving the blessed smell of nothingness. The ship's filters scrubbed the air so well that the ship was almost odorless. Torrin swallowed to work some moisture back into her throat.

"What's our status?"

"We have arrived in the Nadierzda system, Torrin," the AI informed her. "I have queried the buoys outside the asteroid field and have received the safe route through the field."

"Good," Torrin grunted, her voice cracking from disuse. "What about—"

"The League of Solaran Planets ship, the *Icarus*?" Tien waited patiently until Torrin nodded. "There has been no sign of them, Torrin. They still had not emerged from the nebula when we made our jump into peripheral space. The sensors revealed no other ships along our same course in the periphery."

Sourly, Torrin nodded. She'd always believed that Tien was highly entertained by her need for recovery time. The AI was always so inordinately pleased with herself when Torrin was thawing out. Eyes opening wide as another memory surfaced, she tried to sit up and knocked her forehead on the underside of the lid.

"Dammit, Tien, open this thing!" With one hand to her forehead, she started disengaging the needles and tubing from her legs with the other. "How is Jak doing?"

The lid hissed as the seal was broken and residual gases leaked out. "As can be expected, Torrin, there has been no change to her status. I have not yet brought her out of stasis."

Torrin went limp with relief. Problems in cryosleep were extremely rare but not unheard of. With the run of bad luck she and the sniper had experienced, it wouldn't have surprised her to find out that something had gone terribly wrong with Jak.

"Good. Let's keep her frozen until we land so she can be brought out of stasis with a real doctor present. No offense." She hastened to reassure the AI.

"None taken, Torrin," Tien replied.

By now the lid was fully open and Torrin's eyes had adjusted to the light. It really wasn't that bright, but her eyes were so sensitive from her time in stasis that even dim light caused pain.

"How long were we in?" Torrin asked. She climbed shakily out of the pod, pulling the last of the tubes from where they inserted into the veins of her arms. She cast about until she saw a white robe draped over a nearby bench.

"A little less than two months, Torrin."

That was longer than normal. The smuggler tottered over to the bench on muscles stiff from forced confinement and sat down heavily before pulling on the robe.

"Why so long?" she finally asked when the AI was less than forthcoming.

"A star in our trajectory had gone supernova, Torrin. Even in peripheral space, the ripples rendered that area impassable. I had to reroute our FTL jumps to recalculate a safe trajectory around the spot."

Now that was more like her luck lately. Stars didn't go supernova every day, at least not the ones between her and her destination. It did account for the delay in their journey. The supernova had likely required Tien to make at least two extra jumps, possibly more. Jumping into peripheral space didn't take long, but dropping back into normal space was a longer process. The ship had to slow down enough that it didn't tear itself apart upon reentry. Running through the process more times than she'd planned for would significantly delay them. In this case it had added a few weeks onto their trip.

Torrin worked her legs and arms as she sat, working blood back into limbs that had been blood-deprived for two months. In the cryo process, after the sedative was administered, the sleeper's blood was removed from the body and stored in tanks attached to the pod. Chemicals were then introduced into the body so that the body's tissues didn't freeze solid. It kept pesky things like frostbite from taking fingers, toes, arms or legs. It also took some getting used to when the blood returned. Her tissues weren't exactly oxygen-deprived, but they were no longer used to moving or having blood flowing through them.

Pushing herself up from the bench, Torrin tottered over to the chamber's only other occupied stasis pod. She wiped away the frost rimming the outside of the pod's window and gazed tenderly down on her lover's face. Jak's face was at peace in a way she'd never seen while they were on the sniper's home planet. With any luck, it was a look she would be seeing more often now that they were almost to Torrin's home.

The civil war-torn planet of Haefen was about as different from Nadierzda as two planets could be and still be habitable. Haefen was all shades of blue and full of soaring trees, craggy mountains and hills. Nadi was sandy browns and yellows shot through with verdant greens. What trees they had were stunted by comparison as a result of sandy soil and nearly constant wind. Still, Torrin loved her planet as only someone who had grown up there could understand. The mere thought of rolling plains and meadows topped by tall cliffs sent a wave of homesickness washing over her. She wasn't often homesick, preferring instead to roam the outer reaches of the galaxy, known as the Fringes. She loved her planet, but for years a severe case of wanderlust had kept her unable to put down roots for long.

Slowly, she traced a fingertip over the glass, around what would have been the contour of Jak's face had she been able to touch her.

"Soon, babe. We'll be home soon," Torrin promised quietly.

She stopped in her cabin quickly on the way to the bridge but only to throw on a set of real clothing. She would be damned if she would come home wearing nothing but a flimsy robe. A quick change and brushing of teeth later and she was ensconced in her seat on the bridge.

The monitor in front of her was lit up with the best route to Nadierzda, which lay on the other side of a large asteroid field. The ever-shifting mass of space debris was the planet's first line of defense. The field was dense enough that it was difficult to scan through. Torrin knew for a fact that the planet didn't exist on any League star charts. Everyone who lived there did their best to make sure the League stayed blissfully unaware of their existence.

Because there were so many asteroids in the field, a sophisticated network of buoys and markers had been liberally seeded amongst the floating rocks. When properly queried, the marker buoys would provide a constantly updated map of the best paths through the field. If the buoys were queried without the password, the only output would be a line of gibberish that looked for all the world like the last gasps of some antiquated computer system. Even the buoys had been painstakingly crafted to look like just so much space junk.

Torrin scrutinized the path carefully. She could have let Tien bring them in. With the current map, the AI was perfectly capable of taking them through the asteroid field. It was a point of pride for Torrin to bring them through herself. Truth be told, it was mostly that she really didn't like someone else controlling her ship. While she was in stasis, there was nothing for it. Since she didn't have a way around that, she made up for it by piloting the ship herself whenever possible. Plus, she told herself, if the AI was down, she knew she'd be able to bring them home regardless.

The flight in was as tortuous and winding as ever. It was impractical and dangerous to speed through it, but Torrin was able to take some solace in the fact that she had the record for the fastest time through the field... unless someone had broken it while she was gone. She doubted it, but stranger things had happened. She bumped up their speed a little more. They weren't redlining it by any stretch, but they were definitely pushing the edges of sanity, especially given the way the asteroids drifted around her. The urgency of Jak's situation drove her, desperate, before it. Nothing could happen while Jak was in cryostasis, which should have reassured Torrin. Logic had nothing to do with it, though. She could no more take her time than she could stop breathing.

When they were three-quarters of the way through the field, Torrin switched on her comm system to scan the bands. Communications with the surface were on a variable frequency, another practice designed to hide the planet. If she'd been home remotely close to on schedule, she would have known which frequency to tune in to, but as it was she'd have to scan for it. There had been no point in looking for the frequency outside the asteroid belt; the moving masses of rock broke up most communication unless it was hooked into the buoy network. One frequency in particular seemed clearer than most of the others.

"Control, this is the *Calamity Jane*. Come back."

A burst of static met her words, then the comm crackled to life.

"Torrin! Is that you? You're late as hell!"

The smuggler grinned to hear a voice she recognized. "Nat, is that you?"

"Damn right, it's me. You gone so long you don't recognize your own sister's voice anymore?" Nat sounded like she was having a hard time deciding whether to be annoyed or amused. "You know there were people who were ready to give you up for dead."

"I can guess who," Torrin replied dryly.

"Well, yeah. Nothing ever changes around here. You should know that better than any of us."

"True enough." Torrin's voice turned serious. "Look, I need you to do me a huge favor. We'll be landing in about twenty minutes and I need you to get a doctor to meet us."

Nat's voice sobered immediately. "No problem. I'll get Kiera in. Are you all right?"

"I'm fine. I don't need her for me."

"You becoming a passenger service?" Torrin loved her sister, but she could be overly curious. She'd been on the verge of telling her about Jak, but something held her back. Everyone would know about her soon enough and she wanted to keep Jak to herself a little bit longer. Things were going to get complicated quickly, and she needed a light touch. Besides, the other women on the planet, especially those who'd been born and were living their lives there, viewed new arrivals as fresh meat. Jak would have so many women vying for her interest that she wouldn't know what to do with herself.

Seething jealousy broke her focus for a moment, surprising her. She knew she liked the sniper, liked her a lot in fact. The idea of Jak with another woman made her want to break something. That was new. She'd never felt strongly enough about any of her previous lovers to bother with jealousy. Usually, when they found someone else the separation came as a relief. It meant she didn't have to hurt them by breaking things off. This was something different. She wasn't the jealous one in her relationships. Not her. Not ever!

Torrin took a deep breath. The Ruling Council would want to get its mitts all over her business on this one. The beginnings of the plan that were still percolating in her brain were audacious, to say the least. The less the council knew, the better. There were strong isolationist forces on the council and among the planet's inhabitants. Everything would have to be prepared and presented just so to get the council's approval. Her plan wasn't ready for that, and it wouldn't be until she'd had the chance to go over it with her business partners. It would soon be all over Landing that she had requested a doctor for someone. She would decide later how they would spin the entire situation. Now, though, she had to give Nat something to keep her off her case. All that mattered was getting Jak well and pushing through the deal.

"Hello, Nadierzda to Torrin," Nat prompted her when the silence went on too long. "You there?"

Torrin shook her head. "Yeah, I'm here." She paused again, trying to figure out how she was going to explain Jak to Nat. "I ran into someone who needed my help. The doctor's for her."

Now it was her turn to wait as a long silence fell over the comm.

"I...see," Nat said. Torrin could hear the shit-eating grin in the warmth of her voice and she colored in response. It was a good thing their connection was audio only. The blush would have given her away for sure.

"It's complicated. Just have Kiera meet us when we land," Torrin instructed. "*Jane* out." She terminated the transmission abruptly. She never liked to explain herself to her sister, but for some reason Nat's amusement offended her. A few moments later instructions popped up on her screen, directing her to land in the small spaceport's rarely used emergency services area.

Kiera was a great doctor and she would be able to handle Jak's needs without any problems. Torrin knew they would take the callout seriously.

A ship's AI could handle all but the most severe cases through its onboard medbays. So when someone came in requesting a doctor to meet the ship, it was because something had come up that was more than the AIs could handle.

A few minutes later she cleared the asteroid field. She could see Nadi in the distance, increasing rapidly in size as she barreled toward it. The planet was mostly bands of sandy brown, pocked by interlocking craters of brilliant green. Many centuries before, some hotel company had claimed the planet and had started terraforming it to turn into a luxury resort destination for rich people. The planet's orbit around the solar system's young sun had been altered, warming it up, but more importantly, moving it away from the asteroid belt. Unfortunately, before the terraforming process was completed, the company had gone bankrupt and the planet had been left as is. Torrin had heard it estimated that when the company pulled out, the planet had been halfway to completion. As it was right now, maybe a quarter of the surface was habitable.

Since Nadierzda had seen many collisions with asteroids as a result of its proximity to the field, it had plenty of impact craters. Only the sunken places escaped the constant dust-laden winds that scoured the planet's surface. These provided shelter from the wind which had wiped out the other verdant areas. Even so, every year they lost a little more arable land to the wind. One of the reasons Torrin was so set on making money was so they could finish terraforming the planet before the remaining habitable areas became choked by dust and sand.

"Tien, are we cleared for landing?" Torrin asked the AI as the planet's surface filled her main viewscreen. They were going to enter the upper level of the atmosphere soon and she wanted to make sure she had a clear shot. She was going to bring the *Jane* in hot. The faster they got to the surface, the faster Jak would be taken care of.

"Affirmative, Torrin. All flight traffic has been diverted from our entry vector."

"Good." Torrin gritted her teeth as they hit the atmosphere. The ship's speed made for a turbulent entry, but she could handle a little bumpiness if it meant seeing Jak again that much sooner. She kept a close eye on the hull integrity readouts. If something had compromised the hull in the nebula, the stresses of atmospheric entry were when it was most likely to show up. Their descent slowed and the buffeting eased. To her relief there were no hull issues.

They broke through the sparse clouds into a dust storm in the upper atmosphere. Torrin was accustomed to flying in such weather, but today the annoyance she typically felt with the storms threatened to flare into full-blown anger. She didn't have time for this bullshit.

"We are cleared to land immediately, Torrin," Tien informed her. Torrin nodded tersely in acknowledgment and applied herself to piloting the ship into Nadi's small spaceport as speedily as possible.

The spaceport stood at the edge of the only settlement on the planet that was big enough to properly be called a city. The locals referred to it simply as Landing. According to local legend, this was where the planet's discoverers had first landed. Their first touchdown had been less than controlled, but, as Torrin had often joked, Crashing wouldn't have been as catchy a name for the settlement.

They broke through the clouds and the green of Landing's main crater yawned beneath them. The main crater itself was hundreds of kilometers wide, not to mention the stretches of interconnected craters that spread out from the main crater like beads on a particularly haphazard necklace.

Today's flight path brought them in over the city. She could see its long, low buildings. Unlike other planets, where large buildings were typically built up, on Nadierzda they dug down into the surface. Tall buildings were at the mercy of wind that carried with it particles of fine sand and dust which eroded tall structures very quickly.

The grid of the streets below suggested that whoever had laid out the city had an extremely organized mind. The layout was all geometry and ninety degree angles, but with enough variation that it had a certain severe beauty. It always reminded Torrin of the ancient Earth artist Mondrian.

Finally the spaceport hove into view. *Jane* screamed over it and Torrin gripped the yoke then twisted sharply, skewing the ship steeply to the left, then down in one motion. With an extra flourish on the controls, she brought the ship to rest mere meters from the walkway. She cut the engines and disengaged herself as an umbilical walkway extruded itself from the side of the spaceport to adhere to *Jane's* nearest airlock.

As she walked down the hallway toward the airlock, she heard hissing as pressure equalized. Tien must have released the locking mechanism.

Torrin was greeted with a babble of voices. A tall woman with cinnamon-hued skin and many long black dreadlocks looked down at her. Torrin wasn't short by any stretch, but Kiera always made her feel self-conscious about her height. Her gray eyes startled Torrin whenever she saw them for the first time in a long while.

"Torrin," Kiera called out to her. She opened her arms and enfolded Torrin in a long hug, pulling her head back to bestow a warm kiss upon her cheek. Yes, they'd been involved, but that had been many years ago. That was one relationship where Torrin had managed to hang on to the close friendship that had evolved from their amorous encounters.

Torrin surprised and horrified herself by bursting into tears.

CHAPTER TWO

Kiera tightened her arms around Torrin.

"Frozen hells, I'm sorry," Torrin tried to apologize through hiccupping sobs.

"It's okay, you have nothing to worry about," Kiera reassured her. The others on the medical team did their best to pretend they were somewhere else. She knew a few of them by sight, but only one other by name. Fortunately, the only one in the group she'd actually slept with was Kiera.

"You must really care for her."

The smuggler nodded. She was trying to bring herself back under some semblance of control, and talking about the situation threatened to burst the floodgates open again. Through it all, Kiera kept her in the warm, comforting embrace.

"I think I'm good, thanks," Torrin finally said after a few moments. The sudden flood of tears was embarrassing in the extreme. She wasn't usually a crier, but there she was being comforted by one of her exes while her current lover was on ice right down the hall. Awkward didn't even begin to describe how she felt. She stepped out of the circle of Kiera's arms and gestured down the hall.

"She's still in cryostasis. I thought it would be best if she was thawed out with you guys there." The tears threatened to rise once more. Her throat was tightening and she cleared it roughly. "You can get the particulars from Tien."

Kiera pressed a gentle hand on Torrin's forearm. "It's all right, we've already queried your AI on the condition of the patient. We're ready to proceed whenever you are. She'll be at the clinic. You can meet us there after you've taken care of things here."

"I'll go with you." The doctor looked a little shocked at the statement.

"What? Tien is perfectly capable of locking the *Jane* down." Kiera stared at her, both eyebrows raised. Their short relationship had fallen apart after Kiera had accused her of caring more for the ship than for her. Frankly, the accusation had contained more than a grain of truth to it, more like a mound of truth, really. At the time, it was a convenient excuse to get out of a relationship that was already causing her emotional claustrophobia to flare up.

"If you say so." The doctor turned to address the small group of waiting women. "Ladies, you know what to do. Let's get the thawing process started while we take the patient back to the clinic."

The waiting women moved into purposeful action. As one, they swarmed down the hall to the cryochamber.

"Her name is Jak," Torrin felt compelled to tell Kiera. "Do your best for her."

"We will, Torrin. She's in good hands."

"I know."

* * *

Jak could hear muted voices buzzing above her head, back and forth. She strained to hear what they said but couldn't make anything out. She floated in dark emptiness and the voices were the only stimuli she could discern. All around her was darkness. Her limbs felt very far away. With effort, she thought she might be able to move them, but it seemed like far too much work.

"You're in a bit of a fix, aren't you?" A familiar voice spoke to her out of the darkness nearby. A young blond man with a familiar grin stood at her right when she turned her head. He was standing on nothing and was surrounded by the shadows.

"Bron!" Jak exclaimed. She tried to reach out to him, but her so-distant limbs were too slow to react. "What are you doing here?"

"That's a good question," he replied, raising an eyebrow at her. She'd always hated when he did that. Behind that raised eyebrow she knew he was laughing at her and she hated being laughed at. Now, however, she couldn't remember seeing anything as wonderful and welcome as that sardonic eyebrow.

"Are you going to tell me about the mess I made? That's what you've done every other time I've seen you since you died."

"I think you already know what kind of a mess you're in. I wouldn't be here otherwise."

"So you won't lecture me about hooking up with Torrin?"

"Does she make you happy?" He tilted his head and fixed her with an uncharacteristically serious gaze.

"Yeah, she does," Jak said. "Happier than I've been since you died, maybe even before that."

"I'm not going to tell you I think it's right, but it's nice to see you happy. But that's not why I'm here." His eyes were still on her, piercing through her skin and into her soul as if he was willing her to come to some realization.

"Then what?"

Bron sighed. "You never were one for any kind of metaphysical discussion, were you?" He shook his head and grinned. "You've always been the practical one. I was the dreamer. Jak, I'm here for you, if you want." He held out a hand to her. "All you have to do is come with me and this will all stop. The hurting will stop and the loneliness, the isolation. We'll be together again."

She stared at his outstretched hand for a moment. It seemed so simple. Everything would be over and she'd never be alone again. She started to reach her hand toward his. The limbs that had seemed so far away before now obeyed her without even the slightest hesitation.

Her hearing suddenly intensified. In the echoing darkness she could hear voices, raised in alarm.

"Damn it, she's coding!" A woman's voice exploded above her head.

"Get that suction in there, she can't breathe. Her lungs are filling with blood." A second female voice barked orders to the first. Jak didn't feel anything; all she could hear were the voices. Her hand wavered, hesitating.

"Stay with us, Jak," the first voice ordered. They knew her name. *Where am I?* She couldn't remember the last time she'd heard a woman's voice other than Torrin's.

"Jak, baby, you need to be strong." As if her thoughts had summoned Torrin, the smuggler's voice sounded in her head. *She's begging. Why is she begging?* Desperation gave Torrin's voice a ragged edge that burrowed into her. "Come on, Jak! I need you to come back to us."

A small warm spot suddenly bloomed on one of her cheeks. Jak raised her fingers to her face and the tips came away wet. *Crying. Torrin's crying over me.* If she went back, she wouldn't be alone. Torrin was there.

Jak turned to face Bron and lowered her hand.

"I can't," she said simply.

"I know," Bron replied, smiling a gentle expression she'd never seen on his face when he was alive. "I know, but you had to know also. You have something to live for now. I can't say I approve, but I'm glad you won't be alone."

"When did you get so wise?"

The sardonic smile was back. "About the time I took a sniper's bullet to the throat. Be good to yourself, sister-mine. And don't take things so seriously. You'll have a much better time." He faded, growing steadily less distinct.

"Bron, wait!" Jak cried, reaching toward him with both hands. "Can't you stay for a little while longer?"

"I'm not the one going," she heard him say faintly, so quietly she almost couldn't hear him. "You are."

She only had a moment to wonder what he'd meant before her vision exploded into brightness. Strange shapes surrounded her, and a form loomed over her, masked and swathed in white. Pain hit her like a sledgehammer. Her chest was on fire, and she tried to suck in a breath, rib cage heaving. Arms grabbed her suddenly flailing limbs and held her down. Alarmed at the restriction, Jak fought back with everything she had.

"She's back," the first woman's voice issued from behind the mask. "Keep her still so she doesn't hurt herself."

Jak felt warm hands on her face and her wildly rolling eyes met Torrin's over a face mask. She would have recognized those moss-green eyes anywhere.

"It's okay, Jak," Torrin assured her. "They're trying to help."

Trying to help. Surely Torrin wouldn't lead her astray. Jak relaxed her struggles and the hands holding her down gripped her less tightly.

"We're going to give her something to put her to sleep so we can help," the first voice said. "Is that okay?"

Jak nodded even though it seemed to her like the question had been directed at Torrin. The smuggler nodded as well and warm lassitude swept over Jak. Darkness threatened to overwhelm her. She resisted as long as she could before letting go and falling back through the darkness. The feeling of hands warm upon her cheeks went with her into the dark.

* * *

Torrin sat on a hard bench and leaned her head back until it thumped gently against the wall. Her eyes were shut, and she was exhausted. Kiera had permitted her to be in the room while they thawed Jak, and things had gone sideways very quickly. Apparently the damage to her lungs had been more acute than anyone had realized, and when she came out of cryosleep the damage became unexpectedly and catastrophically active.

While Torrin was glad she'd been there, it had been one of the hardest things she'd ever had to do. Seeing Jak like that, looking so small on the clinic bed with all those people working to keep her alive, had sliced into her heart. There had been a point when she'd thought Jak was gone; her vitals hadn't even registered on the monitors. Everyone on the medical team had kept laboring over her, though, and suddenly she'd been back. Torrin still wasn't completely certain that Jak had really been awake, but seeing her eyes open and locked onto hers had been heartening.

The bench creaked and shifted as someone sat next to her. She opened her eyes to see Kiera sitting next to her. The doctor also looked exhausted, but she'd taken the time to change out of her blood-spattered steri-scrubs.

"That was close," Kiera said.

"I wasn't expecting things to go bad so quickly. What happened?"

The doctor shook her head. "At some point during the cryogenic process, crystals formed in her lungs. Her blood should have been removed during the process, but from what I could tell, some of it pooled in her lungs and couldn't be completely removed. When it froze, it crystallized and lacerated the surrounding lung tissue." She shrugged. "When she thawed, the lacerated tissue hemorrhaged."

Her words hit Torrin in the chest like a mallet. In trying to save Jak, she'd almost killed her. Some of what she was feeling must have showed on her face because Kiera leaned over and placed a hand on Torrin's arm.

"Torrin, you couldn't know this would happen." She squeezed Torrin's forearm reassuringly. "You made the best decision you could under difficult circumstances. The best thing you could have done is what you did. It's also a damn good thing that you waited until we were there before thawing her out."

It helped a little bit to hear that from the doctor, but guilt still writhed within her.

"Besides, I know she means a lot to you," Kiera continued. "Waiting to thaw her must have been hard to do."

"Can I see her yet?" Torrin was uncomfortable with Kiera's insight into the situation and tried to change the subject. From the look the doctor gave her, she hadn't succeeded.

"You can go and sit with her. She'll probably sleep for a while yet."

"I'm used to that," Torrin said. It felt like she'd spent half their relationship waiting for the sniper to awaken.

"If she does wake up, make sure you keep her calm. She's stable for now, but if she gets upset or stressed, that could change."

"Don't worry, I'll be good."

"That's what I'm worried about." Kiera laughed, then stood and clasped Torrin's shoulder in a brief squeeze. "Come and find me when you're ready to talk."

Torrin crossed the hall to peer through the small window in the door. She could see Jak's form on the bed. The sniper was hooked up to a frightening array of equipment. So far things hadn't gone at all like she'd expected. Instead of introducing Jak to the world she called home, she'd almost killed her instead. After watching her lover sleep for a few more moments, Torrin couldn't take it any longer. She crossed into the room, doors hissing open to grant her entrance.

From up close, Jak didn't look any better. She wasn't a large woman and the room's machinery dwarfed her. A tube exited the side of her rib cage, shuttling blood away from her lungs so she could breathe. The lower half of her face was covered by a clear half-mask that pumped oxygen into her lungs.

Torrin pulled a chair up to the side of the bed and reached carefully around all the tubes, wires and other pieces of machinery to take Jak's hand. It was nothing close to what she wanted to do. If she could have, she would have crawled onto the bed and cradled Jak to her, but not with all that equipment. She didn't want to accidentally kill her again.

The door hissed open and someone knocked gently on the doorframe. She turned her head to see Nat standing in the doorway.

"You look like shit," Nat told her bluntly as she crossed the room to join Torrin by the bed.

"Thanks so much," Torrin replied. "I'm doing my best to stay upright right now, so cut me some slack."

Nat perched on the arm of the chair. Her warm brown eyes gazed worriedly down on her sister. As usual, her chocolate-brown hair was cut short, though not nearly as short as Torrin's hair currently was. Nat ran a hand over Torrin's scalp and she irritably ducked her head out of the way.

"That's short."

Torrin snorted. "I didn't have any choice in the matter."

"Never thought I'd see you with hair this short. You trying to match your girlfriend, or are you finally picking up on current fashion? I think you might've overdone it." Nat reached back over again and rubbed her hand over the auburn stubble on Torrin's head. She grinned cheekily when Torrin glared at her.

"She's not my girlfriend. Not exactly. Or not yet. I don't know. Like I said, it's complicated."

Nat turned her head to watch Jak speculatively where she lay, oblivious. "If she's not yours then maybe she'll have some time for me. She's cute and obviously closer to my age than yours."

"She's not available! You leave her—" Torrin stopped abruptly when she realized that Nat was grinning down at her again. "You little…" She shook her head and turned her gaze back to Jak.

"You must be tired," Nat noted. "You never let me win an argument.

Look, why don't you go get some sleep. You know cryostasis by itself is hard on the body. And with everything else you've had to deal with, you look ready to keel over. Or if you want to stick around, you could fill me in on your not-girlfriend."

Sleep sounded like a really good idea, a much better idea than filling Nat in on all the gory details. Torrin didn't want to leave Jak alone; she knew what it was like to be a stranger on a strange planet. Still, her eyes drifted shut at the mere thought of rest.

"I can't," she said, shaking her head to clear it. "I need to be here when she wakes up."

"So sack out next door. The room's empty and I can get you if she comes to. It doesn't look like she's going to wake up any time soon, though."

Try as she might, Torrin couldn't come up with a good reason not to go take a nap.

"Fine, but you need to come and get me as soon as she so much as twitches." Torrin stood, and it was her turn to look down on her sister. "I mean it, Nat. Come and get me, don't use the opportunity to interrogate her about…whatever. She's in no condition for that right now."

By the smile on Nat's face, Torrin knew that Nat could read what she wasn't saying perfectly well. Nat knew Torrin didn't want her interrogating Jak on their relationship and Torrin's refusal to even admit to it amused her to no end.

"Don't worry, I'll come and get you," Nat said. "You might tell me her name, so I don't need to ask her before I get you."

"Jak, okay? Her name is Jak." Torrin crossed the small room and stood in front of the open doorway. She looked back over her shoulder at the too-small form in the bed. Nat had turned to look over Jak's still body.

"Nat?" Her sister glanced over her shoulder. "Thanks."

"You got it. That's what sisters are for, after all."

CHAPTER THREE

The darkness that had enfolded her in its embrace was receding again. Jak had floated there for a while, warm and safe, but she was afraid of what she would face when the darkness let her go completely. Awareness returned to her one sense at a time. First to come was sound. It was mostly quiet, which was a relief after the chaos into which she'd previously woken. All she could make out were a rhythmic whooshing noise and repetitive beeping. They weren't loud, but they were persistent. For a while she was content to lie there and listen to the noises.

As she listened to those sounds, the darkness lightened. Her eyes were closed, but the space she was in must have been well lit. She tried to open her eyes for a few seconds, but they didn't want to cooperate and she had no desire to force them. The smell of antiseptic tickled her nostrils. She must be in a hospital or clinic of some sort, though there was a strange difference to the scent. It was a little fruity, almost, but that wasn't quite it. Under the antiseptic was dryness. It smelled hot and arid, like sand that had been out in direct sun for hours. It was nothing like the damp loaminess of the forests that Jak was used to experiencing. She wanted to smack her lips, but her body still wasn't responding.

As her sense of touch returned, she could feel sheets under her fingertips. They were smooth and soft, a far cry from the rough linens she'd had to sleep on while in the army. They felt a little like the sheets she'd had when she was a little girl, before her mother died. Her mother had liked nice things, but after she died, her father didn't seem to want them anymore. Whether it was because he couldn't afford them or because they reminded him too much of his dead wife, nice sheets hadn't stayed for long.

With touch came tightness in her chest. Her lungs were inflating and deflating on their own, but she wasn't quite able to draw a full breath. Iron bands were clamped around her rib cage. With the awareness of tightness, an ache bloomed. It rose in her like a wave until the pain crested and she was, unfortunately, completely aware.

The beeping she'd been hearing picked up speed and her eyes popped open. She tried to put a hand to her chest, but her limbs still weren't responding properly. The best she was able to do was flop her right arm over a few inches.

An unfamiliar face swam into view. The concerned eyes that met hers were warm brown beneath delicately arched eyebrows. Her skin was dusky in a way Jak had never seen before. It was a far cry from the pale skin she was used to seeing back home. The woman looked like she'd spent a lifetime out in the sun. A nose that was too strong for its own good jutted out over lips a smidgeon too full.

"Jak, it's okay, I'm a friend." Her voice was low but pleasant, almost furry. The accent was clipped and reminded her of Torrin's, the vowels open and the rhythm lilting, with sharp consonants. The woman, little older than a girl really, pushed herself up. "I'll be right back."

Jak tracked the girl with her eyes as she hurried to the other side of the room where a door opened of its own accord and she disappeared into the hallway. Jak couldn't make out what she was saying, but she was calling out to someone. Moments later Torrin appeared in the doorway, eyes heavy-lidded from sleep. The smuggler rushed to her bedside and perched in the recently vacated chair. She took Jak's hand. The incredible pain in her chest didn't exactly go away, but with Torrin there, it was a little easier to bear. The rapid beeping slowed a little bit at Torrin's touch.

"Jak, I'm here," Torrin said, rubbing the back of her hand with a thumb. "How are you feeling?"

She took a breath to talk, but pain seared through her chest again. Torrin caught her wince and turned to the young woman standing beside her.

"Nat, go get Kiera," Torrin ordered. "She's in pain." She recaptured Jak's hand. "You don't need to say anything, it's all right."

Lying there and being unable to fend for herself was quite a foreign concept to Jak. She was used to relying on herself, especially since Bron died. She wasn't sure how she felt about Torrin hovering over her. On the one hand it was gratifying to know Torrin cared for her that much. At the same time she was a little testy that she couldn't simply get up and take care of things on her own. While she struggled with the foreign feeling of being dependent, the door hissed back open and a tall woman with skin even darker than Nat's came in. Nat walked through the doors on her heels, her forehead creased with concern. The woman wore a white coat with a multitude of pockets; strange instruments protruded from many of them. Her long hair was in a multitude of knotted locks that were pulled back so they cascaded down past the middle of her back. Beads on the ends of the locks clacked and clinked softly as they moved against each other. Her eyes were so dark that Jak couldn't tell where the pupil ended and the iris began.

"How are you feeling, Jak?" the tall woman asked. Jak recognized her voice from when she'd come to during all that pain and confusion.

"She's in pain, Kiera," Torrin answered indignantly before Jak could say anything. Torrin subsided quickly at Kiera's impatient glance. "Sorry," she said, her face contrite though the intensity of her eyes belied the word. Jak couldn't believe it. She hadn't seen Torrin back down to anyone before.

Kiera turned back to Jak.

"Hurts," she whispered. It was the best she could manage; talking any louder would have required a deeper breath than she was capable of. "My chest."

The doctor nodded. "That's to be expected, I'm afraid. The freezing process for cryostasis damaged your lungs rather severely. We had to open your rib cage to get them healed enough that you wouldn't drown in your own blood." Kiera produced a tablet from her pocket and manipulated the touch screen. With a flick of her wrist, she transferred the image on her tablet to the wall opposite Jak's bed. She started pointing out various details and sites on an enormous scan of Jak's lungs. Jak tried to follow the explanation, but the pain in her chest made it impossible to focus on anything for very long.

Kiera looked over and realized she'd lost her patient's attention. Her eyes softened as soon as she became aware of Jak's agony.

"I can give you something for the pain, but like any drug it has side effects." She turned to Torrin. "I wish you'd brought some of the stimulant she took. Some drugs hang around in the system for a long time. You really never know how different pharmaceuticals will interact, especially not ones developed on other planets."

Jak had started nodding as soon as Kiera had mentioned a drug for the pain. The doctor was arrested in her aside when Torrin once again redirected her attention back to Jak.

"Very well. I'll have a nurse bring the painkiller to you. Make sure to let someone know if you're having any problems." She smiled wryly at Torrin. "Though I imagine we'll be hearing about it right away."

Torrin's face was suddenly suffused with color. She was blushing. *Is she embarrassed by me?* The thought brought more pain, though a different type than Jak was already feeling. The beeping monitor behind her sped up again and Kiera looked down at her in concern.

"The pain must really be getting to you. I'll have someone come right in." The tall doctor strode through the doorway and out of sight down the hall.

"Don't worry, babe," Torrin said, pulling Jak's hand against her chest. "You'll feel better soon."

The first woman had been standing quietly in a corner of the room, but with Kiera gone, she moved in to stand next to Torrin.

"Babe?" she asked Torrin, her voice light and full of mirth. "You do have it bad. The only pet name I've ever heard out of you is the one you used when you were putting me to bed."

Torrin grimaced up at her, cheeks slightly flushed. "Jak, let me introduce Nat. She's my baby sister. We were both raised by the same women, more or less." She wrinkled her nose at the young woman. "If she's being a particular pain in your ass, you can call her *mozhka*. It means 'gnat' in Old Russian. You know, like the insect." Torrin reached out and ruffled her sister's close-cropped hair.

Jak nodded tiredly at the youngster. Nat probably wasn't that much younger than she was, but she had an irrepressible air that made her seem much younger. Of course, she probably hadn't grown up in the middle of a civil war. Jak hadn't had much of a childhood, and she knew she tended to act and seem older than she was, certainly older than she looked. That was normal on Haefen. She only knew because some of the oldsters would lament the loss of their children's innocence and hope for a day when the war was behind them.

A short woman bustled through the door with a glass vial in her hand. She was in her middle years with a plump, matronly look to her.

"Jak," she smiled warmly down at her, "I'm going to give you something for the pain, all right?"

That sounded like heaven and Jak nodded as eagerly as she could without sending any more pain through her chest. The woman stood next to her and affixed the vial to a port branching from a long, thin tube that ran from the wall into Jak's chest, right below her collarbone.

"This will make you feel so much better," the nurse chattered away. "Almost as good as this one does, I'm sure." She winked at Jak and pointedly ignored Torrin. There was a strange expression on Torrin's face. She seemed torn between shame and rueful amusement.

Almost as soon as the medication was administered, the pain began to fade. The agony drained away in a slow ebb. She inhaled, reflexively bracing herself for discomfort. There was some pain, but it was removed, like it belonged to someone else.

"Better, dear?" the nurse beamed down at her. "Good. You make sure to call for me if you need help. Name's Bethenny." The nurse gave Torrin a sharp look before bustling back out of the room.

"You'll have to excuse how women act around Torrin," Nat put in before Torrin could say anything. "Either she's a sex symbol to them, or they're annoyed because she's a sex symbol to others." If Jak hadn't been looking at Torrin, she still would have heard the eye roll.

"Nat, don't you have somewhere else to be?" Torrin asked pointedly.

"Nope." Nat smirked back at her sister. "But you do. Mom said to have you stop by to see her as soon as you can. I'll keep Jak company while you head home."

"No way," Torrin protested. Jak could see the sibling bond between the two of them, despite the age difference. It reminded her a bit of her interactions with Bron. The thought brought a lump to her throat, but it was smaller than it would have been even a few weeks ago.

"She said if you don't come see her right away, then she'll just come to you."

It was amazing exactly how white someone could get when all the blood drained from her face. Jak had heard of people going pale but had never actually seen it. Torrin's dusky skin lost its luster and she swallowed convulsively. She didn't understand why Torrin wouldn't want to see her mother. She would give almost anything to see her own mother one last time and actively trying to avoid her made no sense at all. Either that, or Jak really was embarrassing her. That made more sense to her, though it didn't make her happy.

"Torrin," Jak whispered. "I'll be okay, you should go."

"You'll understand when you meet her," Torrin assured her. "She's… difficult to explain. I don't want to leave you, but there are things I have to deal with." She shot a look at the still-smirking Nat.

"She'll be fine with me," Nat told her. "Now get going before Mom comes looking for you."

Patting Jak's hand, Torrin stood and leaned over the bed to kiss her on the forehead.

"I'll be back as soon as I can," she promised. She practically walked backward from the room so she could keep her eye on the sniper a little while longer.

"Wow, she's got it bad," Nat remarked when the door had closed and Torrin was safely out of earshot. "A whole bunch of people are going to be pissed off that she's not on the market anymore. She's different with you than the others."

"Others?" Jak whispered.

"Nothing you need to worry about," Nat said, chagrined. "Torrin's going to kick my ass, for sure."

"What others?" Jak was quietly insistent.

"Nothing bad," Torrin's sister said soothingly. "Women are always panting after her. She doesn't stick around for very long between trips and she always has a different girl when she's here."

"Always girls?"

"Well, yeah." Nat's tone was that of someone explaining that water was wet. "Who else would she sleep with?"

"What about men?"

The laughter that overtook Nat at Jak's question was as surprising as it was loud. She laughed so hard her chair rocked and it took a visible effort to keep from falling over.

"Seriously," Nat wiped a tear from her eye. "Torrin, sleep with a man?" She snorted inelegantly, trying to get herself back under control. "Even if she wanted to, which she doesn't, it wouldn't happen here. There are no men on Nadierzda. There are a few boys, but they're all under six years old."

No men? She hadn't seen any since waking up, but then she hadn't seen many people at all. Now that she thought of it, she'd never seen a female doctor before. Of course, before Torrin, she hadn't seen a female merchant either. This was a very strange planet. With Torrin gone, she felt very alone. Nat continued to chatter on about her sister. Any other time Jak would have loved to hear more, but it was hard to think of anything beyond the fact that she was all by herself on a planet full of strange women with strange ideas. The only person she thought she knew was turning out to be almost as much a stranger as the rest of them.

CHAPTER FOUR

The painkiller had nicely smoothed the sharp edges off everything she was feeling, not least of all the pain. Jak floated along in a pleasant daze as she listened to Nat chatter about nothing that really interested her too much. At one point, she dozed off and when she came back around, Nat had still been talking. Even though she wasn't really listening, she was able to get the gist of Nat's conversation. Torrin was her idol, for all that Nat teased her constantly when she was around. She really wanted to go into business with Torrin and see other worlds like the smuggler did. It was hard for Nat to believe that Torrin had finally settled down with someone.

Jak wasn't sure about that. It wasn't like they'd discussed anything, and she was still certain that her feelings weren't right. While she couldn't deny that she had an intense sexual attraction for Torrin, that didn't mean it was right to act on it. Torrin's pull was so much easier to resist when she wasn't around, but even with Torrin gone, Jak still yearned for her. Knowing that as soon as Torrin came back, she would feel immensely better also served, illogically, to make her feel worse.

She must have dropped off again because when she woke up Nat was gone and Torrin was there. Torrin slouched in the chair next to her bed, her feet up on the bed's rails and her chin pillowed on her chest as she slept. One hand was in Jak's, the other lay limply in her lap.

With her eyes closed she looked so much at peace that Jak was content simply to sit there and watch her sleep for a while. It reminded her of the times in the wilderness when she'd lain awake because of the stims and Torrin had slept, pressed against her. She had burned for Torrin's touch even then, without ever having known its sweet pleasure. Now that she knew the pleasure Torrin's touch could bring her, her desire burned hotter than ever. Torrin's hand in hers was her focal point. It helped move away the last vestiges of the terrible pain that even the medicine couldn't touch.

Time flowed over them, barely touching them as they sat there, holding hands. Torrin finally stirred and opened her eyes to find Jak watching her. A smile dawned on her face. She was always beautiful, but when she smiled that beauty held a warmth that warmed Jak in her bones. Jak hadn't seen much of that smile lately and she wanted to see more of it.

"Hi," Jak whispered.

"Hi yourself," Torrin greeted her back. She moved over to perch on the edge of the narrow hospital bed.

"How are you feeling?"

"Better. Pain's mostly gone."

"Good. I hate seeing you in pain. I'd rather be the one in that bed. Having to watch you go through it and knowing I can't do anything to help is making me crazy."

"You help. You're here." Torrin was running a hand up and down Jak's thigh, but she liked a little too much where she was touching her. "Please stop."

A flash of hurt chased across Torrin's face and Jak felt terrible.

"It's too good." Jak hastened to explain. "Can't do that right now."

"Naughty girl." Torrin scolded her, understanding Jak's discomfort immediately. "I think we'd both be in trouble if I tried something like that right now."

"You don't know the half of it, Torrin Ivanov." Kiera's voice rang out from the doorway. "My patient isn't up to that right now. It'll be quite some time before she is." The doctor seemed mostly amused, but a hint of a rebuke ran beneath the surface of her admonishment.

"She might be your patient, but she's my girlfriend," Torrin reminded her cheekily.

Girlfriend? Jak was confused. Was that what they were? She enjoyed Torrin's company, and she definitely enjoyed making love with her, but she didn't want the smuggler to feel tied down. If what Nat said and the nurse implied were true, then Torrin was used to having a whole lot of women at her beck and call. Jak didn't like the idea of Torrin going with other women, but what say did she have when she hadn't known her for more than a few weeks? They'd really only been sleeping together for a little over a week, after all. Did any of those other women expect to have some rights to Torrin? She would have to disabuse them of the notion if they did. She wondered where her rifle was.

Something about her reasoning didn't seem quite right, but it was nearly impossible to think through the haze of drugs floating through her system. She was floating.

"Jak, when you're a little more lucid, we'll discuss therapy options," Kiera informed her. "Is the pain bearable now?"

The sniper nodded, then got distracted by the refraction of the light around the lit wall panels. The lights danced and shifted, changing colors and breaking apart, then rejoining.

"She'll be like this for another couple of hours," Kiera said in answer to Torrin's concerned look. "This is why we don't use these drugs unless we have to."

"It's okay," Jak declared muzzily.

"I'm sure it is," the doctor replied. "I'll be back in a bit."

With the pain mostly gone, Jak found it a little easier to talk. The oxygen mask on her face didn't help speech a whole lot, but Torrin seemed to understand her perfectly.

"Are you really feeling better?" Torrin asked quietly, running the back of her fingers along Jak's jawline, one of the only places that wasn't covered by medical equipment.

The sensation of Torrin's fingers on her skin heated Jak from the inside. Her touch always made everything else that was happening seem easier to face.

"Jak, honey?" Torrin cupped her chin and gently swiveled her face until Jak looked into the smuggler's eyes. "Focus on me now. You're feeling all right?"

Jak nodded, then got lost in Torrin's eyes. *Have her eyes always been that green?* They were a shade of shimmering emerald that rendered her literally breathless. She so wanted the smuggler for her own. How would Torrin react to Jak's jealousy? Better not to say anything. Sharing her would be better than not being with her at all.

"Lie back, babe," Torrin instructed and gently eased Jak back to a lying position. She didn't remember sitting up, but she must have. Torrin pushed Jak's outstretched arm to the bed. Carefully, Torrin arranged herself until she was lying next to Jak, almost but not quite snuggled around her. It felt so nice and Jak drifted for a while, not quite asleep but not really awake either.

"How's your mom?"

Torrin looked down at her, surprised Jak was still awake. "I didn't go see her. I let her know I would touch base when you're feeling better. I'm sure she's out with her precious herd of goats. There's nothing as important as them, apparently. Anyway, I went and made sure that Tien and the *Calamity Jane* were well taken care of. After that, I came right back to you."

"Oh." Jak's eyes drifted shut. "Will she be mad?"

"Probably, but that's my mom." Torrin launched into a monologue on her mother's sins, but Jak wasn't paying attention. Sleep was a greater force than she could battle and she let it pull her under.

The next time she woke, Torrin was still curled up next to her. One of her arms was thrown over her chest, and she'd managed to drape one leg over Jak's. It was a familiar position. The few times they'd actually slept in the same bed after making love, Jak had awoken to find that Torrin had claimed her as a life-sized cuddle toy. Torrin's proximity was reassuring, but the weight of her arm on her chest was producing some discomfort. Carefully, she reached over and disengaged Torrin's arm, sliding it off her. Torrin gurgled an incomprehensible sound of displeasure and moved her arm back, this time across Jak's abdomen, below the rib cage. She pulled herself closer, nuzzling into Jak's neck. Since the arm across the abdomen wasn't causing the discomfort it had been, Jak let her be.

She lay there, enjoying the closeness they were sharing. Misgivings still lurked at the back of her brain, but she didn't stop to examine them. Everything was just right and she didn't want to ruin it.

After a while the door slid open and the doctor walked briskly in. She came to an abrupt stop when she saw them.

"That's not a good idea," Kiera said with a rueful shake of the head.

Jak shrugged. "Feels good to me."

The doctor smiled crookedly. It might have been Jak's imagination, but she thought she saw a shadow of pain behind Kiera's eyes. She moved over to the bed and shook Torrin's shoulder. The smuggler opened her eyes, yawned, and then smiled up at Jak.

"I'm moving," she said to Kiera and unfolded her long body from the narrow hospital bed, careful to avoid jostling Jak.

The doctor chose not to take Torrin to task and focused instead on Jak. "I want to talk about your therapy. Are you better able to focus now?"

"Much," Jak said.

"Good," Kiera murmured as she perused the chart at the foot of Jak's bed. She flipped back and forth between a few screens on the tablet. "I want to put you through some quick-grow sessions. It'll encourage the tissue in your lungs to heal at a faster rate and will probably halve your recovery time. Well, your base recovery time."

"Base recovery time?" Torrin asked.

"Yes, base recovery time. It'll heal the lung tissue, but she'll still need therapy to increase her lung capacity back to something resembling her original state. There's no shortcut for that therapy, I'm afraid. That'll be some old-fashioned PT."

"Will I be all better after?" Jak whispered. While she was definitely feeling more lucid, the pain was creeping back. Nothing like it had been when she'd first woken up, but enough that she had to be careful about talking.

"There's a good chance you won't regain full lung capacity," Kiera replied frankly. She looked Jak right in the eye. "Your capacity must have been nothing short of amazing, judging by how long you were able to function as the tissue in your lungs was destroyed." The doctor shrugged. "At this point, we simply can't tell. You may get back to full capacity or you may gain something like what most people consider full capacity. There's also a chance, though I think it's small, that your lung capacity will be greatly reduced."

Jak was quiet as she considered what Kiera had said. She appreciated that the doctor had leveled with her, but the frank appraisal frightened her. The level of activity she was used to engaging in was quite vigorous, and she didn't want to compromise that. Losing even some of that would change her, but how much? Torrin had been attracted to her as she was on Haefen. If she wasn't able to do the things she had there, would the smuggler still find her attractive?

"Hey, we'll get through this," Torrin reassured her, judging rightly by Jak's expression that she wrestled with the uncertainty of her prognosis. "Don't worry, I'll help out however I can."

Covering the smuggler's hand with her own, Jak gave it a quick squeeze and smiled wanly up at her.

"Let's do it," she said to Kiera.

"Excellent!" The doctor beamed over the tablet at Jak. "We'll get you in for your first treatment early tomorrow. Try to get a good night's sleep. The therapy will take a lot out of you." She slid the chart back into its slot at the end of the bed and looked at the two of them.

"Torrin, I'll need you to be out of here by sixteen hundred hours. Jak needs her rest." With that, Kiera swept out of the room.

"You can go now if you want," Jak offered. The offer hurt, both in the breath that it took to form it and in the anticipation of being separated from her lover for any longer than necessary.

"No way," Torrin said. "I've waited a long time for us to be together in a place where we can both be ourselves."

What did that even mean? How could Jak really be herself in this place? There was no constant struggle, no danger just over the horizon. She had a lot more time to confront things in herself that she wasn't sure she'd like. She wasn't even sure who she was, not really. Without the constant struggle against an implacable enemy and concealment from her own people, she had no idea how to act. She had no purpose without anyone to kill or anyone trying to kill her; she was adrift, aimless.

Oblivious to her turmoil, Torrin had launched into a list of the things they would do once Jak recovered. Most of the activities, Jak had never heard of. What was base jumping? Sail planes? She nodded numbly as Torrin went on.

* * *

Torrin stayed with Jak until the end of Kiera's allotted time. It was late in the workday when she left, but she decided to swing by the office to see if any of her partners were around. There was a good chance that at least one of them would be. The people she worked with had almost as many workaholic tendencies as she did. Beyond that, she really didn't want to go home to an empty flat. That had never been a problem before. Before Jak, she would have stopped at one of the bars on the way and taken her pick of one of the willing and eager women there. For a change, Torrin didn't want meaningless sex with someone she would drop as soon as the next trip came along. She wanted Jak. Since that wasn't possible, the office was her next best option.

She rode her bike slowly through the city streets. The clinic wasn't too far from her workplace and she wasn't in any hurry. She perused Landing with new eyes as she imagined what Jak might think of her home. Compared to some planets she'd been on, the main city wasn't overly impressive at first glance. It hugged the contours of the land, becoming part of it instead of thrusting upward toward the sky like so many overcrowded inner-world planets. Torrin was proud of how her people worked with what the planet gave them. They were caught in a delicate struggle as dust and sand threatened to choke Nadierzda. Even so, the inhabitants did their best to work with what they could.

An open square lit with bright lights and full of women dancing and laughing beckoned to her. The shared merriment might distract her from the worry she felt for Jak. She was tempted for a moment but quickly decided against stopping and roared on. A block away, a group of women spilled out, laughing, from a staircase. The stairs went down to the mag-train, which was the main method of transportation for most of those who lived in Landing. There was always talk of connecting it to the other towns on Nadierzda, but the logistics were a nightmare almost impossible to overcome with their small population. Nothing survived for long in the shifting sands that covered much of the planet's surface. Keeping the mag-rails clear of sand would be a Sisyphean task, one that nobody could conceive how to tackle. The trains were limited within their complex of craters; transportation to other crater systems was done by air.

She pulled up in front of a low building in the office district. They were close to the spaceport but still a fair haul out from the warehouses. She waved her hand in front of a wall-mounted scanner. The scanner read the microchip implanted under the skin on the back of her hand. A high beep was followed by a clunk as the lock disengaged and the front door hissed open smoothly. She stepped inside and followed a short hallway past an elevator. Ignoring that, she let herself into a narrow stairwell. She'd always found stairs to be quicker. At least they required less waiting than the elevator did and she desperately needed to burn off excess energy. Trotting down the stairs two at a time at her usual breakneck clip, she reached the third lower level in a hurry. There were two other levels below this one. The lowest one was devoted almost entirely to a pumping system and backup generators. Though the planet was mostly sand, there was water on it—or rather in it. There was too much for it all to have been a byproduct of the aborted terraforming efforts. It was mostly locked right below the surface, where the sand was saturated by water and formed a hard crust. In order to keep water from seeping through the walls, pumps ran nonstop and were backed up by extra generators. Even the backup generators had backup generators.

The door on this level was nondescript and a little battered. Nothing about it suggested that on the other side was Troika Corporation, Nadierzda's most powerful and successful trading corporation. The address was hard to find, the office equally difficult to locate, and that was the way Torrin liked it. They didn't do business with any kind of walk-in contracts. All their business came from offworld, and there was no way any of their customers would find their way to the main office. Troika Corp. had half a dozen satellite offices on various worlds throughout the Fringes. Customers came in through those locations. If the goods their clients were interested in obtaining were exotic, difficult or downright dangerous, the requests were forwarded to Torrin and her two partners on Nadi. It was the perfect setup, really. No one off the planet had any idea how big their enterprise was, which suited Troika Corp. just fine. The illusion of insignificance protected them more than any standing army ever could.

Another wave of her arm in front of a scanner secured Torrin entry to the offices. As she expected, the series of interconnecting rooms was quiet at this time of day. This far underground, she always expected it to be dark, but the light strips were enhanced with ultraviolet light and the offices were lit up as if it were afternoon. The light had been carefully calibrated to mimic a sunny afternoon on the surface. Her employees were going to be as comfortable underground as she could make them and the light didn't hurt her disposition either.

As she worked her way deeper into the office, she passed the occasional woman at her desk. There were usually upward of thirty women working for them. More if business was especially busy. When the home office started getting overcrowded, the partners started planning to open a new satellite office.

Torrin made sure to nod a greeting to each of the women she saw, but she didn't slow down to engage in chitchat. She'd already fielded enough inquiries over her whereabouts the past day and a half. The story would make the rounds on its own soon enough, and she was tired of repeating herself.

At the far end of the cubicle farm were three solid wood doors, each of equal size and elegance as the others. The only variations were in the color of the wood. She stopped in front of a door with deep red overtones and a light gray grain. The contrast had always appealed to her, yet she found herself thinking of the blue tones of wood on Haefen. Maybe she would look into procuring enough lumber to have a new door constructed. The partners changed up the colors of their doors occasionally. It was one of the perks of making so many offworld trips. Though, truth to tell, none of the others made nearly as many trips as Torrin.

She let herself through the door and into the lushly appointed office. The furnishings weren't overdone, not like the monstrosities that had been endemic in the decoration in Hutchinson's mansion. The Orthodoxan colonel had apparently never come across a piece of furniture that couldn't be embellished. He'd been set on having nothing but the best, which had unfortunately included Torrin. Fortunately for her, Jak had put a bullet through his skull before he could act on his avarice. Torrin shuddered slightly when she remembered how close she had come to being Hutchinson's brood mare. That Jak had actually been sent to take her out should have bothered her, but it didn't. Jak had proven her devotion to Torrin many times over since then.

By contrast, it would have been obvious to any visitor to Torrin's office that the room had been furnished with her comfort in mind. There was an overstuffed couch against one wall, the velvet upholstery only now beginning to betray signs of heavy use. Torrin was known to take frequent naps on that couch. Sometimes she even slept the night there, especially if she was trying to avoid a woman whose heart she was short of breaking.

The couch wasn't her destination this time; instead she sat at the desk. It managed to be large and elegant at the same time. The cushions on her chair gave slightly and conformed to her body. The ergonomic smart-gel cushions developed on Circe-VIII made for the most comfortable furniture she'd used anywhere. They were extremely expensive, but she hoped that by opening up the market on them, the price would come down. If not, as long as she had access to them for her own use, she still counted that contract as a win.

As she sat down, the computer panel inset into the desk's surface sprang to life. A quick glance showed her that one partner was still in the office. The other had probably gone home at a reasonable time. She was recently married and spent as much time as she could afford with her new wife.

Moments later there was a peremptory knock at the door before it burst open. A short, dark-haired dervish whirled into the room, threw her arms around Torrin's chest and squeezed. Even though she barely came up to Torrin's shoulder, somehow she managed to lift the smuggler out of her chair.

"Audra, whoa!" Torrin's laugh was breathless. "You're crushing me."

"That's what you get," Audra said, giving her another squeeze before letting go. "We don't hear from you for weeks and weeks. You're way overdue."

"I know, I know. Believe me, I've been hearing it enough from everyone."

Audra Kalinin stepped back and looked Torrin up and down. Her eyes were light blue, so pale they were almost colorless. She was the best negotiator Torrin had ever met. Under her eyes, her opponents were weighed and measured, and most of the time they came up short.

"I'm too skinny, I've heard that too."

"It's true." Audra reached her hand up to rub the stubble on Torrin's scalp. "The hair is new."

Torrin yanked her head back, out of Audra's reach. "I know." She knew her tone was curt, but she was getting tired of the sideways looks and the remarks. It was only hair. It would grow back. Why was everyone making such a big deal about it? It didn't change who she was. If she kept telling herself that, she might even believe it.

Audra grinned cheekily at her. She knew she was getting under Torrin's skin. She tilted her head and stared. "There's something else going on, isn't there?" Audra considered her a little longer. "I can't put my finger on it, but there's something different about you."

Try as she might, Torrin couldn't stop herself from coloring slightly and the tips of her ears heated. A grin spread slowly across Audra's face until it threatened to split.

"It's a girl, isn't it?" The ice of Audra's blue eyes danced as she chortled at Torrin's discomfort. "So you've finally settled on one. Your days of sampling from the buffet are done and you're ready to settle down with one dish for the rest of your life."

"Trust you to make this all about food." Audra was known around the office for her voracious appetite, for food among other things, especially the finer things. Torrin enjoyed herself, sure, but Audra took hedonism to an art form. For the amount of food Audra could put away in a sitting, nowhere was it evident on her rail-thin body. She threw herself headlong into exercise and physical activity the same way she did the other things in her life. No one worked harder, raced faster or loved more completely than Audra.

The little firebrand merely shrugged in reply. "Did you meet her on your mysterious trip?"

"Yes."

Audra looked on expectantly, waiting for Torrin to elaborate, which she had no intention of doing. It was much more entertaining to let her partner squirm.

"You know, you really need to start letting us know where you're going on these little scouting expeditions of yours." Torrin blinked at her, taken aback by the sudden change of subject. "This latest stunt scared the crap out of Mac and me and brought additional scrutiny from the Ruling Council. You know they think we couldn't hack it without you."

Torrin scoffed at the idea. "That's a load of crap and you know it. You two would be fine without me."

"I know that, you know that, even Mac knows it, but the rest of the planet doesn't. For better or worse, you're the face of the company."

Taken aback at Audra's shift in mood, Torrin was silent for a moment. Audra was sometimes mercurial, though seriousness wasn't a mood she typically settled on. It was one of the reasons she and Torrin got on so well; both had an almost pathological inability to take things seriously. Their third partner, Mac, was serious enough for the three of them.

"Maybe I didn't have a good reason to be careful before. I never figured anyone here would miss me that much."

Audra hooked her foot around the leg of the nearest chair and pulled it toward her. She collapsed into it dramatically and delicately pressed the back of her hand against her forehead.

"Oh dear me," she gushed. "I am so unloved that if I fell into a black hole no one would even notice. Except your partners. And your employees. Family. Friends. Jilted ex-lovers!" By the end of her sally, Audra was back on her feet. "Face it, Torrin, you've touched a lot of lives here. You drift in and out, but everyone notices you. Those who don't want you wish they could do half of what you do without even noticing that you're doing it."

Audra's speech was impassioned and Torrin was sure she meant what she said, but it was hard to hear. She'd always functioned perfectly well believing she was free and had no ties. Now, not only did she have Jak, but she was finding that she'd had more strings tied to her limbs than she'd ever known. Her partner's words had her feeling almost physically uncomfortable, claustrophobic even.

"Look, I'm not saying you need to tell us what you're doing every moment of the day," Audra said. She'd known Torrin for a long time and had probably read her discomfort in the stiffness of her body. Audra knew all of Torrin's tells as well as Torrin knew hers, which was why they never played cards with each other. "All we want is to know where you're going on these trips and when we should send someone after you."

"I'll think about it," Torrin said. "But you know I work best when I have a lot of discretion."

"Well, for your girl's sake, you're going to need to start telling us. She deserves to know."

"I don't know." Torrin paused and sneaked a glance over at Audra, gauging her reaction. "I'm thinking of taking her with me."

Audra collapsed back into the chair, hand pressed to her chest. She took a couple of heaving breaths before finding her voice. "It must be true love. You won't even share a ship with your sister for anything longer than a half-day trip." Torrin's partner pushed herself up on the arm of the chair and pushed chin-length black hair out of her eyes. "So what's her name then, this mystery woman of yours? When do I meet her? Is she mentally defective?"

Unable to help herself any longer, Torrin laughed and wrapped her arms around her partner and gave her as big a hug as she'd received.

"I missed you, short stuff. If you have some time, I'll fill you in on everything."

"For you, partner-mine, I have all the time in the world."

CHAPTER FIVE

Two hours later found them seated next to each other on the couch, sharing a bottle of Myrrandian scotch. They'd made a significant dent in the bottle and Torrin was feeling no pain. From the way Audra was draped with boneless grace over the arm of the couch, she felt pretty good herself.

"Tha's quite the story," Audra said, pulling another swig from the bottle. They'd started out using tumblers but had long since abandoned them to drink straight from the source. "So what're you gonna do now?"

"I'm not sure." Torrin leaned back and rested her head on the wall behind the couch. She studied the panels on the ceiling. "We needa get the plans for the cyberne-, cyber…metal-thingy implants looked at by someone who c'n manufacture them. I also needa get the shipments I promised to those Devonites. Plus find out who set me up."

"Set you up?" Audra rolled her eyes over at Torrin.

"Yup. Neal's intel was way off. Plus, Tien's databanks didn' match the planet. Can't both be by accident."

"Sure you're not being paranoid?"

"Doesn' mean I'm wrong."

Audra flapped her hand at Torrin. Everyone knew Torrin's favorite saying. "First part's tricky," Audra contemplated the ceiling alongside her partner. "I'll do that. I'm waaaaay better at negotiating than you are. You get the shipments together."

"No problem. I want the shipments double-teamed, though." Audra snickered at the unwitting sexual reference and Torrin rolled her eyes. The move made her head spin and she turned her head with exaggerated care to look over at her partner. "I don't jus' mean the delivery ship either. They need the extra ship. The picket around Haefen isn't going to be that light forever. If the *Icarus* hasn't been reinforced already, the damn Leaguers will make sure of it soon."

"Tha's not gonna make Mac happy. You know she hates anything that eats into our bottom line."

"I know, but I won't be happy if we lose anyone. Besides, the score we have with the implants'll have her turning cartwheels." Both women stopped, looked at each other and burst into peals of laughter. The idea of staid and sober Mac doing cartwheels was laughable.

A familiar chime sounded in Torrin's ear. If she wasn't mistaken, that was her mother's call-signal. She rolled her eyes and sat up.

"Hold on, I gotta take this. Mom musta finally gotten my message. She prob'ly wants to know what's going on with Jak and me."

"Don' we all." Audra snickered but subsided quickly and put on her most innocent expression when Torrin gestured at her to be quiet.

"'Lo, Mom."

"Torrin?" Irenya's voice sounded as disapproving as usual. "Is that you? You sound different."

"Of course it's me, Mom. It's almost impossible to call the wrong person on these things. I'm sorry I'm not who you were expecting, but then I never have been."

Audra's mouth went round with surprise followed by a big grin. She flashed Torrin the high sign, goading her on.

"Are you drunk?"

"Mebbe."

There was a long silence on her mother's end and all Torrin could hear was measured breathing. "I was hoping you would be willing to come over here tonight and tell me and Raisa about your latest trip. We were worried about you. You were gone much too long this time."

"Yeah, well. I ran into a bit of a pickle. Nothin' I couldn' handle. It's all good now, and I'm going to make us stinkin' rich!"

"I'm glad to hear it," Irenya said after a long pause.

Torrin could tell she was getting under her skin. *Good*, she thought.

"Nat told Raisa you brought someone with you. We'd like to meet her. I'm hearing some strange rumors about the woman."

Suddenly tired of the game, Torrin sat up straight. For a moment. She listed to the side and put her hands on the couch to steady herself. "So you're gonna give her the third degree? That's nice. She's in the hospital. She almost died."

"I'd heard she'd been injured, but I thought they could patch her right up. What are those autodocs good for if not getting people back on their feet right away?"

"You of all people should know that not everything can be fixed with an autodoc. If Jak ever meets you, it won't be until she's fully recovered. You won't see me until then either. I know what she needs from me right now, and tha's for me to be with her every step of the way."

"Torrin Mara Ivanov, you will not speak to me that way!" Irenya thundered in her ear. Torrin winced and shook her head at Audra. Her partner seemed torn between horror and hilarity.

"I have to go, Mother. Jak needs me and I'm gonna do what you couldn't. I'm gonna be there for her. I'll let you know if I plan to come see Raisa." She didn't give Irenya any time to say anything and simply disconnected.

"Torrin, what in frozen hells did you do that for?" Audra lapsed into helpless giggles. "Your mom's gonna kill you!"

"Her? I'm not afraid of her." Torrin looked around, her eyes wide. "Where is she?"

Audra chortled even harder, holding her sides and Torrin joined in. Her cheeks hurt from laughing so hard, but every time she made eye contact with Audra, the giggles rolled through them all over again. Eventually their mirth subsided, and Torrin continued, wiping tears from her eyes. "Back to Mac. I know the initial outlay'll be huge, but we got tech that's way more advanced than what the core worlds can manage. Think of it, for a change they'll have to come to us." Gloating wasn't the prettiest of emotions, but Torrin didn't care. The idea of the uppity inner-world populations procuring their implants from the Fringes made her rub her hands with glee. They were going to make a killing.

"You know we needa take this to the Ruling Council, right?"

The smuggler groaned and clapped one hand over her eyes. "Do we gotta? They'll ask us so many questions, want a report, then probably convene a subcommittee, blah, blah, blah. By the time they decide to move, the inner worlds will probably have developed their own metal-thingy tech." She flopped onto her back and draped her legs over the arm of the couch. She held out a hand for the bottle in Audra's hand. "Besides, aren't you the one who told me it is better to beg forgiveness?"

"Than ask permission? Yeah, I know. But I don't think they'll be that bad, 'specially if we let them know this could be the last push that finally gets us able to afford terraforming."

Torrin took a long swig from the bottle and rolled until she could see Audra again. "We needa spin it right then. What's that new intern's name? The one who does our PR and junk?"

"Mollie?"

"Yeah, her. Let's get 'er on this. We need to have it 'accidentally' leaked that we have this new product we wanna develop and it'll make us a boatload, maybe even enough to terraform. Then we go to the Ruling Council. Give 'em long enough to hear the rumors so they have no choice except to summon us."

"That could work. I'll have her start on it tomorrow, first thing."

"Jus' tell 'er she can't use any official channels, and don' tell about the Devonites. Council won' be happy we're dealin' with their sort. It's the kinda thing that'll drive 'em out the hatch. Oh, and if Mollie can pull this off, we need to give her a bonus or a raise or something." Torrin took another gulp of scotch. She hadn't thought the alcohol was really affecting her, but when she sat up, the office tilted crazily to one side.

"I needa get home," Audra announced and stumbled to her feet. "Konnie isn't gonna wait on me forever."

"Still with 'er?" Torrin slurred. "Thought you said she's makin' you crazy."

Her partner shrugged. "She keeps me warm at night and she's fun t' fool aroun' with. It's not like we both don' know it's gonna end, so I'll have fun while it lasts."

Torrin nodded slowly and waved as Audra walked, a trifle unsteadily, through the door. She helped herself to another swig of scotch, then held the bottle up to the light and contemplated the blood-red liquor inside. Between the two of them, they'd managed to almost empty a mostly full bottle, though she'd been responsible for most of the imbibing. She held her liquor better than Audra, but then she also topped her partner by more than thirty centimeters and outweighed her significantly to boot. It was nice, she was so hammered that she wasn't nearly so worried about Jak. She was just happy that she hadn't burst into tears while relaying the story to her business partner.

It seemed silly to leave a finger of alcohol in the bottle so she downed it in one long swallow. Lying on the couch as it spun lazily around her seemed the right thing to do. How long she stayed there, she wasn't sure. Eventually she dropped off in a drunken stupor.

* * *

The rising sun had woken Jak early, slanting through the window on the door and spilling across the floor. She noted that it didn't seem quite as bright as it could get on Haefen. What little she'd glimpsed by craning her neck to see through the window, she thought that when the skies were clear here, the sunlight still looked a little dim. The sand and dust in the atmosphere created a perpetual haze. From what she'd seen so far, the sun was out more often though not as strongly. Haefen's climate was often rainy and overcast, but when their sun was out, it was out.

She'd been watching out the window in her door for quite a while now. Nat had been in to visit with her for a little bit around breakfast. Torrin's sister had regaled her with more stories of growing up with a big sister like the smuggler. Torrin was quite a bit older than Nat—by a good twenty years or so, if Nat was to be believed and Jak wasn't sure she did. There was no way Torrin could be in her mid-forties. Despite the age difference, they'd gotten into their fair share of scrapes together. They both seemed to go out of their way to give their mother fits. Irenya? She thought that was what Nat had called her, but she'd uttered the name in hushed tones like she was afraid of getting in trouble. The stories hadn't been quite so amusing without Torrin. *Where is she?* She'd been waiting all morning to see her, but there had been no sign of her lover. If she was out with another woman, Jak was going to have to line the wench up with a headshot. If she had no head, she wouldn't have eyes for Torrin, then would she?

That probably wasn't the best way to deal with an obstacle. She wasn't in a war zone any longer and she needed to stop thinking like she was. Still, the idea of Torrin being intimate with someone else made Jak itch to hurt somebody. *If she's not with another woman, then where is she? What other reason can she possibly have not to be here?* Jak had thought maybe she meant a little bit to Torrin. The more tangled her thoughts got over Torrin's unexplained absence, the worse Jak felt. She wanted to pull Torrin in closer, but she knew she had no real hold over the woman. Who was she to lay such a claim on Torrin?

The door opened and Jak whipped her head around. Disappointed, she assayed a small smile to Kiera.

"Are you ready for your first dose of quick-grow therapy?" the doctor asked. She pulled the tablet out of its slot at the foot of the bed and swiped through Jak's vitals. What she saw had her smiling slightly and nodding her head. "Your vitals look much better than they have any right to. I see no reason to delay things."

"Well, almost no reason," Jak said quietly, pointedly looking around the room that was empty but for the two of them.

"You were hoping Torrin would be here." The doctor turned what should have been a question into a statement. She regarded Jak for a moment. "I'm sure she'll be here soon." The way her eyes shifted away at the end of the statement made Jak wonder how much Kiera really believed her own words.

"It's okay," Jak decided. "I want to go ahead with the treatment, even if she can't make it."

"Good woman." Kiera smiled encouragingly. "We're going to take you to the quick-grow lab." She nodded at the older nurse who was standing outside the door in the hallway.

The woman came in and disengaged Jak from the wall and started plugging the various tubes and cords back into the bed. Noticing Jak's curious gaze, she nodded toward a large box at the foot of the bed.

"Your bed has an internal power source that autonomously powers the various pieces of equipment you're hooked up to. You'll be fine for up to a day without being hooked back in to a hard power source."

She finished disengaging and re-engaging the various tubes leading into and out of Jak's body before she reached down and pressed her hand over a small panel. The bed settled minutely, not enough to jar Jak, but enough to let her know something had happened. A motor engaged and the nurse was able to easily wheel her out of the room and down the hall. With so much equipment built into the bed, it must have weighed quite a bit, but the nurse handled it without any indication of effort.

They proceeded down the hall. To Jak's disappointment, there were no other windows along the hallway. Instead, she was treated to sterile, light green walls. The shade of green was nice enough, she supposed, but she really missed the outdoors. Even if she couldn't see the trees she'd grown up with, being able to see the sky and the sun would have made her feel better.

They finally passed a large window on their way to the quick-grow lab. Through it, Jak got the impression of low buildings, topped by a sandy blue sky. The view matched the smell of warm sand she'd started to associate with Torrin's world. She wasn't able to catch more than a glimpse before she was wheeled into a large lab full of tubes similar to the one Torrin had put her into on the ship.

"What are those?" Jak asked when they stopped.

"Those are quick-grow capsules," Kiera replied. She pulled the tablet from the end of the bed and reviewed Jak's vitals again. "We're going to put you into one of the big ones. From there we'll fill it up with grow-gel. Wherever it comes in contact with damaged tissue, it'll encourage new growth."

"But my damage is inside?" Jak turned the statement into a half-horrified question. She had a sick feeling that she knew where this was going.

"You're going to be inhaling it," Kiera said, confirming Jak's fears. Catching the look on Jak's face, she hastened to reassure her. "Don't worry, the gel has been oxygenated for your treatment. It'll be a little strange at first, but your lungs will adapt quickly."

The last thing Jak wanted to do was get back inside one of those tubes. Only Torrin giving her no other choice had gotten her into the cryotube in the first place, and without her there now, Jak wasn't sure she could do it.

"You'll be fine," the doctor reiterated when Jak didn't seem overly convinced. "We'll be right here if something goes wrong."

"No offense, doctor, but the last time I went into something like that, it didn't end so well."

"I suppose it's fitting that we'll be healing the damage using similar technology then."

That was an angle that Jak hadn't thought of. She'd never flinched away from danger before, and she wasn't going to start now. When Kiera asked if she was ready, she simply nodded firmly in response. Inside, she was anything but certain, but there was no sense in broadcasting her insecurity.

There were two other nurses and a doctor in the room. When Kiera felt Jak was ready after checking her vitals one last time, she motioned the others over. Quickly they swarmed her and removed all the tubes going into and out of her body. Without the breathing assistance, Jak was quickly winded, but the team moved so quickly to get her into the tube that she almost didn't notice. She also hadn't noticed that she was completely naked until the tube began filling with a viscous green gel. The doctors and nurses shut the hatch on the tube and she was barely able to see the gel pouring in around her feet. It glimmered emerald in the light and it was cold. So cold that her feet and legs started to ache, but just as quickly the pain passed to be replaced by a mild tingling sensation.

The gel level rose and enveloped her. Despite Kiera's assurances, she couldn't help but try to keep her head out of the goo for as long as possible as it oozed slowly up her neck and over her face. Even when she could no longer keep her head above the green, gelatinous surface, she tried to hold her breath. It was an exercise in futility as her lungs demanded air much too quickly. Try as she might, she was suddenly gasping, trying to gulp in air, but all that came in was the emerald gel. She coughed at the unfamiliar intrusion into her lungs, then suddenly she could breathe. In fact, she felt better almost immediately, the pain from her lungs was gone.

There was a tap on the glass and when she looked up a familiar face looked in at her.

"Torrin," she tried to say. Without air over her larynx, there was no sound. Torrin caught her eye and smiled. Well, she tried to smile. She looked terrible and Jak wondered if she was getting sick herself. She only hoped that she hadn't gotten the smuggler sick.

"We're going to keep you in there for an hour," a tinny voice filtered to her ears through the gel. She recognized Kiera's voice and nodded. This was going to be interesting. Claustrophobia was something she'd rarely experienced, but she was getting every indication of it now. It was great to be completely pain free, but she felt a powerful urge to move. Experimentally, she raised her arms to see how much room she had. She'd barely bent them before the backs of her hands brushed the sides of the container. If she'd had any air in her lungs, she would have sighed.

Torrin was still watching her, and she placed her hand, palm out, on the small window hatch. Jak wormed her way around and placed her own hand on the other side of the glass. Even though they had no direct contact, she was still relieved that Torrin had made it.

An hour later, Jak was being helped out of the tube and back onto her bed. The hour spent locked in the tube had been pure torture. The only thing that had made it bearable was Torrin's presence. She didn't know what she would have done had Torrin not been there.

Torrin still didn't look good. She flinched visibly at every noise and was more than a little green around the gills. She soldiered bravely on, but it was plain that she was suffering. Jak was pretty sure now that Torrin was hungover. Bron had come back to their room in similar condition on more than one occasion.

"Are you okay?" Jak asked after the gel had been cleared from her lungs. Getting the goo cleared out had been an involved process with tubes and suctions being inserted down her throat. She had to admit it felt good to be breathing air again, but it was pretty amazing how quickly she'd acclimated to breathing a thick liquid.

On the other side of the bed, Kiera snickered quietly. Torrin shot her a venomous glance and winced again when she turned her head too quickly.

"I'm fine." Torrin glowered. "It's nothing that won't fix itself in a while. Or someone could fix it for me." She glanced back over at the doctor.

"You know my philosophy on hangovers. You had the fun, you earned the pain. It's no more than you deserve, after all."

Torrin shook her head gingerly and kept Jak's hand in hers as they left the lab. The trip back to Jak's room was quick. She'd intended to ask if they could linger by the window for a little bit, but she was exhausted. Her breathing did seem to have improved. One of the nurses had set the mask back over her face, but the oxygen flow wasn't as strong as it had been. The color of the walls was rather soothing, she thought. Her eyelids felt particularly heavy and she closed them to rest her eyes for a little bit.

When she woke up, they were back in her room. Torrin was talking over her to Kiera.

"It's perfectly natural," Kiera replied to Torrin's question. "Her body is under a huge strain right now while it's being forced to regenerate damaged tissue at such an accelerated rate. She'll sleep a lot until we're done with therapy."

"How long will that be?"

"Most likely about a week. She's responded really well to the first treatment. It's no surprise, really. She's extremely fit and with a high level of conditioning."

Seeing that Jak was awake again, Torrin leaned over and kissed her forehead. Jak smiled tiredly up at her.

"Still good?" Torrin asked.

"Tired."

"Well, sleep as much as you need to. I'll be here when you wake up."

"All right." Jak closed her eyes once again and lapsed quickly back into sleep.

* * *

Torrin watched Jak drift off to sleep again. Despite Kiera's assurances, she still fretted over her lover. Jak had been through so much, but she always kept going. It was gratifying that she had yet to see the terrible bleakness in Jak's gaze that she'd glimpsed a few times back on Haefen. Once before, she'd seen that look on someone who thought she had nothing to live for. She knew Jak had plenty to live for, and she was going to prove it to her. There was no way she was going to let her slip down the path that led to…She refused to acknowledge the final thought and purposely steered her mind away from even considering it.

The headache that bludgeoned her temples was something else. It had been a long time since she'd been this hungover. Come to think of it, Audra had been there the last time too. She needed to stop letting her business partner lead her merrily down the path of debauchery. It was good that Audra was such a handy scapegoat. Torrin had known she was in trouble as soon as she woke, but exactly how much trouble hadn't been truly evident until she'd bent over in front of the sink to wash her face. Her brain had come screaming in from the back of her skull and bounced off the inside of her forehead. She moaned slightly as she recalled the pain.

It was too bad that she had too much to do to really wallow in her misery. She needed to get back to the office to continue discussion on the plan of attack she and Audra had started the night before. They'd had a brilliant conversation, and Torrin hoped that Audra remembered more of it than she did. However, Jak waking up alone in the hospital room was the last thing she wanted.

Standing by the bed and watching Jak sleep, Torrin took a deep breath to steel herself and activated the subdermal transmitter behind her ear. Pain, intense and sharp, pierced her skull at the transmitter's location. Using the device with a hangover was agony, but there was too much to get done in too little time to wait until she recovered.

It was likely that Audra was at least in as bad a shape as she was, so she contacted Mac first. The woman was a morning person anyway, so it was no surprise when she answered after the first tone.

"Hello to you, Torrin!" Mac chirped at her cheerfully. Torrin grimaced. Every tone of Mac's voice grated through her head. It felt as though someone was rubbing salt into an open wound inside her brain.

"Mac," Torrin replied with judicious care. "The three of us need to meet. I have to fill you in on my latest run and there are some things we need to get out ahead of."

"I'm happy to. I've been more than a little curious about your activities. I'll get the conference room set up."

"No. I'm over at the clinic. We'll meet here."

"Are you all right?" Concern dripped from Mac's voice.

"I'm fine, but I can't leave at the moment. Meet me here in an hour."

"Got it." Mac signed off abruptly after the last statement. In anyone else, Torrin might have thought she was angry, given the abruptness with which she ended the transmission. With Mac, it was just the way she was. Her business partner wasn't really that interested in other people. She was interested in numbers and processes. While she could muster up interest in others when they were someone she actually cared about, when she was given a task to focus on, that almost always took priority. The only exception Torrin had seen in Mac's attitude was toward her wife.

For a moment she sat without moving, unwilling to incur the next round of agony by contacting Audra. It was so nice to sit in the silence and relative darkness of Jak's room. The only sounds were the low, repetitive noises of the machinery she was hooked up to. Being there with Jak was very soothing even though the sniper was currently dead to the world. At least she seemed to be sleeping easier.

Torrin heaved a sigh and reached up behind her ear again. This time the tones went on for a good half a minute before Audra finally answered.

"What is it, Torrin?" she moaned. "This better be good."

"We need to meet, the three of us," Torrin said tersely. "Meet Mac and me at the clinic in an hour."

Audra's only response was a grunt before she terminated the transmission. That was fine with Torrin and no more than she'd anticipated. She had no worry that Audra wouldn't show up.

Since she had an hour before her partners arrived, this was as good a time as any to catch a little nap. She put her feet up on the bars running along the hospital bed and slouched down in her chair. Folding her chin to her chest, she sighed and dropped into a doze almost immediately.

When the chime in her ear went off, Torrin had no idea how much time had passed. It couldn't have been much; she still felt like something that had been scraped off the underside of a manure cart.

"What?" she asked roughly. It was only Nat, and she didn't feel too much need to be polite to her sister when she felt so terrible.

"And hello to you. Sounds like you're hungover, which explains the call I got from Mom first thing this morning."

"What are you talking about? I couldn't talk to Mom yesterday. She wasn't home."

"Mm hm." Nat's tone was so dry it would have crumpled up and blown away in the slightest breeze. "How much did you drink last night, anyway?"

"A bit. Audra and I were celebrating." It had been more than a bit. Torrin couldn't remember the last time she'd opened and finished a bottle with someone else in one sitting. The drink had been well-deserved, and no one could tell her differently. She'd made it back home in one piece. She'd brought Jak back with her, and if she was not the picture of health yet, she would be soon. Troika Corp., and by extension Nadierzda, was going to make a shipload of money which would solve a whole heap of problems. So yeah, a drink had been exactly what the occasion had called for.

"Mom called you last night, remember? She says she did and she's beyond angry at you. I don't think she's been this mad since you snuck off to join the militia, or so I've heard."

"That's crazy. I'd remember if I'd had it out with her—" Torrin snapped her mouth shut on the rest of her protest. It was fuzzy, but she had the sudden feeling that Nat might be telling the truth. Her stomach lurched and she groaned.

"Memory coming back to you?"

Torrin could hear the grin in Nat's voice. There was no reason her sister had to be enjoying her discomfort quite so thoroughly. "Maybe. I think I told her Jak was sick."

"So? Half the crater knows she went to the clinic when you got here."

"I may have said something about staying by her side, not like she did with Mama."

"Oh, Torrin." All traces of amusement were gone from Nat's tone. "You didn't."

"I think so." It had been a low blow, Torrin knew that. There was no way to take it back now. She owed Irenya an apology. Nausea stirred within her at the idea. How was she supposed to do that? *I'm sorry I said you weren't sad enough when your wife died.* That wasn't going to do it. There was no way out of the dreaded family dinner now and the worst part was that she'd brought it on herself. She'd delay it as long as she could, though, and hope that by the time it happened Irenya would have let go of some of her anger. It could happen. Torrin snorted. Sure it could, and maybe they'd find a freshwater oasis in the middle of the sands.

"I should go," Torrin said.

"Let me know when you're going to dinner. I'll come with to run interference."

"Thanks." Torrin disconnected their call. Gratitude for her sister's offer filled Torrin. It wasn't often that they were able to have each other's backs, but Torrin was glad that they could. If Jak was up to it, she'd bring her along also. Between her sister and her girlfriend, she might even survive dinner with her mom and stepmother.

Exhausted by the exchange, Torrin dipped her head to her chest. She nodded off into unpleasant dreams where her knife-wielding mother chased her around the dinner table while Jak and Nat sat by, laughing and keeping score.

CHAPTER SIX

A gentle hand on her shoulder woke her. Torrin blinked a couple of times, then looked up into Mac's sober face. The woman was about as plain as they came, but with an intensity to her eyes that didn't match the rest of her face. Everything else about her was average and completely unmemorable. Her eyes were washed-out gray, her hair a nondescript brown. She kept her hair long, but Torrin had never seen it in anything other than a ponytail, and she'd never seen a hair out of place. Everything about Mac screamed precision and neatness, down to the smallest crease in her clothing.

Mac handed her a container. "From the way you sounded, I thought you could use this. Then I talked to Audra and I knew you'd need it."

Torrin slid the lid off the container and inhaled deeply the bitter vapors within.

"You are a lifesaver," she said gratefully. She took a quick swig of the highly caffeinated concoction. Bitrian was dark brown—almost black—and had a thicker consistency even than cocoa. Aside from the darkness of the liquid, it was nothing like the coffee that was sucked down on so many other worlds. The drink was made from the bark of a local plant and was extremely bitter, but with a fruity aftertaste that she preferred to coffee. Torrin sighed as she felt the stimulant perking her up.

"I hope you have some of that for me," a rough voice groused from behind them. Audra looked terrible. Torrin expected that she looked equally as bad. Dark circles stood out like bruises under the small woman's bloodshot eyes. Her hair stuck out at funny angles. It was obvious from her condition that she'd rolled right into bed when she'd gotten home. She was still wearing the same clothes she'd had on when she left the office, and they were now heavily creased and rumpled.

Mac wordlessly held out another container and Audra seized it eagerly. She slid open the container's top and slurped eagerly at the steaming liquid inside. Closing her eyes, she stood there for a moment.

"Hot," was all she said.

"Let's take this outside," Torrin said. "I don't want to wake her."

"Her new girlfriend," Audra stage-whispered to Mac. They both craned their necks around Torrin to get a better look at Jak's slumbering form. Torrin stood and shooed them from the room.

In the hallway, Torrin rustled up three chairs and set them up by the door to Jak's room. She set the door to remain open and positioned herself so she could see her lover. If Jak woke, Torrin would be at her side in a flash.

"She looks a little young," Audra observed, her voice studiedly neutral. "How old is she? Sixteen, seventeen?"

"She's older than that. Early twenties. And she was forced to grow up quickly." Torrin wondered why she was being so defensive. She had hooked up with women younger than Jak. Not younger by much, and not very often, but it had happened.

Audra nodded knowingly and Torrin found herself blushing; the tips of her ears burned.

"I didn't bring you two here to discuss my love life," she said, more harshly than she'd intended. She closed her eyes and breathed deeply through her nose before continuing. "We have a lot of business to sort out and not a lot of time in which to do it. When the Ruling Council gets wind of this, we need to be able to hit the ground running."

"What Torrin's trying to say," Audra explained to Mac, "is that the payment she received for our services, while substantial, is…complicated."

Mac pulled her tablet out of a pocket on the inside of her jacket. She quickly toggled it on, frowning slightly as she started opening screens. Her fingers danced over the display with a grace that Torrin envied. No one could manipulate a tablet like Mac. On a few occasions, Mac had tried to teach both of her partners some of her techniques, but they were so far beyond either of their capabilities that Mac had quickly decided things were better off as they were.

"Explain," she directed Torrin as she manipulated her way through the multitude of accounts and spreadsheets that comprised the company's records.

"It's a great opportunity," Torrin started. "But we basically need to start a new industry on the Fringes to get the full potential out of it. I have full schematics, plans, and the underlying research and development for cybernetic implants that are decades, maybe even centuries, more advanced than anything even the League has."

The announcement shocked Mac enough that she paused in her activity and glanced up at the earnest Torrin and grinning Audra.

"The initial outlay will be enormous," Mac said, her voice expressionless. Torrin could see the gears spinning behind her eyes as Mac tried to wrap her head around what would be required.

"But the payoff will be huge," Torrin countered. "In a few years, we'll be able to corner the market, if not before then. Everyone will be coming to us for the technology. It's highly unlikely that anyone will be able to reverse-engineer it for quite some time."

She pulled her own tablet out of her pocket. Hers was much smaller than Mac's. The uses to which Mac put her tablet were far beyond anything Torrin had any wish to do with her own. If she needed to do something more than her little palm-sized unit could manage, she would either have Tien run it, or she would do it herself at one of the bigger units at her home or office. She opened up the index list to the documents and sent it to both of her partners.

Mac started scrolling through the list immediately. Audra took another gulp of bitrian, then pulled out her own unit.

"This is extensive," Mac said. "Very extensive."

"Holy crap," was Audra's contribution to the conversation.

"So what do we need to make this happen?"

"What could spike our wheels here?"

The questions were right on top of each other and Torrin answered Audra's first. "There's a lot, potentially. For one thing, the Devonites are a rather repressive society, at least when it comes to their treatment of women."

"I thought you said the Orthodoxans were the assholes on the planet."

"They are." She ignored Mac's glance. Fortunately, the possibilities represented by the numbers on her screen quickly recaptured her partner's attention. The less she had to recount of her time with Hutchinson, the better. "They are so much worse than the Devonites, there's almost no comparison. But that doesn't mean the Devonites are saints. It just means the Orthodoxans are really, *really* terrible."

"That's no good. If the Ruling Council finds out we're dealing with a bunch of backward pigs, they're going to have problems justifying our use of the technology."

"I don't think they're all bad, in fact there are a number who show a lot of promise, but I don't think I'll be able to explain the subtleties of what's going on. The fact is, I have a contract with them and we will supply them with their equipment and weapons, but will the council look at the implant tech as fruit—"

"—Of the poison vine?" Mac finished for her. Her brow was creased, but she didn't look up from her tablet. "Very likely, and if they're as bad as you're saying I don't know that they're wrong."

"But look at the good it will do for us," Audra said. "We've never been so close to finishing Nadi. As it was, we were going to be pushing it. You'll be able to tell us best, but I think with what we have here, we could complete terraforming a good decade ahead of schedule. You know how much every year counts."

"Clearly, we need to manage what the council finds out about our newest venture," Torrin said. "They're going to want to be hip-deep in it. We'll have to go off-planet to start production."

Audra stood up and paced back and forth in front of them. The hangover hadn't kept her down for long. Torrin wished she could bounce back as quickly, but she was still recovering from cryostasis. Getting plastered right after coming off ice was not the smartest thing she'd ever done.

"The big liability is your girlfriend," Audra said finally. When Torrin opened her mouth to protest, Audra held up her hand. "Hear me out. She's the only one who can contradict our characterization of the Devonites. Will she be on board for some subterfuge?"

With a cringe that she immediately wished she could take back, Torrin shook her head. "Jak is a lot of things, but a gifted liar isn't one of them. If it doesn't have to do with her gender, Jak can't lie worth a damn." Once again, she was aware of Mac's curiosity. Audra would fill her in, probably sooner rather than later.

"That's unfortunate." Audra perched on the edge of her chair for a moment before getting up again. "So we spin what we have to work with. She's the selfless woman who helped you out of a really tight place. We play up how bad the Orthodoxans are—"

"Which won't be hard," Torrin said. "They really are that bad."

Audra nodded without missing a beat. "And we don't mention the shortcomings of the Devonites. Your Jak becomes a war hero as well as someone who saved your life. We focus on her good qualities. You said she's a good hand as a sniper, right?"

"And then some. The woman is a wizard with a rifle."

"Good. Let's make sure people focus on her and not on her people. We have a hero and a nation of antagonists. She'll be the darling of the masses here."

Torrin nodded slowly. It made sense and would give them some breathing room, enough to get their venture off the ground before the council could stick their collective noses too deep into it. How would the extra attention sit with Jak, though? She had shunned the spotlight back on Haefen, but surely that would be different on Nadi where she didn't have to hide her true self. Still… "We should have it be known that she's very humble. That will explain any reticence she might have about talking about herself."

"That's good. That's really good!" Audra rubbed her hands together with glee. "This is coming together, and I know exactly who to start out with."

"Who?" From the look on Audra's face, Torrin was fairly certain she already knew the answer.

"Nat, of course. She's perfect. She's a giant gossip and people will assume she got her information from you. We'll seed it a few more places, but with Nat spreading it around, we won't have to do much work."

"So can we talk about how feasible this whole thing actually is?" Mac's dry voice put a visible damper on Audra's good mood and she plopped back into her chair.

Torrin opened her mouth to answer Mac, but she turned her head when she thought she heard her name being called. There it was again.

"Torrin?" Jak's voice barely carried through the open doors.

"We're going to need to get back to this, sorry." Torrin got up and crossed the hall to the doors. Audra pushed past her into the room. "Audra! She's not ready for visitors."

Her partner took no notice of Torrin's hissed admonishment. Instead, she walked up to the side of the bed and leaned over the railing.

"So you're the woman who's tamed our wild Torrin." She stuck out her hand to Jak, who eyed it warily for a moment before grasping it. Audra shook it and Torrin appreciated her care. "Torrin's told us so little about you, but I can see how you attracted her eye."

Jak blushed, her discomfort painfully evident in the red of her cheeks.

"Jak, this is Audra, one of my business partners." Torrin glared at Audra. "Though for how much longer remains to be seen."

The only response to her threat was a wide grin. It was strange how much better Audra looked now that she had the chance to give Torrin a hard time.

"Good to meet you," Jak said politely, her voice labored and her face still flaming.

"This is Mac, our other partner." Torrin waved her over from where she'd been standing patiently by the door.

Mac came over to the bed and shook Jak's hand, her face grave. "I'm thrilled to meet you," she said, her words in complete contradiction to her expression.

"Likewise." Jak's response was equally dry.

"So what implants do you have?" Audra's eyes sparkled with poorly suppressed curiosity. "You'll help us demonstrate their effectiveness when the time comes, right?"

"I guess so." The look Jak shot Audra was a little suspicious. Torrin realized that her naturally standoffish nature wasn't going to be overcome so quickly. The thought made her a little sad. She slid her fingertips over the back of Jak's palm, then interlaced their fingers.

"Is there anything I can get you?" Torrin asked.

Jak shook her head. Her eyelids were drooping again. "Just wondered… where you were."

"I'll be right here while you fall asleep." Torrin looked up at her partners and tilted her head toward the door. They nodded and withdrew quietly, Audra raising her hand in quiet farewell, though Torrin wasn't sure Jak saw it. "When you wake up, I'll be right outside the doors, okay?"

"Okay." Jak's eyes drifted the rest of the way shut and her breathing resumed the even rhythms of sleep almost immediately. Torrin watched her sleep for a long time. Regretfully, she relinquished Jak's hand and joined her partners in the hall.

* * *

Over the next week, Jak's condition improved steadily. The quick-grow therapy was very effective; she could feel immediate improvement after each session. By the seventh day of therapy, Jak was breathing totally on her own and had begun to feel more like herself.

She was also getting restless. There had never been a time when she'd been cooped up inside for so long. The walls got a little closer each day, and she was starting to bridle at what she saw as Kiera's overcautiousness.

It didn't help matters any that Torrin was busily working away. The smuggler was at the clinic and spent each one of Jak's waking moments with her. Jak also knew that while she slept, which was still frequently, Torrin worked with her business partners. The three of them had set up an impromptu conference center in the hallway outside her room. Audra and Mac would stop in to say hello. Mac was unfailingly polite, but distant. Audra made her laugh with her outrageous stories and cheerful flirtations. The stories she told about Torrin were endlessly diverting. When Torrin was there looking disgruntled, they were even more enjoyable.

The view out the window on the way to her quick-grow therapy had gotten less jarring. Her eyes were becoming accustomed to washed-out colors of this planet, but it was no less alien to her. She missed the soothing blue of home. Still, she was eager to see what Nadierzda might have to offer. Most of all, she yearned to feel the wind on her face, not the cool but stale breeze from the vents by the ceiling. If she was going to make this planet her home, she needed to take it in and she couldn't do that if they wouldn't let her out of the room.

Aside from the brief distractions of the visits of Torrin's partners, Jak was heartily tired of the same four walls, the same faces and the same assurances that she would be up and about soon. "Soon" always seemed to be right around the corner and she had lost patience. One thing she'd learned was that nobody was going to do anything for her. If something needed to change, she had to do it herself.

"How are you feeling?" Kiera asked. As usual she was flipping through the tablet at the end of the bed.

"Good," Jak replied. "When can I get out of bed and look around?"

"Soon. Very, very soon." Kiera strode over to the wall and pushed a couple of images to the wall display. They were scans of Jak's lungs. The first one Jak recognized from the first day, the second was new.

"As you can see," Kiera said, "your lung tissue is regenerating nicely. There is some scarring, but it appears minimal. I'm extremely pleased with your progress so far."

"So what's the next step?" Torrin asked from her usual seat next to Jak's bed.

"Well, you're going to need some intensive physical therapy." Kiera turned to address Jak directly. "Your lung capacity is extremely diminished. It's one of the reasons you're tiring so quickly. Therapy will help with your lungs, but we won't know for a while if we'll be able to get you back to where you were before this."

"Can we start today?" Jak asked eagerly.

Kiera laughed indulgently but with such warmth that Jak couldn't take offense. "I'm afraid not. You still need to recover from the effects of quick-grow therapy. Let's give it a few days until you're not falling asleep in the middle of your dinner."

Torrin leaned over toward her and clasped her hand.

"Give it time, baby. Let's get you well and not rush things and put you into some sort of setback."

"Listen to your girlfriend," Kiera said. "She gives much better advice than she takes."

Jak squeezed Torrin's hand in response but didn't say anything. It was all well and good for them to tell her to sit tight, but if she didn't move soon, she was going to explode. Kiera thought her a model patient because she sat there and took the doctor's directions and didn't challenge her. Jak hadn't been so successful at what she did because she rushed a stalk, though. All she needed was an opportunity.

As soon as Kiera took her leave of them, Torrin squeezed herself onto the bed next to Jak. She'd been admonished for such things more than once by the doctor, but she didn't seem to care. Jak relished the chance to be close to her. The warmth of Torrin's hand on her cheek was nice. Even nicer was when the smuggler leaned over and pressed her lips to Jak's. It had been so long since they shared more than a quick peck that Jak had almost forgotten how soft Torrin's lips were and how nice she tasted. She parted her lips and allowed Torrin's tongue to slide between them. Arousal flamed to life in her belly, sending warmth lapping throughout her entire body.

Torrin groaned and arched against her, then stopped herself, pulling back. Jak moaned, an inarticulate noise of protest.

"If I don't stop now, I won't be able to stop at all." Torrin laughed shakily. "I don't think you're quite up for that yet."

"Why don't you let me make that decision?" Jak murmured, sliding her hand up under Torrin's shirt to cup one of her breasts.

"Stop that, you tease." Torrin swatted halfheartedly at Jak's hand.

"You sure you want me to stop?" Jak pinched Torrin's nipple gently, rolling it between her fingertips. Even through the fabric of Torrin's bra, she could feel the nipple harden instantly.

"I'd almost forgotten how easily you turn me on," Torrin groaned. "But we really need to stop." Gently she took Jak's hand and disengaged it from her breast.

"That's fine. But the next time I get my hands on you, I'm going to make love to you so thoroughly your head explodes."

Torrin flushed at the thought and seemed to be reconsidering, but she still shook her head. Instead she turned on her side facing Jak and pulled her against her. Their bodies fit together perfectly. The warmth and Torrin's proximity were making Jak drowsy.

"You know what would make this perfect?" Jak asked.

"Hmmm?"

"If you were naked." She was rewarded by the vibration of Torrin's rib cage as she laughed. Torrin squeezed her gently.

Jak lay there for a little longer.

"I know you've been working from here," she finally said a few moments later. "That must be a pain. If you want to go to your office, I won't mind."

"Are you sure?" Torrin asked. "I didn't want to leave you alone here, especially not after I almost missed your first treatment."

"It's fine," Jak assured her. "I'm mostly sleeping anyway, not exactly the most exciting thing to be watching."

"It would help. There's going to be some shit hitting the fan soon." Torrin levered herself up on one elbow to look down at Jak. "You sure you're okay with this?"

"I wouldn't have said anything if I wasn't."

"All right. But I'm going to stick around until you fall asleep. I'm enjoying this too much right now to stop."

"That's..." Jak yawned hugely, jaws creaking. "...fine." As comfortable as she was, it wasn't going to be long before she dropped off. There would be time to look around soon enough after she woke up. Settling in, she closed her eyes and drifted off.

* * *

When she woke, Torrin was nowhere to be found, and the bed was cold except where Jak was lying. The hall door was shut. Torrin always left it propped open whenever she met with her cronies out there, so she could come back in as soon as she saw Jak awake again.

Satisfied that she was alone, Jak swung her legs over the side of the bed. The previous day, they'd removed the oxygen mask and the tube that brought her nutrients and kept her hydrated. She'd been especially happy to see the nutrient tube go. It was as thick around as her pinky and the nurse had been forced to reinsert it through unblemished skin, regrown every time she returned from therapy. Second only to the oppressive closeness of the quick-grow pod, the reintroduction of the nutrition tube into her abdomen was her least favorite thing about therapy.

Jak flexed the muscles in her legs in anticipation, then carefully pushed herself out of bed. As she'd expected, her limbs were quite weak, the muscles atrophied. She held onto the side of the bed and let go experimentally. Almost immediately, her knees buckled, and she clutched the edge of the bed to keep from collapsing. Steeling herself, she let go a second time. Her legs wobbled but held. Taking a deep breath, she took a step. It was slow and took more effort than she'd anticipated, but her legs still supported her weight, if shakily. Slowly she made her way across the room to the cabinets to the left of the door.

Trying not to think about how hard she was holding on to the cabinet top to keep herself from face-planting, she opened the top drawer. The drawer was filled with hospital gowns. Those weren't going to get her very far. Besides which she was heartily sick of wearing them. As she pulled open the second drawer, the door to her room hissed open.

Nat strode through the door toward the bed. Realizing it was empty, she turned to find Jak standing guiltily in front of the cabinet. Nat grinned in delight.

"You're making a break for it, aren't you?"

"Well, not exactly..." Jak hedged, trying to come up with a good reason to be out of bed and rummaging through a cabinet.

"It's about time," Nat crowed. "I don't know how you did it, sitting there and letting them tell you what to do. Poking and prodding while you sat there and took it."

"So you're not going to stop me?"

"Not bloody likely. But you're not going to get far in that." Nat indicated Jak's clothes with her chin.

"I know. I'm trying to find some decent clothing."

"I doubt you'll find any street clothes in there. If you can hold on for a little bit, I'll get you something to wear, then I'll show you around town a bit."

"Won't you get in trouble if we get caught?"

Nat shrugged. "Won't be the first time. Besides, this'll be way more fun than watching you snore."

"I don't snore!"

"Sure you don't." Nat smirked and ducked out of the room.

Well, this is promising. At least it was promising as long as Nat wasn't selling her out to the doctor right about now. She had no choice except to trust the girl, so she waited. Her short sojourn across the room had taken more out of her than she'd expected it would. By the time she made it back to the bed her legs were shaking so badly that she collapsed as much as sat on the soft mattress.

About thirty minutes later Nat came back into the room. She held a small duffel bag and started pulling out articles of clothing.

"You're shorter than I am, so the clothes won't fit real great, but it's better than that thing." She tossed Jak a pair of pants and a shirt. The weave of the clothing was much finer than what Jak was used to on Haefen. The shirt felt almost slick, it was so smooth. Nat pulled out a pair of underwear and a bra and tossed those to her as well. She sat down in the chair and waited expectantly.

Jak wasn't sure what to do. There was no way she was going to disrobe in front of Torrin's sister. The fact that she'd been naked in front of Kiera still troubled her. She had hidden it for so long that revealing it to anyone made her skin crawl. Whenever she went without her breastbinder, she felt like everyone was staring at her.

"Do you mind?" Jak finally said.

"Mind what?" Nat looked puzzled. Realization dawned, and she grinned while Jak blushed slightly. "Modest, are we? That won't last too long around here. But if it'll make you more comfortable..." She swiveled around in the chair until it pointed in the opposite direction.

Jak scrambled into her borrowed clothing as quickly as she was able, which wasn't very. Nat had been right, the clothes did fit strangely. The bra was a new experience for her. After a little maneuvering, she was able to negotiate her way into it. It fit very snugly, and she felt a little less exposed, though far from relaxed. The rest of the clothes were another matter. Not only were the arms and legs a little long, but the chest was rather tight. She shortened the arms and legs easily enough by rolling them a couple of times, but the tightness over her breasts bothered her. She felt like she was calling attention to them. Again, she wondered where her breastbinder was. As often as she'd cursed the thing, at the moment she really missed it.

The clothes felt odd also. Their cut was different than what she was used to, the fasteners unfamiliar and the cloth strange.

Nat swiveled back around when she heard the rustling stop.

"Looking good," she said.

Jak grunted sourly. She felt ridiculous, but if it was going to get her out of the room, she was willing to put up with it.

"Let's get going then," Nat said when it was clear Jak wasn't going to say anything.

It took less time for Jak to get herself levered out of the bed this time. Her legs felt a trifle steadier than they had. She barely wobbled at all as they walked slowly out of her room.

"If someone you know walks toward us, look over at me and talk casually. Whatever you do, don't act like you're guilty of anything, that'll draw their attention more quickly than you shouting at them."

Jak nodded and clamped her teeth on an acerbic comment. She had been trained to insert herself into almost any situation. Usually that had translated to wilderness environments, but she had been trained to infiltrate urban environments as well. If there was one thing she knew, it was how to pass unnoticed.

Even though she was curious about the clinic, she couldn't look around too obviously. She did her best to commit the layout to memory, however. There was never any knowing when intimate knowledge of the interior of a building would come in handy. She hoped there wouldn't be any raids and Torrin had given no indication to expect any, but it didn't hurt to be too prepared.

CHAPTER SEVEN

They walked right out the front door without any acknowledgment, let alone any kind of a challenge. The clinic wasn't overly busy, but she didn't recognize the few doctors and nurses they passed. The large waiting room they passed through before getting to the exterior doors was populated only by a handful of women. Jak saw absolutely no men. The only people they saw were female. It didn't make her uncomfortable exactly, but it felt like something was strangely amiss. She'd been around men almost to the exclusion of all else for so long that to be in the company of so many women was making her twitchy.

They passed through the clinic's doors and only Jak's instincts kept her from stopping to rubberneck. The first thing that hit her was the smell. It was like taking a deep breath of the inside of an oven and she wondered if there was any water on the planet at all. Her nostrils dried out instantly and she wrinkled her nose while looking around. The sky was the same dusky blue she'd seen through the window, not the brilliant blue that she was used to back home. Against the dusty-looking sky, the green of the trees really glowed. They were an emerald color that didn't look natural in a tree. In fact, the whole spectrum of colors was more vibrant because they were true colors, not simply different variations on blue. She looked left toward the huge cliff face rose that rose in the distance. Bands of browns and yellows shot through the rock. The top of the cliff was higher than anything she'd seen before. As she looked more closely, she could see what appeared to be canyons carved into the rock.

"Watch your feet," Nat said, taking her elbow and guiding her around a large flowerpot. Apparently Jak hadn't been doing as well as she thought in the not-rubbernecking department. She dropped her gaze and checked out her immediate surroundings. The overall impression she got of the city was one of flatness. The buildings weren't very high, the tallest ones maybe three stories high. There were plants everywhere. That bright green was shot through by brilliant flowers in every imaginable hue. The plants added variation to what could have been a very stark design of straight lines and squares. It should have been boring, but it wasn't. Many of the buildings were accented with architectural details, borders and murals. Each accent gave the building the character that was absent in their unvarnished overall design.

It was all so foreign to her eyes. Everything looked off. *She* felt off. She'd hoped that getting a better look at the planet would help her feel more at home, but it was only helping to solidify exactly how different she was and how out of place. Nothing about this place was right.

"Do you want to know more about my home?" Nat asked. She had a hand on Jak's elbow to steer her around any obstacles. As tightly as she was holding on to her arm, though, Jak was certain Nat's hand was there as much to keep her from falling over as it was to move her around planters.

Nat's hand was dark against her skin. Jak stared at it for a moment, then scanned the small crowds of women who eddied this way and that around them. There were women with the same skin tone as her and Torrin, but there were easily as many women of differing shades, including some who were darker even than Kiera. Jak hadn't known people came in any other shades than pale.

"...terraformed."

The strange word caught Jak's attention and she realized that Nat had decided to give her Nadierzda's background, even though Jak hadn't said anything.

"Once the hotel company went belly up, Nadierzda floated out here. Along with the company's records, the planet was lost. Good for us, really. Who knows what some core world corporation would have tried to get going here if they'd known about it."

"So you don't like the League either?"

"What's to like? It's not like they've done anything for us. We're better off without them and we get along just fine, thanks anyway. Besides, I don't think they would've gotten on well with our ancestors. They weren't exactly the most law-abiding women in the galaxy."

"Were they smugglers like Torrin?" Jak thought these mysterious women must have had a lot in common with her. There was more than a little nose-thumbing of authority from Torrin.

Nat laughed. "Not even. They were straight-up pirates. The story goes that they had quite a fleet and were really well-organized a few star systems over. They got a little too successful, though, and a bunch of worlds banded together to take them out. The fact that they were all women and had the nasty habit of taking all the female slaves with them when they attacked a ship or settlement probably had something to do with how pissed off everyone got at them. Men. You take away their toys, and they decide they hate you."

"Pirates with hearts of gold?" This was starting to sound more and more like a fairy tale. She thought maybe it was based on one her mother would tell them. Robbing Hood and his Many Men, or something like that.

Jak's skepticism must have come through because Nat shook her head. "They definitely were in it for themselves and their families. Aside from liberating the slaves, there was nothing soft about them. Anyway, the pirate fleet scattered to avoid the fleet after them. One ship came this way and tried to lose its pursuers in the asteroid field. They must have clipped an asteroid, or maybe they were damaged by the ones chasing them, I'm not sure. Different people have different versions of that part. I think they probably clipped a rock, but getting damaged while destroying another ship definitely sounds more exciting. They came down somewhere around here and decided to stick around for a while. A crash landing will do that, I guess."

Despite her skepticism, Jak was getting drawn into the story. Hearing about the exploits of women awakened a thirst in her that she hadn't suspected existed. Stories about women who were more than window dressing or the object of men's affection were new to her. "So were they okay? What happened to the other ships?"

"Most of the rest of them eventually tracked them down. They figured out the planet was hard to find and didn't seem to be on anyone's star charts, so they decided to colonize it. Most of the pirates were from Ancient Russia, part of the same extended family. They called the planet Nadierzda, which means 'hope' in Old Russian. Whether they were hoping no one else would find them, or they thought the planet would be a new hope for the former slaves, I don't know."

It was quite the tale. Jak wasn't sure what Nat meant by Russia or Russian, but that seemed neither here nor there. She was glad to get some background. It helped her reconcile some of the alienness of the landscape and the people in her mind. They were different than she was, that was true, and none of them could share her experiences, but they hadn't sprung fully formed from the ground either. To be reminded of that was comforting.

She wished Torrin were there with them. She was the one who should have been rattling on, letting her know about this new place she expected Jak to share. Instead, she seemed to have her heart set on wrapping Jak up as snugly as possible. Jak didn't need to be kept safe; she needed someone to help her deal with the newness of her situation.

Silence had grown between her and Nat, and Jak was content to let it. Nat was nice enough, but her cheerfulness was the last thing Jak wanted to deal with. Torrin's sister was only trying to help, but it didn't change the fact that Torrin should have been there instead.

"I'm really glad I caught you breaking out of there," Nat said a while later.

"What do you mean by that?" Jak asked, immediately suspicious. Was Torrin's sister about to turn her in?

"I was starting to wonder why my sister had gone for a complete wimp, so different from her usual type of girl. She mostly likes women who are fiery. You know, who don't take any crap."

"So she's had a lot of girlfriends?" Jak didn't really want to know the answer, but she was compelled to ask all the same.

"Not exactly," Nat replied blithely. Jak heaved a mental sigh of relief. Perhaps she'd been misunderstanding the veiled and not-so-veiled references to Torrin's love life. "I mean she would have to go with them for a while to be considered girlfriends. They were mostly women she would have sex with for a few weeks, then she would leave town and move on to someone else when she came back."

Jak stopped dead in her tracks. Was that what she was to Torrin? Someone who was only around to play with before she found something more interesting? Ahead, Nat came to a stop and looked back when she realized that Jak was no longer with her. Catching the look on Jak's face, she backtracked over to her.

"I'm sure that's not what's going on with you two, though. She's never brought anyone back with her before and she seemed really broken up when you were really sick. Plus, it's not like her to stick around when she isn't getting any."

"Is that supposed to make me feel better? 'You must be okay because she isn't having sex with you.'"

"Um, yes?" Nat looked down at the ground and tried to wear a hole in a paving stone with the toe of her shoe.

Movement in the sky caught Jak's eye, and she allowed it to distract her from her line of questioning about Torrin.

"What's that?" she asked, pointing to a small oblong object flying high above. As she watched, wings flared out and it swooped in a lazy circle, climbing higher and higher.

Nat brightened up when she saw where Jak was pointing. "It's an ultralight aircraft. There's a group of women who fly them. It drives the Ruling Council nuts. They're of the opinion that it's extremely dangerous."

"There's someone in there?" Jak's eyes glowed. Being able to fly above everything would be almost as good as being back in her forests. Already, she could feel the solitude she would have on the heights. Being able to see so much but to be almost invisible from the naked eye would be amazing. She manipulated her left ocular implant to zoom in on the ultralight. "Can we do that?"

"Sure, I can talk to some people about getting you up there." Nat looked over at her, a little surprised at her excitement. "You're really amped about that, aren't you?"

Jak nodded, still watching the aircraft. She drank in every detail she could make out.

"Let's keep going," Nat suggested. "I think there's something else you'll like to see."

They kept on down the road and turned left down a side street. Torrin's sister led them in what felt like a circle. Eventually, they stopped in front of a grassy open area. Stunted trees lined one edge of the grass. Nat led her across the wide, grass-filled expanse to the far end. A shimmering force field separated them from an even larger grassy area. Gratefully, Jak sat down when Nat took a seat under one of the trees by the force field. Even that relatively short walk had taken a lot out of her.

"So why did you help me make a break for it?" Jak asked idly as she watched Nat peel the bark from a twig that had fallen off the tree.

"I know what it's like to be cooped up." Nat pulled off another strip of bark. "Anyone can see that you've been going stir-crazy, stuck in that bed. I could tell that you were ready to get out of that holding pattern, get back on with life. Torrin doesn't always see things like that. She decides what's best for you and goes with it. She won't give me a fair shake either. I hate working comms at the spaceport. Instead of getting to do the fun stuff, I make it so other people get to."

"How do you mean?"

"I've been asking her to give me a shot working with her for over a year now, but she won't even discuss it with me. All she'll say is I'm not ready, but how can I prove if I'm ready or not if she won't give me a shot?"

"You know, I'm not even really sure exactly what she does. I mean I know she's a smuggler since that's how I met her, but that's all."

"Were you supposed to make a deal with her?" Nat asked, changing the subject.

When talking to Nat, Jak had become accustomed to her habit of redirecting conversations whenever she got distracted by something more interesting. She would probably come back around to her previous tack and with as little warning.

"Oh no." The idea was so preposterous that Jak barked a laugh. "No one was supposed to trade with her, not as far as my superiors were concerned. I was sent to kill her."

"You were?" Nat stared at her, eyes wide. She leaned away from Jak. It was a little shift, but Jak picked up on it immediately. "Wow, she didn't tell me that. Not surprising, I guess. But still. Wow."

"Well, yeah," Jak said. She needed to convince Nat that she had no evil designs on her sister. She had only been following orders, but not very well as it turned out. "A supply of new tech for the Orthodoxans could have easily swayed the war in their direction."

"So you went out and killed whoever you were told to?"

"That is—was my job," Jak said, wondering where the line of questioning was going. "It's not like I wanted to. Snipers don't make the call on the target. All we do is pull the trigger."

"Then why didn't you shoot my sister?"

"I don't know, not exactly. When I found out she was a woman, it kind of threw me. I've never killed a woman before, only ever men. The Orthodoxans don't value women, so there's no point in killing them."

"Are they really that bad? Torrin told me a little bit, but I thought maybe she was exaggerating. She does that sometimes, when she's trying to make a story more exciting." Nat leaned back against the tree's trunk and watched Jak through half-lidded eyes.

"They're worse. Most of what Torrin knows is what I told her, and she doesn't know the worst of it."

"Then why anyone thought it was a good idea to send a female to trade with the Orthodoxans, I don't know. It seems like a good way to get rid of someone." Nat looked thoughtful for a moment. "She's more than a smuggler, really. She and her partners run one of the most successful trading houses in the Fringes. They have offices on over half a dozen worlds and they're always looking to expand. It's one way that women who don't fit can leave here."

"Women who don't fit? What does that even mean?"

"So what do you know about Nadierzda?"

"Almost nothing aside from I'm here and I haven't seen a man yet."

"Miss them?" Nat asked slyly. She snickered at Jak's look.

"Not hardly. But it's weird not to see any and to see so many women doing all the things I was taught they weren't suited for."

"You get that a lot out here. A lot of places on the Fringes are really backward when it comes to how they treat women. Though not usually as bad as your Orthodoxans."

"They're *not* mine."

Nat shrugged and continued. "Just because they aren't usually as bad doesn't mean that there aren't some who are. We don't usually see whole planets of them, though. There are a lot of slavers in operation out here, and most of the time they traffic in female slaves. We rescue a lot of girls from that life and they end up here. Torrin's biological mother was one of those. I guess she was already pregnant with Torrin when she was brought here. She must have been in rough shape when she came in. I was told she died shortly after giving birth. I don't even know what her name was. I don't know if anybody does, even Torrin. Her moms adopted her right after she was born."

Jak nodded. That made sense with some of what Torrin had told her while they were still on Haefen. "So were you born here then?"

Nat nodded. "I was. My mom came from offworld also. Raisa. She's Irenya's current wife."

Jak must have looked as confused as she felt. She didn't consider herself a stupid person, but she was having problems untangling the mess that was the sisters' family tree. Who was Raisa again?

Nat grinned. "Families here get really confusing if you're not used to it. There's no stigma attached to adoption. In fact, most families rarely go more than a generation without adopting in a new daughter. Tamra and Irenya were Torrin's adoptive mothers, but Tamra died shortly after Torrin joined the militia. Irenya then married Raisa and they had me. Simple, right?"

Jak snorted, then coughed. "Sure." Simple as tracking a bullet's drift through changing crosswinds.

"I can draw you a diagram if it helps."

"I think I'm good."

"Excellent. So some women, mostly from off planet, don't want to stick around on a planet full of women who are mostly dykes. That's where Torrin's company comes in. They also keep their eyes out for women in trouble and send them on here."

"So everyone here likes…" Jak hesitated, her upbringing warring with her desire to know. "They like sleeping with other women?" Her voice was high, almost squeaky with surprise.

"Not a hundred percent. Some women are bi, some are so damaged they probably won't have sex with anyone ever again. Some women leave when their sons get too old to stay here. Torrin's company makes sure they have access to good jobs and prospects in other Fringe settlements. There are no males over the age of six on Nadi." Nat looked Jak in the eye. "You didn't think you were the only one, did you?"

The question floored Jak. She had been thinking exactly that since the first moment her attraction to Torrin had reared its head. From the way Nadierzda's other women acted around the smuggler, she knew intellectually that it must not be the case, but she believed in her heart that there was something wrong in her, twisted.

Some of her struggle must have shown on her face because Nat patted her reassuringly on the shoulder.

"There's nothing wrong with you. There's nothing wrong with feeling like you do. Hell, if she weren't my sister and wasn't a huge pain in my ass, I'd want her too. If you think there's something wrong with you for feeling like you want to be with women, then you're saying there's something wrong with most of the women on this planet. And I don't recommend voicing that opinion where they can hear you because they'll probably kick your ass for saying it."

Nat opened her mouth to continue but closed it again. She rolled her eyes and looked up at the sky.

"Looks like we're busted," Nat said cheerfully, all traces of seriousness gone. "Torrin's pinging me, wants to know where we are."

"Does she sound pissed?"

"Yeah, but don't worry, she'll get over it. I'm sure she'll blame me for everything." Nat looked up, searching the sky for something. "We'll go back in a second, I want you to see this."

Jak craned her neck to see around the tree's branches, joining Nat in gazing skyward. A small point swooped slowly toward them. It grew slowly larger as it got closer and Jak had to engage her ocular implant to bring it into focus. It was another ultralight, though this one looked smaller and less robust. She watched with wonder as the small aircraft came toward them. On completely silent wings, it floated past them to land on a paved strip with effortless ease. Jak couldn't tear her eyes from the small vessel. She'd never seen anything more like freedom in her life.

* * *

"What the hell were you thinking?" Torrin turned her back on Nat and pinched the bridge of her nose between her fingers, trying to calm down. Even though her sister was across the room, she wouldn't look at her. She didn't trust herself enough to get near Nat. There was an excellent chance she would end up throttling her.

"It's not her fault," Jak said quietly from the bed where Kiera was looking her over. The too-large clothing she had obviously borrowed from Nat had been removed and she was back in a hospital gown. Torrin could tell she was exhausted from the way she lay there allowing the doctor to poke at her.

"She knows better than to pull this shit," Torrin griped. "There's no excuse."

"Oh please," Nat shot back at her sister. "Not that long ago, you would have suggested it yourself. You need to stop wrapping your girlfriend in gauze. She won't break." She looked like she was about to say more but quieted at a glance from Jak.

"She almost did." *And it was all my fault.*

"I don't need you to fight my battles," Jak said. Nat's head whipped around, dismay in the curve of her eyebrows. She opened her mouth to speak, but Jak forestalled her. "Not you, Nat. You, Torrin."

The statement surprised Torrin. *Does she really feel like that? Like I'm trying to fight her battles for her?* In her mind's eye, she could still see Jak hunkered down, tongue between her teeth, skin stretched over her face and eyes bright with fever. Even then, she squeezed off shot after methodical shot. Half dead of fever, and she was still driven to fight. When would Jak realize she didn't have to fight all her own battles, that she had someone willing to take up the cause on her behalf? Torrin would have to demonstrate that Jak could rely on her to help keep her safe.

"So how is she?" Torrin directed the question at Kiera, ignoring the way Jak's lips tightened.

"Not too bad, considering. She's slightly feverish and her breathing sounds a little labored. It's likely the result of overexertion, but we'll keep an eye on her."

"See, she's fine." Nat pushed herself away from the wall to one side of the door and ran one hand through her hair. By the gesture, she'd been more worried than she was letting on.

"No thanks to you."

"Enough from the two of you." Jak issued the order from the bed. Her voice was quiet, but there was a whipcrack of authority in her tone. She was usually so reserved that it was easy for Torrin to forget she'd been a noncommissioned officer in the Devonite army. "Nat, I'll talk to you tomorrow. Don't forget your promise."

Nat nodded and turned on her heel, leaving the room without any further words for her sister, though the angry look she sent her was clear enough. Kiera took the opportunity to slip out. She sent a significant look in Torrin's direction, trying to send her a message, but Torrin had no clue what she might be after. When Torrin stared back at her blankly, Kiera just shook her head and followed Nat out of the room.

"Come here." Jak's voice was even quieter, but the sharpness was gone. She patted the edge of the bed. Torrin joined her and took Jak's nearest hand between her own.

"What are we doing here?" Jak asked.

"We're waiting for you to get better," Torrin replied. The answer to the question was pretty evident to her.

"That's not what I meant." Jak plucked at Torrin's fingers with her free hand. "I like spending time with you and I'm pretty sure you like spending time with me. Even when we're not—you know." She blushed and waved a hand vaguely in the air. "But I feel like you're trying to keep me a secret. If your partner hadn't shoved her way past you into the room the other day, would you have introduced me? I can't tell if you're embarrassed by me or what. Is it that you don't want to be seen with me in public?"

"Is that what you think? That you embarrass me?" Where had Jak gotten that idea? It was so obvious how she felt about the sniper. "You don't embarrass me, but you have to understand, I have something of a reputation around here. You don't embarrass me. The way I used to be and how people are going to react, that's what embarrasses me."

Jak looked unconvinced but nodded slowly. "Nat told me all about your planet's history. None of the women your people look up to are pushovers. I won't be one either."

Torrin winced. She should have been the one showing Jak around and filling her in. She'd completely misread the situation and misplayed her hand badly. If she wasn't careful, she would drive Jak away and someone else would snap her up. "If it'll help convince you, I can start introducing you around. I was only trying to spare you some of the prodding. After all, you're getting enough of that here." Jak didn't smile at the sally and kept watching her with those big blue eyes. Sighing, Torrin soldiered on. "Look, this town is like a village a quarter its size. Everyone knows what everyone else is up to, and they all have an opinion which they'll happily share whether you want it or not. Besides, it's not like you've really been up to it."

"That's the other thing," Jak said. "You need to stop treating me like I'm going to break. I can't deal with that."

"I know that, but after what happened on the ship, the thought of losing you…" Torrin looked away, the red of Jak's blood painting the cryotube a horridly vivid memory. It had run from her mouth and down the tube, dripping to the floor.

Jak squeezed her hand, reacting to the pain that Torrin couldn't conceal. "Try not to get carried away, that's all I ask. I got along fine before you came along and I could again if I needed to." Her eyes darkened and it was Jak's turn to look away.

Torrin let loose a series of curses inside her head. The bleakness yawned again in Jak's eyes as she'd spoken of getting along without her. Now that they were on Nadi, the darkness was supposed to go away. Obviously, she needed to work on that. Jak was painfully independent, and Torrin wondered if she should loosen up a little bit. Their relationship was so new that it was tender in some places and raw in others. The strain of Jak's illness on top of the move to an unfamiliar world wasn't allowing their relationship to unfold as she would have liked. Her plans of taking Jak around, showing her the sights and ensconcing them in various romantic locations to make love, had gone up in smoke, erased by the terror of almost losing her. As she thought about it, Torrin could feel the tips of her ears heating and hot embarrassment flooded her face. Though it pained her to admit it, Nat and Jak were right. She should have been the one to take Jak out.

"Look, once your fever is gone, I'll take you out and start showing you around. My sister was right. Don't tell her I said that, though. I'll deny it completely."

"She's young, but she seems to have a good head on her shoulders," Jak said, gracious in her victory. "And I'd like that. Having you show me around, that is."

CHAPTER EIGHT

"The Ruling Council is very concerned about your plans," said the buttoned-down woman standing in front of the three partners. Torrin eyed her carefully, trying to conceal her active dislike. Alyx Rosnowski was the Ruling Council's official representative but not a member of the council itself. There was open speculation on Nadierzda that she was positioning herself for the next open council seat.

"So we've gathered," Torrin drawled. "Hopefully we can allay some of their fears."

"I hope so. The rumors going around Landing have created concern among the council's members that your latest business venture will expose the planet's existence."

"We've put together a quick presentation." Torrin stood up and pulled a chair out for Alyx. "If you'll take a seat, we can get to it."

The representative folded her body into the chair. Tall and painfully thin, she reminded Torrin of an insect. Coupled with eyes that were slightly too large, an unfortunate habit of rarely blinking and the way she cocked her head, Torrin was always reminded of the Earth praying mantis. At one time it had been believed that the mantis ate the head off her mate during copulation. As she watched Alyx, Torrin could believe the representative would think that was a good idea, especially if she could gain some political benefit from the act.

She smiled thinly as Torrin pushed the seat in. Pulling out her tablet, she fussed with it on the table a little bit to make sure it was perfectly aligned.

Mac stood at the front of the conference room and pushed the presentation from her own tablet to the wall. Audra had actually been forced to go back through the presentation and make it a little less perfect. Mac, in typical fashion, had completed the presentation days ago and had been tweaking it ever since, trying to get it as perfect as possible. She had actually thrown her hands up and walked out of the office in disgust when Audra insisted it be less polished. The point was to make sure the Ruling Council thought they'd caught the three of them unprepared. If they caught wind that they were being subtly manipulated, the whole business could be torpedoed. Mac looked slightly uncomfortable at the front of the room. She still wasn't happy presenting something that was less than perfect. Fortunately, her discomfort actually helped the image they were trying to project.

"If you have any questions about the origin of the technology, you can ask Torrin." Mac swung into the presentation, body stiff. "Suffice it to say that we expect to be able to revolutionize the cybernetics industry, not only here on the Fringes, but among the inner worlds as well."

Torrin had a sanitized version of her acquisition of the tech ready to go. There was no reason for her to get into the entire business and how Jak fit in to it.

Thinking of Jak made her smile slightly. Jak was recovering nicely from the unscheduled jaunt she had indulged in with Nat a few days earlier. Her sister was right, though it still pained Torrin to admit it, even in the privacy of her own thoughts. She should have been bringing Jak out long ago, regardless of Kiera's protestations. The doctor wasn't used to dealing with women like Jak; her typical patients weren't the well-honed machines that Jak was. If she'd been thinking, she would have suggested that Kiera think of her more like one of the rodeo riders and less like the typical city-dwelling women she usually treated. The realization only furthered Torrin's self-recrimination; she knew what kind of a woman Jak was, and she was definitely not the kind who suffered being cooped up lightly. It was a huge oversight on her part and she was doing her best to make it up to Jak.

The previous night, the two of them had gone for a slow walk outside the clinic. Nadierzda was really at her best at night in Torrin's opinion. During the day, the wind was hot and carried dust on it that got into everything and coated every surface with fine grit. At night, when the sun went down, the air grew more humid. The wind, hot as air from a baker's oven during the day, was cool and smelled of damp grasses at night. Most of the Landing's population agreed with Torrin about the superiority of Nadi's climate at night and socialized in the evening, with women gathering in every other square to talk and laugh and pair up.

As the two of them had wandered slowly through the streets of Landing, Torrin had introduced Jak dozens of times. Her lover seemed oblivious, both of the envious stares and the admiring ones. Admiring stares because Jak was very attractive in her own right; with her bronzed skin, short blond hair and piercing blue eyes, she easily turned many heads. Envious stares came from those who credited her with tying down Torrin and taking her off the market. Overall, Torrin was happier with the envious stares than the admiring ones. She hadn't thought of herself as the jealous type, but with Jak she wanted everyone to know the two of them were very much together.

When Jak had tired, they'd found themselves part of a quiet gathering. They'd both sat and listened as women sang quietly, accompanied by musicians on local instruments. Many of the songs were ones Torrin had known since childhood, but hearing them with Jak made her consider them anew. Occasionally she heard a song she hadn't heard before and she knew it had come from women newer to Nadi. Some were of the opinion that new arrivals to Nadi were a danger, but in her opinion the new arrivals kept the population from stultifying. Nadi's vitality and success came from the influx of new ideas and new cultures. She'd seen too many Fringe societies that had stopped evolving and, like Haefen, had become mired in some truly horrid traditions.

She'd tried to cuddle with Jak, but the sniper had frozen as soon as Torrin made a move that could have been interpreted as being the slightest bit intimate. Torrin tried to understand that Jak couldn't instantly take down the walls she'd built around herself on Haefen. A lifetime of locking people out to preserve her secret wasn't going to be undone in a couple of weeks. Still, as the night wore on and the music continued, Jak unbent enough to scoot over to her lover. By the end of the evening, she was settled comfortably between Torrin's legs and leaning back against her chest. All Torrin had wanted to do was take Jak back to her flat and make love to her. Hopefully Torrin would actually survive that long. *Is it possible to die of unrequited arousal?*

"Torrin? Torrin!" Hearing her name jolted the smuggler out of her reverie. Her cheeks were warm from her remembered arousal, and a curl of heat slowly unfurled in her belly.

"Glad you could join us," Alyx said with malicious glee at Torrin's red cheeks. "Now that you're paying attention, perhaps you'd like to explain how you came into possession of these schematics."

"Well, Alyx," Torrin replied, an easy smile on her face, "I engaged in negotiations with the military head of government of the Devonite people on the planet Haefen. We were able to reach a mutually beneficial arrangement, part of which was the schematics for creation of the implants."

Lips pursed as though she'd gotten a whiff of something particularly foul, Alyx regarded Torrin steadily. A faction on council disapproved heartily of any military connections. Usually, the disapproval amused Torrin to no end. Nadierzda had been settled by pirates, very successful pirates. If the council thought those women had been that successful by asking nicely and strewing rose petals about, then they were seriously deluded. At the moment, all the disapproval did was irk her. Their plan was a good one and she wasn't going to let it be derailed by a few prudish old ladies.

"We're prepared to turn over a copy of the schematics to the local research community for their perusal." Audra inserted herself smoothly into the conversation when the silence lengthened uncomfortably. "I think they'll agree that we don't have the capabilities to develop it here."

"I've taken the liberty of forwarding a copy of our proposal to the members of the Ruling Council as well," Mac added. "A number of them will be able to evaluate the proposal on its own merit. We are, of course, standing by to clarify any points that might seem…murky."

"I see." Alyx eyed the trio carefully. "Your preparation is admirable. I'll report my findings to the council. I'm sure they'll be in contact." Primly, the scrawny woman stowed the tablet in her bag and pushed back her chair. Neither Torrin nor any of her partners made any move to help her up. Without any further comments, Alyx swept out of the conference room.

When she was well out of earshot, Audra let out a loud sigh. "Do you think we pulled it off?"

"I'm not sure, we'll find out soon, I expect." Torrin glanced over at Mac. "Good call sending out proposals to the members of the council. There's no way that Alyx can sweep this under the rug."

"Oh. Yes. I need to do that before I forget."

Audra and Torrin looked at each other.

"You mean you lied to her?" Audra asked, her voice cracking in incredulous surprise.

"Well, yes."

"You never lie," Torrin said. "I didn't think you knew how."

"Just because I generally choose not to doesn't mean I don't know how," Mac said. "Frankly, after running the numbers not only for this opportunity but also the outfitting of Haefen for space travel, I've concluded this is our best chance to finish the terraforming on Nadi."

Torrin was impressed. Mac was rarely this impassioned. The last time she'd heard her so fired up was right before Mac had proposed to her then-girlfriend.

"You know we don't have that much time left. Every year, more water sources are choked off by silt and more arable land is claimed by sand. By my calculations, if we don't move on this in the next ten years, we'll lose Nadi. Well, I'm not ready to leave."

"That right there," Audra crowed, looking at Torrin and pointing across the table to Mac. "We need to get her up in front of the council in an open session."

Nodding slowly, Torrin looked back and forth between the two of them. "Let's get your employee in here, Audra. The one with the talent for marketing. We have word to spread."

"Will do." Audra chewed on her lower lip for a moment. "We need to talk about which councilors we want to target for…special consideration."

"Bribery?" Mac's voice was as stiff as her back. "It's a good proposal. Can't we assume that we'll be able to get it through without having to resort to that?"

Torrin sighed. She wanted to believe the proposal was strong enough to stand on its own merit, but she knew the reality of Nadierzdan politics. "I'm sorry, Mac, but I think Audra may be right." She raised both hands when Mac opened her mouth to protest. "I hope we won't have to, but we need to be prepared in the event that a couple of councilors hold out for compensation. It wouldn't be the first time." She looked over at Audra. "I'll contact the councilors individually in a few days and see where the sticking points are and which ones can be overcome monetarily."

"I'll look into our funds and see where we can pull clean money for payoffs." Mac pushed herself away from the table and left the room without a further word, her back straight.

Torrin shared a sad look with Audra. They'd discussed the unfortunate level of corruption on the Nadierzdan council before. While Torrin believed with all her heart that Nadi was superior to other Fringe worlds in many ways, they weren't perfect by any stretch.

Not every member of the council was crooked, but there were members who were in it for themselves or solely for their constituents, rather than the interests of the entire planet. Those councilwomen would require extra persuasion, either in credits or in favors for their district. The issue was too important to be derailed by a few shortsighted women.

* * *

The physical therapist was trying to kill her. The woman cheerfully cranked up the speed and incline on the treadmill. Jak was already running along at a clip barely short of a sprint. The addition of incline and another three kilometers an hour of speed wasn't fair. She gasped, inhaling deeply, feeling her breath catch with a slight wheeze at the back of her throat.

Screw this, she thought and collapsed theatrically against the guard bars, then oozed over the side, landing in a crumpled heap next to the machine.

"Nice," the therapist said dryly and tossed her a towel.

Applause from the door drew her attention as she toweled her short hair dry. Peering out from under the towel, she saw Nat and a stranger walking toward her, clapping.

"That was very convincing," Nat said, her wide smile revealing the dimples in her cheeks.

"Thanks," Jak replied brightly. "I do have a lot of experience to pull from."

"Oh yeah." Torrin's sister deflated visibly.

"I'll see you tomorrow, Jak," her therapist called to her.

"Not if I die of exhaustion first, Joan," Jak called back to her. "Help me up, would you?" she said to Nat.

The stranger quickly grabbed her hand and pulled Jak to her feet before Nat could intervene.

"Jak, this is Tanith." Nat's normally open expression was guarded. "She wants to talk to you about a couple of things. Also, she's the one who can hook you up with the ultralights if you're still interested."

Tanith was standing a hair too close for Jak's comfort, and the sniper sidled back half a step. She still had Jak's hand in hers and she pumped it briskly in greeting.

"It's really good to finally meet you, Jak. Everyone in Landing has heard so much about you. Is it true you have over a hundred kills to your credit?"

Taken aback, all Jak could do was shrug. The majority of the women she had met so far, with the exception of Torrin and her sister, had a marked aversion to violence. In truth, she had no idea how many men she'd killed. It could have been a hundred. It could as easily have been three hundred or more. It was only a job. She'd gone where she was told and killed who she'd been directed. Until Torrin, that was.

Tanith regarded her a moment, curly blond hair framed by the sun streaming through the windows behind her. She was still close enough that Jak could see the freckles dusting across her nose. She topped Jak by a fair number of centimeters, and her frame was one of compact muscle. There was a graceful economy to her movements, which Jak had seen before in some of the men in her unit. Those men had been trained to kill with their hands, and they'd been good at it. Tanith reminded her uncomfortably of them.

"You don't need to be modest," Tanith said. "No one's going to be able to disprove you, so go with it." She bumped Jak with her shoulder and smiled broadly to show she was joking.

"Most people here seem uncomfortable with what I've done," Jak ventured cautiously. She finished toweling herself down. As usual after one of her physical therapy sessions, she was exhausted and in a full sweat, but it was worth it. She'd seen definite improvements to her condition. After four days of PT, she could now walk at a normal pace without feeling like she was going to collapse after a few steps. Still, her recovery wasn't moving fast enough to satisfy her. Any kind of a sustained run wore her out much too quickly, and for someone who had been used to running cross country for a few days or more, the reduced capacity upset her. Irritated all over again, she tossed the towel into a receptacle in the corner.

"A lot of the women here have seen too much already." Tanith shook her head sadly. "That's where I come in."

"Tanith commands the militia's ground forces," Nat interjected.

"That's right. It's one of the reasons I wanted to talk to you. I'm hoping you'll be willing to help out with training the women in distance shooting. They're adequate, but I know there's so much more that they—we—can do."

"I can do that," Jak said. It would be nice to be out shooting again. She missed the focused sense of purpose when all she had to worry about were herself and the rifle. The world narrowed until all that mattered was her, the weapon and her target. Sometimes it even felt like she and her rifle were one. At those times, life seemed so simple.

"Excellent. When Nat mentioned that you were interested in going up in an ultralight, I thought perhaps I could barter lessons with you. You teach a group of my women to shoot like you do, and I'll teach you to fly like I do." Tanith smiled, white teeth flashing against her sun-bronzed face. "I think you'll find the women of the militia will understand you a lot better than the majority of Nadierzda's population does. They aren't afraid to stand up for what they believe in."

"I can't do anything until I clear it with my doctor," Jak cautioned.

"No problem. I don't want to get in the way of your recovery." Tanith raised her hands. "That's obviously the most important thing for you right now."

"Torrin should be by soon," Nat noted neutrally.

"Then that's my cue to leave. Thanks for agreeing to help out, Jak. I'm in your debt." Jak's hand was seized between Tanith's two strong palms and pumped vigorously. "Let me know when you're cleared and we'll get started." She turned and walked toward the doors.

Jak watched her leave and was struck by a sudden thought. "Tanith! What was the other reason you wanted to meet me?" she called after the departing militiawoman.

Tanith turned and grinned, walking backward between the doors. "I'd heard you were cute. I wanted to see if that was true." She winked in Jak's direction, then spun jauntily and disappeared around the corner.

Jak chatted with Nat while changing out of her exercise clothes. She was feeling a little less self-conscious about changing in front of Torrin's sister. To Nat's amusement, which she never failed to share, Jak still insisted on turning away when she pulled off her shirt.

"Was that Tanith I saw on her way out of here?" Torrin asked as she strode through the doors.

Nat muttered something a little too low for Jak to hear and turned around to face her sister. "It was. She was asking Jak for some help training some of the militia members."

"So what is she really up to, I wonder?" Torrin asked, staring out the doors.

"She could be up to exactly what she says she is."

"Yeah." Torrin snorted, a frown creasing her brow. "That would be a first."

"She isn't all bad, you know. She does a great job with the militia and the soldiers she commands really love her."

"You don't know her like I do. You don't have to scratch the surface very hard to find the rot on that one."

Jak quietly finished getting dressed. The argument between the sisters made her acutely uncomfortable. It was obvious that Torrin had a beef with Tanith, and she decided not to say anything about the ultralight lessons. There was no point in upsetting Torrin any further.

While the two of them were distracted, she did up her breastbinder. On a visit to the *Calamity Jane* a few days previous, Jak had grabbed it from the corner of the cryostasis room where it had been lying since Torrin had put her in the cryotube. For something that she'd grown to hate so much while she'd been forced to wear it on Haefen, she'd really missed it on Nadi. It felt so strange to have her breasts out there and visible where everyone could see them. She wasn't worried that someone would discover her gender, but she felt so much more secure when she wore it. It was also getting to be time to get her hair cut. The ends were starting to curl a bit. The way it framed her face was getting to be much too girly.

As she rolled up the sleeves and legs of her clothing, she was aware that Torrin was standing right by her. A broad grin creased Torrin's face when she looked up.

"What?" Jak asked as she leaned in toward the taller woman. Torrin kissed her lingeringly on the lips and Nat made a noise of disgust behind them. They ignored her.

"You look like a little kid wearing her mom's clothes. What do you say we get you some properly sized clothing today?"

"I can't afford that. I don't have any money." Jak was a little embarrassed at the state of her financial affairs. She'd never had a lot of money on Haefen, but none of the other soldiers had either. What they'd needed had been provided and aside from the spending money that was distributed monthly, there had been no reason to worry. Most of the men had spent their money on women and drink, but Jak had squirreled hers away. She hadn't saved a huge amount, but it would have been useless on Nadi anyway.

"Don't worry about it, I'll cover you."

Jak didn't care for that idea at all. She'd never been beholden to anyone, and she didn't know that she wanted to start now. The debts her father had owed were what had gotten her and Bron kicked out of their family home after he died. She wouldn't be put in that situation again.

"Besides, I didn't tell you about your cut of the profits from the Haefen deal."

"What profits? I don't work for you." Jak looked at Torrin, mystified.

"Let's call it a finder's fee. We pay our intermediaries a small percentage of the deals their tips bring in. Without you, I wouldn't have made my way to the Devonites. You stand to get half a percent of the profits we make from that deal. And that deal is going to drown us in credits. If it makes you feel more comfortable, I can track what we spend and you can pay me back when the money starts coming in."

It seemed reasonable, but Jak still felt too much like a charity case. The need for her own clothes was a pressing argument though. Almost as pressing was the need to find her own revenue source. Tanith had mentioned lessons; maybe there was something there.

"All right," Jak finally conceded. "But you need to track it down to the centicred. I'm not going to owe you anything."

Torrin twined her fingers through Jak's and drew her out through the doors. "You know I don't mind."

"It's not about what you mind."

Nat had followed them out the doors. "I'm going to take off. Mom's been bugging me to stop by for dinner."

"Me too." Torrin grimaced. "She really wants me to bring Jak. I don't know if she's recovered enough for me to subject her to Mom."

"I'm right here, you know," Jak pointed out. "I don't mind meeting your mom."

"You will," Torrin said darkly. "But I don't know how much longer I can put her off."

"You mean you don't know if you're ready to grovel after what you said to her," Nat said.

"Well, yeah." Torrin's face darkened with embarrassment. Jak wondered what exactly Torrin had said to make her mother so angry. "Would you be?"

"I wouldn't have said it. You know Mom is easier to handle if you maneuver her around to your way of seeing things. You of all people should know that, instead of always trying to go head-on at her."

"That never seems to work for me. She likes you better anyway, and lets you get away with whatever you want."

Nat smacked her on the upper arm. "You know that's not true. If you'd get your head out of your ass where she's involved, maybe you'd see that you're her favorite. You always were."

Torrin massaged her upper arm while glaring at her sister. "She's got a funny way of showing it."

Nat shook her head in exasperation. "You're not much better."

"It would be nice to talk to Raisa again."

"I'll let them know you're thinking of coming over soon," Nat offered.

"Let me take care of it. You get stuck in the middle between us too much as it is. Besides, you already said you'd run interference and I intend to take you up on that."

Nat shrugged as if to say she didn't mind. Torrin reached over with one arm and hugged her quickly. The move surprised Jak a little; she hadn't noticed a whole lot of visible affection between the two of them. Usually, affection took the form of constant bickering. Nat didn't seem surprised, though, and she hugged her sister back warmly.

"I'll see you later, Jak. In new threads, so I can get mine back, I hope." Nat waved at her and took off down the hallway, heading toward the clinic's entryway.

Still holding hands, Jak and Torrin walked back to Jak's room, where they dropped off her workout clothing. While she was stowing her clothes, Kiera stuck her head in.

"You're here, good. I wanted to go over your discharge orders with you." She came the rest of the way into the room. "You're doing really well. Not coming along as quickly as you want, I know, but for anyone else, your recovery would be nothing short of miraculous."

"I just don't feel like I'm there yet," Jak complained. "I still get winded quickly and my muscle tone is shot."

"It's going to take a bit yet. I want you to continue coming in daily for physical therapy as we try to rebuild your lung capacity. I'll write up an order to work on your overall strength as well. But as I see it, you're well out of the woods. You haven't needed any breathing assistance for almost a week. The tissue in your lungs has mostly healed. The little bit that still needs to heal can do so on its own without any further medical attention. It's past time you got out of here."

Numbly, Jak nodded. It hadn't occurred to her that she would be leaving the clinic. At least, she'd thought about it, but not as anything that would be happening soon.

"This is great, babe," Torrin said. "You can finally move in with me. We'll be able to spend a lot more time together." She grinned lasciviously and Jak blushed.

Kiera chuckled. "Remember, she's not back a hundred percent. Don't get carried away and put her back in here."

"So we're good to—"

"Yes, yes," Kiera forestalled her before Torrin could finish. "Make sure you take it easy. Honestly, Torrin, I really don't want to know about your sex life." Her tone was exasperated when she finished.

"Got it," Jak said, face flaming. She didn't know if she would ever get used to the easy way the women bantered about sex. It wasn't something she'd ever heard talked about much, and the idea of two women having sex, even though she was one of them, still made her uncomfortable.

"Stop at the front desk. Torrin, the discharge nurse will get Jak's instructions to your tablet."

"Thanks, Kiera," Torrin said as the doctor departed the room. She looked down at Jak. "That's one more thing we need to get for you."

"I suppose…" Jak wasn't enamored of the idea. She used Torrin's tablet on occasion, but the interface still felt very clumsy. It had been so much easier to plug into the computers back home using the port on her hand.

"Let's get going. I promised to take you out to get some clothes, and I'm really excited to get you moved in to my place."

"Let's skip clothes shopping and head right to your place." Jak looked up at Torrin, face hot from being so forward, but she didn't care. She'd waited far too long to feel her lover moving against her to wait any longer than she had to.

A slow smile spread over Torrin's face and her eyes darkened. "I like the way you think."

Jak lifted her face to meet Torrin's mouth as it came down to cover hers. Arousal pooled between her legs and her thighs trembled slightly in anticipation.

CHAPTER NINE

The door slid open in front of them. Torrin barely noticed, her lips nibbling their way down Jak's neck to the collarbone peeking out through the too-wide collar of her shirt. She glanced up at the soft noise and urged Jak through the doorway without breaking the lock of her lips on the column of Jak's neck. Jak moaned once in protest at being forced to move and again when Torrin removed her lips.

"More," Jak gasped, her fingers grasping the lapels of Torrin's short coat and pulling Torrin against her. Torrin kept moving, swinging Jak around and pushing her against the wall to the side of the door. Her nipples ached where they pressed against Jak through her clothes.

"I can't wait any longer," Torrin whispered. She traced Jak's bottom lip with the tip of her tongue. Her arousal flared even hotter at the sounds she was drawing from Jak and she dropped her hands to rest them on Jak's hips. Jak rolled her hips against Torrin, who couldn't hold back an answering moan. The pressure on her mound was delicious and Torrin undulated her hips in response to Jak's movements. She slid her hand to the waistband of Jak's pants, seeking out the fastener. Jak panted, tilting her hips toward Torrin in tacit encouragement, then lifted her arms and slid them around Torrin's neck.

"So what's keeping you?"

The quiet question burned through Torrin's blood, and she pulled Jak roughly against her and lowered her head. She speared her tongue past Jak's willing lips and plumbed the hot depths of her mouth. Jak moaned into her mouth and Torrin slid one hand down the front of her pants. She growled in frustration when all she could do was drag wet fingertips through damp curls.

Torrin pulled her mouth from Jak's. "Off. They need to come off."

Instead of complying, Jak slid her hands up her side and under the coat, seeking out her breasts. Her palms rubbed over Torrin's nipples and they hardened painfully, becoming twin aching points of sensation. Jak sucked at the side of her neck, and Torrin's hips twitched into Jak's, both of them groaning at the feeling.

"I mean it, babe. I need you. Now."

Jak showed no signs of having heard the order. Her hands were busy pulling Torrin's shirt out of her waistband and sliding it over her abdomen, up along her rib cage.

Unable to get through to her eager lover, Torrin fumbled at the fasteners, finally getting them open. She yanked Jak's pants and underwear down Jak's thighs and her pussy clenched powerfully when the musky scent of Jak's excited sex hit her nostrils.

"Baby, baby…it's been too long." Torrin's skin tingled as Jak slid her hands under her bra and over bare nipples. Somehow, her nipples tightened even more and Jak's touch both soothed and enflamed the ache in her nipples and the fire that pooled between her legs. Wetness flowed between her thighs. She couldn't get Jak's pants down any further without disengaging from her. When she tried, Jak dug her fingertips warningly into the underside of Torrin's breasts.

"Don't even think of it."

"Then lose the pants."

Jak kicked the pants off without relinquishing her hold.

"Finally," Torrin groaned. She slid her hand down, running her fingers through wet curls, parting Jak's lips and dipping the tips into Jak's opening. Jak threw her head back with a gasp, again rolling her hips to give Torrin better access. Torrin closed her lips over the delicate skin of Jak's neck, kissing and biting. She swirled her fingertips through the abundant wetness of Jak's pussy. Poised with two fingers at her opening, Torrin paused before slowly pushing in, reveling in the feeling of Jak's innermost flesh yielding and squeezing around her fingers. The warm softness of her pussy drew her in and she moaned. Jak echoed the sound and pushed against her, drawing Torrin's fingers deeper inside.

Torrin paused for a moment, feeling Jak's heartbeat through her fingers and marveling at the sensation. It was amazing how much better this felt when she deeply cared about her partner. Slowly, she pulled her fingers out until the tips lay nestled right inside Jak's entrance before sliding them back, in one smooth motion. Jak shifted forward to meet her thrust. She gasped and moaned as Torrin increased the speed and power of her thrusts. Torrin could feel the pressure building between her legs. From the contractions squeezing her fingers, Jak was close and so was she.

"More, Torrin. Johvah, I need it, I need it so bad." Jak's barely coherent pleas penetrated the fog of sex and Torrin pulled out completely, then pushed back in with three fingers, filling Jak up. "Oh, yes." At Jak's broken whimper, Torrin's pussy clenched and she rocked her hips against Jak, grinding her center against Jak's hip, seeking friction as she moved within and against her.

"Torrin, I'm coming. I'm..." With a wordless cry, Jak lifted her legs, wrapping them around Torrin's waist, trapping her hand within as she shook and spasmed around Torrin's fingers. The intensity of Jak's orgasm pushed Torrin over the edge, the delicious tension inside her exploding through her body, and she cried out. She barely had the presence of mind to lock her knees and brace them against the wall before pleasure wiped out all thought in a tsunami of sensation.

Torrin came back to herself to find Jak still wrapped around her. She still had one hand deep in Jak's pussy, the other wrapped around her waist, holding her steady. Torrin's knees trembled and she withdrew her fingers with a reluctant smile.

"I need to let you down before I drop you."

Jak laughed, a slight wheeze coming through at the end. "That's romantic."

"More romantic than dropping you."

Shakily, Jak disengaged her legs from around Torrin's waist and straightened. "That was different. We've never done it like that before."

"I'm sorry, I couldn't wait to get you in the bedroom. I didn't hurt you, did I?"

Jak leaned forward and placed a kiss on her jaw. "Far from it. I wanted it as bad as you did." She looked up, eyes dancing wickedly. "In fact, I still want you." She pressed a kiss to Torrin's mouth that made her weak in the knees all over again. "If you don't want a repeat of what just happened, you'd better lead on to the bedroom."

With a laugh that did nothing to disguise the desire she felt, Torrin grabbed Jak's hands and pulled her along to the bedroom. The door had barely opened before Jak was pushing her down on the bed, her hands already stripping off Torrin's shirt. Torrin lay back and returned the favor, wanting to see Jak naked before taking her again.

* * *

Torrin stretched, reveling in the afterglow of an extended romp with her lover. Jak really was amazing. When Jak had first come to her bed, she hadn't been an experienced lover, but she constantly surprised Torrin with her enthusiasm and inventiveness. She was a very quick study, and Torrin immensely appreciated her willingness to experiment. Her body tingled as she recalled Jak's fingers stroking within her as her lips closed over Torrin's clit, sucking and tugging. She'd lost track of the number of times she'd come already, but damn if it didn't feel like she might be up for one more.

Pushing herself up on one elbow, she propped her head on her hand and looked down on the naked body of her lover stretched out beside her. Jak's fair skin was a glowing contrast to the dark sheets creased beneath her. A faint sheen of sweat covered her body. She was still too skinny, but she'd gained enough muscle that she was no longer as frighteningly emaciated as she had been when they'd arrived on Nadierzda.

"What are you thinking?" Jak asked drowsily. Exhausted from their exertions, she looked moments away from sleep.

"I'm so glad you're better now."

Jak chuckled quietly. "You're just happy we can do this."

Torrin laughed along with her. She loved the warmth of Jak's laugh and heard it too seldom. "I'll admit I did miss this. I'd have to be crazy not to." She sobered and looked down at Jak. "But I didn't know what to do when I thought I was going to lose you." Torrin reached out and took Jak's hand in hers and placed it over her heart.

Jak smiled. Was that sadness in her smile? And why, when Torrin had opened herself to her did she see the bleakness creeping back into the corners of the sniper's gaze? Jak blinked and as quickly as the bleakness had come, it was gone.

Maybe I imagined it?

Rolling over to face her, Jak lifted her head and kissed Torrin, her tongue sliding between Torrin's teeth and stroking over her tongue. The simmering arousal in Torrin's belly burst into renewed flames. She pressed herself against the smaller woman and moaned as she felt wet, naked flesh moving against her. Fingers gripped her hair, drawing another moan from her.

Gasping, she pulled her lips away from Jak's. "We probably shouldn't, you're still not completely well."

Fingers plucking at one nipple quieted her and the feel of Jak's mouth kissing its way down the side of her neck distracted her. Nothing else really mattered except the sensations Jak could draw from her. The heat between her thighs could no longer be denied and she gave herself over to her lover.

A long while later, Torrin slipped out of the bed. Jak was dead to the world, so sound asleep that she didn't even stir when Torrin disentangled their limbs. She stood at the side of the bed for a while, smiling as she watched Jak sleep.

She padded through the flat, completely naked. She often roamed her home in the nude. There were no windows for people to look into, so why not? A quick survey of the kitchen revealed that she had no fresh food, and she didn't feel like reconstituted fare. Instead, she prepared a mug of bitrian and took it to the couch in the living room. There, she covered herself with a throw blanket and picked up her tablet.

Things were proceeding well. Audra's intern was seeding the local net with enough hints of rumor and innuendo about their latest venture that things were starting to take off on their own. Already, someone was circulating a digital petition to bring the matter to the council. They'd already gathered a few hundred signatures; this would get the council's attention in a hurry.

Leaning back, she got down to work. Their ducks needed to be lined up when the council demanded an explanation. The presentation they'd given to Alyx had been purposely flawed and slapdash. They wanted her to report to the council that the partners had something, but not how far along they were in the planning stages. In actuality, Mac had been so busy with her contacts that it would take very little to get the project off the ground. All they needed was a few in-person meetings with investors, a visit to some potential manufacturing sites and the hiring of their workforce.

Audra had been instrumental in bringing a number of the local research and development scientists into the project. She was good at choosing people who had enough ambition to try an exciting new project, but who had enough common sense to keep a lid on things. The R&D group had developed prototypes from the schematics and blueprints she'd brought back with her from Haefen. They were already running them through rigorous computer simulations. Only when the devices had passed the simulations with flying colors would they start experimentation with lab-grown tissue. From there they would move on to rolling out the first prototypes for humans. The computer and tissue simulations would work all the kinks out. The tentative advancements in stem cell research made during the twenty-first century had evolved into a science those early experimenters would barely even recognize almost eight hundred years later. A few adult human cells could be grown into a fully functional organ or system. Since the first pieces they would develop would be ocular implants, the scientists were busily cultivating human eyes for study.

Torrin continued working, pulling up files on her tablet, working them into the presentation, making calls to people on the project and touching base with them. Everything had to be just so. She lost herself in the work. This was where she thrived. Making money. Manipulating things until the outcome was exactly what she wanted it to be. It was only another negotiation after all.

It must have been a couple of hours before Jak came out of the bedroom, yawning, with a sheet wrapped around her. Torrin loved the way she looked, hair rumpled, eyes half lidded with an aura of satisfaction around her for which Torrin alone could claim responsibility. It didn't hurt that the sheet clung to the sniper's body in interesting ways, accentuating curves on the body she seemed so embarrassed by. Torrin wished that Jak would understand how attractive she was. It was such a shame that she wasn't comfortable in her own skin yet. Hopefully more time with the women on Nadi would help her accept herself.

"Working?" Jak asked, bleary-eyed. She settled herself at the other end of the couch and tucked her feet under her rump.

Torrin nodded and finished up on her tablet, laying it on the table. "Yes. Things are coming to a head, and we need to be out in front of the Ruling Council so that we can get things off the ground in a timely fashion."

"Why won't you hire your sister?" Jak asked.

"Umm, because she's too young." Torrin looked over at her, taken aback by the question.

Jak snorted softly. "She's older than I am and she has a head for this, you know. And it only makes sense, she's been watching you at it most of her life. You should really give her a chance."

"You can't compare yourself to her. You've had experiences she could never imagine. Did she put you up to this?"

"No, but I think you're missing a huge opportunity. Besides, she worships you and only wants to make you proud."

"See," Torrin said triumphantly. "I can't hire her. If she feels that way, it wouldn't be fair to the others."

Jak dismissed her objection with an eye roll. "To hear you say it, half the women on this planet worship you, and you work with them well enough. Besides, I know your company is big enough. Make sure you're not her direct supervisor. Put her under Mac or Audra."

"I don't know." Torrin could feel herself wavering, wanting to give in just to please Jak. She'd always sworn that she wouldn't let any of her lovers dictate how she worked and she'd never even had the slightest desire to let that happen. But now, Jak seemed so reasonable and it was

something she wanted. Maybe it wouldn't hurt. What was she thinking?
"I don't think it's a good idea."

"Suit yourself." Jak shrugged. "But she did bring up an interesting question. Who in their right mind sends a woman in to do business with the Orthodoxans?"

Torrin sat there, staring at Jak. Nat's thoughts mirrored her own and showed a depth of maturity she hadn't expected from her sister. It was no accident that Torrin had ended up on Haefen. Even if she could believe that Neal hadn't set her up, there was still the matter of faulty background information in Tien's files. Someone was trying to get rid of her. It was the only thing that explained the strange discrepancy between the information in Tien's database and the reality of Orthodoxan society.

The only ones who knew about the problems in Tien's databanks were the AI and her partners. Nat had put all of that together without having access to that damning piece of information. There might be more to her sister than enthusiasm and trouble, after all.

"It seems I do have something to talk over with my sister after all," Torrin said aloud.

CHAPTER TEN

The air was warm and dry and carried along with it the smell of dusty plains. From her vantage point, Jak could see for kilometers in three directions. Nadierzda's cratered landscape made for some splendid vistas. She still missed the majestic trees of Haefen, but there was beauty on Nadi too. From her vantage on the edge of a cliff looking out over the farmland that surrounded Landing, brilliant greenery contrasted starkly with the warm yellows and reds of the crater walls. The constant winds on Nadierzda had carved fantastic shapes into the rocks. Pillars of stone rose in the distance along the edge of the crater, supporting boulders that looked much too large for the slender stone columns that held them.

She sniffed the air. There was an odor on the wind that she hadn't smelled before. That wasn't too unusual. She was new to the planet and unfamiliar with most of the animals here. She'd been surprised both at the lack of diversity and the number of large predators that made up the local wildlife. Apparently, the planet had been seeded with the idea that part of it would be a big game hunting preserve. There was definitely large game to be had, though most of it steered far clear of human civilization. The other animals existed mainly to keep the game animals fed. The planet's original terraformers hadn't cared too much for diversity; rather they'd concentrated on creating a playground for the ultrarich, or so Torrin had told her. The biodiversity of the planet was extremely low; it held maybe ten thousand different animals.

Whatever it was she'd smelled, the trace was gone. She carefully surveyed the surrounding landscape, keying in her implant for maximum magnification. It was a mere fraction of what she could manage even with the least of her rifle's scopes, but it magnified her vision more than four-fold. Everything seemed normal and she relaxed.

There was a stunted forest of what could very generously be called trees growing almost to the cliff's edge. The so-called trees here didn't impress her much. Their foliage was sparse and they were maybe twice as tall as she was. So much light made its way past the leaves that the underbrush flourished. It was actually very difficult to navigate with any speed. As was her habit, she left as little sign of her passing as possible, which slowed her even further.

Still, this small corner allowed her to do some hunting. She was far removed from the demands of the training she was in charge of. At least she had something to keep her occupied now. When she'd been approached to train Nadi's militiawomen, she'd been a little hesitant. It turned out that she not only enjoyed running training sessions, but she was good at it. The chance to give back to the planet that was taking her in didn't hurt either.

If only Torrin weren't so preoccupied with her project, Jak thought. She missed her lover, though she tried to be understanding. Torrin was busy, Jak knew that, but she was getting tired of her making plans for them and then canceling at the last minute. Even more than the cancellations, the knowing looks from other women when she showed up somewhere alone were starting to irritate her. Everyone expected Torrin to screw around on her. Even though she was fairly certain Torrin wouldn't do any such thing, it was hard not to get suspicious when she blew off yet another dinner.

Nat wasn't around much either. While she'd been gratified that Torrin had taken her advice on hiring her sister, it meant that Jak hardly got to see her. Nat had thrown herself into learning the ropes at Troika Corp., which didn't leave much time for Jak. She wasn't going to complain, but all the time without anyone to distract her wasn't a good thing. Her thoughts strayed into areas she didn't like to consider, areas she'd thought she was past. Bron's death gnawed at her even more now that she couldn't do anything to find the sniper who'd killed him.

The only thing that was keeping her from going completely stir-crazy was the sniper training gig she'd picked up with the militia. Tanith had been more than happy to take her on as an independent contractor. She'd also done her best to convince Jak to enlist.

"Come on," Tanith had said, her tone wheedling. "We can really use you. You're head and shoulders above any of our other instructors when it comes to distance work."

It was true; they had no one who could come close to her abilities. In fact, in the two weeks since she'd started training the Nadierzdans, she'd become convinced that most of the women took the militia as a bit of a joke. They treated it like they were on some sort of morale-building holiday. Most of them had been extremely unprepared for her brand of training and discipline.

Enlisting would have made sense, but something held her back.

"I don't think so," Jak had replied. "I'm still a member of the Devonite Armed Forces. It doesn't feel right to join up with someone else."

"It's no problem. There are no Devonites here, so I don't see that there will be any conflict."

Tanith's breezy dismissal should have helped put her mind at ease, but instead it had firmed the decision in her head.

"Not right now, thanks."

"Fair enough, but if you change your mind, the offer will still be open. I can't offer you quarters on base as a contractor, though."

"That's fine, I have somewhere to stay." Remembering the two women's mutual antipathy, Jak had thought it best not to bring up Torrin's name. Tanith had nodded as if she understood completely and they'd left it at that.

Just like that, Jak was working for the Nadierzda militia. Torrin hadn't been happy to hear about her decision. In fact, her displeasure had turned into their first fight.

"Why would you want to do that?" Torrin had bellowed. "You don't have to do that anymore."

"Maybe I wouldn't have to do it if you were around," Jak had yelled back. The way Torrin's face had fallen when she said that had torn at Jak's heart. It hadn't been true, at least not completely. The fact was, this was something she knew how to do and she was good at it. It was all well and good that Torrin had promised her a tidy sum from the Troika finder's fee, but sniper training was a way she could be useful and a way she could start to give back to the planet where she was starting to feel more at home.

The problem was that Jak was constantly questioning herself and her motives. Had she agreed to work with the militia because it was something she enjoyed doing, or was it because it was all she'd ever known? Who was Jak the Nadierzdan? She couldn't be the same person as Jak the Devonite, or could she? It was a question that could and did spin her mind in circles, trying to get hold of an answer, any answer that might shed a little more light on who she really was.

She'd made up her mind not to say anything else to Torrin on the subject. She wished she had the words to make her understand, but it was obvious her lover didn't see where she was coming from. Loneliness and needing to feel useful were much of what had driven her to work with the militia, but she'd also found a community there. The gash in her heart opened a little wider as she remembered Torrin's inability to accept her decision.

Since there had been no game to speak of, she decided to head back to base. From the angle of the sun, it was getting close to the morning's training session. She'd slipped out of the base before the sun had even been above the horizon and she'd have to hurry to get back in time.

Jak jogged slowly through the field outside the militia base. Her lungs still weren't up to par, and she couldn't manage a sustained run for any significant period of time. The best she could manage was this trot, barely faster than she could walk. When she was halfway across the field, a deep roar built overhead until it rattled her bones. She looked up to see one of the extremely rare deep space vessels come cruising in for landing. The downdraft from its engines flattened the grass around her and pushed down against her body, even though it was still a hundred or so meters in the air.

It was a sleek thing, dark and dangerous. The only other space vessel she'd seen had been Torrin's. At the time, it had impressed her greatly. Where the *Calamity Jane* hinted at violence, this ship stripped away all pretense. It bristled with at least a dozen hull-mounted weapons. Where Torrin's ship had been a matte black, this one had a menacing sheen to it. It wasn't built to blend into space; it was built to rip through it and anything else in its way. Having finally seen one of these ships in person, Jak found herself partially revising her poor opinion of Nadierzda's militia.

The ship landed inside the base's walls and the deafening roar of the engines was rapidly muted. Jak picked up her pace and headed to the closest gate. The sentries at the gate nodded to her.

"Ma'am," the near one said.

"What's that ship?" Jak asked, wheezing slightly.

"It's the *Nightshade*." When Jak still looked confused, the sentry elaborated. "It's one of our ships that tracks down the more egregious bastards on the Fringes. You know, slavers and the like."

Jak nodded slowly. "Got it. Thanks, soldier." She made her way into the base proper and stopped in her room in the barracks, securing her mid-range rifle and picking up her long-range one. Rifle in hand, she exited the barracks at a trot. A run would have indicated to anybody who saw her that she was running late. As an officer now, she was keenly sensitive to how she appeared to the lower ranks. She hustled up the street and headed for the square, checking the chrono on her wrist. The chrono in her implant was still set to Haefen time and she had no way to reset it. Jak had grown accustomed to ignoring the constant reminder that she was no longer home. Her training session was in less than fifteen minutes. If she was going to be on time, she'd have to hurry.

A knot of six women crossed the square toward her. They carried themselves completely differently than the other soldiers she'd seen so far on Nadierzda. These women were actual soldiers, not women doing their best to pass as such. They moved with an ease that was impossible to fake. She had no doubt that if one of them got the drop on her, she would be hard-pressed to defend herself.

She nodded to the hard-bitten women and received a respectful nod in return. Clearly, they recognized something in her as well. They all carried rucksacks and she surmised that they were from the *Nightshade*.

"Who was that?" she heard one of them ask as she passed them.

"I don't know," came the reply. "But I wouldn't mind finding out. She's cute."

Jak shook her head. They were like soldiers anywhere, on leave and already looking for a way to pass the time.

When she arrived on the range, she discovered most of her group was already there, waiting. They clustered in small groups, gossiping about the women who'd recently arrived. Normally when Jak arrived on the range the women were ready to go, but the day's events had thrown off the normal order of things. Even though Jak's early morning jaunt had been enjoyable and she was in a decent mood, she expected the women to behave as professionals, not as teenagers on their first campout. She wasn't going to put up with it.

"Everyone, hop to!" she called. There was a delay before the women complied and even then some of them still whispered amongst themselves.

"Since you seem to be having problems focusing, we're going to have to go back to the basics."

A collective groan rippled through the small group. Basics meant inspections and even though she hadn't put them through an inspection since the first few sessions, she was going to now.

The inspection resulted in more than a few pushups being meted out as punishment. The infractions were minor, but even minor dirt or corrosion on a weapon could result in malfunctions and jams. If they'd let their weapons go this badly in ten days, she would have to think about reinstating regular inspections or at least spot inspections to keep them on their toes. This was merely one more aspect of the lack of professionalism that bugged her about the militia. Real soldiers would have known that and taken it to heart. These women treated the whole thing as a lark.

Tanith wasn't with the group. Typically, she never missed a session; she was very interested in becoming a good sniper and she worked hard at it. It had been a surprise to see her in the first group. Even though Tanith had suggested she take on the training, Jak had never thought she would be a part of it, especially given her elevated rank. As head of the Nadierzdan ground forces, Major Tanith Merriam was outranked by only a handful of women. Jak supposed she must have been called away by the arrival of the *Nightshade* and her crew.

"Take your places at one hundred meters," she barked after completing the inspection. The hapless women whose weapons had been less than pristine continued their pushups and the others hunkered down in prone shooting positions. She worked them down the range until they hit twelve hundred meters. Jak was actually very proud that her trainees could consistently hit their targets at that range. First one, then other women started missing their targets. Scowling, she looked up to see what the issue was.

Tanith stood a little way off to one side of the range with two unfamiliar women. They hadn't been part of the group she had passed on the way to the range, but they carried themselves with the same unconscious poise and professionalism.

"Since you can't keep your focus today, I'm letting you go early." A small sound of relief moved through the group. "However, you'll be making up the time tomorrow. I won't have you screwing things up because you can't keep your heads. We'll talk about this at length tomorrow. Dismissed!"

The women got up and straggled off down the range, many of them turning frequently to catch more glimpses of the two women. Jak made her way over to the three observers.

"Major Merriam, do you want to introduce me to the two women who completely distracted this morning's training group?"

Tanith smiled broadly. "Certainly, Captain Stowell. May I introduce Captain Yozhin and Lieutenant Krikorian?"

Jak nodded to the two women and grasped and shook each woman's hand as she offered it.

"I hope you'll excuse us, Captain," Lieutenant Krikorian said. "I wanted to see what you've managed with your training program. We haven't even been back two hours and we've already been hearing about the amazing things you're doing."

The lieutenant was a lithe woman just shy of her middle years. Small amounts of gray threaded the brown hair at her temples and fine lines creased the corners of her eyes. They crinkled pleasantly as she smiled at Jak.

"Please, call me Jak."

"Thanks, Jak. You can call me Olesya. Captain Yozhin goes by Axe. If you're feeling adventurous, you can even ask her why." Olesya grinned widely and Jak found herself smiling back. She liked this tall woman with the easy smile.

"You don't need to ask," Axe grumbled. "All you need to do is look." True to her words, the woman had a nose like a hatchet. It dominated her face and gave her a fierce look that was further accentuated by a livid scar running back from one eyebrow and disappearing into the hairline of her extremely close-cropped hair. She was younger than the lieutenant, which surprised Jak a bit. They seemed close, though.

"Jak, these two are the ranking members of their Banshee squad," Tanith said. "They're interested in what you've been teaching us."

"It's good to meet someone else who has some serious training," Axe said. "We mostly engage in shipboard fighting, so the extreme distance stuff doesn't work so well for us."

"We're always happy to get more tips when it comes to accuracy and distance though," Olesya said, and the captain nodded. "We were very impressed with what we saw earlier."

Jak scowled. "It would have been more impressive if they hadn't been falling all over themselves to get a better look at you."

Olesya laughed again. "We have that effect on people sometimes. You should see us when we leave the base for some liberty. The women mob us. It's gratifying, but not very restful."

"We can rest when we're dead," Axe said. "I'm up for enjoying myself when I'm home. We never know how long that's going to be. Sometimes we get to stick around for a month or so, and other times we're turning back around and heading back out in less than a week."

"Big words from the married woman," Olesya said, teeth flashing white in a wide grin. Axe rolled her eyes.

"Jak knows a little bit about how you guys are treated," Tanith said with a half smile on her face. "She's experiencing it firsthand now that she's dating Torrin Ivanov."

The lieutenant whistled. "That'll do it. Tor's very popular still, and she hasn't been one of us for a good fifteen years now. She and I joined up at the same time. How is she?"

"Good enough," Jak replied stiffly. The line of questioning made her uncomfortable; she still wasn't used to people knowing the details of her and Torrin's relationship. "I don't always see her that much."

"She's been very busy," Tanith broke in delicately. "You know how Torrin is."

Olesya crooked a smile and nodded. "Some things never change. I remember the one shore leave we had when she managed to sleep with a half a dozen different women in a week. Gave herself the last day off, called it her day of rest. She'd spent the whole week in bed, don't know what she felt she had to rest for!"

The Banshee captain elbowed Olesya in the ribs and the lieutenant playfully slugged her back. Axe shook her head and nodded over at Jak.

"I don't think that's the kind of busy the major was referring to," Axe hissed. She'd tried to keep her voice down, but Jak still heard her plainly. The lieutenant looked Jak in the eyes and quickly subsided. The four of them stood awkwardly for a few moments.

"So what are the Banshees, exactly?" Jak finally asked when the silence stretched a little too long.

"We're small groups who go out and break up sexual slavery rings, mostly," Olesya said. "We occasionally do other tasks, but our main function is to rescue women who've been enslaved."

"For example, we just raided one of the transport vessels of an asshole named Connors who calls himself the Sultan of Slavers," Axe added. "We were able to rescue fourteen women, ten of them pre- or barely-pubescent girls who were on their way to be sold to the highest bidder on one of the Fringe worlds. Those women and girls will be able to have normal lives and live here for as long as they want to or relocate once they've recovered."

"You mean, they live here?" Jak was floored.

"Of course they do," Tanith said. "Beyond the normal ways a population grows, the rescued girls boost our population."

Normal ways a population grew? It occurred to Jak that she'd never thought to wonder where the little girls she saw in the arms of their mothers came from. Without men, how were they reproducing? Before she could puzzle that out or ask about it, another thought hit her like a slap. They rescued women, and there were thousands of women on Haefen who desperately needed it. Nadierzda could act as a refuge for those women once they were liberated from the Orthodoxans.

"So how many groups of you are there?" Jak asked Axe.

"There are only ten units who are active at any given time. We have a few training groups, but that's it."

"Oh." That wasn't going to be nearly enough.

"Are you interested in enlisting with us? We're always looking for good women who are willing and capable. There wouldn't be a huge call for your uber long distance shooting, though."

"I don't know about that." Olesya broke in before Jak could respond. "We do run operations on the ground, and her talents would be extremely handy in those situations. It's only ship-to-ship boarding actions don't have those kinds of distances." The lieutenant started pacing. "In fact, if we were to concentrate more on ground operations, we could do a lot more good. Think about how many women we could save if we could hit more of these bastards at their point of operation, instead of having to wait until they move their 'merchandise.'"

"We've been over this, diversifying to ground operations would mean making bigger units and recruiting in specialists we don't currently have access to."

"Like snipers?"

Jak felt warm fingers on her left elbow and looked over to see Tanith standing right next to her.

"Let's move on," Tanith said quietly. "They're barely getting started. I can't tell you how many times I've heard this argument between them."

Jak allowed herself to be drawn away from the bickering women.

"Hey, Jak," Axe called as they left. "I meant what I said. We're going to be coming by for training. If you see anyone you like, tell me and we'll line them up for more intense work." Jak nodded back over her shoulder and waved to the two of them.

"They're pretty impressive, aren't they?" Tanith asked when they were almost back to the barracks.

"The Banshees?"

"Well, yes, but those two especially. Please tell me you're not interested in joining up with them. If you enlist with anybody, it should really be with the planet-bound militia. We need your talents the most."

Jak was taken aback at the quick subject change and shook her head. "I don't think they can really use me right now. If they were to come up with something where my talents could be put to use, I'd have to seriously think about it."

"I have some ideas about putting your talents to use right here. I've been talking with General Lethe about having you start a sniper school. You could lay the groundwork for training sniper-scout teams. The Banshees are our only special operations units and it's past time to change that. We really need to shake up the whole organization. I've never been happy with the militia designation the council has hung around our necks. It gives the ladies an excuse not to take themselves seriously."

Jak nodded slowly. It was very strange to have so many of her thoughts parroted back to her, almost word for word. "I get where you're coming from. But you have nothing to scout or fight here. The whole planet is under your Ruling Council's control."

"We don't have anyone to fight against now, that's true. What happens if someone decides to invade? We're not prepared to mount any kind of sustained resistance. The council seems to think that if we can stay hidden, we'll be all right. But there's no way we'll stay hidden forever. We could be discovered tomorrow, or twenty years, or even two hundred years from now." Tanith was clearly impassioned about the whole thing. They'd arrived at the barracks, but instead of going in she was striding back and forth by the front steps, eyes flashing. "Torrin's pushing us into the galaxy. If we don't act now, she's going to get us killed or worse. And if she's not the one who pushes us out there, sooner or later the planet's going to do that for us. At that point, we may have to be prepared to take what we need to survive."

"I need to go stow my gear," Jak said, pushing past Tanith at the mention of her girlfriend's name.

Tanith followed her into the building and down the barracks to her office.

"I know you hate hearing bad things about her, I'm sorry."

"It's fine." Jak shut the door to her gun locker and slid the locker between her desk and the wall with her foot.

"It isn't, and I'm sorry. Torrin and I don't always see eye to eye. Besides, I know you're not really happy with her now either. I hear you've been heading out to go hunting a lot."

"So? I haven't missed any of the training sessions."

"Something's obviously eating at you. I want to make sure Torrin's treating you right."

Jak shot her an irritated look, and Tanith stepped back, her hands raised.

"I know she's busy right now but I think you're becoming isolated. I'd hoped that you'd be making friends with some of the other women. I feel like I'm your only friend, and with Torrin so busy, you have to be a little lonely." Tanith cocked an eyebrow at her, daring her to disagree with her assertions. "Being alone isn't always a bad thing, but I think it could help to talk to somebody. I can get you the name of a good shrink. She sees a lot of the Banshees when they come back from missions that go sideways."

"I don't need to see a psychologist." Jak could feel herself blanching at the idea. Spilling her innermost thoughts and secrets went against everything she'd been living since she'd barely been an adolescent.

"I really think it could help. You need to talk to someone."

"I'm doing fine. I'd like you to leave now." Jak looked Tanith in the eye. The other woman's face tightened momentarily, then smoothed out.

"Okay. Have it your way. But I'm here to talk if you want to, even if you don't want to talk to a professional." Tanith left the room and closed the door quietly behind her.

There was no way she could talk to someone about what was going on, not when she only dimly understood it herself. Once again she was alone in the midst of crowds of people. When Torrin was there it didn't feel so bad, but when she wasn't... Opening herself up to anyone meant giving them the opportunity to slide a knife between her ribs and twist. She leaned back in her chair and stared at the ceiling. As usual, the ceiling gave her no answers.

* * *

"Sight. Aim. Fire!" Jak's light voice rang out across the firing range. It was echoed by the sound of plasma impacting a dozen targets. The sound was completely different from what she was used to, but she was getting accustomed to it. Instead of the familiar sharp report she heard when she fired her rifle, it sounded like a heavy impact, almost like something hitting a slab of meat. It had taken her a little bit to get used to firing a plasma rifle. She'd mastered it quickly enough, though it would never supplant her preference for the chemical propulsion weapons she'd grown up with. For one thing, plasma didn't slice through the air in the same way. Try as she might, she had yet to match the distance at which she could be accurate with her regular rifle. She doubted it mattered to anyone but her. Before she'd started training them, her beginning class hadn't been accurate at half their current distance. The current group of women was a completely different kettle of fish. They were already accurate at her beginning class's current range and this was their first class.

She looked down range and twitched her implant to give her the best magnification. The targets were five hundred meters away. Most of the women had scored decent hits. One of them had missed completely. A quick glance confirmed that it was the medic. The woman seemed to be there for a lark. Jak appreciated her medical talents but wished she would find somewhere else to be if she wasn't going to take things seriously.

Two targets had burn marks right in their centers. She didn't have to look to see who had been that successful. It had been the same two all morning. Tanith and Perez. The major had an advantage, she'd already been working with Jak for a couple of weeks and she'd invited herself along to the Banshees' class as soon as she'd learned Jak was giving it. She worked hard at the craft and it showed. Perez reminded Jak a bit of herself and not only in looks. Perez was almost as short as Jak and her hair, though dark, was just as short as the sniper's. She was rather flat-chested when compared to Jak and she found herself envying Perez her lack of endowment. Jak still hadn't reconciled herself to her breasts and was only occasionally appearing in public without the breastbinder. She knew Torrin wished she would get rid of it completely, but it helped keep her anxiety levels down, especially in new situations. Nadierzda was one new situation after another for her.

Perez had taken to sniping as if she'd been born to it. Apparently, she'd been one of the best shots in the Banshee unit. Jak's fingers itched as she contemplated how much better Perez could get under her tutelage. So far, Jak only needed to show her something once and she could apply it right away. Jak couldn't wait to see what Perez would do when they started working in the field. Range work was all well and good; it kept their skills sharp. Jak spent as much time as she could on the range, but nothing replaced fieldwork.

A couple other of the women showed some promise. If she was lucky, she'd get a core of four to six women who would be able to take her training and apply it to their marksmanship. Fieldwork would help her home in on her hand-picked core of sniper trainees. Being out there with like-minded women would be a new experience for her.

It would have been nice if Torrin could find the time to come out with her. The wildlife here was so different from what she was used to on Haefen and offered new challenges. Being able to experience a part of Nadi that she was coming to appreciate would have been that much better with Torrin. Jak cherished the time she spent with her lover, but she understood that hunting might not be Torrin's favorite thing to do. Torrin's favorite things tended to be much more exuberant and she closed her eyes against the sudden memory of Torrin's mouth on her nipples, Torrin's fingers spreading her lips before…

Embarrassed that her mind had wandered to the previous night's love-making, Jak focused again on the targets. Aside from the medic, another woman was doing almost as poorly, though Jak didn't know why. Hamilton had barely grazed the edge of her target, leaving only a dark smudge on the border.

"Hamilton, did you exhale before you squeezed the trigger?" Jak called.

"I did not, sir!" Hamilton's voice was chagrined.

"Remember to do that," she snapped, exasperated. "Now all of you! Sight. Aim. Fire!"

Again she was answered by a dozen impacts. Plasma flared in her line of sight and was quickly doused. The results were pretty much the same, though Hamilton had managed to hit the target this time, if barely.

"Everybody up. We're going two hundred meters that way."

A cluster of groans met her order. Most of the women had partied late into the night. Even though it was early afternoon, a number of them were still feeling the ill effects of the previous night's overindulgence. They didn't appreciate being run up and down the range. The Banshees straggled to their feet from their prone positions, some without any problems. Some, including Hamilton, were having more trouble.

"Hamilton," Jak barked. The Banshee stopped her trudge with a cringe, her shoulders tight, almost up around her ears. "Let me see your hands."

Grumbling under her breath, Hamilton held both hands out toward Jak. Her fingers trembled visibly, even though Jak was a few meters away.

Jak covered the distance between the two of them and stretched up to put her mouth next to the soldier's ear. "If you ever show up for one of my sessions in this shape again, I'm going to hand your ass over to Axe. I don't give a rat's ass how much fun you had last night, but I'm not going to waste my time on training someone who is probably still hammered."

"Yessir." Hamilton flushed as she meekly agreed. Tanith was standing next to the hapless Banshee and turned away to conceal a smirk. A moment later, she turned back and slapped Hamilton playfully on the behind and said something in a low tone. Hamilton looked over at her gratefully and smiled.

"Pick up the pace," Jak hollered, taking grim pleasure at Hamilton's visible flinch. "Quick time!" She led the pace at a brisk jog until she judged they'd gone another couple hundred meters. She was winded at the end of the short jog and tried not to catch her breath too obviously.

"You doing all right?" Tanith asked quietly as she came to a stop nearby.

"Yeah, I'm fine." And she was fine. This was an improvement over where she'd been two weeks ago when she'd first started assisting with training. There was no need for Tanith to continue treating her so solicitously.

"Okay, Banshees, let's get into position. Show me what you've got, and try not to make me feel like I've been wasting my time."

The women dropped with alacrity and assumed their prone shooting positions with some degree of competence. They ignored her final sally.

"Sight. Aim. Fire!" The sounds of plasma impact were muffled by distance. She only made out about half a dozen plasma flares and zoomed in on the far-off targets. Seven women had hit their targets. Surprisingly, Hamilton was one of them. Not surprisingly, Tanith and Perez had hit their targets dead in the center once again.

In her drill instructor's voice she read off the names of the women who had hit the targets. The women grinned at each other.

"Those of you who missed, you owe me twenty pushups. The rest of you, back another hundred meters." The five women who'd been singled out groaned but assumed the position quickly and started counting out their pushups. The other seven got up and jogged further down range. By the time the women had reached their next spot, the first group had finished their pushups and was jogging down to observe the others.

"Here's how it's going to go, ladies. As long as you keep hitting the targets, you're still in it. If you miss, you owe me pushups. Last one standing gets—"

"A kiss?" She was interrupted by a suggestion from one of the prone women. Surprised, she turned to survey them but couldn't figure out who made the suggestion. The suggestion had been barely loud enough for her to hear, but not loud enough that she recognized the voice. A smattering of snickers greeted the suggestion.

"In your dreams," she said dryly to the group's further amusement. "Last one standing gets to rub it in the faces of the others until the next time we do this."

There was a chorus of disappointment from the group on their bellies. It was mostly joking, but there was an undercurrent of seriousness that Jak found perplexing. When Torrin had told her there were a fair number of women who were interested in her, she'd blown the thought off. Working with the militiawomen had opened her eyes. She was constantly fending off offers, some subtle, some decidedly less so.

"Settle down! And sight, aim...fire!"

As a group they worked their way down. The other four women quickly fell out of the competition. As a reward, the further they progressed from the targets, the fewer pushups Jak demanded from them.

At twelve hundred meters, only Tanith, Perez and, astoundingly, Hamilton were left. Hamilton was the next one eliminated and Jak let her forego the pushups. It must have taken the Banshee some herculean self-control to overcome the effects of her massive hangover. That she'd been able to pull herself together was nothing short of astounding. Grimly, Hamilton stared Jak in the eye before dropping and giving her twenty anyway. Smiling, Jak shook her head.

Perez and Tanith battled it out for another two hundred meters before Perez finally missed the target from fourteen hundred meters. Tanith jumped up with a whoop and Perez slowly got to her feet. Jak watched them closely as the other women clustered around to congratulate the two of them. It didn't escape her notice that they congratulated Perez just as much as Tanith. A couple of the women barely acknowledged Tanith's achievement and went right to Perez instead. She supposed it must be difficult to be taking training with a commanding officer and wrote off the snub as discomfort because of Tanith's rank.

"All right," she said. "We're done for the day. Let's head back. Make it quick time, then hit the showers."

Full of smiles, the women trotted off, still congratulating each other. Jak jogged back after them. For a while she was able to keep up, but halfway back to the barracks she was forced to slow down. Trying not to feel too bitter, she let the group get ahead of her as she followed at a walk.

She walked into the compound slowly. She turned a blind corner and almost ran into Tanith.

"You were right about being in my dreams," she said. "I wouldn't mind collecting my reward."

"You know I'm with Torrin," Jak said, uncomfortable with the comment.

Tanith grinned, teeth flashing white against her tanned face. "I'm only letting you know your options. You know, in case things don't work out."

"I'm not worried about it," Jak snapped.

"It's okay, I believe you." Tanith crossed her arms and looked down at Jak. Her eyes implored the sniper to believe her. "It's hard to believe that the old Torrin isn't lurking somewhere. I'd like to believe that it's for real. You deserve to be happy."

"Thank you for your concern," Jak said stiffly. "But it's completely misplaced. Torrin and I are doing fine, great in fact."

CHAPTER ELEVEN

Jak walked away more slowly than she would have liked and made her way to her small office in the barracks. In a few quick moves she shed her fatigues and stowed them in an upright locker in the room's corner. Aside from the fact that it was in a barracks, the place had little in common with her room back at Camp Abbott on Haefen. For one thing, the colors were all off. The shades of green and sandy brown that made up the camouflage here were still foreign to her eyes. When outside, the dearth of blue in the landscape still surprised her on occasion. The room was tiny and cramped, though, and that small similarity to her previous quarters was close enough that she spent very little time there. If she had work that needed to be done, she usually brought it back to Torrin's flat.

Jak tried not to dwell on Tanith's words. She knew Torrin had a checkered past with the women of Nadierzda. There were still too many of them who mooned after her, though Torrin's exes seemed to take it all in stride. The ones who made Jak uncomfortable were the ones who shot her dark looks, as if they were blaming her for taking Torrin off the market before they had a chance to sample her charms.

The walk home was uneventful. She could have taken one of the small buses that ran between the militia base and the center of town, but the walk was good for her and helped rebuild her lung capacity. Women passed her and smiled or called out a greeting. She smiled tentatively in return or nodded but never stopped to engage them in conversation. Almost everyone was very friendly, but she still felt as though she was a step removed from all of them, like there was a force field between them. She could see them and they could see her, but none of it was quite real. The only women, aside from Torrin and Nat, with whom she was making any connection were the group of militiawomen she was training and the Banshees.

She let herself into the flat. It was late, the training had gone late into the evening, but there was no sign of Torrin. As usual, when Torrin wasn't there the flat felt cold and too large. Sighing, she helped herself to some food in the kitchen and settled herself on the living room couch.

Over the past few days, she'd had little contact with the smuggler. Apparently things were coming together at work and she had next to no time for Jak. All they had lately were late night lovemaking sessions followed by sleep. Tanith's words gnawed at her while she sat alone on the couch.

She tried to keep herself busy. For a while she distracted herself with reports. The tablet interface still felt foreign to her and she struggled with the hardware. After a few hours she gave up and headed into bed. Torrin's bed was huge and felt even bigger when she was the only occupant. It took her long hours to fall asleep and when she finally drifted off, her sleep was interrupted and disjointed. Bron made multiple appearances in her dreams. Sometimes all he did was stare at her; other times she had to relive his death all over again.

The weight of her broken promise to his ghost was still dragging at her. There were mornings when it was all she could do to pull herself out of bed. Only the knowledge that she had a training session to conduct or that she might get to see Torrin kept her going. The only thing that didn't feel like an effort was spending time with her lover or heading out on the hunt.

Torrin climbed into bed sometime in the wee hours of the morning with a whispered apology. The smuggler pulled Jak's naked body against her own and stroked her exposed skin with a feather's touch. With Torrin's warmth against her own, Jak finally dropped into some restful sleep.

Jak woke as the room lightened. There were no windows; the flat was a few stories below ground, but the lights had been programmed to mimic the progress and warmth of the sun in an attempt to acclimate the women living underground.

She stretched, reaching out for Torrin, but her hands met only air. A quick glance showed her rumpled sheets but no Torrin. Head cocked, she listened to see if the smuggler was still in the flat, but heard nothing. The frequency with which Torrin slipped out of her life was increasingly distressing. Jak would be damned if she was going to try tying Torrin down, but she wished she was more of a priority to her. Her feeling of being adrift in this strange world intensified painfully.

Another day was upon her. She should have gone to the base, but she had no intention of doing so. There was only one thing that would help get her feet under her. Quickly donning some clothing that wouldn't stick out too badly in the Nadierzdan landscape, she pulled the rifle out of the bedroom closet. She needed to go lose herself for a while.

* * *

The warmth of Jak's body curled against her back when she'd woken up had come close to convincing Torrin to stay in bed. Thankfully, Jak was doing well with her recovery and seemed to be assimilating well. While Torrin wasn't exactly thrilled that Jak worked hand in hand with Tanith, she understood that Jak was doing something that was hers alone. She needed to trust Jak, but she would never trust that woman.

As she groomed herself for the day, she watched Jak sleep. It always amused her how absurdly young Jak looked when she slept. All the substantial cares of her life fell away as she slumbered. The furrows on her brow smoothed out and the serious expression gave way to one of peace. Torrin only wished that she could see that relaxation on her face when Jak was awake. Once again, she was tempted to crawl back into bed and to wake her lover in spectacular fashion. Her pussy clenched at the idea and she took half a step toward the bed before stopping herself.

They were so close, she told herself as she pulled herself away from the bedside. It would only be a little longer. Her source inside the council had told her they would be summoned any day, and they'd sent out their "gifts" to the councilwomen who could be swayed to their side. A small conservative core on the council would never cast a vote their way, and Torrin saw no reason to try convincing them of anything. She chose to concentrate on those who could be bought.

The presentation was complete, the prototypes were coming along. Troika hadn't started tissue tests yet, but the prototypes were working as advertised in computer simulations. Fortunately, they wouldn't need a working prototype to demonstrate the implants: they had Jak. All they needed now was a public forum in which to unveil them and to lay before the women of Nadierzda the plan that would allow them to keep their home planet from being slowly choked to death by dust and sand.

Her bike called to her in the flat's small garage and she succumbed to its sleek charms. She still missed the bike she'd left on Haefen. When she had the time, she would soup this one up also. Climbing on, she gunned the engine and tore out into the street. Because of the early hour, there was no traffic to speak of. Her ride to the office was shorter than normal.

Audra's head popped out of the door to her office when she approached. A broad grin creased her face and she winked at Torrin. The smuggler noticed that her partner's hair was mussed and her clothes were rumpled and crooked, like they had been pulled on in a hurry. Whatever news Audra had must be good if her partner had cut off an assignation to let her know.

"You look refreshed," Torrin said.

Audra's grin widened. "Just celebrating. The council's summons came down this morning. They want to see us for the evening session in three nights."

"It's about time. We've been ready to go for a week. I thought we might have to kidnap one of them and implant a prototype to get their attention."

"It seems we finally got through to them. The campaign finally moved them." Audra shot an indulgent look behind her into her office. At the look, Torrin knew who her partner had hooked up with. Reaching past Audra, she pushed the door open slightly. A young woman reclined on the sofa, partially covered by a blanket.

"Mollie," Torrin called in greeting and the intern raised a hand in reply. "You're terrible," she accused her friend. "She reports to you. Or she did. Now we need to reassign her to someone else."

Audra shrugged, not repentant in the least. "She's good at what she does. You know how competence turns me on."

Torrin rolled her eyes and headed for her office. "Call a meeting in a few hours. We need to get everyone rolling."

She'd barely gotten seated to review the latest reports on the prototypes when there was a knock at the door.

"Come," she called and the door hissed open in response to her voice. Two women stood on the other side of the threshold.

"Hazel, Rudrani," Torrin said in greeting and stood up to welcome the two women. They both had a hardened air around them, and they scanned the room for threats even though nothing was likely to attack them there. If Audra was turned on by competence, then she would have been panting after the two women. Torrin knew for a fact that not only could they manage anything thrown at them, but they would get it handled without breaking a sweat. "How did the first delivery go?"

"No problems," the darker of the two said. She had a hooked nose and intense, deep-set eyes. After Torrin, she had been one of the most eligible single women on Nadi. Now that Torrin was out of the running, she must have been getting a lot of action. "You were right, they were a little squirrely at first. They settled down after we gave them a few demonstrations."

"Good." Torrin turned to the other woman. "Hazel, any issues with the picket? Was it still the *Icarus*?"

Hazel nodded, her shock of white-blond hair flopping into her eyes. She pushed it back absently. "It was the *Icarus* all right, but they didn't even know we were there. Easy in, easy out."

"Be careful with that one. Her captain is good, and I don't want to lose either of you."

"About that, Torrin." Hazel pushed her hair back again, even though it hadn't gotten in her face. "I can't go on the next run. Or probably the next one after that."

"For crying out loud, Hazel." With exasperated voice and rolling eyes, Rudrani broke in. "Her wife's about to have their baby. She wants to stay home for a while to help raise her."

Hazel reddened uncomfortably when Torrin sent an amused look her way.

"You don't strike me as the playing house type," Torrin said. "But if that's what you want, we can find work for you to do around here." She was pretty sure this domestic phase wouldn't last very long. Hazel was one of the butchest women she knew and Torrin couldn't envision her being happy for long, surrounded by little girls.

"I'd appreciate that."

Torrin nodded and turned back to Rudrani. "We have a number of shipments to go before we've met our obligation to the Devonites. You're going to need a new partner." She leaned back in the chair and surveyed her employees for a moment, thinking. Nat wasn't really ready, but this was as good an opportunity as any. She had to learn sometime and Rudrani was one of her best. If anyone could show Nat the ropes and keep her in one piece, it was Rudrani. Leaving Nadi was something Nat wanted more than anything else, and Torrin could empathize. She'd been ready to leave the planet's surface at Nat's age also, but she had lacked the opportunity. Reaching up behind her ear she activated her subdermal transmitter.

"Nat, come to my office." An assenting grunt was the only reply she received before her sister cut the transmission. Nat wasn't very happy with Torrin's management style. Torrin was harder on her sister than any of the other employees. There was no way she wanted her sister to be tainted by accusations of favoritism, though she was probably going to hear about this decision. Nat deserved the chance, though; she'd been putting up with Torrin's toughness admirably well. For Nat.

She chatted amiably with the two women while waiting for her sister. A few minutes later, Nat strode through the door.

"What do you need, Torrin?" There was a slight edge in Nat's voice.

"I'm giving you a new assignment."

Nat rolled her eyes in response but wisely refrained from saying anything. One thing Torrin wasn't going to allow was anyone to weaken her position, especially not in front of other employees. They'd had one particularly bad row a couple weeks after Nat had started. If Jak hadn't taken her sister aside to talk some sense into her, Nat's employment with Troika Corp. would have been very brief. Jak had also taken Torrin aside and told her to be easier on Nat.

"You're taking over the Haefen run with Rudrani. Hazel is going to be taking some time off—" The rest of Torrin's words were cut off when Nat stepped forward and threw her arms around her. The other two women grinned widely as she squeezed Torrin.

"Nat. Nat? Nat!" Torrin hollered at her sister before she would let go.

"Thank you, Torrin! Thanks so much, this is going to be awesome. I'll make you really proud, you won't regret this, I promise."

Torrin let her babble on with gratitude for a little while longer before interrupting.

"You need to get everything in order here," she said. "If there's anything that you need to take care of, do it today. You and Rudrani are leaving for Haefen the day after tomorrow. You'll make a stop at our suppliers first, then on from there."

"Got it. I'll just be going now, if that's all right?"

Nodding, Torrin hid a grin as her sister bustled out the door.

Nat stopped in the doorway and looked back at her. "You know this means you can't duck out on dinner with Mom any longer."

Torrin swore and Nat flashed her a cheeky grin before heading out. It was true—she'd run out of time. If Torrin let Nat go off without the family dinner, her mother would blister her ears for sure. As it was, she was already going to catch it for the drunken rant she still couldn't quite remember. Her employees were smirking at her when she looked up. They seemed very entertained by her sudden change in mood.

"You keep your hands off my sister, or I'll blast you out an airlock at low altitude," Torrin said conversationally to a still-grinning Rudrani. Hazel guffawed and punched Rudrani in the shoulder. Rudrani's grin widened.

CHAPTER TWELVE

The walk from the road looked incredibly long, longer than it actually was. Torrin stood in front of the white fence that surrounded the always perfect yard. The long, low house of her childhood looked the same as it always had. Like always, the sweet sound of chimes swaying in the wind drifted across the yard to where they stood. This was nothing she was looking forward to. Her relationship with her mother was...complicated. Introducing Jak to the mix was going to be interesting.

"Are you ready for this?" Torrin asked.

Beside her, Jak was pale. Her recovery was coming along well, but she still lacked the glow of complete health. Truth be told, she almost looked paler than when she'd first woken up in the clinic. She betrayed her nerves at meeting Torrin's parents in the way she swallowed hard at the question. Torrin had seen her less worried before taking Orthodoxans on by herself. In fact, Torrin would have given a lot to avoid this dinner as well. She wasn't quite ready to face Hutchinson again instead of dinner at her mother's place, but it was close. If she was this nervous, how could Jak not be? Torrin made a mental note to support Jak however she needed to during dinner.

"As ready as I'll ever be." Jak's voice was muted and Torrin had to strain to hear her.

"Let's get this over with." Fingers entwined with Jak's, Torrin swung open the gate and walked down the tidy path to the front door. She knocked quietly at the door and waited. They didn't have to wait long. Footsteps hastened to the door and it swung open. A woman of middling height surveyed them through the open door, focusing first on her, then on Jak. She nodded her head decisively, black hair flopping forward in front of her eyes.

"Torrin, how are you?" she asked, flipping her hair out of her way. "Your mother was beside herself."

"I'm fine, Raisa. Any rumors you may have heard are mostly untrue."

Raisa laughed, flashing white teeth before pulling the smuggler into a tight embrace. Torrin found it strange that these days she was closer to her mother's second wife than she was to her own mother. Raisa was willing to take her for who she was while her mother was constantly trying to fit her into a mold she wasn't suited for.

"You don't even want to know what rumors we've heard." Raisa squeezed Torrin against herself one last time before letting her go. "But it isn't like you to have been so late without something being seriously wrong. She worries. We both worry. She shows it differently than you do, but she cares very deeply for you. You would do well to remember that." She looked up at Torrin, her eyes speculative and lifted her hand to gently brush at Torrin's temple, where she would have had strands of hair that had escaped from behind her ear.

Torrin shifted at the pointed remark. Apparently Irenya had passed on at least some of what she'd said. Raisa didn't seem too angry about it, but Irenya's fury had probably been towering and likely still was. Jak shifted uncomfortably behind her, drawing Raisa's attention. Before she could do more than look up, Jak found herself engulfed in a hug. Torrin bit her lip to keep from laughing at the way Jak's arms stuck out in rigid discomfort before she bent them to awkwardly return the embrace.

"You must be Jak." Raisa stepped back, her hands on Jak's shoulders, to get a better look at her. "We've heard so much about you." She turned her head to look at Torrin and wink. "Very nice, dear."

Jak's face flamed bright red. "I hope it's good things," she mumbled.

"Of course. The crater's a-twitter with news of your presence. Nat's been going on about you too. It's so nice to finally meet one of Torrin's girlfriends." Raisa leaned forward conspiratorially. "You're the first, you know."

"Come on, Raisa, you know that's not true." Torrin's voice rose in protest.

Smiling, Raisa rolled her eyes. "The first one in twenty years, then." She wrapped an arm around Jak's shoulders and shepherded her inside, leaving Torrin to trail along in their wake. Jak shot a look back at her, one eyebrow raised in question, and Torrin cursed Raisa's chattiness. Now she was going to have to have that talk with Jak about her dating life, a topic that could have waited forever as far as she was concerned. She didn't like thinking about Galya, let alone talking about her. Some wounds were still too fresh, even after twenty years.

"Come on in. Dinner is almost ready. Your mother's out bringing in the goats, but she should be back soon."

The house was immaculate as it had been since Mama had died. Irenya, one of her adoptive mothers, had supported the family through farming and crafting. She kept goats and milked them for the production of cheese. She also sheared the goats for wool. The wool was a much-sought-after commodity and commanded good prices at the markets. It kept her out of the house most of the time and busy in the countryside where she watched over her flock. By contrast, Tamra—her first wife and Torrin's Mama—had always been around. She hadn't been the best housekeeper, but she'd always had time for Torrin. Some of Torrin's happiest childhood memories were of the time she'd spent with Mama.

Irenya had hoped that one of her children would follow in her footsteps. Nat hadn't been born yet, so from the beginning she'd pinned her hopes on Torrin. When Torrin had made it clear that she wanted nothing to do with farming or crafting, Irenya had been extremely angry and had made her displeasure well known. For years, Torrin couldn't do anything right and was scoffed at and browbeaten, but to no avail. Torrin had moved out of the house as soon as she finished school to put in time with the planetary militia. She had taken leave when Mama got sick and had spent the better part of a year nursing her and caring for her before she died. Irenya had spent her time with the goats. On the day of Mama's funeral, Irenya and Torrin had come to blows.

"Get the fuck out until you can show me some respect!" Irenya had screamed at her.

"How can I show something I don't have?" Torrin had shot back over her shoulder.

By the time she talked to Irenya again, Torrin was starting to make a life and name for herself as a merchant and smuggler. She only came back into her mother's life when Nat was born. There was no way she would ever understand what a warm, vibrant woman like Raisa saw in the emotionally distant and focused Irenya, but Raisa seemed happy and her mother was looser with her around. She was a much warmer mother to Nat than she'd ever been to Torrin.

Even with the reconciliation, Torrin had been in her childhood home only rarely since the funeral. Raisa's touch on the place was visible in the decor. The differences were in subtle departures from what Torrin remembered as a child. A painting that Tamra had in a back bedroom was up in the family room. Raisa had a taste for the pottery that was crafted on Nadierzda and sought after across the galaxy. A number of large pieces decorated a half wall with their graceful lines and brilliant glazes. There were members of the aristocracy on dozens of planets who would have killed to have possessed so many pieces and of that size and quality. They probably would have cried to see them gracing the home of a farmwife.

Torrin was ensconced in the corner of a sofa, Jak pressed against her side, twin cups of pungent tea warming their hands when Raisa set a plate of cookies down in front of them.

"You're too thin, you know that?" Raisa said accusingly when Torrin didn't immediately go for a cookie. With a small smile, Torrin helped herself to a cookie and nibbled on it while sipping at her tea.

"It's been a rough few weeks," she admitted carefully.

"Don't tell me now," Raisa admonished her with a smile. "You'll only have to repeat it when your mother comes in." She turned the smile onto Jak. "You could use some meat on your bones also, dear."

Jak gave her a wide-eyed stare and reached for a cookie. She broke off a piece and popped it in her mouth. Liking what she was tasting, she bit off a larger chunk and chewed away hungrily.

"So how are you then?" Torrin asked.

"I'm very well. My weaving has been going especially well, and I've been producing some high-quality fabric." Raisa indicated a loom, barely visible through a low doorway. "With the dyes that I get at the market, I can make some incredible fabrics. Irenya wants me to package them for you to sell."

"Of course she does," Torrin snapped a piece off her cookie. "If it makes a buck, Mom's after it."

"Sounds like someone else I know."

"It's different with me. You know why I'm doing this." Even to her own ears, Torrin's protests sounded hollow.

"All I'm saying is for someone who didn't want to follow in her mother's footsteps, you're not around to see much of your family either."

"But—" Raisa's hand forestalled any further arguments. Torrin subsided grudgingly.

"You need to patch things up with your mother. She won't be around forever, and with your life the way it is, one of you is going to die without fixing things with the other. Your last trip backs me up on this one. So does what you said to her." Raisa captured Torrin's eyes with her own. Torrin was the first one to look down.

A knock at the front door broke the tension. It opened before Raisa could do more than look up.

"Hello?" Nat's voice floated through the entry hall to the living room. "We're in here," Raisa called back. She stood and greeted Nat as warmly as she had Jak and Torrin. Nat enfolded her in a big hug and squeezed back enthusiastically. Raisa's ability to accept her wife's adopted daughter as easily as her own biological daughter always amazed Torrin. For her part, she knew she preferred Raisa's company to Irenya's and she supposed that there might be some favoritism toward Nat in her stepmother's heart, but she'd never seen it.

"Cookies!" Nat pressed a quick kiss to Raisa's cheek and bounded into the room and plopped herself on the other end of the couch. She reached forward and helped herself to a handful of cookies.

"Don't eat them all, Nat." Raisa stood with her hands on her hips, but the smile on her face belied the sternness of her voice. "We have guests."

"We do?" Nat's voice was muffled by a mouthful of cookie and she looked around, slightly confused. "Oh, her." She swallowed to clear her mouth. "Jak doesn't count. She's pretty much family already." She smirked over at Torrin, knowing how the dig would affect her.

Hoping the smile on her face wasn't too sickly, Torrin reached for another cookie. Torrin wasn't sure how she felt about Nat's breezy acceptance of Jak into the family. She knew she wanted Jak to stick around. Jak had already been with her longer than most of her hookups and she had no desire to change that, but Nat seemed to think they were already married off.

A door opened and closed at the back of the house, putting a damper on Nat's teasing. They both knew what was coming. There was no way Irenya would take the news of Nat's departure well.

Torrin rose quickly when Irenya joined them in the living room. After pausing to brush cookie crumbs from her lap, she awkwardly embraced her mother. The hug she'd shared with Raisa had been much more heartfelt, which probably seemed strange to anyone who knew the dynamics of the family. Torrin wondered what Jak made of it. Irenya sat down on the chair across from them. Raisa perched on the arm of the chair and draped an arm around Irenya's wiry shoulders.

"So," Irenya started formally. "How was your trip?"

"It was all right," Torrin said, but she didn't elaborate any further. So far her mother hadn't made any mention of their latest fight. If she was going to ignore it, then so was Torrin.

"It couldn't have gone that well if it took you an extra couple of months to get back," her mother pointed out.

"I closed the deal. There were a few complications, that's all."

"Oh, well as long as you closed the deal." Irenya's tone veered sharply into the sardonic, and Raisa placed a warning hand on her knee. Torrin's mother shut her mouth sharply on the rest of her words.

Her mother always had more to say. However she heard about the events from Torrin, Irenya was going to decide that all had gone wrong because she'd wanted to go to space to seek her fortune and find adventure. They'd had this conversation so many times Torrin felt she should be able to recite it by heart.

"This is Jak, by the way. My girlfriend." Irenya's lack of interest rankled and Torrin was determined to do this right. If it also deflected some of the attention from her trip, all the better.

"I'm glad to meet you," Irenya said, raking Jak with shrewd eyes. Torrin had seen Irenya give a sickly member of the herd a very similar look. Jak was being weighed and measured, but Torrin's mother wouldn't be sidetracked. "So what happened then?" Irenya prodded.

"Well," Torrin took a deep breath. All at once, she decided to be completely candid and get it out in the open. The faster she told the story, the faster she could get the recriminations over with. "I'm sure Nat told you about me getting in trouble on my latest run and Jak bailing me out. It's true as far as it goes, but there's more to it."

"I was sure there was," Irenya said. "With you there pretty much always is more to the story."

Torrin smiled tightly. Her mother wasn't making any of this any easier and they hadn't even gotten to the hard part. "Fine. I was held captive by a psychotic colonel who wanted me to be the chief wife in his harem, got rescued when Jak shot the colonel, got dragged through the wilderness to make a deal with the other side, then dragged her back through the wilderness to my ship. Haefen was the most misogynistic, backward backwater I've ever had the misfortune to visit, but for my pains, I'm going to make Troika Corp. more money in one run than I ever have before. Oh, and Jak was actually sent to kill me, not the colonel. I'm so glad she didn't or I wouldn't have her as an amazing girlfriend." She smiled brightly at her mothers' shocked stares.

* * *

Jak shifted on the couch, suddenly feeling like her skin was too tight. After Torrin's bombshell, Irenya and Raisa stared at the two of them, gazes skittering back and forth. Whatever had possessed Torrin to tell them the particulars of their meeting in that way? Beside her, tension radiated from Torrin. She relaxed a little bit when Jak slid her arm through the crook of Torrin's elbow.

"Is that true?" Raisa's voice was soft with concern.

"What the hell, Torrin?" The irritation in Irenya's voice smothered her wife's quiet query. "How could you get yourself involved with someone who was trying to kill you? This is the woman whose side you couldn't leave? The one you were too busy with to come see your own parents. It really is different than it was with Tamra. She never tried to kill me. Torrin, are you thinking with anything other than your groin?"

"Mom, it's not like that." Nat broke in, trying to smooth things over.

"Then what is it like, exactly?" Irenya's eyes bored into Jak. She quivered on the edge of readiness, prepared to leap up and defend her daughter from Jak's slightest sign of aggression.

Unsure how to answer, Jak glanced over at her lover. Anger shivered along the rigid line of her jaw. Her eyes snapped with the intensity of the emotion.

Sure that Torrin was about to say something she would regret, Jak jumped in. "I didn't make the call. That's not how it works. Snipers go where they're told and take out who they're told. Only, when I saw Torrin, I couldn't pull the trigger." She had no idea what else was going on. Clearly she'd missed something, but she could at least take the heat off Torrin about her intentions.

"Really, Mother." Torrin's voice was light, almost conversational, but Jak knew she was simmering inside. Jak ran her hand up and down Torrin's arm in what she hoped was a soothing gesture. "Not only did she contravene her orders, to her own likely detriment, but she rescued me. Without her, I would still be in serious trouble on Haefen, and she could have gotten into serious trouble for helping me."

Irenya's face softened and she looked back at Jak appraisingly.

Raisa leaped into the conversational void and smiled at Jak. "So how are you liking Nadierzda? Are you getting to know the place?"

"I like it very much." Jak nodded emphatically, grinning like an idiot. "Nat's been very helpful in showing me around." She smiled down the couch at Torrin's sister. "It's too bad she won't be around much longer to give me the official tour of every bar and restaurant in Landing, like she said she would."

"Nat's going somewhere?" Irenya sat up straight and glared at Torrin.

Torrin winced and shot Jak a quick look. She had gone pale. Apparently she had just let the aetenberan out of the cage. Her face bloomed with heat and she looked down at her hands. *How was I supposed to know? It would have been nice to know that. Does Torrin tell her ma anything?*

"She's making a delivery run. One of my crews lost someone." When Irenya looked ready to explode and even Raisa seemed taken aback, Torrin clarified hastily. "We lost her to her wife. They're about to have their first daughter and she wants to be home for her family." She smiled tightly. "Admirable, isn't it?"

Torrin simply couldn't seem to resist needling her mother. Raisa might be Torrin's stepmother but she clearly had a better relationship with her than with Irenya. It was odd that she should be so estranged from her.

"I've been wanting to go out for a long time," Nat said. "You know that, Mom. I'm stoked that Torrin is giving me the chance. I'll finally have the chance to see other planets and meet other cultures firsthand, instead of through her stories."

Neither of them had mentioned that Nat would be heading to Haefen, the same planet where Torrin had had so many problems. Jak wasn't going to say anything, not after the look she'd gotten when she accidentally busted Torrin and her sister. It was interesting, and it made her stomach sink a bit, how easily Torrin skirted the truth with her mother. Had her lover done that with her, avoided difficult or inconvenient truths? How well did she really know Torrin, and why were things so much more complicated here?

Irenya's brow lifted slightly in the face of Nat's enthusiasm.

Torrin pounced on the opportunity. "She's going out with one of my best women. Rudrani will show Nat the ropes but will keep her out of trouble. It's why I'm sending her out now. There really isn't anyone better."

Nat nodded vigorously from her end of the couch. "It's true. Rudrani is the best! She's already been getting me up to speed on the ship and the best way to stow cargo."

"There goes any hope that one of you girls will take up here after I'm gone," Irenya said softly. She didn't look angry anymore. Her brow was still creased, but it looked more like sadness to Jak.

"I'm sorry, Mom." Nat got up and crossed over to Irenya. She perched on the other side and wrapped her arm around Irenya's shoulders. "You know I never would have made a good goatherd. Those things hate me. I think they want to eat me."

"They probably remember how you used to strap on that old riding helmet of Torrin's and go down and try to butt heads with them."

Nat laughed and threw both arms around her mother, hugging her exuberantly. "I only did that a few times."

Irenya grinned hugely and suddenly all trace of stern matriarch was gone. She ruffled her hand through Nat's hair, making it stand up at all angles. "Are you sure your Rudrani will be enough to keep this one out of trouble?" she asked Torrin. "Do you have a few Rudranis?"

Torrin shared a smile with them. "Just the one, I'm afraid. Don't worry, I've given Rudrani strict instructions to bind and gag Nat if she gives her too many issues."

The sudden turn from argument to banter was enough to give Jak a lump in her throat. This was what she missed most, what had been missing from her life since Ma died. She and Bron had given their father a hard time, but it hadn't been the same after she was gone from their lives. The bonds of family were what she had been living without for too long. They'd been torn from her one at a time until she was all alone, and to see them in front of her again but not be able to participate was almost more than she could bear. Did Torrin realize how lucky she was? She must not, or she wouldn't have avoided her mothers for a month after getting back to Nadierzda. Jak's eyes prickled and she bit the inside of her lip. She would not start crying in front of these women whom she'd just met. She would not!

"Now that we've settled that, I'd like to know why Torrin isn't the one showing you around Landing." Raisa bent a gently chastising look on her stepdaughter.

"She's very busy right now," Jak said. "It's okay, I understand."

"Yeah, Raisa," Torrin said defensively. "Jak understands."

"She shares a lot in common with her mother," Raisa continued, ignoring the way Torrin's face stiffened at the comment. "When she's neglecting me too much, I find I need to do something to get her attention. Something low-cut usually does the trick."

"Mom!" The outraged cry was drawn from the throats of both daughters and Raisa shared a wide grin with Jak.

"So I know you had to be a soldier on your home planet." Irenya leaned forward to engage her. "What are you going to do now that you're here?"

"I'm working with the militia. They don't have anyone with my skill set so I'm training a class of women in long-distance marksmanship."

"Really?" The twist of her lips signaled Irenya's disapproval even though she didn't give voice to the criticism.

"Mother…" Torrin's voice prickled with warning and Irenya looked over at her.

"I have a right to my opinion."

"Maybe you don't need to let it out right now."

"It's okay, Torrin." Jak tried to reassure her.

Torrin took a breath to respond but couldn't get a word out before Irenya cut her off.

"Why would you even want to keep doing that? Wouldn't you rather be involved in something that brings life or something that improves people's quality of life? If you keep on with the militia, then you're good for one thing, and that's killing."

"Irenya!" Raisa hissed at her wife, but Irenya ignored her.

"Here we go," Nat muttered, burying her face in her palm.

"Mother!" Torrin's eyes flared angrily at her mother, but there was no stopping her.

"We don't need more warmongers here. This used to be a peaceful planet, but the more of you interlopers we get, the more war-like we become. I have to tell you, things sure have gone downhill."

"That's funny," Jak said from between gritted teeth. "Nat told me that Nadi's first settlers were pirates. Doesn't sound too peaceful to me.

Besides, if you stopped letting new people in, you would be down one daughter."

"And a wife," Raisa said quietly.

"Bah." Irenya was unmoved. "We should have closed things up fifteen years ago. With Torrin and her new business ventures all over hell's half galaxies, we could be discovered at any time. We should pull everyone back to the planet, close down our interstellar travel and do only what we must to protect ourselves. Everything we need is right here."

"That's enough, Mother."

"No, it isn't, Torrin. We're better off on our own, without the likes of her." She pointed accusingly at Jak.

"Let me tell you something, Mother. Nadierzda is dying. The precious planet you want us to barricade ourselves on is choking to death."

"Twattle. That's a myth."

"No, it isn't. But we have the power to make it a thing of the past. Do you know why we have that opportunity? Because of Jak. Without her, I would be dead, or worse, on Haefen and you'd be sitting here wondering what happened to me. Without the possibilities that her advanced technology offers us, you would also only be decades from choking to death on sand."

Irenya stared at her, shocked at Torrin's words and her vehemence. She opened her mouth to respond but closed it with a snap when Raisa put a hand on her forearm and gently shook her head.

"I've heard you bitching about the silt that clogs the watering holes your goats use. Didn't you say that it's worse now than it was when you were a kid?"

"I suppose. I have to clear out the watering holes every few months instead of every few years like my mother had to."

"See, it's only going to get worse." Torrin stood up, leaving Jak alone in the corner of the couch. She missed Torrin's comforting presence against her, but she was glad for how she drew away Irenya's intense eyes. "I've been told that the more of the planet that gets reclaimed by the sands, the faster the rest of the green spaces will be taken over. People think, based on how slowly the rest of the planet was swallowed, that it'll be a couple of centuries before we're buried."

"That's not the case?" Irenya sat back in her chair, eyes thoughtful.

"No, Mother. It isn't." Torrin stood at the far end of the room, hands on her hips as she looked out the living room window. She dropped her head. "We have thirty, maybe forty years, tops."

Irenya sat up in the chair, her back ramrod straight in shock. "Why haven't we heard anything about how bad it really is from the Ruling Council?"

"They're looking into it." A bitter smile twisted Torrin's lips as she turned and leaned against the windowsill. "They don't want to let the truth out because they don't want to start a panic."

"It's getting damn close to being time to panic." Nat was uncharacteristically sober. She crossed the room to perch on the other arm of Irenya's chair. Her mother wrapped an arm around her waist and squeezed Nat reassuringly.

Jak was struck by the tenderness of the gesture and how the family banded together around Irenya for support. All of them, except Torrin. Jak yearned to be included, to allow the family's strength to bolster her own. Torrin didn't know how lucky she was.

"And you can fix it?" Raisa wrapped her hand around Irenya's, watching Torrin.

"If we get the money within the next ten years, we can get the terraforming completed." Torrin came back and sat down next to Jak. "We *can* get the money. Between what we've made through Troika Corp. over the past fifteen years and what we'll make through the implant technology I brought back from Haefen, we'll have enough." She smiled, her eyes bright. "Can you imagine it? Nadierzda, completely green, no sand left."

Her family echoed the smile.

"How can I help?" Irenya asked.

"Spread the word. The Ruling Council is dragging its heels. They're worried that this new technology will pull Nadi from hiding."

"They're right to be concerned. You know my feelings on it."

Jak was relieved that the tenor of the conversation was calming down. She'd known from the little that Torrin had said about her mother that there were issues. It made no sense to her. Jak would have given pretty much anything to have any of the members of her family back.

"I do." Torrin's smile had a bit of an edge to it. "But if we don't do anything, we'll be hiding ourselves from the galaxy on a dead hunk of rock, fighting to keep from being torn apart by the sands. What happens then? We get spread across the Fringes, each taking up residence on a world where we don't know how we'll be treated? We'd lose what we have here."

"I hate to interrupt," Raisa said, standing up. She kept her hand in Irenya's until the last possible moment before reluctantly pulling it free. "But my nose tells me dinner's almost done. We should move this outside."

Nat jumped up immediately.

"It's no surprise that the mention of food gets your sister moving," Irenya said to Torrin.

The gentle teasing surprised Jak, but Torrin just laughed.

"Thanks, guys." Nat turned to her. "Come on, Jak. I'll show you where we're eating." She led Jak through the house and out into a small courtyard. The roof extended far over the courtyard, shielding the small area from sun and blowing sand. Large potted plants lined the corners while long boxes lined the walls full of flowering vines climbing up the walls.

"Houses in the country usually have courtyards like this," Nat said, taking note of Jak's interest. "We don't have them so much in Landing, all the buildings together act as wind blocks, but out here, the only thing to block the wind is the house itself."

"It's cooler than I thought." Jak noticed a small fountain bubbling away in the corner. To her delight, she discovered that the small pond below the fountain was stocked with colorful fish.

Soft voices announced the arrival of Torrin and her mother. They had their heads together in a quiet but intense conversation. Seeing Jak over by the pond, Irenya broke into the first genuine smile Jak had seen on her face. It looked strange; the skin at the corner of her eyes crinkled and her cheeks revealed dimples. Jak had assumed that Torrin's mother was a cheerless woman and the dimples surprised her.

"Do you like it?" Her smile grew as she joined Jak. "I built it for Tamra, my first wife. She used to sit out here and watch the fish for hours."

"It's very nice," Jak said. "I can see why she enjoyed it."

"She did. After she got sick, she didn't always have the strength to come out and sit, but she would always ask after her fish. Fortunately, Raisa doesn't mind it." Irenya sighed, staring into the depths, her face back to the soberness it seemed made for.

"Dinner's ready." Raisa's voice floated over to them, saving Jak from needing to say something. Nat and Torrin rushed to help her, bustling back and forth, setting dishes of food and plates on the table. In a few short moments, the table at the center of the courtyard was full of food. Nat yelped when Raisa rapped her knuckles for trying to cadge vegetables from a serving dish.

"Let's go save Nat from starvation." Irenya pitched her voice loud enough for her youngest to hear and pretended not to see the mock-glare she received. She accompanied Jak to the table and waited as she took her place. Waving to the rest of her family, she took the seat across from Jak.

Laughing and chatting, Nat and Raisa sat while Torrin followed more quietly. She slid into place next to Jak and leaned over to give her a quick kiss on the curve of her jaw. Jak's face heated at the display of affection. Not for the first time, not even for the hundredth time, she wished her embarrassment didn't show so easily. To her left, Nat snickered at her discomfiture and Jak punched her under the table. Nat grunted but did nothing to hide her continued smirk.

There was controlled chaos as Torrin's family helped themselves to food and somehow Jak's plate was filled without her even realizing it. The food looked wonderful and smelled even better. It was the usual mix of sweet and spicy that she was coming to realize was essentially the regional cuisine on Nadi. The spice had been especially hard for her to get used to. Compared to here, the food on Haefen was bland, especially the MREs she'd eaten half the time.

After she'd eaten enough to blunt the edge of her obvious starvation, Nat looked up and glanced around the table, a wicked gleam in her eyes. Jak wondered what she was up to. She'd known her long enough to realize that there was very little Nat couldn't joke about and her favorite target was her older sister. In some ways, she made Torrin seem downright sober by comparison.

"So, Mom, what do you think of Torrin's new look?"

Torrin flashed her a look of peevish irritation. It hadn't escaped Jak's notice that Torrin was getting sick of the comments about her hair. Jak reached up and ran her fingers through the short hair on the back of her head. Her own hair was much longer than she was used to, but it didn't bother her too much: Torrin seemed to like it longer. Beside her, Torrin dropped her hand after making the same gesture. The grin on Nat's face widened as she watched them.

Irenya shrugged, barely glancing up from her plate. "It's a little shorter, so what. It'll grow back."

The look of gratitude on Torrin's face was hard to miss, and she shared a glance with her mother. Nat speared a vegetable on her plate with extra vehemence, disappointed not to be getting more of a rise out of Torrin.

Silence settled around the table as Torrin and her family dug into the food in front of them. Finally unable to take the quiet for any longer, Jak turned to Raisa.

"So if you have no men here, how do you have children?"

Raisa's eyes widened, and she hastily swallowed the last of the bite in her mouth before wiping her mouth with a napkin. "Children? You're interested in having children? That's wonderful news!"

Across the table, Irenya frowned slightly and leaned toward Torrin. "Do you think that's a good idea? You two haven't known each other that long. You should give things a little longer before you take the plunge."

Aghast that her question had been so misinterpreted, Jak shook her head vehemently. Her cheeks were so hot that she thought her face was about to burst into flames. "No, that's not why I was asking."

"What? No!" Torrin's panicked refusal would have been funny if Jak hadn't also been on the hot seat.

"I was only wondering. Nat told me that there are no men here, but I see women with small children, and I was confused."

"Oh." Raisa sounded disappointed and she sat back in her chair, a move that Irenya mirrored, though her face betrayed relief rather than disappointment. "Children end up on Nadierzda in two different ways. A small minority of them end up here because their mothers were impregnated before they were rescued by the Banshees. Our children are a perfect example of both ways." Her gentle smile encompassed Jak along with Nat and Torrin.

"Torrin told me her mother was rescued from off-planet."

"Her bio-mother was, but she died a few hours after Torrin was born. Irenya and her first wife adopted her. After she passed on, I married Irenya, then we had Nat. She came about from a fertilization procedure. Are you familiar with cloning?"

Jak nodded.

"Well, instead of fertilizing an egg with genetic material from the same person, we use genetic material from the other mother. So essentially, we're fertilizing eggs with eggs, not sperm. Does that make sense?"

"I think so. Does this mean that the only children you can have this way are girls?"

"That's right." Irenya picked up the thread. "No way to introduce Y chromosomes into the mix, and besides, who needs them? We get along perfectly fine without men here. Things are peaceful; we settle our disagreements in a civilized fashion. We don't need a bunch of testosterone-laden men who only think with their genitalia trying to tell us what to do."

"So what happens to the boy babies? The ones who come with the offworld women?" Jak straightened, slightly alarmed. If they were so anti-men, what were they doing to those children?

"Relax." Torrin placed a hand on Jak's knee, soothing her. "We don't do anything to them. Their mothers are welcome to stay here for a few years until they've recovered from their ordeals. Then we find them new homes offworld."

"It's true." Nat's words were muffled around her mouthful of food and she chewed, then swallowed before continuing. "Torrin and the rest of us at Troika Corp. work our asses off to try to find them good places to live. Usually, they end up getting jobs with Troika also."

"Oh, okay." It made perfect sense and Jak relaxed, glad she hadn't accidentally uncovered Nadierzda's dark secret. She chided herself for being so suspicious. It was hard not to be, coming as she did from Haefen where misogyny was a national pastime. Nadierzda seemed too perfect to be true; there was no way any society could be this perfect. As the women chatted around her, Jak tried to shake off the dark disquiet that closed around her. Could any place be as perfect as Nadi seemed to be? Maybe she was looking for the speck in the pudding, but as much as she wanted to believe things could be this great, part of her couldn't stop looking for some kind of corruption beneath the surface.

CHAPTER THIRTEEN

"Did you get everything packed?" Torrin stood next to Nat in her quarters on the *Melisende*. There wasn't much in there beyond the clothing that Nat was currently stowing. Rudrani was nowhere to be seen, which was fine with her. She didn't need any of her employees witnessing the sendoff of her little sister.

"Of course I did." Nat rolled her eyes. "Clothes, weapons, some entertainment. What else do I need?"

"There isn't much more. Did you have anyone go over your weaponry with you? The last thing you want is to be in a tight spot with a faulty plasma pistol."

"Jak cleared all my weaponry. I'm sure it'll be fine."

"Good." Torrin watched in silence as Nat finished stowing her gear. She chewed idly upon a cuticle. Unable to keep quiet any longer, she tried a new tack. "Watch yourself with the Devonites. They aren't like anybody you're used to. You must never be alone in their presence. Make sure Rudrani is with you whenever you have to deal with them."

Nat turned toward her, hands on her hips. "Torrin, I can handle myself. Did you tell Rudrani the same thing?"

"Actually, yes, back on her first run to the Devonites, and I've just told her again." Torrin crossed the small room and took her sister by the shoulders. "There's no guarantee she'll be dealing with the same men as before or that one of them won't decide to try something anyway. I want you both back in one piece. I worry about the safety of all my employees, but you can't blame me for being even more worried about you. Besides, if something happens to you, Mom and Raisa will skin me alive. Then they'll stop being nice."

"That's true." Nat threw her arms around her sister and squeezed hard. "I'm so glad you're letting me do this." She let up on Torrin's rib cage after she started to struggle. Excitement shone in Nat's eyes. "I'll make you proud, I promise."

"You already do, sister-mine." It was true. Torrin's chest was tight with the pride she felt for her sister. She had no worry that Nat wouldn't be able to discharge her duties. Her worry was for the crap the Devonites might give her. As long as she and Rudrani stuck together, they would have no issues. Torrin would have put money on them over any Haefonians.

"Thanks, Torrin." Nat's eyes were suspiciously shiny and Torrin was fairly certain hers were in the same condition. "I'm going to miss you."

"I'll see you in a couple months, tops. The time will go much faster for you, one of the benefits of cryostasis."

"True. When I get back I want to hear all about the demonstration with the council. Also, make sure you take good care of my cats."

"I've got you covered on both bases. Jak is thrilled to have them around, so I guess they're not all bad."

Rudrani stuck her head through the doorway. "We've been cleared to take off. Cargo is stored, all we need is your carcass off my ship, Torrin."

"She's my ship, Rudrani. I just let you borrow it." One final squeeze of Nat's shoulder turned into a last hug. "I'll get out of your hair."

"Love you, Torrin."

"I love you too, Nat."

The *Melisende* took off easily in a cloud of dust and blowback. Torrin watched as long as she could until the ship disappeared from view. It would have been really nice to have one of Jak's ocular implants right then. She stayed at the window for a little while longer until she was certain Nat and Rudrani were well underway.

It was so easy to tell Nat that she cared for her, she thought as she left the spaceport. Why was it so hard to say those three little words to Jak? The sniper was the one for her, of that Torrin was certain. There was no one else she wanted to be with, though time with Jak was few and far between right then. No matter how stressed out and exhausted she was over the monumental project she was directing, a mere few minutes with Jak and she felt like herself again.

She needed to tell her, that was all there was to it. Even as she resolved to do so, Torrin could feel hesitation dragging at her. As good as it felt when they were together, she was getting the feeling that Jak was pulling away from her. It was never for long, but there was a reserve when they were first together that was new. It seemed like Jak was somewhere else for a bit and it took her a little longer to come back every time.

Torrin disliked the toll the implant project was taking on their relationship, but how could she do anything differently? Hundreds of thousands of women were depending on her. Jak had to understand that this was simply how things had to be for now. It wouldn't be forever. In a few months, six at the most, she would be able to hand over a lot of the day-to-day operations of the project. It was only now, in the project's nascence, that Torrin had to be so heavily involved.

Satisfied with her reasoning, Torrin made her way to the office. She still had work to do before the demonstration. Jak would be great, Torrin had absolutely no reservations in that matter. The whole planet had to know how great Jak was and how impressive the implant tech was. The Ruling Council couldn't be allowed to sweep the demo and the following discussion under the rug. What they needed was the planetary media to be out en masse. She was fairly certain Mollie had notified them, but a personal invitation from one of the heads of Troika Corp. couldn't hurt. She had a busy afternoon in front of her. Torrin's steps quickened with anticipation. They were so close.

* * *

Jak crouched, careful not to silhouette herself against the hill's crest. On the other side of the crest was an animal she'd never seen before. She sneaked another glance. It drank from a shallow pond at the bottom of the hill. Watching the way its paws sank deep into the mud at the pond's edge, she was glad she was downwind of the animal. She could see its long claws digging into the mud and had no problem imagining the damage the animal could cause.

It looked vaguely like a bear, but it was so much larger than any she'd ever seen. Powerful shoulders dwarfed hindquarters. Wicked teeth were visible in its mouth as its tongue snaked out to drink more water. The wind shifted and she held her breath, hoping it hadn't gotten her scent. The bear-thing lifted its head and sniffed at the air. The shaggy fur along its back was so coarse it almost looked like quills. She heaved a sigh of relief when it lowered its face back to the pond. As brutal as the animal looked, she would still rather have faced it than to have to deal with Torrin's mother again. Sure, the previous night's dinner had ended well enough, but Irenya was an imposing woman, and Jak was fairly certain she didn't consider Jak good enough for her favorite daughter. Torrin could go on all she wanted about the problems she had with her mother, but Jak hadn't missed the proud looks Irenya had bestowed upon her when Torrin wasn't watching.

Clearly, Irenya hadn't felt the same about Jak, especially after she'd spilled the beans about Nat's departure. Torrin, or Nat for that matter, should have clued her in about that. How was she supposed to know that they hadn't told Irenya? Heat suffused Jak's face all over again as she recalled how irate Torrin's mother had been. Even Raisa hadn't been too happy about it. What else had Torrin conveniently forgotten to tell her? Not liking the direction her thoughts were taking, Jak considered the animal again.

What this animal was doing so close to the tiny village at the edge of the crater, she wasn't sure. In her experience, most large predators avoided human settlements. Humans didn't get on well with dangerous animals. There was something fascinating about this one. It moved with strength and confidence. That much raw power in one place had her captivated. Jak didn't doubt that the beast was at the top of the local food chain.

Finished drinking, it wandered off a little ways, then licked mud from its forepaws with a broad pink tongue. The mud came cleanly off the dark brown fur on its paws. Its coloring seemed designed to blend in with the surroundings on Nadierzda. Spots of lighter and darker brown dappled its coat.

She watched transfixed until it suddenly gathered its legs under it and took off at a lope. It ate up ground and the earth barely touched its paws before it gathered itself again and sprang forward in its rhythmic pacing. In mere moments it was far enough away that she lost sight of it, even using the magnification of her enhanced eyes. She pulled out her rifle and dialed in the scope and watched until it had gone far beyond even its range.

Peace filled her and she relaxed for first time since the uncomfortable meal. The only thing missing was the chance to share with someone else what had happened. She wished Torrin were there with her. Jak smiled and sighed. She wasn't sure how she could feel such happiness and sadness at the same time. Not that long ago, she would've been wishing for Bron. Maybe she was finally moving beyond losing him. She wasn't sure how she felt about that.

The sky above her was a washed-out blue, nothing like the crystalline shade of Haefen's heavens. She turned onto her back to watch thinly stretched clouds whip by. Coming out here had been a good idea, and she sighed, reveling in the feeling of freedom. No responsibilities, no obligations, just her and the wilderness. Exactly the way she liked it.

Then why did she feel so lonely? The sense of freedom evaporated and suddenly she missed Torrin terribly. The best days of her life had been while they traveled through the Haefonian wilderness together. Maybe she could convince Torrin to take an afternoon off work and they could come out here together. They wouldn't have to hunt, but simply being there with each other and no one else would do them both a world of good. Torrin wasn't what she would call a natural hunter, she never seemed particularly interested in it. That didn't mean Jak couldn't teach her to move through the wilderness without leaving a trail a blind man could follow or scaring away all the game over three square kilometers.

When it came down to it, any excuse at all would have done. She ached to spend time with Torrin doing more than making love. Not that their lovemaking was something Jak wanted to give up, far from it. Rather she wanted to share her joy in Nadi's wilderness the same way Torrin had shared her love of...

Her love of what, exactly? Sex, maybe. So far all they'd shared was a bed. Nat had shown her more of the planet than Torrin had. The lovemaking was fine. Better than fine, actually. Jak's cheeks heated and a corresponding glow flared in her belly. But was that all there was? Was she anything more to Torrin than an enthusiastic bed partner?

There had to be more to their relationship than that, right? There would be, she told herself—just as soon her lover wasn't so busy with her business. The rationalization rang hollowly in her mind. Jak shook her head to regain some equilibrium. The feeling always evaporated when she returned to Landing, but usually when she was out here with none but the trees and animals for company, she was at peace. The wilderness was one of the few places she felt like she was being truly herself, and Jak wanted Torrin to get to know her authentic self.

She lay in the grass a while longer before sitting up slowly. She did have responsibilities after all, and being out there was an indulgence. One she could afford on Nadierzda, true, but she was unaccustomed to giving in to her own indulgences.

Still, this interlude had been good for her and she felt better equipped to take on whatever might come her way. Day-to-day life on Nadierzda was still a mystery. Her life had gone from being extremely structured to something much more free-form. She still wasn't sure what was expected of her or what her purpose was. Standing, she looked around to get her bearings and trudged back toward Landing.

An hour later saw her making her way past the very lax security of the base's front gate. These women played at being soldiers. None of them had the type of discipline that was instilled by necessity. Part of her was glad they hadn't needed to develop that, but the rest of her worried. They wouldn't stand up against a determined force. She didn't doubt that they meant well, but a resolute enemy wouldn't crumble in the face good intentions.

Gratefully, she slipped into the office she'd been assigned. Some days it seemed like the only place on the planet that was hers alone. Torrin's apartment was nice enough, but it was Torrin's. There was very little sign of Jak's presence, though she'd been living there for weeks. It made Jak sad, that she had so little visible impact on Torrin's life. At the same time, it wouldn't take long for her to move out of there if she had to.

The cover of her tablet glowed slightly; she had a message. She smiled when she heard Torrin's voice through the speakers.

"Hey, babe." Jak's smile widened at the excitement in Torrin's voice. "Sorry I had to go before you got up this morning. Don't forget the Ruling Council has summoned us to demonstrate the implants tonight. We'll need you to do your thing and impress the pants off them. I know you'll be great! I lo—I'll, uh, see you tonight."

Torrin had stuttered at the end, like she'd wanted to say something else but had decided against it at the last minute. Jak wondered what she'd meant to say. Was Torrin going to tell her that she loved her? She wasn't sure how she felt about that. She certainly loved the smuggler, but for some reason she couldn't force herself to say those three simple words to her lover. Torrin saying them first meant Jak wouldn't have to go out on a limb and risk irrevocably damaging their relationship.

After all, it wasn't like they'd ever sat down and talked about what they had. Not having it spelled out made Jak feel like it was less concrete, less binding. Becoming Torrin's lover hadn't really altered her anxiety over their relationship. More accurately, she wasn't so concerned about the nature of it, not after having met so many of Nadi's women who seemed so very happy and natural in their relationships to each other. The reason for her anxiety had shifted, it seemed. Where did she really stand with Torrin? She was asking herself that question a lot these days. Torrin was a busy woman and she was doing important work. There was no question that Jak felt needed and cherished when they were together, but that was happening with less and less frequency as the days passed. The time Torrin seemed able to carve out when Jak had first left the clinic no longer seemed an option.

When she and Torrin were together, it felt like there was nothing they couldn't handle; it was where she was meant to be. When they were apart, though, doubts crept in. The longer they were apart, the more her doubts multiplied. Was the slow erosion of their relationship, whatever its status, a less painful option than the abrupt way in which Bron and her father had been torn from her life? How long would it take to move her things out of Torrin's place if it came to that? she wondered.

Though she hadn't fired her weapon, she stripped it down to clean it. She was sitting at the desk, bent over the pieces of her rifle when there was a quick knock at the door and Tanith stuck her head in.

"There you are," she said, smiling. She took a seat and lounged in the small room's only other chair. Tanith seemed to be able to take her ease no matter where she was. Her relaxed nature was infectious, and Jak could see how most people felt comfortable in her presence. Most of the time, Jak felt that way around her, but every now and then Tanith did or said something that put her back up. She was fairly certain that Tanith didn't do it on purpose. The woman didn't even seem to notice when she did it.

"You weren't on the range this morning," Tanith said. "The women were disappointed. You know how they look forward to getting instruction from you."

"It wasn't a mandatory session. It was a chance for them to get a few more hours on the range."

"Mandatory or not, they all showed up."

Jak bit her lip. She'd expected a handful, not to have her whole novice class to be there. "Sorry about that, I needed to take some time to clear my head after meeting Torrin's family. Torrin's seeing her sister off, so it seemed like as good a time as any."

"That's all well and good, but you need to do right by these women. They look up to you and they're eager to learn. As your employer I need to let you know that this lapse has been noted." Tanith looked at her reprovingly.

"Don't you think I know that?" Jak shot back, the day's pent-up tension releasing at once and giving her words more venom than she intended. "Your militia needs all the help it can get. It wouldn't stand for a day against some of the shit I've seen rained down. And what I do with my own time is my affair. I may work for the militia, but you don't own me. No one owns me but me."

Tanith looked shocked at her outburst. "Is everything all right?" She leaned forward, her eyes concerned.

"Yeah, it's fine," Jak said miserably. The outburst wasn't something she'd planned, and she could feel her face heating as Tanith regarded her sympathetically.

"Really? You don't seem fine."

"Really, I'm okay. It's more that..." Jak trailed off. She wasn't sure if she wanted to air her issues to Tanith. The woman was the only sympathetic ear she had right now. Torrin was always gone, working. Since Torrin took Nat on as an employee, Jak had hardly seen her. Now Nat was heading offworld, if she wasn't gone already, and Jak was already feeling the absence of one of the few women who knew her. The women of Nadierzda seemed friendly enough, but she'd isolated herself for so long that she didn't know how to break out of her own shell.

Tanith stood and came around the back of the desk. She put an arm around Jak's shoulders and squeezed lightly.

"I never see Torrin anymore. I know she's busy with the big cybernetics project, but I miss her." Jak let her head fall back against Tanith's arm. "I don't know what to do. I barely know anyone, and the one person who should be around isn't. When it comes down to it, how well do I even know her? We have fun together, when we can be together, but I can't get below the surface before she clams up. She knows every little thing about me, but I can't even find out about her first serious girlfriend, the one no one will talk about. She's blown me off every time I've asked her. And now I'm being a whiny ass to someone I don't even know that well."

"I don't mind," Tanith assured her. "I understand how you must feel. It can't be easy to come into a new place like this where you don't know the people or the culture. You need to get to know some people, expand your circle of friends."

"How do I do that?" Tanith looked at her askance, and Jak plowed on, desperation wavering in her voice. "I mean it, Tanith. How do I do that? I've spent so many years keeping people away so they wouldn't learn my secret. I don't know how to let anyone in. Torrin let herself in and that was hard enough."

"Wow, I had no idea. I knew you'd been through some stuff, but I didn't know."

"You have no clue." Jak leaned forward, curling in on herself, rifle forgotten. It hit the desk with a clatter that made her jump. Tanith's hand rubbed soothing circles on her back.

"The first thing you need to do is ditch this thing." Tanith's fingers plucked at the edge of the breastbinder. "Free yourself of it and free yourself of who you had to pretend to be back on your home planet."

Jak nodded slowly. It made a certain amount of sense. The binder was like a security blanket. It wrapped her round and gave her comfort, but it also anchored her in the same emotional place she'd been in on Haefen. While she kept herself safe, it also shielded her from others.

"Next, we'll introduce you around. And I know you've been itching to get up in one of the ultralights. I'll see what I can do to get you your first lesson. Now let's get you up and get you out of here. You're never going to meet anybody by hanging out in your office all day." Tanith stood and removed the remaining pieces of rifle from Jak's lap, then grabbed her hands and pulled her up.

* * *

The range buzzed with excitement. Jak looked around at the groups of women gathered to watch. It was strange to be on the range in the middle of what was almost a carnival atmosphere. From off to one side, she watched the gathered throngs, her sniper rifle slung over one shoulder. They were so carefree, most of them. If she looked closely, Jak thought she could pick out the ones who had been brought to Nadi from offworld. She imagined she looked much the same as they did, reserved and standoffish. Afraid to let go for fear she would be slapped down again. At least she hadn't gone through the horrors she imagined they had. Jak's mind flashed back to the Orthodoxan women she'd witnessed. Her imagination had unfortunately fertile ground to play in.

One of the women she'd mentally tagged as being from offworld—damaged goods, just like her—was swept up in a one-armed hug by a woman standing near her. They smiled at each other and the woman was drawn into the cheerful conversation and banter. Jak watched, bemused, as the woman smiled and laughed with the others. Maybe there was hope for her too.

"What are you thinking?" Torrin asked, sliding her arm through Jak's.

"Yeah," Audra said, appearing next to Torrin. "You looked awfully serious."

Jak lifted a shoulder. She wasn't prepared to discuss the isolation that wrapped around her, stifling her in its emptiness. Bron's absence seemed especially acute at that moment, surrounded though she was by people. Maybe if it had been Torrin and no one else, but she didn't know Audra that well. "Just hoping I don't screw this up."

Torrin scoffed openly. "No way in hell. This range is half what I've seen you do with my own eyes. You'll be fine."

"I don't know." Jak tapped nervous fingers along the edge of her rifle strap. "I don't usually do this with an audience."

"You'll be fine," Torrin insisted and pressed a gentle kiss to the side of Jak's face. Jak worked to keep herself from flinching, but she was sure Torrin noticed the slight tensing of her shoulders. She was fairly certain that Audra hadn't noticed or she would have heard about it for sure. These public displays of affection still made her uncomfortable, like she was painting a target on her back.

"So what are we waiting for?" At least they were doing the demonstration at night. It wasn't nearly as oppressively hot. So far, she'd found night on Nadi to be lovely, but the day was much too hot and dry for her taste, and there wasn't nearly enough shade. Lights were set up along the hastily erected bleachers where the women gathered.

"The Ruling Council will be fashionably late," Audra said. "They can't do anything without making it into a grand entrance." She dug her elbow into Torrin's ribs.

Torrin slugged her playfully in the shoulder. "What are you trying to say?"

"Nothing." Audra massaged her shoulder with a wounded expression that was magnificent in its exaggeration. "Except maybe you should run for Ruling Council one of these days. You already have some of the instincts."

"You little..." Jak watched, bemused as Torrin let go of her arm and did her best to wrap Audra in a headlock. Her superior reach should have made it easy, but somehow Audra kept slipping out of her grasp. They'd both had close-combat training, that was obvious. From the way they moved with each other, each so familiar with the other's moves, Jak suspected they still sparred together. She hoped sparring was all they did together, then kicked herself mentally for even thinking Torrin would be unfaithful to her with Audra.

Mac appeared next to them without so much as a whisper of sound. "You two," she hissed, "get a grip, the council's going to be here any second."

"About time." Audra hastily patted her hair into a semblance of order. The chin-length strands were in minor disarray after her tussle with Torrin.

Torrin raised her hands to bring her hair back under control, then dropped them when she realized her hair was still cropped short. It had grown out a little bit, but not enough that it required fixing. Jak didn't doubt that Torrin was cursing the narrow-minded bigots on Haefen. It wasn't Torrin's fault they couldn't accept a woman in a position of authority, and it certainly wasn't fair that she'd had to sacrifice her long hair to their misogyny.

"Come on." Mac tugged at Audra and they walked toward a break between the bleachers. A raised dais with a table and empty chairs waited for them. Torrin slid her arm through Jak's again and followed her partners.

"Watch this," Torrin whispered in Jak's ear. As usual, the close contact sent shivers down Jak's spine. Arousal bloomed in her abdomen and she felt warmth pool between her legs. This was going to make things interesting; she'd never taken her shot when horny as hell. Jak concentrated on her breathing. Best to settle her heart rate now.

"Watch what?" Jak asked when she was a little more in control of her faculties.

"The council's faces when they realize how many people are here." Torrin chuckled, satisfaction warming her tone. "I'm sure they wanted to slide this one under the carpet. Fat chance of that happening now." She nodded to a few knots of women pointing strange equipment at the dais. Jak was almost certain it was recording equipment, but it was different enough from what she knew that she could have been mistaken. "The press is here too. Audra's intern did a bang-up job on getting everyone mobilized."

"Press?" Jak's palms moistened and her heart rate quickened again, but not from arousal.

"Yep. Your little demonstration is going to be all over the planet pretty much as soon as it happens."

"Torrin." Jak's voice cracked and she swallowed before continuing. "You said this would be a little thing. I shoot the target for the council, I go home." She stared at the presswomen. They stared back at her and pointed. First one camera, then others swiveled to point at her. Her breastbinder was back in her room at the barracks and she wished she was wearing it. Everyone was going to see her, to know who she was.

"Jak, baby." Torrin took her by both shoulders and swung Jak around, away from the cameras, to face her. "You're going to be great. I know you won't miss. Hell, I don't think you could even if you tried."

Jak shook her head frantically, then remembered the watching cameras and stopped herself. "It's not that. Everyone will know who I am."

"So?" Torrin cocked her head in confusion. "Is that what you're so worked up about? So what if they know who you are? No one here is going to hurt you."

"You don't know that! Anonymity is safety." She repeated the mantra of her childhood. Her father had drilled it into her on numerous occasions. *Fit in, do your job, keep your head down and no one will notice you. Only then will you be safe.* His voice rumbled in her memory. The usual comfort she felt at his voice pricked out of existence when the babble of women's voices surged again.

"The council's here," Torrin said. She bounced on her toes, manic energy moving through her. "It's showtime."

CHAPTER FOURTEEN

Torrin grabbed Jak and pulled her over to stand in front of the dais. It was hard for Jak to see and she refused to go up on her tiptoes. There was no sense in seeming overanxious, even though she was. The crowd parted and the combined voices swelled. The timbre of so many women's voices was very different from the tone of the crowds Jak was used to. Somehow, they sounded so excited. Her memory of the crowds of servicemen on Haefen was one of oppressive discomfort; the mere memory caused her palms to sweat.

With stately grace, one after another, seven women climbed the steps of the dais. They stood waiting behind the long table until they were all there. As one, they sat, except for the woman in the middle. A matronly looking woman of not-quite-advanced years spread her hands and looked around. The crowd stood mostly behind her, but she included as many of them in the gesture as she could.

"Welcome, all." The woman smiled, laugh lines deepening in her face. "This little demonstration seems to be getting a whole lot of attention." Laughter greeted her statement and the laugh lines deepened further. Not all the women on the council shared her amusement at the situation. Jak watched with interest as one councilwoman in particular looked exceedingly angry. Her neighbor laid a hand on her arm and her face cleared immediately, leaving her looking mildly interested.

"Without any further delays, let's begin. For the record, will the councilors please identify themselves?" she asked in formal tones. Her voice rang through the crisp night air.

"Councilor Mashir."

"Councilor Travkin."

"Councilor Ararat."

"Councilor Tachay."

"Councilor Jakande."

"Councilor Pavlenka."

"And I am Councilor Yozhin. It is the common year 4129; two hundred and seventy-two years, thirteen months and five days since the founding of Nadierzda. We are in this hearing to explore the advisability of Troika Corporation's new business venture." An excited hum rippled through the anxiously waiting crowd. Yozhin raised her voice to continue. "I will remind the crowd that this is an open demonstration, but it will be closed if disturbances slow its progress." She ran her eye over the crowd. The noise level might have abated slightly, Jak couldn't tell, but Councilor Yozhin turned away from the gathered women to address Torrin and her partners. Jak stood to one side and back a few paces, hoping not to be noticed. She sneaked a quick glance over at the watching cameras. They were all pointed their way and she looked away hastily.

"Is this the woman we've heard so much about?" Yozhin asked.

"It is, Councilor." Torrin reached out an arm and snagged Jak by the elbow, drawing her up to stand next to her. "Councilors, this is Jak Stowell from the planet Haefen. She is prepared to demonstrate the efficacy of the implants we want to develop. Her people developed the technology behind the implants and she is fitted with a number of them."

The sour-looking councilor—Councilwoman Tachay, Jak thought—leaned forward. "Has the presence of these implants been confirmed by a medical professional?" Her tone was biting and Jak stiffened. Torrin tightened her hand around her elbow for a second before letting go.

"Yes, Councilwoman. Dr. Kiera Massin has checked her. You have received her report, the details are in there."

The councilor sat back with a grunt. She glared at Jak. Offended by her tone and irritated by her implication, Jak stared back, her face as impassive as she could make it. Bron had laughed that she could win a staring contest with a stone with that face, and Jak used it to her best effect now.

"How will the demonstration work?" asked another councilor.

"Stowell will take her spot at the far end of the range." Torrin pointed to the targets that had been set up a dozen meters past the end of the bleachers. "She will aim at those targets in complete darkness, using only her implants to see through the darkness." Bright lights had been brought in to light up the audience's area. "The lights will be extinguished for the demonstration."

"And her rifle doesn't have an infrared scope?" Tachay asked, her tone a shade this side of aggressive. "Has that been independently verified?"

Jak was going to be lucky not to end up with bruises on her arm from the amount of pressure Torrin was putting on the joint. Jak turned her head toward the councilor in time to catch a look verging on outright hostility. It was hard to tell if the angry gaze was directed at her or at Torrin.

"We have checked that, Councilwoman Tachay." Audra stepped over to Jak and held out her hand. Jak stared at her for a moment, not comprehending, before sliding the rifle from her shoulder. "We're happy to have someone check it again." Audra approached the dais where Tachay snatched the rifle from her and turned.

The crowd murmured as a member of the council's bodyguard took the rifle and peered through the scope. Jak held her breath. She was pretty sure the woman didn't know much about the kind of weapon she was handling. All Jak could do was hope that she didn't fiddle with it too much and throw off the alignment and calibration. After a few moments, the bodyguard handed the rifle back to Tachay.

"What's the verdict, Captain?" Yozhin asked before Tachay could say anything.

"The rifle is free of any night vision technology that I'm familiar with. Also, the scope is fairly rudimentary. I doubt it would be able to dial in to fifteen hundred meters without additional augmentation."

Audra held out her hand, smiling sweetly at Tachay. Disgruntled, the councilor tossed the rifle to Torrin's partner. Jak bit her lip, watching as Audra juggled the rifle and blew out a small sigh of relief when she kept it from dropping to the ground.

"Thank you, Captain." Yozhin turned back to the small group in front of the dais. "Is that the extent of the demonstration?"

"Almost, Councilwoman," Torrin said. "The doctor's report also indicates that Captain Stowell hasn't received a subdermal transmitter. To demonstrate her aural implant, we will be letting her know when to start the demonstration verbally, with no mechanical amplification, save that which her implant allows her." Torrin smiled sweetly at Tachay before she could raise any objections. "You are invited to send someone with her to the end of the range to confirm that the signal is impossible to hear with naked ears."

"We want to make sure the integrity of the demonstration is maintained." Tachay was pious in her pronouncement. "The captain of our bodyguard will accompany Stowell."

"Ma'am." The captain frowned at Tachay's direction and Jak felt a small twinge of sympathy for the woman. No bodyguard wanted to leave her charges. She didn't push the issue though.

"If that is all?" Yozhin asked. At Torrin's nod, she turned to the crowd. "Everyone should take their places. The lights will be extinguished soon."

"That's your cue," Torrin said. She leaned forward and pressed a quick kiss to Jak's lips. "For luck, not that you need it." Letting go of Jak's elbow, Torrin went to take her place to the side of the dais, her partners accompanying her.

"We might as well get this over with," Jak said to the bodyguard. "Come on." She started the long walk to the end of the range.

The night closed around them quickly as they left the spectator area. Jak switched her implant over to nightvision, but the bodyguard captain was slowing her down. Even with both of Nadierzda's moons being out, her eyes were taking a while to adjust.

"Here, Captain." Jak guided the bodyguard's hand to her elbow.

A grateful grunt met her gesture. "I'm Hawlis," the captain said after a moment.

"Charmed."

Her dry response was met with a quiet chuckle from Hawlis. "I'll be able to eat out on this for a couple of weeks."

"What do you mean?"

"Everyone wants to know more about you. The quiet, enigmatic woman who…"

"Tamed the great Torrin Ivanov?"

The chuckle was louder this time. "You've heard."

"It gets to be a bit much after a while."

"I bet. There are as many women interested in you though. You're different than what we're used to. Women are either born here, or they're rescued from trying circumstances." A slight pause gave Hawlis away as she searched for an appropriate term to call the women.

"I wasn't exactly a rescue case."

"No, rumor has it you were the one doing the rescuing."

Jak shrugged, uncomfortable at the direction the conversation was taking. "The rescuing was more or less mutual, when all was said and done." She didn't want to label Torrin as weak and found herself coming to her lover's rescue once again, giving her the due Jak felt Torrin deserved.

"I'd love to get dinner sometime and get the whole story from you."

Was Hawlis coming on to her? Jak couldn't quite tell, but she certainly seemed much too interested in Jak Stowell.

"Only as professionals," Hawlis hastened to add when the silence stretched on too long. Jak thought she detected disappointment in her voice. With relief, she saw they'd almost reached the end of the range.

"We're coming up to my spot. Can you see well enough?"

"I can."

Without any further discussion, Jak disengaged herself from the bodyguard and waited while she settled herself to one side before settling in a prone position. The lights were out downrange and Jak peered through the scope on her rifle. As Hawlis had pointed out to the council, the scope's magnification wasn't enough on its own to be useful in picking out the targets. She dialed up the magnification on her implant, adding to the scope's capabilities. The targets jumped into sharp focus and she swept her gaze down the range, watching for changes in wind speed.

It was a long distance to be shooting over. Jak's mind was already clicking through the requisite calculations. She almost didn't have to consider them consciously anymore, but there were times when she forced herself to go through the arithmetic gyrations, to consider them to make sure they were accurate. This was one of those times. The shot she was about to take was one of the most important ones of her life. The stakes were so much different than any shot she'd taken before, and Jak appreciated the feeling that she was about to use her gift to possibly bring life about, instead of taking it. If the demonstration was successful, Torrin's project would get the green light and the planet could be saved.

Before the uncomfortable dinner with Torrin's family, Jak'd had no idea that Nadierzda was slowly choking itself to death. Irenya had been ignorant of the true extent of the danger as well, but Jak had seen how entrenched her isolationism was. If she was any indication, it would take some serious persuasion to move the more conservative members of the Ruling Council. Torrin had mentioned some of their issues with particular council members, and Jak didn't envy her at all. She had little interest or patience for politics; her approach to problems tended to be very direct. On the other hand, Torrin professed to hate politics, but Jak had noticed that she was usually exhilarated after meetings with individual councilwomen.

Jak sighted down the range to the target, lifting her aim to allow for the bullet to drop over the distance. The wind was fairly consistent from east to west and Jak compensated by moving her aim right. She wished the targets were the silhouette shapes she was used to, but Audra and Mac had argued forcefully that a certain faction on the council wouldn't approve of developing implants that could be used for military purposes. The isolationists tended to be very antimilitary as well. The bulls-eye shape was traditional, but not what she was used to practicing with.

Her aural implant was turned to its highest setting. She could hear every breath Hawlis took from five meters away. Even so, when the signal came, it was barely audible.

"Take it away, Jak." It was Torrin's voice, and Jak smiled slightly, her shoulders relaxing as minute tensions she hadn't recognized drained away. She took the time for one last gauge of wind speed and ambient temperature. After a couple of minute adjustments, Jak stuck her tongue between her teeth and bit down gently as she squeezed the trigger.

The rifle roared in her ear and the bullet was away. She saw it strike the first target, a hair off from the center point. As soon as it hit, Jak's attention flowed over to the next target. On automatic pilot, she sighted on the second target and pulled the trigger. Another crash shook the night, the muzzle's flare lighting up their lonely end of the range. Relying on years of training and muscle memory, not to mention raw talent, Jak sighted and loosed on the last three targets.

Finished, she took a moment to survey her handiwork. The first and fourth targets were the slightest bit off from center, but the other three were as close to perfect as she'd ever done. Satisfied, Jak pulled the flare gun from the back of her pants and rolled to one side. She pulled the trigger and a green flower of light bloomed over their heads. Moments later, the lights came back on by the bleachers.

Hawlis got up and strode over to her, offering her palm. Jak grabbed the proffered hand and allowed the bodyguard to pull her to her feet.

"That was impressive," she said as they started their walk back to the bleachers.

"How do you know? You couldn't see what I did."

"I know someone who knows her craft. You barely had to think about that, did you?"

Jak lifted her left shoulder. "I've had a lot of practice."

"Sure you have."

They walked back to the waiting crowd in silence, Jak evading any attempts to draw her into further conversation. The attention was making her edgy, and the closer they got to the crowd and the waiting cameras, the more nervous Jak became. Sweat dripped down her spine and she tried to force herself to calm down. *No one on Nadi wants to hurt you.*

"How did I do?" Jak asked Torrin as they drew abreast of the Troika Corp. partners.

"You were amazing." Torrin rubbed her hands together with glee, grinning widely. "Each one was practically a bull's-eye. And the speed. We could hear the bullets hitting the targets. The council was amazed when we turned the lights back on."

Jak risked a glance over at the dais. The seven members of the Ruling Council were engaged in a heated discussion. With some relief, she noted the press had their cameras trained on the council and not on her. At the edge of the crowd, a wave pulled her attention. Tanith caught her eye and motioned her over.

"I'll be right back."

Torrin nodded absently. She was watching the women on the dais in their argument.

"What's up?" Jak asked.

"You look beat up. If you want to get out of here, I can give you a ride home. I imagine Torrin's going to be hanging out for a while yet."

Jak gave her a grateful smile. Having to stick around the gathering for much longer was enough to make her want to punch something.

"Let me see what's going on, but I'll probably take you up on that. Thanks, Tanith."

"No worries, Jak." Tanith favored her with a benign smile. "You're one of us now."

"Well, still. Thanks." Jak was on her way to rejoin Torrin when she heard her name being called from the raised platform.

"Where is Jak Stowell?" Councilwoman Tachay's voice was louder than it needed to be, Jak thought. She didn't sound the least bit happy either.

"I'm here, ma'am." Jak hastened out in front of the table, mindful of the eyes upon her. Once again, she was the center of attention. She came to her full height and saluted, remembering the Nadi militia's salute at the last minute. She wasn't truly a member of the militia, but it was a gesture the council would recognize. As long as she kept her eyes on the dais, she could pretend that she wasn't being watched by so many unknown eyes. Dimly, she was aware of Torrin and her partners arranging themselves behind her. She was grateful for the show of support.

"Did she maintain the parameters of the demonstration?" Tachay's words were for the captain of her bodyguard, but Jak felt Torrin take half a step forward. Torrin stopped and Jak wondered which one of her partners had held her back.

Hawlis stepped up beside Jak and snapped off her own salute. "Yes, she did, ma'am."

"There were no attempts to deviate from the plan?"

"None." Hawlis skewed a glance over at Jak before continuing. "I've never seen such a display of marksmanship. Captain Stowell is, without a doubt, one of the finest markswomen I've ever seen. Even with her obvious skill, there is no way she could have seen the other end of the range using that rifle without augmentation of some kind."

Jak could feel her cheeks heating at the praise and she kept her eyes fixed on the space between Councilor Yozhin and the councilwoman next to her.

Tachay's only answer to the praise was a sour grunt.

Yozhin stood and rapped on the table. All eyes moved to her, much to Jak's relief. "Now that we've had a demonstration, we need to discuss the viability of your business plan."

Mac took a step up next to Jak. "Of course, councilors. If you will look at the documents that were sent to you last week, we'd be happy to answer your questions and address your concerns."

Audra and Torrin moved past Jak, watching the council with intent eyes.

Hawlis looked down at her and winked. "I think they're done with us."

"Thank Johvah."

With a quick look of confusion for Jak's quiet exclamation, Hawlis clapped her companionably on the shoulder. "I need to get back to my post. I meant everything I said, by the way. Your skills are nothing short of remarkable. I'd be happy to train with you anytime."

The praise meant far more to her coming from a fellow professional; it was also easier to take. "Thanks. Let me know when you have some free time and we'll get something figured out."

Hawlis gave her a final nod of thanks and left, skirting the edge of the platform and disappearing. Jak scanned the crowd and saw Tanith at the edge, further out than she'd been originally. It would be so much easier to slip away unnoticed and Jak blessed the major's thoughtfulness. Her own girlfriend was too busy with politics to notice that she was taking off. As she slipped away from the group, Torrin looked up and gave her a small smile that disappeared as quickly as it had appeared. Looking uncharacteristically serious, Torrin cocked her head at Jak.

Was Torrin trying to tell her something? There was no time to ask and Torrin had turned her attention back to the women on the dais. The sound system had been switched off; the Ruling Council's grilling of Torrin and her partners was at least somewhat private. With interest, Jak noticed that most of the women who had attended the demonstration had made no attempt to leave. They knew what was at stake. So did Jak, but she'd done all she could. It was time to get out of the public's eye.

"Let's get out of here," Jak said to Tanith.

Tanith was kind enough to drop Jak at Torrin's flat. She let herself in using the keycard Torrin had procured for her. Without a microchip implant, she didn't have access to a number of things. The idea of having a piece of machinery mechanically inserted under her skin made her feel a little twitchy. She much preferred the way her people did it, and she'd been shocked to find out that the rest of the galaxy actually had to stoop to physically opening people up to insert implants. It was no wonder that anything but the simplest implants had never caught on in a big way.

The lights came on as Jak walked through the front door and Nat's two Earth cats ran out to greet her. Somehow Nat had talked Torrin into taking her cats when she left to make the run to Haefen. As usual, Resi came right up to greet her while Tesser hung back a little bit. He would be right underfoot as soon as she turned her back. She had to admit it was nice to have living beings in the flat, especially when Torrin wasn't around. Torrin seemed to be warming up to the cats also. Jak had actually caught her throwing a toy for Tesser to pounce on, then gut with his back claws.

She wandered through the flat to the bedroom so she could change out of her street clothes into something more comfortable. The council meeting had been exhausting. She lay down on the bed for a moment and closed her eyes.

Jak came awake all at once. There were two warm bodies pressed on either side of her. Tesser shifted when he realized she was awake and his bone-deep purr rumbled against her rib cage. She moved a hand to pet him. How long had she been out, and where was Torrin?

Resi noticed the attention Tesser was getting and stretched for a moment before wandering up Jak's body to head butt her face. She was also purring. Jak pushed herself up from the bed and wandered into the kitchen to check the cat food dispenser. Sure enough, it was empty. While she was topping it off, she heard the door open.

"I'm in here," she called and Torrin appeared in the kitchen's doorway. "How was the wrap—"

Torrin kissed her thoroughly and came up for air breathing raggedly a few moments later.

"I owe you an apology," Torrin said. "I should have told you how big this thing was looking to get when I knew—"

Moments later, it was Jak's turn to be breathless.

"Never mind," she breathed. "I'm so glad you're home." Just like that, her irritation with Torrin evaporated. It was impossible to stay angry with her when they were together.

Torrin grinned and threaded her fingers through Jak's hair. Jak closed her eyes and luxuriated in the feeling. There were some advantages to having longer hair, part of her mind supposed. The rest of her was only interested in one thing and she stepped closer to Torrin.

"What did you have in mind?" Torrin whispered her lips next to Jak's ear. Her breath sent delicious whispers down Jak's spine. Instead of answering, Jak slid her hands under Torrin's shirt and ran them along the base of her rib cage. Goose bumps sprang into being wherever she touched.

Torrin gave a wordless growl and scooped Jak up and slung her over her shoulder. Unable to control her laughter, Jak lapsed into giggles as Torrin transported her to the bedroom. She dumped Jak onto the bed and crawled on top of her, pressing Jak's body down into the mattress. Arousal flooded Jak's system at Torrin's weight and she moaned.

"I love the noises you make," Torrin said, sliding her hands under Jak's top. "They get me so fucking hot." She raked her nails up Jak's abdomen, leaving gooseflesh in their wake.

Jak lifted her hips, pressing them against Torrin, seeking the friction she craved. Torrin closed her hands over her breasts, wrenching another moan from Jak and teasing already hard nipples through the fabric of her bra. Unable to keep her hands to herself any longer, Jak tugged Torrin's top out of her pants. She reached between them, searching for the fastener on Torrin's pants.

"Oh no you don't." Torrin dropped her head and covered Jak's lips for a kiss that curled Jak's toes. Jak nibbled delicately on Torrin's lower lip and pulled gently. Torrin let out an unsteady laugh as she surfaced for air. She attacked the side of Jak's neck, kissing, licking and biting, leaving motes of heat that expanded on Jak's skin. Each one felt like it had a direct link to her groin and Jak's hips strained upward in response to each.

"Johvah, Torrin." Jak slid her hands down the back of Torrin's pants. Firm muscles flexed beneath her fingertips and she squeezed. Torrin's hips thrust against hers and Jak groaned as fresh wetness flooded the already damp space between her thighs.

"Stop that." Sharp teeth dug into her shoulder where it met her neck. "Tonight's about you. Lie back and enjoy it."

The sentiment was nice, but Jak needed to feel Torrin against her now. She was already so turned on, it wouldn't take much for her to come. She bared her teeth in frustration when Torrin lifted her hips, depriving Jak of the delicious pressure on her center.

"I need you now, baby," Jak gasped. "Give it to me."

"Patience." Practiced fingers flew down her shirt, opening Jak's chest to the chill air of the bedroom. Torrin dropped a kiss to the top of her shoulder before kissing her way down Jak's chest to the swell of her right breast. Aching nipples begged for attention, straining against the thin material of her bra. When Torrin closed her mouth over her right nipple, Jak pushed against her, half sitting up.

"Down." Firmly, Torrin pressed her back against the bed and growled in frustration when she realized she couldn't reach the clasp on Jak's bra from the position they were in. She sat back, straddling Jak's hips. Jak closed her eyes, undulating her hips against Torrin, pressing her center up into Torrin's. Then the weight was gone, Torrin rolled off her and Jak's eyes snapped open.

Hands, demanding yet gentle, pulled her up on the bed. They were everywhere, unclasping her bra, unfastening her pants before sliding them over her hips and down her legs. In a brief flurry of activity, Jak found herself completely naked, looking up at Torrin who stared down at her, not moving, watching her wordlessly with eyes dark with need. Jak stared back, unable to move from the intensity of the gaze.

Torrin stood, drawing Jak with her, never saying a word. Her clothing felt strange against Jak's bare skin, but Jak only barely noticed as Torrin lowered her head and captured her mouth, sliding a deft tongue past her lips to stroke deeply in Jak's mouth as her hands roamed Jak's body. They broke apart, breathless and panting. Torrin slid her hands down to Jak's hips and turned her around so her ass was nestled against Torrin's clothed hips.

"Bend over for me, baby." She put her hand on the back of Jak's neck and gently pushed down. Jak's hands hit the mattress and she gripped the sheets as Torrin's hand wandered slowly down her back and over her rump so lightly she barely felt it. Her hips jerked and pleasure shot through her core when hands gripped her cheeks and squeezed roughly. Jak bit her lip and rocked back, seeking more.

"You like that?" Torrin squeezed again, digging fingers into the taut muscles.

"You know I do." Jak almost didn't recognize her voice, breathy and overflowing with need. It was nothing like the rough growl she'd affected for so long. Only Torrin could coax these sounds from her.

"Do you like this?" Jak could hear the smile in Torrin's voice and she lifted her hips as Torrin's fingers slid between the cheeks of her ass, lingering momentarily over the pucker of her anus then down to her pussy. Torrin's fingers slid easily through the copious wetness that gathered there. "I guess you do." She teased Jak, sliding fingers over the outside of her labia, never stopping for more than a moment while Jak rolled her hips, desperately seeking sustained contact.

"Please, Torrin," Jak finally gasped. "I need it so bad. I need you, baby."

Fingers suddenly pressed into her, sliding deep inside her with almost no resistance and Jak groaned at the sensation of being filled so completely. She pressed back against Torrin's hand.

"Then come for me, Jak-baby." Torrin withdrew her hand, leaving an aching emptiness behind before thrusting back in. She curled her fingers, running them over that oh-so-sensitive spot inside Jak, sending a burst of sensation through her groin and Jak met the thrust. She was so close. Torrin kept up the pace, thrusting into her before sliding her other hand around.

When Torrin's fingers closed over her clit, Jak keened aloud, her hips bucking as sensation crested within her. Thousands of pinpricks swept over her skin and poured into and through her. Her voice rose as she called Torrin's name over and over. It was an eternity of pleasure and it was over too soon.

Jak came back to herself slowly, face down on the bed, cradled in Torrin's arms. She looked over her shoulder into brilliant eyes still dark with arousal.

"Your turn," Jak said, reaching for her lover.

* * *

"That was nice." Jak's eyes were closed and she luxuriated in the feeling of having been thoroughly made love to. A warm glow radiated from her limbs and she was content to lie there and be.

"It was," Torrin agreed, propped up on one arm next to her lover. She trailed her fingertips idly over one of Jak's nipples, causing it to stand at attention.

"The demo went over well." Jak cracked one eyelid open barely wide enough to peer up at Torrin's beautiful face.

"With the crowd. I wish I knew what the council thought. Guess we'll have to wait for that." Torrin stared at the back of her hand where it covered Jak's breast. Silence lengthened as Jak waited for her to say something.

"Torrin, is there anything wrong? You're acting a little out of it."

"Am I? I'm sorry." She looked up and smiled crookedly into Jak's eyes. As it always did when Torrin smiled at her like that, Jak's heart sped up. As quickly as the smile came over her face, it was gone. In its place was an unaccountably serious look. "There is something." Torrin paused and stared into space. She looked like she was struggling for the right words, which was completely unlike her. "It's Tanith," she finally blurted out. "I don't want you to spend any more time with her."

Jak was confused. "Wait, what?" Of all the things for Torrin to say to her, this was one she hadn't seen coming.

"She's a bad influence. I'd really rather you didn't see her anymore."

"Torrin, she's one of my only friends. I don't know anyone on the planet except you and a few of your friends. In case you hadn't noticed, you've been a little busy lately. I find a friend and you try to up and tell me I can't spend time with her?"

"You don't understand!"

"Well, explain it to me then." Jak set her jaw and tried not to look as irritated as she felt.

"She's not a good person. Right now she has you completely snowed, but she's only spending time with you to get back at me."

Jak was flummoxed. The explanation made Torrin sound paranoid. She'd seen no sign of Tanith wanting anything from her that she wasn't ready to give. There had been the incident when Tanith had made a pass at her, but she'd backed off when Jak had made the situation clear. It was a good thing Jak had kept the incident to herself. If Torrin was going to act like this after seeing Jak and Tanith leave together from a public event, there was no telling how she'd have reacted to the other incident.

"Why would she need to get back at you? This makes no sense."

"Tanith hates me, Jak. She's hated me for a long time, twenty years or so. She thinks I took something from her a while back and she hasn't forgiven me for it."

"Did you?"

"No! But I haven't been able to convince her. It's been eating at her for almost two decades. She can't be trusted."

"Look, I get that there's some history, but it doesn't have anything to do with me. You need to leave me out of it. I can't exactly avoid spending time with her. She's my direct report in the militia and she's on my training squad." Jak had no intention of limiting her contact with Tanith, not for some long-held grudge between the two of them, but she wasn't going to tell Torrin that. She'd been aware her lover had a bit of a jealous streak. It hadn't eluded her notice when Torrin glared at women who stopped to chat for a while or whose hugs went on a little too long. Torrin was overreacting. Again.

"I get that. But try not to, you know, encourage her."

Jak's eyebrows climbed halfway to her hairline. The last thing she did was try to encourage anyone.

"She doesn't need any encouragement," Torrin hastened to add, correctly reading Jak's irritation. "I know you aren't doing anything, and I don't want her to think you are."

That really wasn't any better, and Jak sat there for a moment staring in disbelief at her lover.

"I need a drink," she finally said and rolled over, swinging her legs over the edge of the bed. Naked, she stalked from the room.

"Scotch," she ordered when she entered the kitchen. One of the cabinets popped open and a bottle appeared in a dispenser. She snatched the bottle and poured herself a stiff drink in a convenient glass. It might have been clean; she didn't pause long enough to check. The alcohol burned going down and she coughed. The burn was replaced by pleasant warmth and she took another swig. She stood there in the kitchen for a few minutes, alone and drinking from the glass.

Arms slid around her waist and a familiar body settled behind her. Torrin leaned her head on Jak's shoulder and pulled her into a warm embrace.

"I'm sorry, babe. I had no right to tell you that you couldn't see someone."

Relaxed, both by the alcohol and by Torrin's presence, Jak melted back into her embrace.

"Damn right you can't," she muttered.

"Can we just leave it at I know her and I've been burned by her before? I really don't want her to hurt you."

"Fine."

Torrin nuzzled closer. "I know I pissed you off. Will you let me make it up to you?"

Jak smiled. That sounded good to her. She didn't say anything. Instead she turned around in Torrin's arms and met the smuggler's mouth with her own.

CHAPTER FIFTEEN

Torrin waded her way through the *Calamity Jane*'s maintenance records. Her head ached and she was in a piss-poor mood, though she still ached pleasantly from the previous night's exertions. Normally, a love-making session with Jak would have put her in an excellent mood that wouldn't wear off for hours, but paperwork was one of her least favorite things to do. Going through old paperwork was even worse. She'd already dealt with it once; going through it again normally would have felt like a waste of time.

This time the paperwork was anything but a waste of time though. Both Nat and Jak had mentioned that her presence on Haefen made no sense. Now that she didn't have the proposal to the council to worry about and Jak was showing every sign of being well on the road to recovery, she needed to get a jump on chasing down what had happened. Neal was on Tyndall, and there was no way she could get to him right away. She'd gotten a relay call back from her factor on Tyndall. Torrin reached forward and activated the replay of the message. Laiya's voice filled the room.

"There's no sign of Neal. I've tried his usual haunts, but he seems to have gone to ground. I'm going to dig a little deeper and get back to you."

The little shit had known something was up with the information he'd sold her, then. She would have to wait until Laiya had a bead on his location. Tyndall didn't have a huge population, but there were a lot of places to hide. Neal would resurface eventually, probably as soon as he started to detox.

Neal was only one part of the puzzle. Why had the information in Tien's memory banks been so wrong? That was something she could look into on Nadi. After doing some digging through the AI's memory, Torrin had discovered that the information for Haefen had been lifted from the record on Oroma-V. Word for word, the data had been copied over Haefen's entry. Whoever had done it was good enough to fool the AI and leave no trace behind. The problem was that she didn't know when the information swap had happened. The last thing Torrin wanted to believe was that someone from Nadi had set her up. It wasn't out of the realm of possibility that the hack had happened on another planet, but the best access would have happened here.

I'm here now. I might as well look into the computer techs who've had access to Tien lately. Torrin located the computer maintenance records and looked them over. She let out a dissatisfied huff. Only two techs had worked on the *Calamity Jane* in the past year. Both of them had access, though she didn't think either one of them had motive. One of them was her slightly crazy ex, one of the few who hadn't taken it kindly when Torrin had broken off their relationship after a week and a half.

Breena's crazy, sure. But she doesn't have the attention span to set up something like this. Torrin pulled up the other record. The other tech was a woman she knew only barely. She'd met her a few times in the course of getting her ship's systems updated. The woman probably had the smarts and the attention to detail required by the scheme, but she had no reason to want Torrin to end up in the hands of the Orthodoxans.

She suppressed a shudder as Hutchinson's lust-contorted face flashed before her mind's eye. Goose bumps erupted over her skin and she rubbed both arms briskly in an attempt to warm herself back up. Going back to the record, she pushed Hutchinson from her mind.

The second tech had the ability to screw Torrin over, but she had no reason to. Unless Breena and the other tech had been working together, she found it hard to believe that either of them could have masterminded and pulled off the scheme.

Still, she needed to rule them out. The best way to do that was to interview them, face to face, where she could gauge their reactions. She was good at reading women, though men not so much. That was it then; she would bring them in. If she didn't get a read off them, she would have to follow up with her informant on Tyndall. Her ship's databases might have been messed with, but the original tip had originated with Neal.

With a quick check of the chrono, Torrin assured herself that she had plenty of time. She was taking Jak out for a thank-you dinner in a few hours and she didn't want to be late.

* * *

The landscape opened up beneath her. From the dizzying height, Jak could see the edge of the round, green crater that made up this habitable part of Nadierzda. The winds buffeted the small craft, and Tanith expertly maneuvered them to find a calmer spot. They were crammed together in the small aircraft; Tanith suspended above Jak in a harness and rig that allowed her to control the ultralight. She was in a separate harness immediately beneath Tanith, but they were close enough for her to feel the heat radiating from the other woman's body. The closeness was a little unnerving, but the view more than made up for it.

Beyond the edge of the crater, shifting sands blew, creating a perpetual tan haze. In the distance, Jak could see another splash of green and beyond that, another. Brilliant green dotted the planet's surface, but even she could tell that much of it was in peril of being swallowed by the shifting sands.

"This is awesome," she radioed to Tanith using a transmitter clipped around her neck. The thrum of their small engine was drowned out by the roar of the wind.

"I thought you'd get a kick out of it," Tanith radioed back, activating her subdermal transmitter.

The sensation was amazing. It was certainly very different from her woods, but there was a sense of solitude up there. Now, more than ever, she really wanted to learn how to fly one of the contraptions.

"Why doesn't the council like you doing this?" Jak asked.

"Safety, mostly, or so they say. The winds are so strong and constant that they think those of us who do this are all going to die probably sooner than later."

"Is it really that bad?"

"No. There are usually a handful of wrecks each year. Most people walk away from them. The only time there's major trouble is if someone goes down in the sands. Sometimes those dunes move so quickly that they can cover someone and tear them apart. Usually, it's inexperienced pilots who have the biggest problems. Over half of the wrecks are from newbies."

"So if they're so set against it, why do they keep letting you do it?"

"It's a great way for us to train pilots. Everyone who pilots any kind of ship, whether it's an intra-atmosphere or deep space vessel, starts on one of these."

"So Torrin had to learn on one of these?"

"She sure did. She was a terror also. Had more than a few wrecks. That woman had no fear. Nothing's changed since."

Tanith actually sounded affectionate, and Jak wondered how much of the two women's antipathy was one-sided.

They swooped around above the crater until the sky began to darken. Sunset on Nadi was almost always spectacular. Torrin had explained that because there was so much dust in the air, it reflected the setting sun's rays and bathed the sky in brilliant oranges, reds and purples. On Haefen, Jak had only occasionally seen a sunset as gorgeous as those she saw almost every day here. Experiencing it from the air only added to her enjoyment. The flight was over far too soon as far as she was concerned. They swooped in for a landing, the ultralight's small wheels catching and pulling them back down to the earth. To Jak, it felt like they were being physically anchored to the earth once more and she was surprised by how much she resented it.

"Where are you headed now?" Tanith asked, pulling Jak's arm back through a harness strap.

"I'm meeting up with Torrin at her office so we can go out for dinner. She's been working to make time in her day for me. I know she's slammed with the planning for the implant manufacturing facility, but it really helps to know she's trying."

"I bet. I think it's great that the Ruling Council gave them the go-ahead to get that up and running. Anything that gets us closer to terraforming is good in my book." Tanith hoisted their harnesses over one shoulder without betraying any visible effort. "Where are you two going?"

"Sakura Season. She's very excited to get in there. I guess it's usually pretty packed."

Tanith quirked an eyebrow. "She's going high class on you. Tell you what, let me stow the gear and I'll give you a ride."

"You don't have to. I can catch the train."

With an airy wave, Tanith brushed her demurral aside. "It's no problem. It's on the way home, and I know how annoying it can be to take the train."

"I thought your home was on base?"

"I didn't say I'm heading to my home." Tanith grinned cockily.

Jak laughed. "Fair enough."

Tanith disappeared into the corner of the hangar. Jak entertained herself by watching the last moments of the sunset. Already, the howling heat of the day was subsiding, replaced by soothing coolness. The air smelled less dry, though it did nothing to approach the rich loamy smell of earth she still missed.

"We're set," Tanith announced, striding over to Jak, two helmets in hand.

The ride to the Troika Corp. offices was uneventful. Tanith wasn't quite as reckless as Torrin could be, but not by much. Jak hopped off the bike as soon as Tanith squealed to a stop. The helmet would not disengage from her head and she struggled with it for a few moments. There was no change; the helmet still stubbornly resisted her attempts to remove it. Finally Tanith realized her plight and came over. She inspected the helmet and rapped it sharply right below Jak's left jaw. The blow was hard enough that Jak's ears rang momentarily, but the helmet snapped open, releasing her head.

"Thanks." Jak tossed Tanith the helmet.

"You kids have fun now," Tanith replied as she swung herself back onto the bike. She roared off in a cloud of dust, and Jak entered the low building's front door and approached the elevator. The building was almost deserted at this time of day and Jak didn't see anyone else until she'd made her way through almost all the cubicles at the front of the offices.

She waved cheerily at a woman in a cube. "Is Torrin in her office?"

"Yep," the woman replied without looking up from her console.

Jak made her way deeper into the suite of rooms and down a dimly-lit corridor to the three partners' offices. She knocked once and pushed open Torrin's door before staggering to a stop.

A leggy blond woman in an extremely revealing dress sat on Torrin's lap and was performing an amateur tonsillectomy on her with her tongue. Jak struggled to breathe. Her rib cage was wrapped in a vise that was slowly squeezing the breath out of her. She didn't want to believe her eyes, but there was no mistaking what was going on. Torrin's hands reached up for the woman's shoulders in slow motion. She wrapped her hands around the blonde's bare shoulders.

"Torrin!" Her lover's name was torn from her mouth in a shriek unlike anything she'd ever heard from her own lips.

Torrin pulled her lips away from the blonde's and stared, shocked, at Jak. *Holy shit*, she mouthed. Jak could read her lips from the doorway. Unable watch any more of Torrin's betrayal and unwilling to let either woman see her cry, she backed through the open door. Hot tears filled her eyes and spilled over, tracing scalding tracks down her cheeks. Blindly, she fumbled her way through the office until she stood in the hallway outside, hands on her knees, heaving for breath and trying not to vomit.

Dimly she became aware of someone saying her name. She looked up through her tears to see Torrin's face and hands imploring her.

"Don't touch me." Jak drew herself up to her full height.

"It isn't what you think," Torrin protested.

"I don't see how it could be anything else. What was going on in your office would have been obvious to a blind woman." Jak dashed tears out of her eyes. She didn't want Torrin to see her crying over her.

"Let me explain—"

"There's nothing to explain. If you wanted to be with someone else, you should have said something."

"But baby—"

"Shut it, Torrin." Jak needed to get away. The walls were closing in on her, and she needed someplace to go where she could lick her wounds in peace. "Just leave me alone."

She turned her back on Torrin and took refuge in the elevator. When Torrin made a move as if to join her, she shut the doors in her face. The ride back up to the surface took an eternity, and Jak had no idea how long she stared out the elevator's door before realizing it was open. She emerged into darkness; the sky to the west wasn't even light anymore. Head down, she started walking. The base was the best place for her to go. There was no way she was going back to the flat.

* * *

Torrin burst through the stairwell door in time to see Jak striding down the road. She wanted so badly to follow her, to explain. How had things gone so wrong so quickly? All she'd wanted was to have a nice meal with her girlfriend. As she'd been sitting there trying to figure out if Breena had sold her out, her ex-lover had stood up in the middle of their meeting and plopped down into her lap, then subjected her to a lip lock. Before she'd been able to do more than barely register the crazy woman in her lap, Jak had walked in and witnessed the whole mess. The timing was incredibly maddening. If Jak had walked in thirty seconds sooner or later there would have been nothing to witness.

Her heart shrieked at her to run after Jak and stop her, to make her understand. Her head told her to let Jak go and blow off some steam. She made her way back into her office. Behind her desk, the crazy blonde lounged in her desk chair. Breena smiled widely as Torrin approached and uncrossed and recrossed her legs, making sure Torrin had a perfect view of the lacy panties she was wearing.

"There you are, lover," Breena said in a voice meant to be smoldering and sensual. To Torrin, it sounded as if she was recovering from a bad cold. "I've been waiting for you. We can pick up right where we left off."

"Get up," Torrin grated, teeth clamped together to keep from screaming at Breena. "I'm not having sex with you. You've caused enough damage already."

"Who me?" Breena was a portrait of outraged innocence. She stood up and sauntered across the office and ran her finger down the center of Torrin's chest. "All I did was remind you who you really belong to. If that little bitch can't deal with a little competition, then she isn't worthy of you anyway."

"Don't you call her a bitch. If I hear you call her that again, so help me..."

Breena flashed a coy smile and arched an eyebrow. "I love it when you get rough, Torrin, darling." She grabbed either side of Torrin's shirt and yanked, fasteners flying across the office.

"Good," Torrin snarled, "then you'll love this." She took Breena roughly by both elbows and shook her. The blonde tried to yank her arm free. Torrin's grip, born of desperation and anger, was immutable as iron, and Breena couldn't shake free of her grasp. With a slight twist of Torrin's wrist, Breena found her arm yanked around behind her back. Torrin marched her through the offices, in front of the stunned eyes of the few women still working. She dragged her into the elevator and held her by the arm, but far enough away that Breena couldn't reach her. Breena still tried and the contortions she managed in the attempt would normally have amused Torrin to no end, but as it was all they did was serve to throw rocket fuel on the flames of her anger.

"Get out of here," Torrin ordered. She pushed Breena forward, through the open door at the surface. Breena turned toward her and smiled, reaching to snake a hand around her waist. Torrin stepped back and rapped Breena's hand sharply with her knuckles. With a jerk and a pout, Breena snatched her hand back.

"Don't touch me. Don't you ever!"

Breena made no effort to leave so Torrin pushed past her. She had no time for the crazy woman. Her head was finally in agreement with her heart and she needed to catch up with Jak. Jogging through the lot, Torrin opened her car door and threw herself into it. She throttled open the engine. The small car leaped into motion and buzzed spitefully down the street. Normally she would have had her bike, but after dinner, she'd been planning to drive Jak out to a secluded spot where they could have spent some quality time together.

On her way back to her flat, Torrin kept her eyes peeled for the sniper. There was no sign of her, and so she wasn't surprised when she walked into the flat to find it cold and dark. The cats bounded over to greet her, but Torrin barely even saw them.

The oppressive silence in her home didn't stop her from searching every room, in case Jak was there. To her disappointment, there was no sign of her. She settled herself on the couch to wait for Jak's return.

After an hour, Torrin came to the conclusion that Jak wasn't coming home. If she'd gone to the base, it would be difficult for Torrin to gain access. She'd lost her clearance when she'd quit the militia. Unsure of her next step, Torrin got up and fetched a glass of parathenol. She needed something for company while she waited alone in her cold, empty apartment, hoping Jak would show up soon.

* * *

Jak's breath sounded harsh, even to her own ears. The walk was definitely overtaxing her, but she didn't care. It was a fitting punishment for getting involved with Torrin. The happiness she'd been experiencing hardly seemed worth the agony she now felt. How could she have been so stupid? Everyone had warned her this would happen, that Torrin was too irresponsible to commit to one woman.

The base was still another thirty minutes away by foot, and it was all she could do to keep placing one foot in front of the other. She'd been walking for over an hour. The tightness of her chest urged her to stop and take a break, but she forged on through the pain. At least when the pain was physical, she could master it. Emotional pain was what she couldn't deal with. The same pain had sent her deep into herself after her brother was killed. This hurt was so intense that she couldn't shove it down deeper into herself. So, even though her body begged her to stop, she kept trudging grimly through the darkness.

She barely noticed when a single light whipped by her in the darkness. Wheels screeched to a halt up ahead, then came about and slowly tracked back toward her.

"Jak? What are you doing out here?" Tanith's voice was muffled by her helmet's visor, and she flipped it up to get a better look at her.

Jak just stared for a moment, unable to process what Tanith was saying through her anguished haze. She must have looked terrible because Tanith hopped off the bike and approached her at a trot.

"I'm heading back to base," she finally responded leadenly.

"On foot? Where's Torrin?"

"I don't know. Don't care either. There was a…fight."

"Oh, honey, I'm so sorry." Tanith placed a hand on Jak's back and started rubbing in soothing circles. She paused in her rubbing. "You sound horrible. I know your lung capacity is still low. I'm not letting you walk the rest of the way back to the base."

"It's all right. I don't mind."

"Well, I do. Here." She thrust the second helmet into Jak's hands and stared her down until Jak finally donned it. "Get on, let's go."

Tired to the bone, Jak climbed onto the bike behind Tanith. She stared blankly into the darkness as they sped through the night. Tanith didn't say much when they got back to the base. She directed Jak to a small but blessedly private room in the same barracks where she had her office. Jak sat on the room's uncomfortable wooden chair staring at nothing while Tanith made up her bed. Tanith clasped her shoulder where she sat.

"I'll be just down the hall if you need anything," Tanith said.

Jak nodded numbly. She supposed she should have felt grateful. Tanith's quarters were on the edge of the base in one of the small single-family houses, and she was making a sacrifice by staying there.

Tanith waited for a moment but left when Jak said nothing.

The small room was no comfort, but at least it didn't make her hurt more. There was nothing of Torrin here. She moved to sit on the bed. Her legs gave out beneath her, dropping her the last few inches. It was too much work to catch herself, and she flopped over onto her back. She lay unmoving on the bed for a while, not bothering to change her clothing. She stared at the ceiling. How could Torrin do this to her? She thought they'd had something special. Everyone had said how Torrin didn't act with her like she had with any of her legions of former lovers. Obviously, the affection had been more one-sided than she'd supposed. Her face burned with embarrassment and she turned to hide her face in the blankets. How Torrin must have resented her constant demands for time and attention. Torrin had probably viewed her as ballast around her neck, tying her down.

Unable to deal with the line of thought, Jak pushed herself off the bed. Being alone with her thoughts wasn't helping. She walked down the hall to her office and snagged her rifle from her footlocker, then headed out to the range. It was her medium-range rifle. The long-range one, her favorite, was still over at Torrin's. She would need to retrieve that. Probably her clothes too, though she really didn't want them now. Torrin had bought those for her, and she wanted nothing of anything that came from her.

Even though it was almost midnight, she wasn't the only one out on the range. A couple of women from her training group worked on the range. Jak had introduced them to spotting earlier in the week and had paired them all off. The bottom half of the class in accuracy on the plasma rifles were designated as spotters for the top half. By now, none of the women was a slouch with the rifle. She had insisted that they keep practicing shooting; after all, they would never know when they would be forced to take on the shooting in a pinch.

She wasn't surprised to see the women on the range. Most of them were fanatical about practicing, and they practiced every chance they could get. Jak had made an offhand comment about getting used to working in the dark, and the trainees had obviously taken it to heart.

Not wanting to talk, instead she nodded at them as she headed to the far end of the range. It was pitch black out there. Both the moons were at their smallest slivers and as usual they were further obscured by diaphanous clouds that scudded hurriedly across the sky.

Mechanically, she sent shot after shot into the target. After she'd destroyed one, she would move one hundred meters further away to repeat the process. The repetition calmed her down as nothing else would. She entered a semimeditative state where the same series of motions anchored her in a blessed nothingness. Check the wind. Sight and adjust for wind speed and distance. Aim. Squeeze the trigger. Ride the recoil. Trace the bullet's path to the target. Adjust. Repeat.

She lost track of how long she'd been out there. She only stopped when distance and exhaustion had severely compromised her accuracy. Her arms trembled from the constant strain. The sky had lightened perceptibly with false dawn. She welcomed the state of pure numbness and dragged herself back to her room where she forced herself to clean her weapon before rolling into bed. She didn't even bother kicking off her shoes. Sleep dragged her down in an instant.

CHAPTER SIXTEEN

"Things not working out too well?"

Jak cringed. She knew what came next and tried to clamp her eyes closed. Against her will, she looked over to see her brother grinning at her. His eyes glittered with amusement. The background faded away and his face snapped into focus with stomach-churning rapidity. His blue eyes pierced hers deeply. She wanted to cry. It had been so long since she'd had the dream. Apparently, it had been too much to hope that it was gone.

"I don't want to talk about it," she said curtly.

"I told you she would be trouble," Bron said, raising the spotter's scope to his eyes and scanning a far-off ridge.

"I don't want to talk about it, I said."

"Who's had your back this whole time?"

"You."

"Then why don't you listen to me?"

"I said I don't want to talk about it."

"You know I won't drop it until you do." Bron kept peering through the scope.

Fuming at his refusal to drop the subject, Jak put her eye to the rifle's scope and scanned the far ridge. As usual, it didn't matter that the end of the dream was predetermined; she still had to try to find the other sniper before he fired and ended it. She'd seen a flash of red the last time. Where had it been again?

"Turn on your cloak," she said absently, still searching the far trees.

"Stop trying to change the subject." He reached up and twisted on the cloak's control around his neck. In an instant, he shimmered out of view. All she could see was a flicker in the air like heat rising off a hot road.

"Why couldn't you let her go when it was obvious you two weren't meant for each other?"

"I can see heat shimmer from your cloak. You should reset it."

"Don't worry about it; it'll be fine. You're trying to change the subject." Amusement warmed his voice again.

Where was that spot? That area looked familiar, the trees sharpened in her mind's eye.

"I loved her, okay? Is that so terrible? I loved her. Stupid as it is, as much as it hurts, I still love her."

Bron snorted derisively. "Could've fooled me. If you love her so much, why are you giving up on her?"

"She stabbed me in the back!" Jak flared in anger while trying to track down the flash she'd seen last time. The distraction robbed her of her anger as the task forced her to clear her thoughts. This was definitely the right spot, so where was the flash of red she'd seen? As if conjured up by her thoughts, she watched as a red round was chambered into a rifle. She dialed back a bit on the scope to bring the sniper into her sights. A kid? What was a young boy doing out here? And with that huge rifle. The boy looked up and met her gaze through the scope.

"Bron, I've got him! On the far ridge by the stand of four trees." As she squeezed the trigger, the boy raised his rifle and shot in one smooth motion. He shimmered out of her view as her round traveled through the space he'd just occupied.

"Bron?" Knowing what she was going to see, but powerless to stop, she looked over. Bron lay next to her, throat gone, ripped away by the bullet. A pool of blood, red and growing oozed toward her. His eyes, still blue, filmed over but held hers accusingly. Darkness blossomed around the edges of her vision and pushed in until only his eyes were visible, then they too were gone. She toppled into the dark, falling forever.

"Bron! Bron!! BRON!!!"

Hands reached out and pulled her from the darkness. Bron's name still on her lips, she lurched forward into a sitting position. Her chest heaved as she tried to catch her breath. She felt like she'd run a marathon and loud wheezing filled her ears.

Shit, that's me.

"Take a drink," Tanith's warm voice urged her and like magic a glass appeared in front of her. Jak grabbed it out of her hands and took a gulping swig. Water trickled down her throat, soothing and calming her. Slowly she brought her breathing back under control.

"You were going through something intense there. Are you all right?"

Jak shook her head. "I'm fine. It's a recurring nightmare."

"It must be a doozy."

"Oh it's a doozy. I get to relive my brother's death over and over and I can't do a damn thing to stop it." Tanith's prying irritated her. Couldn't she see Jak didn't want to talk about it? She supposed she should have been grateful to the woman for pulling her out. Instead she felt annoyed at having to explain something so personal.

Tanith rubbed her gently between the shoulder blades. "I'm sorry, I can't even imagine," she said quietly, and Jak immediately felt like an ass for snapping at the woman, even if it was only in her own head.

"I thought I was beyond it, but I guess I was wrong. Tanith, I want to enlist."

The major blinked at the sudden change of subject. "Why do I get the feeling that whatever happened last night is behind your change of heart? Are you sure this is something you really want, you were pretty adamant before. Why don't we talk about it? You have the day off. I set the trainees to working on the spotting maneuvers you were teaching them."

"I don't know. All you'll do is say that you told me so."

"It's not about me, hon. This is about what I can do to help you get through this." Tanith cupped Jak's chin in her hand and tilted it up so Jak looked her in the eyes. "You don't have to tell me any more than you're comfortable with. I won't judge you."

"I walked in on Torrin kissing some blond asshole."

Tanith sat back as if she'd been slapped. "She did what? That woman is insufferable! Usually she has more grace than that and breaks it off before she moves on to the next one. Of course she doesn't always do that." The bitterness in her final statement was almost palpable.

"Were you and she…together?"

"A very long time ago. I caught her with somebody else. She broke my heart."

"I'm sorry."

"It's not your fault. I only wish I could have spared you the same pain. Come on." Tanith pulled her to her feet.

"Where are we going?"

"Back to her place. You need to get your stuff out of there. A clean break will make all of this easier. Besides, if you're serious about enlisting, you'll have your own space here."

Bron's words rang through her head. This seemed a little off. Maybe she should try talking to Torrin.

"You can try, but I'm sure you'll be wasting your breath."

Jak hadn't realized that she'd spoken aloud, and she tipped her head noncommittally.

"Talk to her or not, we still need to get your gear and your rifle. It'll be easier to do while she's at work. You can talk to her later, if you want. Somewhere neutral would be best."

That made sense and Jak allowed herself to be walked out of her room.

* * *

Torrin awoke slowly. Her shoulder was stiff and her mouth tasted like the inside of her sports bra after a hard workout. To top it off, a dull pain threatened from behind her left eye. She opened her eyes and the pain switched from threat to cold reality. Lowering her eyelids against the light in the apartment did nothing to lessen the now blinding agony in her temples.

For a few moments she tried to come to terms with the pain. When it receded to a point where she was mostly certain she wouldn't vomit, she opened her eyes again. The living room coalesced in her bleary vision. The stiffness in her shoulder made sense. She was lying on the floor in front of the couch. She might have started the night on the couch, but at some point she'd ended up on the floor. Not that she had any recollection of the previous night. Chances were the same that she'd started out on the floor.

It took a little doing, but she levered herself back up onto the couch. Nat's cats were on opposite ends and leveling recriminating stares at her.

"S'not my fault," Torrin mumbled at the felines. What wasn't her fault again? She had the feeling something was missing. Something was very wrong. Why had she gotten so blindingly drunk? She usually had a good reason for that. Her memory churned up the unappealing truth, and her stomach lurched. Jak. She was gone.

Torrin staggered up and into the bathroom as quickly as she could. Bending over the sink, she emptied the contents of her stomach. It was almost all liquid, caustic and stinking of alcohol. Her eyes burned, and she sobbed like a little girl as she held herself up with hands clamped tightly around the edge of the counter.

What was she going to do now? Everything she'd been worried about in the hospital was coming right back at her. The worst of it was that she'd thought they were safe. Jak was getting healthy and healthwise was out of the woods. Then something like this had to happen. It was all a cruel joke. *Please let it be a joke.*

Eventually she realized she was leaning against the sink, head cradled on her arms, crying bitter tears that rolled down the inside of her elbows. Her mama and her first girlfriend were the only women she'd ever cried over. Slowly, she was able to pull herself together. She washed her face, cleaned her teeth. In a half-daze she considered her reflection in the mirror. Her hair, still much shorter than she would have liked, was beginning to grow back in. The top was barely long enough to touch the top of her eyebrows. The auburn strands stuck up in willful disarray. She stared at them long enough to decide that she didn't care.

The office. There was enough work to do there that she could lose herself in it for weeks. She shambled into her bedroom and grabbed the first shirt she could find. It seemed that she'd never bothered to put on a new top since she'd arrived home and decided to seek solace at the bottom of a bottle. The pants would do. They were wrinkled, but she couldn't bring herself to bother. A pair of dark glasses and a hat, pulled low to block out as much light as possible, rounded out the ensemble.

If only her hordes of ravening fans could see her now, she thought. They wouldn't recognize the disheveled wretch. That was fine. She wasn't worthy of their adulation, never had been. There was only one person she wanted to look at her that way, and she had no idea how to fix what had gone incomprehensibly wrong.

The harsh sunlight stabbed through her eyeballs. Even with the hat and glasses, it hammered a spike deep into her brain. Bypassing the bike, she slid into the car and toggled the window tint to its darkest setting. If she'd been a little more with it, she would have overridden the factory setting and taken it darker than the legal limit. But then, if she'd been more with it, she probably wouldn't have needed such a high setting.

The drive to the office was exceedingly uncomfortable. The smallest sounds sent throbs of pain through her head. When she got to Troika Corp., she almost sobbed with relief. Without acknowledging anyone, she strode through the cubicles in the office's front area to her private office in the back. Once there, she collapsed on the couch and dimmed the lights. It wasn't pitch black, but it was dark enough that she could barely make out her hand in front of her face. The headache gradually subsided and she napped fitfully.

A gentle hand on her shoulder brought her back to herself.

"Torrin? Are you all right?" Audra's concerned face hovered over her in the almost darkness.

"Leave me alone."

"I heard there was an incident here last night. And I don't think I've ever seen you this hungover. Are you and Jak having problems?"

Torrin laughed hollowly. "You could say that. If you call her walking in on one of my crazy exes giving me a tongue lock, then I guess so."

"What?" Audra sat back on her heels, confusion written across her face. "You were making out with your ex in your office?"

"No, she was making out with me. Before I could push her off, Jak walked in. I know what it looked like, but I haven't been able to explain it to her. She just left."

"Wow. I probably would have done the same thing in her shoes. Well, after punching you in the face."

Torrin sat up slowly and buried her face in her hands. "I know. I think she's at the base, but I can't get in. I have no clearance. I don't know how to get her to listen to me."

Couch leather creaked as Audra sat down next to her. "Normally I'd say let's have a drink, but I don't think you're ready for that yet. Can I do anything to help?"

Torrin considered for a moment, then sighed. "There's nothing you can do. I'm going to get to work, I guess. I don't have anyone to distract me from it now."

Her partner said nothing. She stood and clasped Torrin's shoulder for a moment. Audra swung the door shut behind her with barely a whisper. Torrin sat for a long minute, then stood and walked over to her desk and powered on the display. At least she had plenty of work with which to distract herself. It was a little paradoxical, really. She had all this work to do because she'd been spending so much time with Jak.

* * *

The keycard actually worked. Jak was a little surprised; she thought perhaps Torrin would have rekeyed the door. Maybe she'd been so busy with her blond piece of ass that she'd forgotten, Jak thought bitterly. The hall seemed quieter than normal. She actually caught herself walking gingerly, as if she were tracking prey back in Haefen's woods. Tanith clomped along solidly next to her.

She opened the door to Torrin's flat. The air that rolled out was slightly stale and held a definite stench of alcohol and lots of it. The cats came bounding over and rubbed eager heads all over her outstretched hands. Tanith surveyed the living room carefully.

"Have you been here before?" Jak asked.

Tanith shook her head. "It's not hard to see something out of place, though." She stooped forward and picked up a shirt where it was piled on the floor. Holding it up to Jak, she could see the front was ripped open. With a sinking heart, she recognized the shirt as the one Torrin had been wearing the night before.

The couch cushions were in disarray. Two of them were on the floor and the remaining three had been pushed to one side. Torrin was always fanatical about everything being in its place. It was one of the areas they'd been in perfect agreement upon. Now it looked like Torrin had had a good time on that couch.

"I need to get my things," Jak choked out and hurried to the bedroom. She dreaded what she might find there. The bedroom looked surprisingly untouched given the events that had obviously transpired in the living room. In fact, it looked like the bed hadn't even been slept in.

They probably had all their fun out there. Clenching her jaw, she pulled open the built-in wardrobe, then retrieved her rifle and pulled the ammunition down from the shelf. Her clothes she pulled out in handfuls... and shoved them into the duffel bag that Tanith had thought to bring. Her eyes were welling up again, and she blindly wedged more clothes in before deciding she couldn't take it anymore and fled the bedroom with as much as she'd managed to pack, hitching the rifle over her shoulder.

"Do you mind if I use the bathroom?" Tanith called.

"Go ahead." Jak did her best not to sound like she'd been crying again.

"Someone had a good time in there," Tanith drawled disparagingly on her return. Dangling from her fingers was a pair of lacy underwear. Jak didn't recognize them as Torrin's and she was well-acquainted with the smuggler's underthings by now. Torrin did tend toward girly, but something that frilly had never seen the inside of her underwear drawer.

Confronted with this last proof of Torrin's duplicity, Jak had to bite her lip to keep the tears from breaking free.

"I need to get out of here."

"Oh shit, I'm sorry, honey." Tanith rushed over to comfort her, clasping Jak to her modest bosom. "Let's get you back to the base." One arm still draped across Jak's shoulders, Tanith led her to the door. Numb, Jak allowed herself to be steered from the flat. How could she have been so mistaken about her lover?

Back at the base, Tanith insisted that she shower. Something about Jak's despondent manner must have spooked her, and she refused to leave the communal shower room while Jak cleaned herself. It didn't really matter, Jak supposed. She'd been terribly body conscious, but it didn't matter any longer. So what if someone else saw her?

"Doesn't that feel better?" Tanith ventured hesitantly.

"I guess so."

"Do you need anything?"

"Just my rifle and some time on the range."

"Are you sure that's such a good idea?"

Jak turned her head and looked her friend in the eyes. Tanith recoiled slightly from whatever she saw looking back at her.

"I'm not going to kill myself if that's what you're worried about."

Tanith flinched. Evidently Jak had uttered aloud exactly what Tanith had been thinking. "Can you blame me for worrying? I hope you won't resort to that. There are more people than you know who would miss you greatly. Me, for one."

"I appreciate that," Jak lied. "All I need is some time where I don't have to think. I'll be fine."

Tanith nodded slowly. "If you need anything, you let me know. I'm staying in the barracks again tonight."

Jak walked past her out of the shower room and into the room she'd been assigned. There she picked up her rifle and headed out to the range. Piercing a defenseless target with dozens of holes wouldn't make her feel better, not exactly. But at least she could lose herself in the mechanics of it. Oblivion was what she craved now, and that was one thing Jak knew she could find on the range.

* * *

The wall rose another meter and a half above her head, but Torrin was fairly certain that if she took a running start, she could grab hold of the top and pull herself over. The sentry had gone by a few moments before and had actually nodded to her as she stood inspecting the wall. Security really was lax. Some of Jak's complaints about the militia's lack of professionalism made more sense, but she wasn't going to complain since it was to her benefit. She grinned mirthlessly; the sentry's familiarity also made it less likely that she'd be shot on sight if caught.

Backing up a little ways, she gave herself enough room to get up to a full sprint before launching herself in the obstacle's direction. Desperation gave her a major adrenaline rush. She was able to easily grab the wall's top with room to spare, and her momentum carried her almost all the way over. With a deft twist of her body, she flipped her legs to the side and landed on her feet on the ground inside the wall.

On base, the night was dark. There were fewer lights than in the city and her eyes strained to see anything in the gloom. Relying on memory, she started off toward the near barracks, hoping that the more seasoned militiawomen were still housed there. As a junior officer, Jak should have her own room in those barracks. Majors and above would be entitled to one of the freestanding homes on the far edge of the base.

Her eyes and ears peeled for sentries or any indication that her presence had been detected, she skulked her way past silent buildings barely visible in the darkness. Torrin had spent a number of years living on base, and she wasn't surprised to see that very little had changed.

Fortunately, she was still friendly with a large number of militia-women, not all of whom had heard about her troubles with Jak. Earlier that evening, when she'd returned to her flat to find all of Jak's belongings gone, Torrin had been ready to crawl back inside a bottle. The remnants of her headache convinced her there might be a better way.

There was really only one place Jak would go, especially now that Nat was gone. It hadn't taken long to confirm that she had enlisted with the militia. Torrin had been pleasantly surprised to find out that she'd been given the rank of captain. Her pride on Jak's behalf had only lasted a moment however. It seemed Jak was reporting directly to Tanith. That was bad news. Tanith would only fill Jak with garbage about how terrible Torrin was. The only terrible thing Torrin had done was not get psychotic Breena off her fast enough. Jak's assignment to Tanith's command made it even more crucial that she get to her lover and explain what had gone wrong. It shouldn't have been a surprise that Jak wasn't making it easy.

The flat had echoed when she'd entered it that evening. Even Tesser and Resi seemed to feel the absence that had opened in the heart of her home. The cats had watched her mournfully from the back of the couch as she made her way through the flat, desperation rising within her every time she opened a drawer or closet to find Jak's belongings gone. It was all gone, Jak had picked up every last piece of clothing, every trinket.

Every piece Torrin discovered to be missing left feeling her more hollowed out inside. It didn't make sense. Jak barely owned anything. Torrin shouldn't have been feeling the absence of those bits and pieces so keenly. And yet, when she'd discovered that Jak's rifle was missing, she found herself on her knees in front of the bedroom closet struggling to breathe over the panic that threatened to choke her. She had realized then, without a doubt, that Jak had no plans to come back.

She needed to find Jak, she decided then and there. Convince her it was all a terrible misunderstanding. If Torrin could negotiate her way through the edges of the known galaxy, surely she could change her girlfriend's mind.

Stealthily she let herself into the senior women's barracks. The first room she stuck her head into was inhabited by a large woman who snored up a storm, mouth agape. Luckily, the woman made so much noise herself that she was unable to hear Torrin. The second room had two occupants, and from the noises she heard when she cracked open the door, they were having a very good time. Blood roared through her ears until she saw that neither woman was Jak. The two had other concerns than her and she closed the door softly.

In the third room, she saw a blond head with closely shorn hair buried in blankets heaped around her. The pit of Torrin's stomach lurched when she realized that Jak had shaved her hair back almost to her scalp. It had been growing in so nicely. The dark blond color framing her face had softened Jak's cheekbones, giving her face an elfin cast. Without the hair,

Jak's cheekbones were too prominent, and with her still too-thin build, she looked like a refugee.

She slipped into the room and crouched down near Jak's head. For a few minutes, all she did was watch as Jak slept. She'd always enjoyed watching her lover sleep. Jak had faced so many obstacles in her short life. When awake, sometimes it looked like the cares of the world had settled around her neck. Asleep, Torrin thought she looked like she must have before her brother was taken from her.

Gently, she smoothed her fingers over the stubble at Jak's hairline. Jak smiled slightly in her sleep and turned her head into the caress. Feeling bolder, Torrin leaned forward and kissed her forehead. Jak's eyes snapped open. For a moment, Torrin thought that Jak looked happy to see her, the corners of her eyes crinkled slightly. A breath later the look was gone, replaced when the bleakness she hadn't seen for weeks flooded back into the sniper's eyes.

"What do you want?" Jak's voice was monotone, stripped of all inflection.

"We need to talk. I want to explain."

"What makes you think you can explain anything? I went to the apartment. I saw."

"Saw what? That I drank myself into oblivion and slept on the couch?"

"Looked to me like you had more than a little fun on that couch. And why was that woman's underwear in the bathroom?"

Torrin rocked back on her heels and stared at Jak. "Wait, what? Underwear in the bathroom? There's no way her underwear was in the bathroom. She hasn't been in my home for years."

"I saw them. How do you explain that?" The blue of Jak's eyes had been darkening steadily since she'd awoken, and they were now the color of fresh bruises.

"Then someone planted it. I didn't do anything, I swear. That crazy bitch Breena kissed me, I didn't kiss her. You have to believe me."

"She doesn't have to do anything you say. Sounds pretty shady if you ask me." Tanith's voice came from the doorway. Torrin's nemesis lounged in the doorway, arms crossed under her breasts. She wore a tight T-shirt that emphasized the muscles of her arms and chest. Torrin had no doubt that she was flexing to impress Jak.

"Stay out of it, Tanith. No one asked you."

Tanith took a step into the room. "It sure as hell does concern me. You've broken the heart of another one of my friends. Everyone else thinks you're something special, Ivanov, but I know better. You're scum."

Torrin unfolded herself from her crouch. "I didn't do anything to hurt either of them. You need to back off before I make you—" With two quick steps, Tanith loomed right in her face. The major wasn't quite tall enough to look her in the eye, but she was doing a good job at filling her field of vision.

"Make me what, Torrin?" Tanith thrust her chin out at Torrin, daring her to take a swing.

Something inside Torrin snapped. Knowing it was a bad move, but not caring, she took Tanith up on the invitation. A quick jab to the stomach followed by an uppercut to the jaw sent Tanith's head back. Pain exploded in her face when Tanith snapped her head forward, impacting Torrin's nose. Blood spurted in an immediate flood, and Torrin reeled for a moment before reaching up with both hands, grabbing either side of Tanith's head and bringing it down toward her rising knee.

"Torrin!" Jak's shout brought her back to herself and she paused. Tanith took the opportunity to sweep her legs out from under her, and Torrin went down in a heap. Footsteps pounded down the hall toward the room as militiawomen were awakened by the commotion. Something hard connected to the bone behind Torrin's left ear. The room's lights winked out to pinpoints.

"Throw her in the lockup" was the last thing she heard before the lights disappeared altogether.

CHAPTER SEVENTEEN

Pain in her head finally woke her. This was becoming too common an occurrence. After a careful peek, Torrin opened her eyes all the way. It took her a few moments to piece together what had happened. She'd known it wasn't a good idea to sneak onto the base to see Jak, but she hadn't been able stop herself from trying. It had been many years since she'd seen the inside of the base lockup. The last time she'd been in here, Tanith had been thrown in the cell next to hers. They'd both been locked up for fighting. This time Tanith was the one who'd locked her up.

She was lying on a hard shelf. It was somewhere between a bench and a bed, and she suspected it had been specially designed to be comfortable as neither. She was alone in the cell, which was probably a good thing.

"Oh good, you're up" came the hated drawl from the shadows beyond the force field.

Torrin forced herself up from the cold metal and winced as pain lanced through the back of her head. Lifting her hand, she probed the large lump behind her ear. Dried blood crusted her hair. A dull throbbing in her face reminded her of the blow she'd received and she carefully fingered her nose. It was mostly numb, which was good because it felt flatter than she remembered.

"How you feeling? Looks like you might have some issues with that nose of yours. Don't worry, you're still awfully pretty." When Torrin ignored her first volley, Tanith continued the taunts. Torrin had forgotten how much Tanith hated being dismissed. Since doing nothing was getting such a rise out of her, she saw no reason to give her any satisfaction. She leaned back against the wall and stared at the small window, high up in the duracrete wall. From the angle and intensity of the sun, it looked like it was probably early- to midmorning.

"Your little girlfriend didn't seem too happy to see you." Tanith threw that one at her with snide confidence. That one hurt, but Torrin did her best to ignore the woman's spiteful barbs. She yawned hugely. Out of the corner of her eye, she caught the spasm of anger that flashed across Tanith's face.

"You're still a shit," Tanith breathed. She stepped up to the forcefield and disabled it at the wall panel. A small, localized force field sprung up around the bench, freezing Torrin in place and holding her hands in place where they'd been wrapped around the edge. "Why don't I show you how I've learned to deal with shit?"

Unable to move, Torrin fought back with the only weapon in her arsenal and ignored Tanith's presence completely. A blow took her across the face hard enough to rock her head back and split her lip, sending more agony driving through her head. Her nostrils flared at the pain, and she hoped her nose would go back to being numb. A small grunt was the only sound that passed her lips. Torrin clamped her lips together, determined not to let Tanith know how much the punch had hurt. Tanith stood above her, slowly shaking out her hand and watching her with expectant eyes. When she was back under control, Torrin pulled her lips wide in a painful imitation of a smile.

"What's the matter, Tanith? You mad because you know the only way you can take me on is if I can't fight back?"

Tanith smiled coldly. "All I want to know is that you're paying attention so I can tell you about all the fun your sweet little Jak and I will have together. She's quite the catch. Beautiful, deadly and surprisingly malleable."

Before Torrin could stop herself, she snorted with laughter. Light flared across her vision, and she immediately wished she hadn't done that. Her eyes watered at the pain in her nose. "Malleable? Are we talking about the same woman?"

"Oh, she's malleable, all right. I'm going to shape her into the perfect little woman for me. When I'm done with her, she won't remember your name, let alone that you two ever shared anything together. Then maybe you'll understand a little better where I'm coming from."

"This old saw again? Tanith, Galya chose me over you more than twenty years ago. I'm sorry she didn't pick you, I wish she had. She got tired of me pretty quickly, left without even saying goodbye. What happened wasn't my fault. I think you've carried this grudge as far as it can go."

"You have no idea how far I can carry this, Torrin."

"Major, you need to release your prisoner to me." Torrin had never been more relieved to hear Audra's voice. Hostility crawled across Tanith's face. For the first time, Torrin wondered how sane the major actually was. She clearly had rage issues. As quickly as it had flashed upon Tanith's face, the hostility was gone when she turned to face Audra.

"Good, it's about time someone came for her. She's lucky that Captain Stowell doesn't want to press charges. I'm taking her recent personal circumstances into consideration, and the militia won't be pressing any charges for trespassing."

"I'm glad you're not pressing charges. It looks like she might have a case if she wanted to bring you up on assault charges however."

Tanith shrugged. "She resisted us when she was apprehended. We did what we had to in order to subdue her."

"I see." Audra didn't sound convinced and stared worriedly at her friend. Torrin tried to smile reassuringly, but Audra's wince told her louder than words exactly how bad she looked. "If you'll release her, I'll get her out of your hair."

"Fair enough." Tanith passed her hand in front of the panel by the door and the localized force field winked out. Torrin rolled her shoulders and flexed the muscles in her limbs. Stiffness and knots of pain told her more bruises were definitely hidden under her clothing. Apparently the militiawomen hadn't been overly gentle in their treatment of her while she was unconscious. Gingerly, she stood. The movement sent a gentle throbbing to her head, but it was nothing compared to the hangover she'd had the previous morning.

Audra waited patiently at the lockup door. She was fidgeting less than normal. Either she'd recently had mind-blowing sex with her latest woman or she was really worried about something. She said nothing as Torrin passed her and fell in right behind her. They walked out of the building in silence.

The lockup was at the far end of the base's main square. Women drilled at various points around the square. They stopped and stared as the two women walked by. Whether it was because of Torrin's bedraggled state or because they knew what had gone on the previous night, Torrin wasn't sure. She remembered how quickly rumors spread in the base's confines and figured it was probably a combination of the two. Glancing down, she decided that she was glad she'd worn black. The blood from her beating wouldn't stain the shirt. Carefully, Torrin shook her head to dispel the random thought before sliding into the passenger seat of Audra's car.

"Your car's been returned to your house. Mac drove it home from where you left it outside the wall last night." Audra powered her own car up, and the doors closed soundlessly around them.

Torrin nodded. "Good, I'd completely forgotten—" Her words were cut off as Audra accelerated sharply, having gained clearance from the gate guards.

"What the hell were you thinking, Torrin?"

"I needed to talk to her, to tell her what really happened."

"You couldn't have waited until you could get to her outside the base? You're damn lucky they aren't pressing charges. What do you think the Ruling Council would have made of that? They could have canceled the whole project based on your unstable emotions. There are more important issues than your love life right now."

"Not to me there aren't. I pissed away my time with Jak by always being at work. Now I don't have her, and I can't even look back on what we had together." Her voice rose steadily until she was screaming at her friend. Audra watched her out of the corner of her eye, keeping one eye on the road and the other on her semihysterical partner in the passenger seat.

"I'm sorry, Torrin," Audra said soothingly when Torrin wound down. "I really am. Mac and I need you with us on the planning process, but I don't think you can do that right now. We need to get you off planet before the Ruling Council gets wind of what happened last night."

"Off planet? Why? I'm fine, I'll be better off here."

Audra laughed sadly. "Jak really does have a hold on you. I never thought I'd see the day when you didn't jump at the chance to take a trip. It'll be for the best. You need to clear your head and you obviously can't do that here."

"I can't believe this! What the hell, Audra?"

"I'm sorry, Torrin. But this is the way it has to be. When you're thinking more clearly, you'll agree." Audra pulled to a stop in front of the clinic. "This should help with some of that. Let's get you patched up, then we'll get you off to Castor III. You look like hell, by the way."

"I figured. Tanith got in some extra licks while I was unconscious, I think."

"She's had it out for you as long as I've known you." Audra shook her head.

"I know. Our friendship ended when we both wanted to go with the same girl. I got the girl, she didn't. She's never forgiven me for that."

Audra opened the passenger door from the console. "Go get yourself patched up. I'm going to get everything arranged from the office. Call me when you're ready to head home."

Torrin stepped out of the car. Turning back, she peered into the car's interior.

"Hey, thanks."

"No problem. Just get your shit figured out."

* * *

The ceiling of Jak's room was incredibly uninteresting. Jak had been staring at it since Tanith and some of the other women had dragged Torrin out of there. She couldn't believe Torrin's nerve. To break into the base and sneak into Jak's room. What had she been thinking? If she hadn't found those damning bits of evidence at the apartment, she might have been inclined to believe the smuggler.

A glance toward the window told her the sun was barely up. She pushed herself out of bed, grabbed her rifle and headed out toward the range. All of the practice she'd been putting in over the past day or so should have been improving her results. Lack of sleep was probably dulling her edge a little bit. Certainly her quickness was off.

The range was silent this early in the morning. She was glad for that small mercy at least. The sympathetic glances of the militiawomen and their solicitous questions were almost more than she could bear. When her brother had been killed, there had been a few statements of sympathy, but beyond that the men had left her alone to cope with her loss however she felt necessary. Everyone here seemed to think she was about to break because of the disintegration of her relationship with Torrin. All things considered, she thought she was handling the mess pretty well.

Her hands shook slightly as she chambered the ammunition. She glared at her stubborn digits and they soon stopped quivering. That wasn't like her. Perhaps she should try to get some sleep.

A few rounds later, she knew something was definitely wrong. She hadn't hit the center of any of the targets. On one shot, she'd missed the target completely. The tremor in her hands was back. What she needed now was some stims, but there was nowhere to get her hands on them here. Ruefully, she conceded that the stims were partially responsible for her current physical deficiencies.

"Captain?" The voice of one of the women floated into her consciousness. It took her a few moments before she placed it as belonging to one of the women in her basic qualification course.

"What is it, Shellin?"

"Are you all right? I heard about your problems with Torrin Ivanov." Shellin's tone was slightly disbelieving. Like many of the women in Landing, she viewed Torrin with pronounced hero worship.

Jak pushed herself up on one elbow and considered the mousy woman standing awkwardly to one side. "It's fine."

"Are you sure?" Emboldened, Shellin approached her. "You aren't the same as you were before you and she…" She started to stoop down to look Jak in the eye but stepped back swiftly. Jak supposed that Shellin had seen how little she cared about her opinion. How little she cared about anything, really.

Sighing, Jak stood. "Really, I'm fine. I'm tired. I haven't really slept since that night."

"It's not my place to say, sir, but you look like hell."

"Thanks. Now if you'll excuse me." Without waiting for a response, she slipped her rifle over one shoulder and left the training range. It hadn't ended up being the refuge she'd been hoping for. A deep longing for the cool, deep forests of Haefen seized her. A homesickness she never thought she'd feel for the planet she'd grown up on threatened to choke her. Forests of any type were what she needed. Sadly, this area of Nadierzda didn't have any forests, not even small woods. Torrin had mentioned that some of the more remote, still-terraformed impact craters were wooded, but they weren't within easy distance of Landing. She had no access to transportation so was limited to the area around the base and in town.

Without thinking about it too closely, she'd ended up back at her room. At least there she could close the door and shut out the sympathetic stares, the prying but oh-so-concerned questions. She closed the door behind her and threw herself down on the bed. Try though she might, she couldn't forget the lightness in her heart when she'd first opened her eyes to see Torrin crouched by the bed. The warmth of Torrin's hand on her head still lingered when she thought about it. Why couldn't she write the smuggler out of her life? More than anything, she wanted Torrin out of her head and to banish the ache in her heart.

A knock on the door woke her from a deep sleep. She didn't remember falling asleep. It was now afternoon, she was able to tell by a quick look out the window.

Tanith stuck her head around the door. "You got some sleep, good!"

Jak grunted groggily in response.

"Well, Torrin was picked up from lockup by her friend. I don't think it was the blonde from her office. It was one of her partners. Audra I think."

Audra *would* be the one to pick up Torrin. She probably thought the whole situation was hilarious.

She'd meant to keep a lid on her emotions at Tanith's mention of Torrin's name, but her face must have given her away. It was very disconcerting for her emotions to be so obvious to others. For years she'd managed to keep her feelings under wraps, but Torrin had battered those walls down far more quickly than she had thought possible.

"I have some time, and I promised to teach you how to use an ultralight," Tanith said. "No time like the present. Let's get you out there."

"Are you trying to keep my mind off her?"

"So what if I am? This is something you wanted to do anyway, so let's do it."

There was no arguing with her logic so Jak nodded and stood up. She didn't even have to put on her boots, since she hadn't bothered to take them off before falling asleep. She shrugged a combat fatigue jacket on over her shirt and followed Tanith out of the room.

* * *

"Where are we headed, Torrin?" Tien asked. "Are we waiting for Miss Stowell?"

"We," Torrin replied, stowing a small pallet of platinum ingots with more force than was really necessary, "are heading to Castor III. Jak will not be joining us. She has decided I am evil incarnate and so has declined the continuing pleasure of my company." She entered the ingots onto the manifest as assorted vegetable matter. Even though she was headed to League space on a legitimate business operation, she couldn't force herself to be completely aboveboard, especially not where the League was concerned.

"I see. Are you all right, Torrin?" the AI sounded genuinely concerned. "I observed that you had unusually high levels of attachment to her."

Torrin rolled her eyes. "I'm not discussing this with you. You need to get a course set in for the Castor system. I'll be up as soon as I finish stowing the cargo."

"Understood, Torrin."

The cargo bay was almost full. Containers and pallets had been crammed into every nook and cranny. She had chosen not to bring any additional vehicles along on the trip. Unlike Haefen, Castor III was heavily urbanized. If there was no public transportation available, she would be able to rent a vehicle. She shifted a couple of containers and wedged a third one between them. A quick glance down the cargo ramp showed she was down to only a couple of items of cargo left to stow. Her personal effects for the journey made up a tiny pile next to the last of the cargo. They looked small and alone, and Torrin focused on getting the cargo bay filled. Everything reminded her of Jak, even piles of inanimate objects.

Fifteen minutes later, she was cabling down the last of the pallets and had activated the retaining fields. She heard footsteps on the cargo ramp and looked up.

"Good luck, Torrin," Audra said. Next to her Mac nodded soberly.

"Come on, guys. It's not like I'm going into exile. It's a short hop to Castor System. If all goes well, I'll be out of there in a few days, a week tops. I'm going to swing by Dowson and look up Neal while I'm in the neighborhood. He has a lot to answer for. Add another week to my itinerary before you come after me."

"You've been those places before and we actually know where they are," Mac said seriously. "You can be sure that we'll send someone to get you if you aren't back in three weeks."

"Yeah, because if you're gone that long, we'll know you got your ass tossed in jail again."

Mac winced slightly at Audra's joking tone, but nodded in agreement. "We need you, Torrin. Don't forget that."

"I already have two moms, I don't need two more," Torrin said.

"The black eye to end all black eyes says otherwise," Audra pointed out. "It looks like Kiera was able to fix your nose though."

Torrin shrugged uncomfortably. The trip felt like a punishment. If her partners hadn't insisted she go negotiate the purchase of land for a manufacturing plant on Castor, she would have stayed around Landing and spent her time trying to convince Jak that the whole thing was a big misunderstanding. For a fleeting moment, the other night when Jak had woken up, Torrin could have sworn the sniper had been happy to see her. One look that had lasted less than a second was all the encouragement she needed. Being off the planet without Jak was going to be torture. All she could do was get to Castor and Dowson as quickly as possible. Then she could try to salvage her relationship.

Audra threw her arms around Torrin and hugged her fiercely. "It's going to be all right," her partner promised in a low voice.

Mac stepped in on her other side and also wrapped her arms around Torrin and squeezed. "We love you, Torrin. Don't worry, we'll keep an eye on Jak."

Torrin closed her eyes. The two women were her closest friends and she had never valued their friendship more than she did now. Knowing they supported her and would keep an eye out for Jak did help. Somewhat.

"Thanks, guys," Torrin said gruffly. "Now let me get on with this."

The two partners let go of her and stepped away. Audra gave her a parting pat on the back and Torrin turned and walked into the cargo bay. Carrying her personal gear, she tossed the two duffel bags into the elevator and pushed the button for the main level.

"Close the door when they're clear, won't you, Tien?" The door hissed open and she walked down the short hallway to her room. "Also, as soon as you clear it with Control, take us up."

"Are you sure, Torrin?" Tien asked, her slightly mechanical voice dubious. "You will need to override the restrictions on my programming."

"It's past time for that. Being a control freak won't stop things from going wrong. Tien, override propulsion and navigation security protocols, clearance code Tango-Alpha-Niner-Seven-Foxtrot. Effective immediately."

"Security protocols overridden, Torrin."

She was of two minds about the security override. If the ship had been able to come to her rescue on Haefen, she wouldn't have been subjected to the attentions of the late Colonel Hutchinson. She also wouldn't have been rescued by Sergeant Jak Stowell, which meant she wouldn't be feeling so utterly crappy right now. On the other hand she wouldn't be setting up what could easily be the biggest score of her career either. The universe was a fickle bitch, that was sure.

With an economy of motion that spoke of a great deal of practice, Torrin stowed her gear and secured her cabin. A quick look around the main level showed that everything was stowed or secured properly. Tien had made sure that everything was cleaned up and placed in an orderly fashion. The cryostasis cabin was immaculate. There was no indication that there had been a major medical emergency there. Anything that reminded her of Jak gave Torrin a little pang, and the cryostasis chamber pulled at her the most acutely, reminding her of the desperation and helplessness she'd felt as Jak nearly bled out as a result of her decision to bring her to Nadi.

Closing her eyes tightly against the remembered images, Torrin set off for the bridge. A quick glance at the main console showed her that Tien was running through her prelaunch checklist.

"We have received clearance to lift off in four minutes, thirty-seven seconds, Torrin."

"That's good. Shoot me your navigation solutions for the trip to Castor III, if you would."

Tien didn't answer, but the solutions appeared on Torrin's console. They were good, but too direct. Torrin made a couple of changes. They would add a few hours to the trip, but it wouldn't be evident to a casual observer which direction they'd come from. It was always possible that somebody who really wanted to know could piece together the last few legs of their route. They would be taking the trip in multiple legs precisely to confuse any such attempts. There was no way Torrin would lead interlopers back to her home, not when she was working so hard to save it. Paranoid she might be, but that didn't mean she was wrong.

During her calculations and adjustments to their route, Tien had cycled on the engines and lifted the *Calamity Jane* from her berth at the space port. Her engines built into a high-pitched whine as they fought the bonds of gravity and rose through the atmosphere. Entering and leaving an atmosphere put some of the highest stresses on space vessels, severely shortening their life spans. One day, Torrin hoped that they could construct and man an orbital space port. Maybe with the money their foray into cybernetics would bring, they would be able to accomplish it. But only after completing terraforming.

In fact, as she thought of it, they might have to construct something like that anyway. The planet's population would need to temporarily relocate during terraforming. That would mean a large number of ships leaving the surface over a short period of time. The pollution produced by so many antimatter-powered space vessels would be intense. Eliminating the need for them to dock on the planet would help to keep them from polluting the planet as they tried to save it. Considering that angle led to other thoughts on the logistics of the relocation process, and she bent over her console to record them.

Below them, Nadierzda's surface dropped away.

CHAPTER EIGHTEEN

"You have a lot of cargo for such a small space," the sable-haired woman mentioned casually. She ran a wand over the electromagnetic manifests on each container, double-checking them against the master shipping manifest Torrin had provided. In a move that Torrin had thought was more than a little anachronistic, she'd insisted on having a hard copy of the master manifest. Torrin had printed out the paper copy that Customs Officer Desseren had on her clipboard and was checking items off with a pencil.

"I have to make do with what I have," Torrin replied and flashed Desseren a charming smile. The customs officer caught the smile and returned it with interest and unconsciously pulled down the hem of her uniform jacket. The move accentuated her impressive bosom and drew attention to the League of Solaran Planets Customs and Trade Enforcement badge. Torrin kept the smile plastered on her face.

"Seems to me you're making do just fine," Desseren returned. "I've never seen such a well-put-together...cargo area."

Time to cool things down, Torrin thought. Otherwise, she was going to have to make good on her flirting.

"I have to admit I was surprised to find a female customs officer on Castor." Desseren was getting closer to the container that hid the pallet of platinum ingots. Torrin was mostly certain that the altered EM signature on the container would do its job, but it had been a while since she'd had to smuggle anything through a League customs shop. The difference on the manifest would be easily explained, and she was well under her limit for the trip, so she wasn't too worried about getting caught. If it worked, she would know the strategy was still viable.

"Five years ago you wouldn't have," Desseren admitted. "Since the League took over, things have been changing. The League doesn't allow for discrimination based on gender and a whole host of other things."

"Hasn't the League been running things for twenty years now?"

"That's true. They allow for a certain period of adjustment, however. Apparently it helps 'backward' populations like ours acclimate to the 'civilization' League membership brings with it." Her voice was acid and Torrin could hear the mocking quotes around the words.

Desseren ran her wand over another couple of containers. She pulled the pencil from behind her ear and made a few more notations on the master manifest, then returned the pencil to its place.

"Seems reasonable," Torrin said, trying to hide her discomfort over the League's policies. The discomfort stemmed in no small part because the policy actually seemed reasonable. Torrin was much more comfortable believing the League's policies were all flawed. Her confrontation with Jak over League policies all those months ago came back to her, and she winced.

"You disagree?" The officer must have caught some of her discomfort.

"Not really, but then I'm from Fringe space. I don't know that I always like someone telling me what to do and how."

"An independent cuss, are you?" Desseren flashed a knowing smirk. She ran the wand over the crate falsely labeled as containing vegetable matter. The pencil came out and she made another notation on the manifest. "Do you always need to be in charge or are there exceptions?" She tried to return the pencil behind her ear, but it dropped out and rolled across the floor, past Torrin to fetch up against one of the containers.

"Let me get that," Torrin said, bending over to retrieve the writing utensil. She straightened quickly when she felt a warm hand running down her right buttock. "Here." She thrust the pencil back into Desseren's still-outstretched hand. She eyed the customs officer's lushly inviting form with regret. She felt no attraction for the woman, instead only an aching void. Thinking of sex only made her think of Jak.

Desseren sidled up to her and ran her finger around the top of Torrin's collar. The high mandarin-style collar went almost up to her chin, and the officer drew a finger along the line of her jaw.

"I'm sorry," Torrin said, stepping back. Desseren moved forward, eyes smoldering. "I'm coming off a bad breakup. I'm really not interested right now."

"Breakup? Who would be stupid enough to break up with a gorgeous piece of ass like you?"

"It wasn't really her fault, but—" Desseren stopped her by placing her finger over Torrin's lips.

"Were you a bad girl?"

"No! Nothing like that."

"Naughty, naughty." Desseren kept moving forward as Torrin stepped back. Too quickly she was stopped by the containers piled against the cargo bay's far wall. Desseren braced herself with both hands against the containers on either side of Torrin's rib cage. "I know how else you've been a naughty girl, Miss Ivanov."

"What do you mean?" Torrin looked around for some way of getting herself out of the woman's embrace without resorting to violence.

"That last container I scanned. It's not vegetable matter. Your EM was good, but we have new scanners." Desseren held up one hand and dangled the scanner at her from the strap around her wrist. With a flick of the wrist, the scanner was in Desseren's hand and she drew it lightly down the front of Torrin's jumpsuit. "They read more than EM manifests. They also scan through the container's surface. Next time you want to smuggle in platinum, you might want to line the inside of your container with what you've claimed on the manifest."

"Did that say vegetable matter?" Torrin laughed hollowly. "I don't know how that happened. Let me clear that up right now. I know I'm under my limit, so we should be able to alter the manifest to reflect the error."

"Sure, we can do that. But then I'm going to need you to open every container so I can visually inspect it. I'm also going to need to search every inch of your vessel to make sure you don't have any contraband."

That was the real sticking point. Tien was a League-issued, military-grade AI. It was illegal for anyone not in the League military to own her. Her signature had been altered to project a civilian-grade cover, but she didn't know how thorough an inspection Desseren was going to insist upon. If she went down to the hull and started pulling hatches off things, there was the chance that Tien's true origin would be discovered. It was a very remote possibility, but not one Torrin could risk. When she got back to Nadi, she would need to talk to Audra to see how they could further conceal Tien's identity. Tien wouldn't be able to help. It was hardwired into her security protocols never to alter her hardware, beyond minor repairs.

"Officer Desseren…"

"JoAnn."

Torrin smiled sickly. "JoAnn, I really wish you wouldn't have to go to all that trouble. Surely we can come up with some sort of arrangement?"

Desseren's smile widened sensually. "You bet your hot ass we can come up with an arrangement." Her other hand moved from the wall and settled on Torrin's hip. She pulled the smuggler against her.

Abruptly Hutchinson's face filled Torrin's vision. She jerked away before she could stop herself. She knew Hutchinson was dead, but the reaction was all instinct. A chill raced through her body and her heart hammered in her ears.

Desseren glared at her, the sensual heat in her eyes replaced with anger. Clearly, she wasn't used to being spurned.

"JoAnn. I'm not ready for what you're so kindly offering. I'm sorry. But I do know how else I can make it up to you."

"You're right, there is one other way, but it's going to cost you. Big."

The smuggler winced. She had no illusions—her involuntary reaction was about to cost her a whole lot of money.

* * *

"Miss Ivanov, you must realize that the turnaround time you're asking for is impossible." The massive gentleman leaned away from the table, wiping his lips with a napkin. The napkin looked tiny in his large hands. The sunken knuckles suggested that he'd made his way with his fists at one point in his life, but the expensive, hand-tailored suit indicated he hadn't had to break heads for quite some time. Of course, all that meant was these days he could afford to pay someone to break heads for him.

"O'Toole, you know you'll be well compensated for your troubles." Torrin did her best to project a reasonable facade. What she really wanted to do was reach across the table and shake him until he agreed to do what she wanted. The faster they went into production, the faster they'd be making money, the faster she'd be back on Nadi working on Jak. "I'm not asking for the impossible. All I want is you to close on the property a few weeks early."

"That will result in additional expenses. The local bureaucrats will demand...compensation."

"I can see to it that their costs are covered, as are your own, of course."

O'Toole made a show of thinking about her proposal, running a hand over the back of his shaven head. He'd been extremely muscular at some point in the past, but success had encouraged some of the muscle to run to fat. His head appeared to sprout right from his shoulders, without the benefit of a neck.

"Miranda, what kind of numbers we talking about?" His secretary jumped at being addressed. She'd been silent for the entire meeting so far, not even eating though O'Toole had ordered her a salad. To Torrin's eyes, the little woman could have benefited from a steak or something else that would have stuck to her bones. If she topped 125 centimeters, Torrin would have been shocked. Her bones were so fine that Torrin wouldn't have been surprised to see light shining through her forearms. Brilliant red hair stood out against the milky-white of her skin. She'd let it grow to directly below chin length and watched the world go by through its protective veil. She had an appealing vulnerability that reminded her a bit of Jak.

Jak again. What was it going to take to get the sniper out of her head? Everything reminded her of her ex-lover. Abruptly, she realized that Miranda had been talking and she hurriedly paid attention to the diminutive woman.

"—and that would bring the total to twelve million credits."

Crap, she'd missed the first part. Desperately Torrin cast back in her mind to see if she could remember what the secretary had been saying but couldn't bring it to mind.

"I'm sorry, could you repeat the first part? I'm afraid I missed it."

O'Toole eyed her speculatively, eyebrow cocked. "Go on, Miranda," he said brusquely. "Perhaps Miss Ivanov will pay better attention to what you're saying this time. Apparently she was distracted."

Miranda flushed and Torrin felt herself matching her. She stared blandly at the mountain of a man, willing her face to stop flaming.

"I said that on top of the cost of the land, the 'expedience fee' the bureaucrats will charge amounts to two million credits. On top of that is the cost of the land at three million creds, equipment at five million, and hiring of workers at two million. That brings us to a total of twelve million credits."

Torrin sat back. She could cover that amount but not with what she currently had with her. Before the customs officer had taken her cut, the platinum she'd brought with her would have barely covered the price. But these types of things always had some wiggle room. It was time for her to earn her keep. Audra might be a better negotiator, but Torrin was a very close second. She grinned and leaned forward. O'Toole caught the look in her eye, and the look in his matched hers in anticipation.

Two hours later after an extended negotiation, Torrin managed to talk O'Toole down by one-third of his price. Part of that had been because she'd come with platinum, not credits. Credits were easily traceable by the League. Platinum could be melted down and reappear in coffers for almost any reason. Torrin's instincts about O'Toole had been right. He might run a legitimate business enterprise, but he hadn't always. Likely, a sizable portion of his current enterprise wasn't exactly aboveboard either. This was the kind of man she wanted to be in business with. Someone who could cut corners, but who had an air of legitimacy. They would have to keep an eye on him and eventually wean him out of their part of the business, but until that needed to happen, both parties would benefit greatly from the partnership. In any case, they wouldn't need to part ways for the better part of a decade.

She made a mental note to have someone dig into his other dealings. Knowing the less savory parts of his business would help to protect their business if the deal went sideways. It never hurt to find out about new suppliers, especially if they operated on the shadier side of legitimacy.

"I'm glad that's over, Ivanov," O'Toole growled. "You've barely left me any room for profit."

Torrin grinned. "There's room for both of us to profit and a chunk left over for the bureaucrats in your back pocket. We're going to make you rich. Richer."

"I know. That's the only reason I'm letting you fleece me like this." He pushed himself away from the table. Their meals had been long since cleared. Miranda had nibbled away at her salad while the two of them had sparred, pausing to pull up numbers on her tablet when asked.

"It's a pleasure doing business with you."

"We're done with business, now it's time for a little pleasure. It's a custom on Castor III for businessmen to take some time off together after a negotiation. It shows that there are no hard feelings over the results and it cuts down on…forced renegotiation, shall we say."

"You mean you get drunk together so you're less likely to knife your competitor in the kidneys?"

O'Toole laughed raucously, his whole upper body shaking with the force of his mirth. "That's direct, but accurate."

"Who am I to go against such a sensible local custom? What do you have in mind?"

"There's a bar I'm fond of. They have an excellent selection of local beverages and some imported alcohol."

"Lead on."

O'Toole stood up and held out an arm for Miranda. His bulk dwarfed her in almost comical proportions. She accepted the arm graciously but dropped it as soon as she was standing. Torrin was left to fend for herself and she was grateful for it. If he'd tried to help her up, she may very well have laughed in his face.

They walked out of the restaurant, the mountainous businessman waving to the maitre d' on the way out. The man nodded at him and they continued on without paying. Torrin made a note to have the employee she assigned to look into O'Toole add the restaurant to the list of assets to investigate.

An antigrav car pulled up as they exited the restaurant's front doors. It hovered in unnerving silence. Torrin was always a little nervous around antigravs. She knew the science behind them and had no reason to believe it wasn't solid, but something about relying on an invisible force to keep something suspended in the air freaked her out a little bit. At least with her ship, she knew that the ship's propulsion would keep it moving, but antigravity struck her as being somehow unsafe.

O'Toole held open the door and Torrin ducked into the car's capacious passenger space. She sat against the far door where she could survey the car's entire interior. Politeness dictated that she should have taken the facing seat, but that would have put her back to the driver. She preferred not to have her back to anyone, especially someone she didn't know.

Miranda clambered in and settled herself next to the smuggler. She had to press herself against Torrin's side to allow O'Toole enough room to squeeze by. Torrin thought it strange that Miranda would sit next to her until she saw how much room O'Toole took up in the opposite seat. He lounged there. She knew he hadn't missed how she had positioned herself, and he seemed to approve of her choice.

The car took off soundlessly, rising and falling gently as it skimmed over the roads. It was a very smooth ride, but it didn't feel quite real. The driver took a corner with enough speed that Miranda slid into Torrin with a small squeak.

"Excuse me," she said and moved herself back over again.

The drive was a short one, but Torrin could tell they'd gone to a much different part of town when she stepped out of the car. Gone were the trappings of high-class luxury, the shine and elegant glitz. The area was more working class and a half step above seedy. O'Toole led them up to the door of a brightly lit establishment. Holograms flickered above the door and windows, looping to promise fulfillment of various vices, the least of which was drinking.

"Do you always bring your secretary on these excursions?" Torrin asked the burly businessman.

"Why not? She earned it." He seemed surprised that she'd care. "Does it bother you?"

"Not at all. It's just not what I expected."

"I'm sure there are many things about me that would surprise you, Ivanov."

Torrin was pleased to hear that he'd dropped the Miss. While some people might have taken it as a sign of politeness, she was fairly certain it was a sign of some subtle misogyny on his part, that he'd been reminding her of her status as a woman and her inherent inferiority. She could only hope that their negotiations had disabused him of his more antiquated notions.

O'Toole held open the door for Miranda and walked in after her, leaving Torrin to bring up the rear. The bar's interior delivered on everything the exterior had promised. A long bar, brightly lit by multicolored strips of light, dominated one wall of the establishment. Beyond that a darkened dance floor was pierced by holograms and lasers. It pulsed with human bodies and a deep bass beat. Above the mass of humanity, narrow catwalks held nearly naked men and women who writhed and ground along to the pounding music.

"Grab one of the booths at the back," O'Toole shouted. "I'll get drinks."

If there were booths at the back then Torrin couldn't see them through the gyrating crowd. Miranda grabbed her hand and pulled her through the throng. Torrin was about to object over the contact until she realized that without it, she likely would have been separated from the petite secretary. As she made her way through the press, men and women alike pressed themselves into her and rubbed their bodies against hers. By the time she got to the table with Miranda, she'd been kissed twice and thoroughly fondled. The atmosphere was electric and she found herself buoyed along by the excitement. Miranda was flushed and her hair was slightly mussed. She'd obviously gotten the same treatment Torrin had.

"It can get a little wild in here," Miranda said, pressing her mouth against Torrin's ear in order to be heard. Torrin slid in on one side of the booth and Miranda followed her. O'Toole would fill the other side completely.

"I can see that," Torrin replied loudly. "It's very...exciting."

Miranda laughed. Her laugh was deep, throaty and caressing. Torrin shivered slightly. She'd never heard Jak laugh like that. She rarely heard Jak laugh at all. And just like that, her burgeoning good mood was snuffed out.

"What's wrong?" Miranda asked, sensing Torrin's sudden change of mood.

"Nothing. I remembered some...thing."

"Someone by the looks of it. Don't worry, we'll make sure you forget her, for tonight at least."

Torrin smiled sadly. "I don't know that it's possible. She really meant something to me."

O'Toole materialized by the side of the table, glasses in his capacious hands. "Miranda, what did you say to sadden our guest so?"

"Nothing a few drinks won't help," Miranda replied with a smile.

He set the glasses on the table. The glasses were small, but he'd managed to bring six to the table. Their contents were a brilliant orange that glowed from within.

"These are a local alcoholic delicacy. They're known colloquially as 'Black Holes' because people tend to wake up the next day with large chunks of their nights missing." He pushed a glass toward her. Torrin picked it up and tried swirl the liquid around. The orange goo barely moved. It seemed to be in a semiliquid, not-quite-gelatinous form.

Miranda grinned. "The texture takes some getting used to. Best way to tackle it is to sling it right down." She put words into action and tossed back the glass O'Toole had placed in front of her. Torrin watched, fascinated as the glow from the drink traced its way down her throat and disappeared into her chest.

She picked up the glass and, unwilling to be outdone by a little slip of a woman, she downed the strange beverage. The Black Hole coated and burned its way down her esophagus. The gelatinous texture ensured that the burn lingered, not unpleasantly. A moment later the alcohol hit her full force. Torrin coughed and slapped her palm down on the table, eyes watering. O'Toole and Miranda shared a chuckle at her reaction. She shook her head. Already, an enjoyable buzz was starting to form.

"Have another," the businessman roared and passed her a second glass. She downed that one also. Her buzz intensified and everything seemed so much more manageable. Miranda downed one and her boss disappeared in search of more drinks.

"What do you think of Castor III?" Miranda murmured into Torrin's ear. The secretary's breath on Torrin's ear sent pleasant shivers down her spine.

"It's something else." Torrin wasn't far gone enough to tell her the truth. That she thought the planet was at an awkward stage between backwater and civilization and reflected badly on both stages. There was enough money flowing into Castor III for a lot of people to do whatever they wanted and not enough regulation to stop them from doing so. It was all part of a regular pattern she'd seen with League worlds new to the organization. In another ten years or so, the major merchant families of the inner worlds would be exerting their influence and creating more regulation until the most viable industries were under their control.

Torrin didn't plan on letting her company's hard work be swallowed up by the powerful merchant families. Ten years was all she needed to gain a foothold in the planet's industrial base and develop a suitable political candidate to resist the families' manipulation. O'Toole might even be a good choice. He certainly had local influence.

"Aren't you sweet," Miranda said. "It's a shithole, but you knew that. You wouldn't be here if it wasn't."

"I don't know what you mean," Torrin protested. "I'm only a businesswoman from the Fringes trying to make it into the big time."

Miranda snickered, her breath again sending more delicious shivers down Torrin's back. "The lady doth protest too much, methinks."

"Did you quote Shakespeare to me?"

"I did. I have a passion for ancient Earth art, especially literature. The fact that you know that also proves that you're more than a simple Fringe spacer. Were you educated in the inner worlds?" Miranda slid closer to Torrin, pressing their hips together and turning her body toward the smuggler's.

"Frozen hells, no." Torrin couldn't hide the disgust in her tone. She shifted to open some room between them, but Miranda cozied right back up to her again. "I'm more than happy never to go that deep into League space. I'm very happy out here on the Fringes."

"So if you're not from the inner worlds, but you're well-educated, what does that make you? I've heard some interesting rumors about an elusive planet full of women who don't bow to any government. Women who craft items of a quality seen nowhere else in the galaxy."

O'Toole's return saved Torrin from having to answer. She pounced on a glass full of an unfamiliar dark liquid and tossed it back. It turned out to be a more conventional parathenol. It reminded her of well-aged bourbon with the heat and smoothness, but there was much more of a kick to it, if not nearly as much as the Black Holes had. She slid a glass over to Miranda, who downed it casually. O'Toole helped himself to a couple of drinks. He beamed genially over at the two of them on the other side of the table.

"You two look like you're getting along mighty fine."

"Oh, we are," Miranda replied. She snuggled in closer to Torrin and ran a hand lightly down her thigh. Torrin started at the contact.

He smiled benevolently. Now that they were out of their negotiations, the relationship between the two of them was completely different. There was a level of deep comfort between them. If it hadn't been for an obvious age difference, Torrin would have figured that they'd slept together at some point in the past.

Miranda seemed to be doing her best to crawl into Torrin's lap. Torrin knocked back another glass of the dark parathenol.

"Do you want to dance?" she asked Miranda in desperation. The little redhead was getting too cozy for comfort. Getting her out on the dance floor would give her a chance to open some space between them.

A gleam lit Miranda's eyes and she agreed eagerly and led Torrin into the crush of human bodies. Almost immediately, Torrin realized her error. There were so many people on the dance floor that Miranda was pressed against her. She didn't have any problem with it either, given how she was dancing against Torrin, grinding into her. Normally Torrin loved to dance, but somehow it felt wrong. She couldn't exactly remember why.

"Loosen up," Miranda said, standing on her tiptoes to yell into Torrin's ear over the music. "Go with it."

It sounded like good advice to her. She was feeling so good and Miranda felt amazing against her. She tilted her head down toward Miranda. A chime rang through her head and Torrin looked up, toward the catwalk with its nearly naked dancers. She realized that a number of them were doing far more than dancing and she gaped at the writhing bodies before remembering that someone was trying to contact her.

"Tien?"

"Torrin, a communications packet has come through from Laiya."

That couldn't be good. Torrin removed her hands from Miranda. How had she ended up with one hand cupped around the secretary's ass? Miranda made a disappointed moue at the loss of contact, but Torrin barely noticed. It was hard to concentrate on what Tien was saying over the thud of the music, not to mention the little hands roaming over her body.

"Miranda, I have to go." She captured Miranda's hands and removed them from her abdomen. "I'm sorry. It was very nice to meet you." Her exit was lame, bordering on rude, she knew it but didn't care. She needed to hear Laiya's message. Looking over the crowd, she saw O'Toole watching them indulgently from the booth. She raised a hand to him. "Say goodbye to O'Toole for me."

"You're leaving?" Miranda pouted prettily. "You can't leave now. We're just starting to have fun."

Torrin shook her head, the room spinning a bit. The invitation was tempting, but she had responsibilities. And then there was Jak. Suddenly, what Miranda was offering held no allure for her at all.

"Sorry, something's come up." Torrin pushed her way through the gyrating crowd toward the edge of the dance floor. She dodged flailing limbs and grasping hands. Finally free of the throng, Torrin made for the door. The cool night air helped clear her head, and she inhaled deeply before raising her hand to activate the subdermal transmitter.

"Tien, play the message, please." She started walking toward the lights of a major thoroughfare not more than a block away.

"Very well, Torrin." After a short pause, Laiya's worried voice filled her head.

"Torrin, the situation on Tyndall's changed. I need backup, the store's been attacked. You need to get someone over here to help out as soon as possible. I don't know if I can protect the store on my own."

"Tien, forward this message through to Audra. We need the Ruling Council to approve a squad of Banshees. Let her know I'm cutting short my trip here and heading to Tyndall right now." Torrin ran for the lights.

CHAPTER NINETEEN

"What you need is a keeper." A putrid stench accompanied the whispered words. They caressed the side of her neck like clammy fingers and fear rose with the gorge in the back of her throat.

Hutchinson. Torrin tried to move but couldn't; her feet were rooted to the ground. She looked down and saw that she was buried up to her ankles. No matter how hard she pulled on her feet, they wouldn't move.

Hardness pressed against her hip and she twisted to get away, but hands like shackles held her still. "When I'm done with you, you'll be addicted to this."

"F-f-fuck off, Hutchinson." Suddenly his face was in front of her, and Torrin screamed at the nightmare that filled her vision. Hutchinson's face was gray but still recognizable. Blood oozed down from the crater where his forehead ended. A fetid miasma rolled over her and she clenched her jaw to keep from retching.

"Deviant filth." The insult came from her other side and Torrin looked over in time to see McCullock pulling back his hand to hit her. Hutchinson grinned and held her arms to her side as the Devonite swung.

Torrin screamed again and sat up, pain flooding her head as if she actually had been pummeled. Her next awareness was of a horrible taste in her mouth. Her tongue tasted like she'd been nursing a bottle of mud, then chased it down with bourbon. It was dry to boot. She smacked her lips experimentally without much relief. The next thing to come to her notice was the dull headache in her temples. She'd been through enough hangovers to know that if she moved the headache wouldn't be dull for much longer.

"Tien, lights," she moaned, wondering what had possessed her to drink so much. The lights in her cabin flashed on, and she clamped her eyelids shut, wondering why Tien had set them to be so much brighter than usual. Between the nightmare and a hangover of epic proportions, she wanted to curl up and die for a little bit. But she had work to do.

"Tien, dim the lights to half power." After waiting a moment for the AI to oblige, Torrin cracked open one eyelid. To her relief, the light no longer stabbed into her corneas. Swinging her legs over the side of the bed, she worked on gathering enough energy to stand. There was a glass of water on the bedside and she grabbed it with trembling hands. She needed to rehydrate and quickly.

Fresh pain exploded in her head when her alarm went off.

"Damn it, Tien! You couldn't have deactivated the alarm when you saw I was awake?"

The racket terminated immediately, and Torrin whimpered in relief.

"Apologies, Torrin. You were most adamant that you be awake when we arrived at our first jump point."

"Damn AI," Torrin grumbled as she stood up. The room stayed upright, which was a relief. Even more of a relief was that her headache didn't get any worse. She looked down at herself. She still wore the same jumpsuit she'd worn to her meeting with O'Toole. No point in changing it now, she thought. She was on her way to get frozen. She felt a grim smile stretch her cheeks. The cryo hangover would be far worse than the one the cryo process would erase, but there was no point in dwelling on that. She needed to get moving. Duty called.

Thankfully, the lights in the hallway were also at half power. Torrin gave Tien a little mental pat on the back as she made her slow and deliberate way to the bridge.

"Let's see your navigation solutions for the jumps to Tyndall," Torrin said when she arrived on the bridge. The main viewscreen changed from a view of points of light hanging on unfathomable blackness to a chart plotting Tien's proposed course to Tyndall.

"Looks good," she said. "But vary the first jump. Let's go out at another vector. No sense giving away all our intentions."

"Very well, Torrin." The ship accepted her changes without any comment, as usual. Sometimes Torrin thought it would be nice if Tien might actually argue with her. The AI tried so hard to pass for human, but her constant acquiescence foiled those efforts. Torrin found herself missing the arguments she'd had with Jak while they'd traveled through the Haefonian wilderness. Everything had been so much simpler when all they had to do was stay alive, just the two of them. She'd known who the enemy was and who she could count on. Her independence was something she'd valued for so long, but right now all she felt was alone.

It was a few hops to Tyndall and she needed to get to the cryochamber. The situation there sounded like a complete mess. She hoped it wouldn't take too long to sort out. Once she had completed her business there, she could head back to Nadierzda and get down to the more pressing business of getting Jak back.

* * *

The slap to her back made her spew her mouthful of beer across the table. The table's occupants broke out into raucous laughter, and Jak wiped her mouth ruefully.

"Sorry about that," Olesya gasped between gales of laughter, "but that was awesome."

"Glad I could entertain you," Jak replied dryly and took another sip of her beer, watching the table's occupants out of the corner of her eye, much to everyone's amusement. Laughter rose above the bar's already high level of ambient noise.

She'd been avoiding Axe's drink invitations for days, content to split her time between her room and the range. Finally, the captain had showed up along with her entire crew. The Banshees, with Jak in reluctant tow, had taken over one of the popular drinking spots near the base. By the shouts of welcome that had accompanied their entrance into the establishment, they were well-liked. It was more social contact than she'd ever been subjected to at one time. In addition to Axe and Olesya, there had been another lieutenant, three sergeants, eight privates, a pilot and a medic. They were all doing their best to drink each other under the table and had welcomed Jak into their banter without blinking an eye. Unfortunately, that resulted in well-timed slaps to the back while she was trying to drink.

She caught Olesya raising her hand again and spun on her seat to fix her with a steely glare. When Olesya burst into another fit of laughter, Jak had to join in.

"You're going to have to get up earlier than that to get the drop on me a second time," Jak warned the lieutenant.

"We'll see about that," the lieutenant replied cheekily.

"So, Captain," Perez broke in. She was a short woman, right about Jak's height and sporting a similar haircut. The amount of alcohol she had consumed was evident in the dark flush of her tan cheeks. "What's your longest kill, anyway?"

"It's hard to say," Jak hedged. The women of Axe's Banshee unit had been trying to pin her down on the particulars. She wasn't comfortable dishing; it felt too much like bragging. "They're usually difficult to confirm out in the field."

"Don't give us that crap. I've known a few women who considered themselves markswomen. One of them once hit a target a couple of clicks out. She was real proud of that."

"I'm sure that was very good for her."

"But not for you, is that right, Jak?" Olesya eyed her closely. The lieutenant was a strange mixture of perception and obliviousness. Jak was starting to suspect that the state of befuddled oblivion was an act.

"It's a good shot," Jak protested.

"C'mon, Captain. Tell us what your best is." Perez wasn't giving up and the rest of the women at the table had caught wind of the conversation and had leaned in to see if Jak was finally going to give up the answer they'd been waiting a long time to hear.

"Perez, don't hassle the captain," Axe barked. "If she doesn't want to say, she doesn't have to."

"But, Captain Axe, I want to know how good she is." Another Banshee added her voice to the request.

"It was a little over four clicks," Jak said into her beer.

"I didn't hear you," Perez complained.

"Holy crap, over four thousand meters," Olesya crowed on top of the private. The women gathered around the table exchanged glances of disbelief, then stared at Jak.

"There's no way," Perez scoffed. Axe cuffed her on the back of the head with the heel of her palm.

"You asked the captain a question. Don't argue with her when she answers you." A trace of doubt lingered on Axe's face, but Jak was happy for the support of the other captain. She looked at Jak. "Do you want her to give you twenty?"

"That's all right. I'd have problems believing it too if all I'd ever shot was those little plasma rifles you all seem to prefer. Bullets slice more cleanly through the air. More aerodynamic than a shapeless mass of flaming plasma."

"I suppose. But then, plasma doesn't punch holes through the sides of ships and open them up to the vacuum."

Jak nodded to acknowledge the point. She hadn't considered that, and it made a certain amount of sense. Avoiding a vacuum-sucking hole seemed like sound advice to her.

"Keep an eye out for Perez," Olesya whispered too loudly in Jak's ear. "She broke up with her girlfriend about a week ago and she's on the prowl. This is her way of getting to know you. Next she'll be challenging you to an arm wrestling match. After that, the next round of wrestling gets even more interesting. She likes officers. Comes off as a top, but she's a total bottom in bed."

Perez overheard every word, exactly as she'd been meant to. She flushed a brilliant crimson and buried her head in her drink but didn't refute any of the lieutenant's outrageous statements. Her squad mates enjoyed her discomfort immensely.

"She's got good taste," a private piped up from down the table. Surprised, Jak looked up into the almond-shaped blue eyes of the blond Banshee. The blonde winked broadly at her and ran the tip of her tongue over her lower lip. This time it was Jak's turn to blush.

"The more you blush, the worse they're going to be, you know," Axe said to her. "They're a bunch of uppity bitches."

"And we're all yours, Captain," the group chorused back at her. They'd obviously heard the complaint before. They raised their glasses to each other and slammed back their beer as quickly as possible. Their mugs were emptied within seconds and one of the women was sent to the bar to get another round. She was the youngest in the group. Olesya was the oldest, but most of the women had the look of experience to them. There was tightness around their eyes that spoke of a keen awareness for their surroundings even though they were unwinding at home. If something went down, the happy, carefree masks would fall at once.

The woman returned with an armful of beer steins. She was wearing half their contents by the time she got back to the table, but she'd brought enough for them all. While the Banshees were busy with their next round of beers, Jak pulled Axe aside.

"I have a hypothetical question for you."

"Hypotheticals?" The captain raised her brows at Jak. "I'm not so good with hypotheticals. Give me a target and a time frame and I'll give you a set of tactics and a strategically sound plan, but that other stuff... That's for the spooks or someone above my pay grade."

"All I need is an idea. How would you go about freeing an entire population of women?"

"An entire population? Jeez, I don't know that we could do that even if we got all the Banshee units together. Why?"

"Where I'm from, half the women on the planet are in slavery as bad as you've seen or worse." With broad strokes she filled Axe in on the condition of the Orthodoxan women. Axe's face darkened perceptibly the longer she talked. By the end of her description, the captain looked ready to punch somebody.

"That's messed up. We could help you out on a small-scale operation or even a series of smaller operations, but you're talking about freeing entire cities." Axe shook her head regretfully. "This would be something you'd have to take to the Ruling Council. Actually, you *should* take it to the Ruling Council. If they know what's going on, they're sure to do something about it."

She placed a comforting hand on Jak's shoulder. "Is this what you came out of?"

Jak shook her head. "No, my family was on the other side of things. My prospects would have been better. Not great, but better. Then my father decided that instead of being his oldest daughter, I should become his youngest son. Joined the army after he died. My brother and I ended up in the sniper corps. He got killed, I got sent out on a mission to kill Torrin and rescued her instead. One thing led to another and now I'm here."

Axe stared at her. "One of these days I'm going to need to get the whole story from you. Sounds to me like there's a hell of a lot more going on there than what you're saying. But not tonight. I'm more than half drunk, and my sweetie's at home waiting up for me."

Jak shrugged and swigged the last bit of beer out of her glass. Maybe Tanith was right. If only she would stop nagging her about talking to a shrink. She did feel a little better for telling some of her story, even in such vague terms. Axe hadn't recoiled in shock but had taken her at face value. Maybe she could open up a little more to these women.

The captain turned back toward the table and plopped her mug down. "That's it, my lovelies, I'm done." A chorus of boos met her statement. She waved them off with a flip of the hand and made her way around the table. Jak marveled at the easy camaraderie she shared with the women of her command. The captain made sure to speak with each of them and to clasp a hand, grasp a shoulder or smack a rump. The women responded well to her; they held her in the highest respect.

On her way by, Axe didn't forget Jak and patted her familiarly on the back. "We'll see you tomorrow afternoon. I know you've got the newbies for your morning training. Besides, half of these bitches will still be hung over by the time we get to you, so best not to push things, right?" Her voice was pitched loud enough for her Banshees to hear her, and they razzed her as she made her way out of the bar.

With the captain gone, the women started splitting off into smaller groups. A group of four decided to play an unfamiliar bar game they called curling. It involved throwing stone disks down a long, smooth surface at the back of the establishment. A couple of groups ordered an obscene number of shots and really got down to the business of getting drunk.

There were a few couples in the unit, and they found themselves some quiet corners where they could make out in peace.

"You wanna arm wrestle?" Perez asked from Jak's elbow. Jak was barely able to restrain herself from jumping. She hadn't heard the private approaching.

"Uh, no thanks, I'm good."

"We can engage in some other type of wrestling, if you want. I'll spot you the first two falls."

"No really. I'm fine."

"Your loss." Perez shrugged and wandered off to join a group of women playing a drinking game that seemed to involve downing shots of parathenol, then balancing the glass on their foreheads.

"Told you." Olesya wandered over, drinking a beer right from the metal canister. "She's nothing if not predictable. Made her way through most of the officers on base with that line. Most of them go for it too."

"Yeah, well. I'm not most officers." *Most officers don't get betrayed by the planet hero.* Jak studied the bottom of her empty mug, then stood up. "I think that's going to be it for me too. I should head back. I do have a morning training session, after all."

Olesya took another pull from the canister, draining it quickly and put it down on the table. "I'll come with you. All this crew is going to do is get drunk, then get laid. I'm getting too old for this shit."

Jak followed Olesya into the cool dampness of the night. They were only a few kilometers from the base, and they started walking in companionable silence.

"So I wanted to ask you something," Jak finally said.

"What's that?"

"Could you get me back to my home planet? You have a ship, after all."

Her question was met with a long silence. "I wondered if you might ask me that," Olesya finally said. "Are you sure it's what you really want? This probably isn't a decision you should make when you're still worked up about Torrin."

"It's my choice. What's your answer?"

"We can't, Jak. I'm sorry. The Banshees go where the Ruling Council sends us, we don't get to make side jaunts. You'd have to convince them, which would be a hard sell. If you couldn't do that, your best bet would be to get a ride from Troika."

Jak flushed. There was no way she would ask Torrin for anything. "That's not happening."

"I didn't think so, but her people are the ones who do the most traveling around the galaxy, after us, of course. If you're really desperate, you might try Tanith. She has her own ship."

"I don't think Tanith is going to give me a ride back home any time soon."

"Probably not. You are her new favorite."

"That's not fair. I do my job and I do it well. She appreciates that is all."

"There was a time she appreciated Torrin too. They were best friends when I first knew Torrin, but they had a falling out not long after they joined up. Something about a girl they both had their eyes on."

Everything kept coming back to Torrin on this planet. The only way she would be free of the woman would be to be free of Nadierzda. "You and Torrin joined the militia at the same time, right?" Where had that question come from? She didn't want to think about Torrin anymore; she was tired of the ache in her heart. And yet, talking about her helped a little bit, even if only for the moment.

"That's right, I joined up a few days after Torrin and Tanith did," Olesya said. "We went through boot together."

"Then why do you look so much…ummm." Jak trailed off, unsure how to phrase the question without potentially angering the lieutenant. Olesya grinned at her.

"Why do I look like an old bag when she still looks like she's in the prime of her youth?"

"That wasn't exactly what I was going to say, but pretty much."

"She's spent way more time in cryostasis than I have, the way she goes traipsing across this arm of the galaxy. I'm gone from home pretty often, but nothing like her. Sometimes I think she's spent half her life in stasis. Keeps a girl young. Also keeps her isolated."

"I guess that makes sense. Do you know why she left the Banshees?" She could feel the lieutenant regarding her in the darkness.

"You have a lot of questions about someone that you're broken up with."

Jak shrugged. She was still incredibly angry with Torrin for the betrayal, but at the same time the smuggler was the one person she felt close to. Hearing about Torrin was a bit like picking at a scab. It hurt, but there was satisfaction in the pain nonetheless.

"After a while she couldn't stand seeing the women we pulled out of those situations. I think she saw her bio-mother in them. The ones we got out were bad, but the ones we were too late to help hurt her more. That's when she started to really pull back from people. Don't get me wrong. She has a ton of friends, people love being around her. She's funny and boisterous, but no one really gets that close. Once that starts to happen, she pulls back. She's been that way for years now."

"So there was never really any hope for us, was there?"

"Now that's an interesting question."

"Why do you say that?"

"I heard that she broke into your room, is that true?" At Jak's nod, Olesya continued. "That's the interesting part. Usually, she up and leaves with no warning or contact. I was surprised to hear that she'd been caught with another woman while she was still with you. I haven't known her to do that before. It's not the nicest thing to bounce from one lover to the next, but she'd always been exclusive with her lovers, even if only for a short time.

"And there's the fact that she came back after you. When the split is made, that's it for her. She's almost always friendly with her ex-lovers. A lot of them actually end up being good friends with her after they get over being hurt. But one thing she's never done before is try to get one of them back."

Jak wanted to say something, but she didn't want Olesya to hear the emotion in her voice. Tears rolled down her face. She didn't know why she was crying. The lieutenant's explanation had made her feel like maybe things weren't so bad after all. Maybe there was some other explanation for Torrin's actions. She wished she'd listened to Torrin when she'd been in her room.

"Are you okay?" Olesya asked.

"I'm fine. Got some dust in my eye."

"Sure you did. Road's real dusty."

Unable to restrain herself, Jak snorted a watery laugh at Olesya's dry tone. Ahead of them, the base's gates came into view, the lights winking at them in the dark. The two sentries nodded at them as they passed through.

Olesya grabbed her elbow at the square. "Barracks are over there." She gestured in a direction that was the opposite of the way Jak had turned. "How much did you drink, anyways?"

"I barely had any."

"Then we need to get you out more often. That went right to your head."

Jak didn't feel drunk, but she didn't say anything as Olesya walked her to the barracks. She'd been convinced that she needed to go the opposite way. But had she been heading to the barracks? She wasn't sure. As she turned to leave, the lieutenant caught her in a large hug. Jak's tears threatened again, but she quelled the surge of emotions quickly.

"Don't worry about it. You'll get this figured out."

"Thanks."

The lieutenant gave her another quick squeeze, then released her and tossed off a quick salute. Jak returned the salute, which still felt odd compared to the one she'd used in the Devonite army. Olesya headed off across the square to the Banshee barracks. She whistled a jaunty tune that Jak vaguely recognized. If the song was the one she knew, the lyrics would have made her blush to hear them. As it was, she just shook her head and entered the barracks. Tanith had been right; talking to someone had helped.

CHAPTER TWENTY

The old-fashioned bell at the top of the door jangled cheerily when Torrin walked into the shop. The Troika Corp. store on Tyndall was small, little more than a glorified convenience store. The usual staples could be purchased there: groceries and basic tools. They shared shelves with more exotic imports, including the beautiful ceramics which were Nadierzda's chief export, not that anyone else in the galaxy knew that, though Miranda's suppositions had come uncomfortably close.

The smell of burned wood permeated the cramped store, and she peered into the gloom trying to find its source. The store wouldn't open for a few hours yet, but she wanted to touch base with Laiya to get a handle on the situation. She had a key and had let herself in the main door. To her left, a board creaked and Torrin ducked as something whistled past her head. She scuttled back a few steps, hands raised in front of her.

"Move again, and you'll get one in the gut. The next one after that goes through your head." A shadowy figure moved out from behind the shelves at the back of the store, plasma rifle in her hands. It pointed straight at Torrin without wavering.

"Laiya, it's me. Torrin." To her relief, the rifle's muzzle lowered a trifle.

"Is that really you? I thought you weren't coming by for a couple weeks yet."

A light flicked on overhead and Torrin blinked in the sudden glare. Laiya stood in front of her, skin dark, with a mass of dreadlocks pulled back into a ponytail as thick around as her wrist. To her relief, the weapon in the shopkeeper's hands was no longer pointed at her, but she hadn't relinquished it completely.

"I was in the neighborhood when I got your relay message. I figured I'd come down as soon as I heard since I was planning on stopping by anyway. Lots of my plans have been disrupted lately." Torrin gestured with her chin. "Have you needed that a lot recently?"

"Unfortunately. Things had been a little off of late, but everything came to a head out of nowhere."

"Off?"

"At first it was nothing I could put my finger on. Sales were down a little, and people avoided talking to me on the street, and there was the graffiti problem. Any one of those things by themselves wouldn't have bothered me too much, but all together and they've been making me jumpy." Laiya hoisted the rifle, hitching it up to her shoulder. "Then a few days ago, someone tried to burn down the store."

"You're kidding!" That explained the burned smell. "Are you okay? Was anything damaged?"

"I'm fine, but I haven't slept since then, not really." Looking closer, Torrin could see the dark circles under Laiya's eyes. She looked exhausted, her eyes dull and half-lidded. "Even though no one's really been willing to be seen talking to me, they all pitched in quick enough when the fire started."

"Not surprising. The buildings are all wood and practically built on top of each other. It wouldn't take much to take out half the town."

"It's funny, though. Things didn't get really tense until I started asking around about Neal."

"Who'd want to protect that lowlife?"

"Someone must. I haven't had any real customers since the fire. Also, the sheriff's giving me the runaround on the cause."

"I'll talk to him, see what I can find out. I have no problems leaning on him if I need to. Any news on Neal?"

"It's funny, I got word yesterday that he'd resurfaced. You were right, the shakes must have gotten to him. He's hiding out in the dirtiest, meanest bar in Dowson. The Posse's Noose, I think it is."

"That's a cut below his usual watering hole."

Laiya snorted in disgust. "Maybe he thinks he's being clever. He's diving head first into a bottle and shows no interest in coming up for air."

"Good, that'll slow him down. He'd better not pull another disappearing act now that I'm in town. I'll have to get after him right away. When will the saloon open?"

"Not for a few hours yet."

"Since I'm here, why don't I fill you in on what's been going on back on Nadi. Then you can give me all the details on what's been going on here." Torrin's thoughts were dark as she followed Laiya into the back. Laiya had every right to be on edge. It would be bad enough without knowing how badly the last deal Torrin had brokered here had almost turned out. For a moment she couldn't tell if she should be enraged or delighted that Neal had sent her to Haefen and into Jak's arms. Time would tell, she supposed. If she couldn't get Jak back, she could always come back and string him up by the short hairs. Her informant had always been a drunk, but it was disquieting to hear he'd taken a sudden turn for the worse. There had to be a connection between that and the false information he'd given her, she knew. The question was if she could tease it out and follow it back to the source. It was unlikely Neal was the mastermind here, not if he was now trying to drown himself in a whiskey bottle.

Laiya led her through the back and up a flight of narrow stairs. The boards creaked loudly underfoot.

"If you need to get that fixed, you can expense it out," Torrin said.

"Actually, I like the noise. No one's going to surprise me coming up these stairs." That made sense, but it underscored Laiya's discomfort and worry. When she'd first been assigned to Tyndall, Laiya had been practically giddy. She was young and the prospect of getting off Nadierzda and seeing other parts of the galaxy had appealed to her. Unlike many of the women who left Nadi through various jobs with Troika, Laiya was a lesbian. She hadn't left Nadi because she didn't fit in, but because she wanted to see more of what life had to offer on the Fringes. The excitement was gone, replaced by a simmering tension.

The apartment above the store was small but cozy. Laiya wove her way through furniture and twitched the curtain aside a hair to glance out into the predawn gloom.

"Nothing," she said, turning back to Torrin, "but it always feels like someone's watching."

"You know what I like to say. Just because you're paranoid…"

"…it doesn't follow that you're wrong." Laiya smiled tiredly at the old saw. Anyone who'd spent any time with Torrin knew it was one of her favorite sayings. A healthy level of paranoia had saved her skin on more than one occasion, and she did her best to impart that philosophy to her employees.

"And you have every right to be paranoid. Apparently someone really is out to get you. Or us."

"You want something to drink?"

"No, it's a little too early for me."

"I was going to brew tea, nothing alcoholic."

"Oh. In that case, I'd love a cup."

Laiya walked over to the small kitchen area and put a kettle on the stove. Tyndall was backward enough that the stoves were gas powered. The ones on Nadi were geothermal, much better for the environment. The old-fashioned kettle came to a boil quickly, filling the room with its cheerful whistle. As Laiya bustled about the tiny space, Torrin made herself comfortable at the kitchen table and filled her in on Troika's plans for cybernetic implants and the implications for their planet and the women living on it. Laiya made the appropriate noises at all the right times, but the third time she dropped a spoon on the floor, Torrin knew she was distracted.

"So fill me in. What exactly has been going on here?"

"Like I said earlier, it was hard to pin down at first." Laiya put Torrin's mug in front of her with enough force that some tea slopped over the brim. With a harried smile of apology, Laiya quickly wiped up the small wet spot. She dropped herself into the other chair at the small table.

"The first thing was some graffiti carved into the side of the building." She blew on the hot surface of the tea, brow creased in concentration. "It said 'bitches go home' or something like that. I didn't think anything of it. It was a pain to cover up since it was carved into the wood, not painted on. But as quickly as I removed it, somebody made sure it was carved into another part of the building. I've been taking it off, but it kept getting put back up. Then they started burning it onto the wall, like they were branding it or something."

"That's not good. Was there any other vandalism before the fire?"

Laiya shook her head, gazing deep into her tea, as if trying to see an answer to her fears in its depths. Torrin took a cautious sip of her own tea and was pleasantly surprised at the full, almost fruity flavor. She didn't usually spend much time on Tyndall, just enough time to check up on the store and touch base with her informants—mostly Neal. This was the first time she'd tried the tea. There wasn't much tea-drinking going on with Neal.

"Is the tea local?" she asked.

Laiya nodded.

"You'll have to let me know where you get it from. This would be a great export, if someone else hasn't sewn it up already."

"You're always looking ahead to the next angle, aren't you?" Laiya smiled.

"That's my job. It keeps us all employed. So tell me what else has been going on."

"That's even harder to pin down. At least with the vandalism, I had something to show the sheriff. But then I started to feel like people were afraid to be seen with me. Like I said, sales are down. It's not that nobody comes in, but I haven't seen most of my regulars for a while. The ones that do come in are in and out in a hurry, and there are a lot of new faces coming into the store. Mostly men. I'm assuming they're coming in from the ranches, but when they're in the store, my regulars barely stick around at all. Since the fire, the only people I've seen are men I don't recognize, and they never buy. All they do is wander around the store watching me out of the corner of their eyes."

"Are the new faces putting the screws to your customers?"

"If they are, it isn't where I can see them. I never see them talking to my customers, but as soon as they see the newcomers, they take off."

"What do the newcomers buy?"

"Almost nothing. Little things mostly, if that." Laiya shrugged unhappily. "I know they're up to something, but what they're doing isn't illegal, but it is strange."

"And this all started…"

"The customers stopped coming in as much four or five months back, not long after you were in town last. The newcomers have been hanging out since I started poking around for you."

Torrin sat back. There was no way that was a coincidence. So, soon after she was sent on a wild goat chase that almost got her killed, someone started moving in on one of her stores.

"Is there anything else?"

"Only that the skittishness has been extending to me when I'm out and about. I knew what I was getting into coming out here. You and Mac briefed me thoroughly. I know the residents of Tyndall are really suspicious of unattached women. Most of the time, it's nothing more than comments about getting me a man, and there was some initial hesitation when I took over for Eirene and Tyler, but that was three years ago. Pretty much everyone has gotten over their reserve. I feel like I've really become part of the community, except that once again I'm being treated like a total stranger."

Laiya sighed heavily and took another sip of her rapidly cooling tea. "It feels like the whole place is holding its breath, waiting for something to happen. Whatever's coming is going to be bad and they know it. That's why I met you with this." She held up the plasma rifle and Torrin realized that she hadn't seen the rifle out of Laiya's reach since she was almost shot downstairs. Laiya smiled, resolve forming on her face, erasing some of the lines of exhaustion. "I'm not going to let them roll over me. If they're going to take me out, I'm taking as many of them with me as I can."

"Well, the good news is, you won't be on your own much longer. I'm here now, and there's a Banshee unit on its way. We'll get this figured out and taken care of."

A tired nod was the only response she got; Laiya's small burst of energy was already spent. In finding out that her ordeal was almost over, Laiya seemed ready to collapse from exhaustion. She must have been going on little more than adrenaline for days now.

"When did you last sleep?"

"I don't think I've gotten a full night's sleep in a week."

"Why don't you head to bed, get some rest. I'll open the store in a few hours. Also we need to call in a permanent partner for you."

Laiya grimaced and stood up, stretching. "I hate to feel like I can't handle this myself."

"This is way outside your job description. If I don't call someone in and something happens to you, I won't be able to live with myself. We have some people who are looking for off-Nadi assignments, so the timing's perfect. Now get yourself to bed. Sleep as long as you need to." Torrin called the last to Laiya's departing back. Her tone brooked no disagreement, and Laiya didn't put up any fuss. She did take the rifle into the bedroom with her.

"Tien, do you read?" Torrin activated the subdermal transmitter.

"I hear you, Torrin," was the AI's steady response.

"Send an FTL packet back to Nadierzda. Bounce it off the usual relays. Let Mac and Audra know that we need somebody out here ASAP. And make sure they send someone with combat experience. I want to leave Laiya in good shape after we get this mess cleaned up." Troika Corp. didn't have too many employees with actual combat experience, but with the situation as perilous as it seemed, it would be worth paying a little extra to have the extra firepower. As far as firepower went, all Torrin had were her sidearm and a vibroknife, her usual weaponry when she was away from the *Calamity Jane*. She had other, more serious weaponry on the ship, but she hoped she wouldn't need it. The Banshees couldn't get there fast enough as far as she was concerned.

The residents of Tyndall were a somewhat misogynistic bunch, though not compared to the Haefonians. They were farmers and ranchers, raising crops and livestock. The entire planet had been terraformed into arable farmland, and almost every available inch was used for that purpose. Torrin was certain the League would have loved to gain a toehold on the planet, but the planet's inhabitants were independent to the point of foolhardiness. There was no central government on the planet but rather tight-knit communities formed at the hearts of hubs of farms or ranches. About the only thing that Tyndallers could agree upon was that they needed to get their crops to a central point so they could be exported off the planet. There was centralized transportation, but that was it, and even that was very much its own community.

The governing structure was unique to what Torrin had seen on the Fringes, but it worked for them. It didn't work very well for outsiders, which was fine with the local inhabitants. It also made for areas where there was little to no legal oversight, which led to thriving businesses of other types. The Troika outpost on Tyndall was barely profitable, and there were certainly many other planets that would have been more profitable locations to set up a store, but Tyndall had a thriving black market. Torrin's smuggling sideline did very well as a result of the connections she'd made there and the information she picked up from time to time. Really, the store was only there so she had a good excuse to keep visiting the planet.

She twitched back the curtain at the front of the apartment. The window looked out onto the street in front of the store. The wooden facades of the buildings across the street were barely visible as the sky continued to lighten. They all looked thrown together from rough-hewn logs. The only thing that looked like it hadn't been built in an afternoon was the elevated rail system that ran through town; that structure gleamed even though the sun had yet to rise. The Federated Transportation Hub, or FTH as the rest of the planet knew it, took its work seriously. Its workers and employees held what would have been called diplomatic immunity on any other planet. They were basically untouchable and formed a community within and without Tyndall's other closely knit communities.

A movement on the street caught her eye. It wasn't a big motion; if it had been any smaller she probably would have missed it. If it had been bigger she would have dismissed it, but its covertness drew her attention. Someone stood in the shadows between two buildings across the street. It was a good hiding place; she could barely make the figure out. She wished she had Jak's implant, to see better in darkness. The shadows would have been no problem for the sniper; she would have flushed out whoever was skulking across the street with one shot. Jak's presence was a steadying one; Torrin knew she could always rely on her. It felt like she was missing her right arm.

She let the curtain fall and turned out the light in the living room, then moved the curtain aside again ever so slightly. The figure was still watching. Whatever had been set into motion with the fire wasn't over yet. Not by a long shot.

* * *

"Good job, Banshees," Jak called out at the end of their latest training session. The Banshees had been wonderful to work with. They were professional and took well to what she had to teach them. If she hadn't known better, she would never have guessed that most of them had been out until all hours of the morning boozing and hooking up. She knew when they'd come back. They hadn't been very discreet and a large group had walked past her barracks singing loudly.

After handpicking the four most promising women, she'd worked on improving their accuracy with their plasma weapons. It wasn't that they were bad shots. Over short and medium ranges, they'd all been excellent shots. Thanks to her training, they were approaching the same level of proficiency over long ranges. They'd also paired up well as sniper teams. Perez and Hamilton were particularly good as a team.

"Good session, Jak." Axe voiced her opinion from where she'd been observing the session at Jak's elbow. She stuck out her hand and Jak shook it. Before she could stop her, the captain swept her into a quick, rough hug and then released her. "So what do you think?"

"Your women are very professional and competent. They're becoming excellent sharpshooters."

Axe nodded sharply. "Excellent. I'd hoped you'd see some promise in them. It never hurts to have a few snipers in the group. If you have no objections, I'd like to continue these sessions every other day while we're here."

"No problem. I'm happy to keep working with them. Do you have any idea when you'll be going out next?"

"Nothing so far. Could be tomorrow, could be three months from now. It's one of the hazards of our profession."

"Don't I know it." The two of them shared a wry smile. Being a soldier looked so glamorous to those who had never actively served. It was far from glamorous. It was dangerous, dirty and, above all, boring. From her experience, it was hours of boredom punctuated by moments of sheer terror. It was all so paradoxical. She couldn't wait for those moments of quiet, but if they went on too long, she got twitchy, like her skin was too tight over her muscles. "There's nothing like adrenaline to let you know you're alive, is there?"

"That's for sure." Axe glanced up at the sun. "Well, I need to get going, time to drop in on the sweetie. She's very demanding of my time when I'm on planet since we never know how long that's going to be."

"Sounds good. I'll catch you later."

Axe nodded again, turned on her heel and trotted to catch up with the four Banshees as they made their way out of the range. They chatted away as they left the area. The informality didn't bother Jak the way it did with many of the other squads of women she'd seen on base. Not a few minutes ago, she'd seen with her own eyes how professional those women could be. They knew when it was time to be serious, but since that time wasn't now they would be damned if they'd let anyone get in the way of them having fun.

"Looked like you were enjoying yourself." Tanith separated herself from the shadow of a nearby outbuilding.

"I guess I was," Jak replied thoughtfully. "They're great to work with. Not that I mind working with the others. It's great to see them coming so far from nothing. But the Banshees know what's at stake. They take everything seriously because they know one day it could save their asses."

"I can see that." Tanith casually rubbed the small of Jak's back. Jak grimaced slightly and forced herself to relax her shoulders. She really needed to get used to the fact that Tanith touched everybody. Just because she wasn't very touchy-feely herself didn't mean that Tanith meant anything by it.

"So what's on your mind?" Jak asked.

"I've been instructed to bring you in for a briefing on an assignment that uses your particular talents."

"Really." Her response came out flatter than she'd meant it to. When she'd been in the Devonite Army, that kind of summons had always meant she was being sent out to assassinate someone. It wasn't the kind of assignment she'd thought would be necessary here on Nadierzda.

"Yes..." Tanith eyed her, a little taken aback by her response. "It's nothing onerous. But I don't think that anyone else on the planet would be able to accomplish it as well as you can. Besides, when General Lethe calls on you, you come."

"Got it. I'll stow my gear on our way by."

Tanith shook her head. "Keep it."

Thoroughly mystified and not a little confused, Jak followed along after Tanith. What could the general possibly want with her skill set here on Nadi? It didn't make sense and it was a little disheartening. There had been something very restful about not having to kill anyone while she'd been on the planet.

"So, you and Olesya look like you're getting along well," Tanith said out of nowhere as they walked across the base to the command offices.

"I suppose. She makes me laugh."

"She makes everyone laugh," Tanith replied darkly. "Make sure you watch out for her. She's cut from the same cloth Torrin is."

"Don't worry about me. I'm not interested in her like that. She's very nice and I think maybe we could be friends." Tanith's response was odd, Jak thought. There was no need for her to warn Jak away from the lieutenant. She had no interest in Olesya as a lover. If she was going to be honest with herself, the only person she was carrying a serious attraction for was Torrin, wounded as she'd been by her betrayal. It was going to be a long time before she would be able to move past that and into another relationship. In any case, her relationships or lack thereof were no concern to Tanith. She bit the inside of her lip to keep from telling Tanith exactly that.

"Oh. Well. Good then. I don't want to see you after you walk in on another one with a lap full of blonde betrayal." Tanith seemed mollified and more than a little cheered up by her response. She was so cheery, in fact, that she linked her arm through Jak's. The contact was very discomfiting and Jak felt her shoulders tensing again in response. With effort she was able to relax and not shrink away from Tanith.

Arm in arm, they crossed the square, looking for all the world like a teenaged couple out courting. Jak found her mind wandering, trying not to think about how close Tanith was to her.

How did she know that woman was in Torrin's lap? The thought popped into her head, and her steps faltered for a moment. She was able to get back in step with Tanith without slowing her down. How indeed? It wasn't like she'd said much of anything to anyone about what had happened; she'd been too shattered that Torrin could do such a thing. Talking about it even now hurt almost as much as it had when Jak had come in on her. It was like the breath was still leaking out of her lungs through a hole in her heart.

Jak stole a sideways glance at the major, who was oblivious to the dark path her thoughts were taking her down. Tanith's face was open and friendly, and Jak gave herself a mental shake. The story of Torrin's betrayal was all over Landing; who knew what stories had been spun. It was probably a coincidence that Tanith knew a detail that Jak hadn't shared with anyone. *Get a grip, Jak.* Tanith was the closest thing she had to a good friend.

Tanith finally relinquished her hold when they got up to the command building. She quickly touched her cap and straightened it, tucking wayward strands of hair behind her ears. With practiced movements, she ran her hands down her fatigues and pulled or tucked everything into place. Jak mimicked Tanith, her own movements as practiced and automatic. She smiled as she realized that the upper echelons of command were the same everywhere. It didn't matter how good a soldier you were. Unless you were fresh off the front lines, you'd better look like crisp and presentable.

"Good?" Tanith asked with a light laugh, fanning her fingers to draw attention to herself.

"Very good," Jak replied seriously. "And me?"

"Almost," Tanith said, brow creased with concentration. She quickly gave Jak a once-over, twitching her collar into place, smoothing her hands over creases. She flicked a piece of lint off Jak's right breast. Jak could have sworn that she'd straightened some of the areas that Tanith had done. Still, Tanith knew more about the general than she did, and it didn't hurt to be prepared for the encounter.

"After you," Tanith said, pulling the door open to admit Jak.

The command building wasn't quite the hive of activity that Jak was accustomed to on Haefen. Of course, Nadi wasn't in the middle of a bitter civil war. As they walked through the narrow halls, they occasionally passed other women and returned their salutes. The command building hadn't looked that big from the outside, but the halls twisted and turned to give the impression that the building was bigger than it probably was. A couple sets of stairs took them up to the third floor. Jak had seen only a few buildings here with three stories and hadn't been inside any of them.

They passed a window on the third floor and she craned her neck, hoping to catch a view out of it. The glass was heavily frosted, and she couldn't see anything through it.

"The wind and sand do that," Tanith explained, unsolicited. "It's why there aren't too many buildings this tall. Apparently, back when the base was first constructed, someone thought it was important for command to be looking down on everyone—for all the good that does when you can't see out the windows."

Another turn of the corner brought them to a pair of double doors flanked by sentries. These sentries looked professional to the core. They were both older women, and they regarded Jak and Tanith with wariness that bordered on the near side of hostility. They paid special attention to Jak's rifle.

"And here we are," Tanith smiled. "Major Tanith Merriam and Captain Jak Stowell, reporting as ordered."

"We'll need your weapon, ma'am," the nearest sentry said. Neither of them moved until Jak slipped off her rifle and handed it to the sentry. The sentry nodded and her partner opened the door grudgingly. Tanith preceded Jak through the door.

"Former Banshees," she murmured to Jak as they walked into the office. Jak nodded. That made sense and explained the calm competence that radiated from the two women.

The office's large waiting room was lushly appointed. An adjutant sat, deeply engrossed in the console inset into her desk. Not so engrossed that she didn't look up and nod to them as they entered. She finished her task before addressing them.

"Major Merriam," she greeted Tanith familiarly but formally. "You must be Captain Stowell." She rose to her feet, both hands on the desk.

"This is Lieutenant Whaley, General Lethe's aide-de-camp," Tanith said.

Whaley saluted smartly and Jak returned her salute just as crisply.

"The general is waiting for the two of you."

Jak was impressed. Whatever the assignment, it must be important. The generals she'd known would keep an inferior cooling his heels for no other reason than to prove their importance, even when they'd been summoned posthaste. The only time she'd gotten in to see a commanding officer this high up the command chain had been when things had gone very wrong or they had an opportunity to capitalize on something that was very time-sensitive.

Whaley led them across the outer office and opened one of the doors at the back. This time Tanith had Jak precede her through the doors. She squared her shoulders and stepped through, eagerness warring equally with concern. She was excited to finally be of use again. In familiar contrast, concern over the upcoming mission rode her like a dark cloud, dampening her excitement with dread.

CHAPTER TWENTY-ONE

A solid, dark-skinned woman in her middle years looked up when Jak and Tanith entered the office. Unlike the two of them, she wore a formal uniform of dark green, one that Jak had so far had little opportunity to see. There was a uniform similar to this one hanging in the small upright locker in her room back at the barracks, but she hadn't had the opportunity to wear it.

Tanith came smartly to attention and Jak followed her closely. They saluted the general with a crisp salute that she tossed back snappily.

"At ease," General Lethe said in a surprisingly deep voice. Jak dropped into the stance and fixed her gaze on a point on the wall right above the general's head. Tanith sat in one of the chairs in front of Lethe's desk.

"At ease means you can take a seat, Stowell," the general said, amusement tingeing her tone. Tanith turned her head to stare at Jak as if she had attempted to turn a cartwheel on the plush carpet.

Jak nodded and dropped into the chair with alacrity. Every time she thought she had this group figured out, they threw another curve. How was she supposed to know that "at ease" meant lounge about in a chair?

"I've heard that you're very…formal, Captain Stowell. You may have noticed that we don't stand on too much ceremony here."

"I understand, sir." What Jak really wanted to say was that the lack of ceremony wasn't something she objected to, but the lax way things were being run spoke of a dearth of discipline and professionalism. However, she wasn't going to gum up her prospects by telling the highest ranking officer in the Nadierzdan army that she didn't think things were professional enough.

"Call me ma'am, Stowell."

"Ma'am." The "sir" had snuck out, a force of habit left over from Haefen. One that she reinforced by insisting her trainees call her "sir."

"Good. Now I'm sure you're wondering why I've called you here." Lethe stopped and watched Jak closely, not continuing until Jak nodded. "We have a situation that needs to be dealt with right away. There have been reports that a Sinosian tiger has been taking livestock too close to one of the area towns. I need you to kill it before it decides that humans are a good supplement to its diet."

Tanith leaned over toward Jak. "Sinosian tigers are huge carnivores. They inhabit the very top of the food chain on Nadi. If we don't take it out, it's only a matter of time before it decides to eat someone. They like to start out with children and work their way up to bigger prey."

Jak nodded. "Ma'am, I see why you need to eliminate the animal, but why do you need my particular skill set?"

"You're quick on the uptake, I like that," Lethe said with approval. "You're absolutely right to ask. If you weren't here, we'd be going after the tiger anyway and I'd expect to lose at least three women to injuries or worse. These animals are extremely dangerous and hard to kill. If we're lucky, you'll be able to kill the tiger from a distance and we won't have to expose ourselves.

"The tigers have an armored ridge of bone that shields their heads, making it difficult to get a kill shot on them. Their musculature is incredibly dense and their skin is very thick. Plasma weapons are next to useless on them. They shrug those shots aside like they mean nothing. They're agile and strong. So far our best tactics have been to get close enough to them to get a vibroknife in the innards, but that's risky."

Jak nodded again. "That sounds like a problem, ma'am. I can see why you'd want to avoid coming in on it."

"I don't know how long this will take," Lethe said thoughtfully. "Sinosian tigers can have a vast range. It takes a lot of meat to feed them." She leaned forward and brought up a map of the crater in which Landing was located and swiped it over to the near wall. A few points of light blinked at the far end of the crater, not too far from where Jak had seen the animal. More points of light blinked further east. From the reported sightings, the animal's range was well over a few hundred kilometers.

"That's a hell of a lot of ground to cover myself, ma'am," Jak pointed out.

"You won't be going alone, Jak," Tanith said. "I'll be going with you. With the general's permission, we'll take an ultralight and a glider so we can cover the most ground possible. I can spot for you when we find the tiger."

Lethe nodded. "That's an excellent plan. Merriam, do what you need to make it happen. Stowell, you need to get yourself outfitted with a radio. I understand you've never had a transmitter implanted."

"It's true, ma'am," Jak admitted. "I've been holding off until the Troika implants are a reality."

"I understand, but it's damned inconvenient. Still, we do have some radios around here. They're mostly used when someone's transmitter is inoperable. Make sure you pick up one of those."

"Yes, ma'am, I've had one requisitioned already."

"That's it then. I need you two to get going on this ASAP. You're dismissed." Turning her attention back to the console in front of her, the general flipped a hand vaguely in the direction of the door. Jak stood smoothly and saluted then spun on her heel and walked out of the room, Tanith on her heels.

"So what's the deal with taking an ultralight and a glider?" Jak asked Tanith as they made their way through the circuitous halls on their way out of the building. "Wouldn't the ultralight alone do it for us?"

"There isn't a whole lot of room for storage in either the ultralight or the glider, so we'll need to wear backpacks with everything we're bringing. Flying tandem in the ultralight won't work if we're both wearing them. So you bring your glider which would normally limit you to the cliffs, but I can tow you into the air with the ultralight. We'll be able to cover a lot of ground that way. Roads are on the scarce side where we're heading. Some of the smaller crater areas don't have any ground access to them."

"That makes sense." Jak grinned suddenly. "Besides, I'll be happy to be piloting the glider."

"I thought as much." Tanith returned her smile and held open the front door. The sun was getting low in the sky, though it was probably still an hour before sunset. "We'll leave first thing tomorrow. There's no point in leaving tonight; we won't be able to see anything from the air. Head back to your room and get together everything you think you'll need. I'll stop by and go over what you have."

"Oh, okay," Jak said with a straight face. She really didn't need Tanith going through her gear. If Tanith had more missions in the wilderness under her belt than she did, she would be very surprised.

"Good deal." Tanith reached out and swatted Jak on the behind. As she'd done every time other time, Jak gritted her teeth. She knew that

Tanith was only trying to be friendly, but the constant contact put her teeth on edge. It was only tolerable because Tanith was like that with all the women she knew. As usual, Jak didn't say anything; she smiled thinly and headed across the square to her barracks.

* * *

Torrin stood behind the counter, eyeing the greasy-looking man who loitered in the aisle by the dehydrated foodstuffs. His long duster hung a hands-breadth above the floor and he watched her out of the corner of his eye as he turned a packet of herbs over and over in his hands.

On the other side of the store, another man hung out by bolts of colorful fabric. He didn't look like the type of guy who would be into crafting. When he caught her watching him, he smiled, showing a large gap where his two front teeth had been knocked out.

So far, Torrin had yet to see any real customers. Sure, she'd seen a couple of folks slow down and peer through the windows, but when they saw one of the men inside, they quickly moved on. No sooner had one man left, then not more than fifteen minutes later another one would wander in. She rapped her fingertips on the countertop, getting more irate by the second.

The first man looked up and met her eye, smirking. For a second, Torrin gripped the edge of the counter, keeping herself from storming up to him. Finally she couldn't take it any longer.

Fuck it. In one smooth motion, she vaulted the sales counter and in two long strides, was up in the greasy man's face.

"You want to put the merchandise down if you're not going to buy it?" This close, she could tell that he hadn't bathed recently. The sour stench of old sweat wafted from his pores.

"Who says I'm not gonna buy anything?" His breath wasn't any better than his body odor and Torrin grimaced.

"Why you givin' old Nate a hard time?" Gap-tooth stood behind her, not close enough to touch but definitely well within her personal space bubble.

"Yeah, why you givin' me a hard time?" Nate smiled nastily, the tip of his tongue pressing against his lower lip. "Maybe I'm gonna buy this." He held up the package, its plastic marred by his dirty fingerprints.

"That's a load of crap." Torrin snatched the package from his hands. "You're not going to buy anything. You and your buddies are here for no other reason than to scare off my paying customers. I'd like you to leave."

Nate's companion laughed loudly and leaned in until she could feel his body's heat against her back. He leaned forward even more until his head was right next to hers. "How do you figure on doing that?" he whispered into her ear, his breath hot on her neck.

Hutchinson's face flashed in front of her eyes, and Torrin exploded into action. With a jerk of her left arm, she slammed the back of her fist into his face, sending him reeling backward, spewing curses as his nose gushed blood down the front of his grubby shirt. Nate gaped at her, stunned by the sudden violence and didn't even raise his hands to protect himself. Torrin shifted forward, burying her fist in his stomach and he folded over, grabbing at her arm. The back of his neck was too tempting a target and Torrin brought her elbow down on it, knocking him to the floor.

Remembering Gap-tooth, she spun on her heel just in time to see him rushing at her. He held a knife out from his side, his fingers shifting on the handle. As he was about to reach her, he jerked back, landing on his rear at the feet of a short, but impressively muscled woman. The plasma rifle at her shoulder was steady as bedrock as it pointed at him. She stepped on his wrist, grinding it into the floor until he let go of the knife.

"Like I said, it's time for you to leave." Torrin reached down and pulled Nate to his knees by the scruff of his neck.

"You should really listen to the lady." The woman's drawl was soft, and Torrin had to strain to hear her.

"Okay, okay." Nate held up his hands and hung in Torrin's grip. He scrabbled to get his feet under him and slunk out of the store, still hunched over from the blow to his abdomen.

Nate's buddy stared down the bore of the weapon leveled at his head. He licked his lips nervously and shifted on the floor, getting his arms under him. The rifle tracked his movements, and he never looked away as he stood up slowly. The woman shifted back, giving him room to head out the door.

"Hey, asshole!" The gap-toothed man stopped, the door half open. "Tell your friends I'm closed down to them. If I see any of you so much as slowing down outside my store, I'm calling the sheriff."

A flicker of amusement crossed his face at her threat and she wondered exactly how deep the sheriff was in their pockets. She hadn't been to see him yet; she'd been waiting until Laiya awoke.

"I take it you're the cavalry?" Torrin smiled at the muscular woman.

"That I am." Her voice was still soft, but definitely warmer. "Banshee Captain Autumn Tate from the *Oleander*, at your service. You're Torrin Ivanov." The last wasn't a question, merely a soft but emphatic statement of fact.

"That's me."

"Looks like I got here right in time."

"I would've handled them."

Tate nodded gravely. "It looked like you were doing all right. I thought I'd step in before you had to break a sweat."

Torrin laughed, surprised at the captain's quiet humor. "That's mighty kind of you."

"I'm good that way."

"I'll just bet you are."

It was Tate's turn to laugh. "I'd heard you were quite the flirt. Careful or I might take you up on that."

In an instant, Torrin's good humor soured. She didn't want the Banshee to take her up on it; she wanted Jak to take her up on it. With a grunt, she walked past the captain and locked the front door, flipping on the closed sign.

"We might as well head upstairs and talk to Laiya. She can fill you in on the bullshit that's been going down."

Without a comment on Torrin's abrupt shift in mood, Tate trailed along behind her and up the stairs to the Laiya's cramped living quarters.

* * *

"So there's nothing you can do?" It wasn't the first time Torrin had asked the question. It wasn't the second or third time either. The town sheriff was being remarkably unhelpful. Torrin had recounted all of Laiya's experiences, plus her own with the man she'd caught watching the store from across the street and the men in the store earlier that morning. Apparently none of it was actionable.

"I'm sorry, missy." The sheriff blew out his long mustache in irritation. Torrin was certain the irritation was at her refusal to drop the issue, not because he was upset that he couldn't do anything about the situation. "Laiya reported the graffiti and I've had someone keep an eye out for anything suspicious. It's probably some kids from the area messing around. As for the fire, there's no indication that it was set a-purpose. Sometimes, these things happen. Frankly, you and your factor sound real paranoid."

Torrin threw up her hands and turned her back on the sheriff.

"We aren't paranoid. Something is going on."

"Whatever you say. But there's nothing I can do about whatever it is you're afraid of." The last statement went beyond his previous evasions and into a decided unwillingness to assist them.

"Fine, but this isn't over." Torrin stomped over to the door of the sheriff's office and pulled it open so hard that it clattered against the office's interior wall and bounced back toward her. She stiff-armed her way through the recoil and stalked through the outer office.

"Don't do anything stupid," came the sheriff's shouted warning right before Torrin slammed the outer door behind her. For a moment she

stood on the wooden porch, seething. His unexpected refusal left her with
very few options. Looking at the sky, she judged the time to be about
noon. With any luck, Neal should already be at his new watering hole.
It was time to look him up and find out why he'd tried to get her killed.

She'd ordered Tate and a small contingent of Banshees to stay behind
at the store, to keep an eye on it. Fortunately, the Banshees had managed
to keep a low profile thus far. Torrin suspected that someone was out there
pulling strings, and she wanted the Banshees to be a surprise if they had to
move on the unknown puppet master.

She had to step carefully on the way over to the Posse's Noose, the
tavern where Laiya had said she could find Neal. A late morning rain
shower had turned the unpaved streets into a morass of mud and puddles.
The occasional passing vehicle had her on a watchful lookout to avoid
getting splattered by a flume of mud. Horses squished their way past her,
and she gave them a wide berth. As was usual on Tyndall, the locals were
going to great pains to stay away from her. There were many suspicious
stares from beneath wide-brimmed hats and from behind fluttering fans.

Dowson was one of the main towns, given that it was the closest town
of any size to the spaceport. Tyndall was a bit of an oddball in that its
spaceport didn't have any kind of commercial establishments connected
to it. The FTH ran the spaceport as its own little fiefdom. Since they
were prevented by planet charter from starting any retail or commercial
establishments of their own, they made sure that there were none within
easy reach of the spaceport. In theory this was to give Tyndall's various
towns and villages an even shake at any offworld money that came
through. In reality, it meant that very few offworlders ever really bothered
with Tyndall or at least not those with any legitimate business.

Dowson saw its fair share of the few offworlders who ventured beyond
the offload points of the Tyndall spaceport, but Torrin still stuck out
like a sore thumb. Conservative dress met drab colors that faded into a
predominantly sepia-toned background. There were days when Torrin
was surprised the whole planet didn't fade into its own background. She
didn't think her outfit was too garish, but the emerald green top looked
neon compared to the neutral tones the locals preferred. Even the black of
her pants stood out since it wasn't charcoal gray or dusty brown.

She made her way across the last intersection gingerly. The Tyndallers
might like everything in brown but that didn't mean she wanted to be
coated in mud up to her knees. Dowson would never have been mistaken
for a high-class resort town, but this area made where her store was look
downright posh. Her store might be dusty-looking, but it didn't look
ramshackle and on the edge of collapse. The Posse's Noose looked like
it was one stiff breeze from toppling over. In addition to a pronounced
lean, it was shabby and needed a good coat of paint. Torrin doubted that

anything less than being razed to the ground would help the old bar. She pulled sharply on the front door. It bound against the floor a bit before popping free and swinging rapidly toward her.

The gloom in the interior was heavy and smoke hung in the air. At the far end of the common room a fire burned sullenly in a smoking fireplace. She peered about to get her bearings. A familiar slumped form occupied one of the stools at the bar.

"Neal," she greeted the man as she took a seat to his left. The man might have been attractive at one time, but years of booze and dissipation had taken their toll. He'd never been a centerfold, but he'd been clean at least. Now his hair was unkempt and greasy, and the stench of stale sweat and alcohol clung to him. Privately, she was shocked at his condition. Laiya had warned her that he'd gone downhill. It seemed she hadn't been exaggerating. If anything she'd been uncharacteristically gentle in her description.

Neal gaped at her, opening and closing his mouth like a landed fish. "Torrin," he finally spluttered, then stopped abruptly.

"How've you been?" she asked breezily.

"Just fine. Why do you ask?"

"Tsk, tsk. That sounds a little defensive there, Neal. Is there some reason you need to defend yourself?" She stared right into his eyes and he flinched away from her gaze.

"Come on, Torrin. You don't know how bad things have been. Can't you cut a guy some slack?"

That was an interesting request from a man who'd done his best to have her killed. She sat back and regarded him levelly. He still hadn't admitted to anything. Neal might be a drunk and currently have the hygiene habits of a Camperus mud-beast, but he wasn't stupid. He was feeling her out to see what she knew before admitting to anything.

"Don't know why I'd want to do that, seeing what you tried to do to me."

"Do to you? I didn't do nothing Torrin, honest. All I've ever done is try to hook you up with the best info possible."

"For which I pay you handsomely. You make it sound like you're doing this out of the goodness of your heart." She pulled the vibroblade out of the sheath strapped to her right thigh. It looked, for all intents and purposes, like a regular knife, but with a matte black blade. Neal watched it come out, sick dread oozing over his features. With a slight flick of her wrist she engaged the knife and a low hum cut through the room's hush. It was a vibration so low that she felt more than heard it. Neal's eyes widened as he too felt the vibrations. The knife's blade was vibrating thousands of times a second. A vibroblade could cut through bone, sinew and tendon with the same effort it took to cut through soft mud.

"You know what this is, don't you?" Torrin asked sweetly. Neal shrank away from her. He opened his mouth to answer, then shut it abruptly.

"Whatcha doin' with my friend Neal, little lady," a voice drawled from behind her.

"None of your business." She'd been watching Neal and had seen the flash of pure terror dart across his face. He might be scared of her, but the man behind her terrified him beyond all reason.

"If you're messin' with my buddy, then you're messin' with me. What do you say you leave his sorry ass be and run along home."

Torrin laid the vibroknife on the bar where Neal could see it, then turned slowly in her seat. A lanky man in a long trench coat slouched behind her, hands stuffed deep into the coat's capacious pockets. His face was unshaven and his yellow grin gleamed sickly at her from the darkness of his cheeks. He was cut from the same cloth as the two men who had been in her store earlier that morning. Torrin would have bet her right arm that he was part of the same group.

"The man and I are having a private conversation," Torrin said. "You can leave at any time or things are going to get ugly."

"What kind of ugly could a pretty young thing like you get to?"

"This is your last warning. Leave."

The man sighed and a stinking cloud rolled over Torrin. She tried not to gag. He sure smelled like his buddies.

"You're the one who needs to be going. My buddy Neal and I are going to have a long talk." He reached for her and she grabbed his hand, forcing the fingers back over his wrist.

"Why you little—"

"Knife!" Neal's shrill cry was all the warning Torrin needed. She twisted his hand harder and slid off the barstool in the same motion. The trench-coated man stumbled forward into her, and she dropped a hip and threw him smoothly over her shoulder. He bounced off the bar and landed in a crumpled heap, groaning loudly.

The bartender reached under the bar but never got any further. Two men seated at a table across the room sprang to their feet and advanced on Torrin. The bartender decided it would be more prudent to duck completely behind the bar. Neal looked like he was contemplating joining him.

"I can take care of two as easily as one," Torrin warned as she pivoted to keep both of them in front of her.

"I'm so glad you feel that way," the man on her right said with a slimy grin and a suggestive tone. He was shorter than his companion, but he was built like a brick shed. They were both cut from the same cloth as the man who'd come to Neal's defense. Like him, they had a less than passing acquaintance with the rudiments of basic cleanliness. Their trench coats were spotted and torn.

"We're big fans of two-on-one action," the other said, drawing his knife from a sheath in his boot. It dwarfed his hand and glinted dully in the bar's low light. His buddy pulled out a pair of knuckledusters and slipped them on.

This was more than Torrin had bargained for. Taking on one unarmed man who wasn't expecting resistance was one thing. Taking on two who had a much better idea what they were up against and who had weapons was a different problem altogether. There was nothing for it now. She would have to get in as many licks as possible and scare them off before they killed her.

She grabbed a dirty glass from the bar and flung it at the nearest man's head. He ducked and she rushed him. A feint at his eyes with her fist was followed up by a sweep of her leg behind his knee. His leg buckled and he went down but not before swiping wildly with his knife. A line of fire bloomed along her ribs followed by slick wetness. He'd landed a decent slice. She dropped back for a second before sliding forward to pay back the favor with a swift kick to his chin before he could get back up. His head snapped back and two teeth went spinning off into the dark corners of the bar. This was the kind of fight she could handle: up close and personal, not picking off unsuspecting enemies from hundreds of meters away. For a distracting moment her mind was filled with the horrific scene from the bridge on Haefen and Jak's face as she methodically took out man after man.

Stars spangled brightly across her vision. Her ears rang and she staggered to one side. The shorter man had taken the opportunity to punch her in the side of the head. She staggered back out of his immediate reach and shook her head to clear it. Her vision blurred, then coalesced briefly before blurring once more. There were two of him approaching her and she didn't have time to determine which one was the real one. She had to finish this now.

With a hoarse cry she rushed at him only to miss him completely. She'd chosen the wrong image and she overbalanced and toppled forward, arms windmilling. His shout of triumph was followed by a sick crack, then a thud.

Torrin turned over to see the pugilist lying in a heap. Neal was still sitting on his barstool, handle of his beer stein in hand. The rest of the mug was in shards around the other man's body.

He shrugged when he caught her watching him. "So we're even now?"

"Not hardly," Torrin replied. "But we're closer." She struggled to her feet and shook her head once again. Her eyesight had returned to normal, but her head felt like it had been cracked open. After a shot like that, she knew she was lucky to be conscious.

"Who are these guys and what do they want with you?"

"Not here. You need to get me out of here, hide me for a while." Neal was shaking on his stool as the enormity of the situation started to sink in. Torrin still didn't know if the men had been there to help him or silence him.

She disabled the still-vibrating knife and slipped it into the sheath before grabbing Neal by the elbow. Before the men could regain consciousness she hustled Neal out of the bar. A handful of the thin plastic sheets that passed for money on Tyndall should have been enough to cover the damage, she hoped. Either she had just ripped the bartender off, or he'd received an unexpected windfall. Either way, she didn't have time to dwell on it now. Outside the bar she scoured the street in both directions. No one stuck out as being particularly suspicious, so she pressed Neal onward. This time she took no care to spare her clothing from the worst of the mud, forging through it instead.

What was it with her and mud? Her first encounter with Jak had been in the muck. The memory of Jak's serious eyes floated into her mind. The look in them shifted to shock, then betrayal. Torrin clenched her teeth: this wouldn't do. There was too much at stake to be mooning over her girlfriend. If she was going to stay in one piece long enough to get back to Nadierzda, she needed to clear her mind. Thoughts of Jak were a luxury she couldn't entertain.

Neal choked slightly and Torrin relaxed her grip on his collar. She forced out a long breath, willing herself to calm down. Once she was done with the mess on Tyndall, she could go home and make Jak listen to her.

Laiya looked up at the jingle of the door and her eyes widened. Torrin knew she must look horrible, covered in mud and blood. Fortunately, there were no customers in the store. Torrin didn't take the time to say anything, but jerked her chin vaguely upward and hustled Neal over to the stairs. Once they were safely ensconced in the upper apartment, she regarded him coldly.

"Sit," she ordered, pushing him in the direction of one of the living room chairs. "Don't move."

There had to be a first aid kit in there somewhere. She banged around hastily in the kitchen's drawers and cabinets and finally tracked down a rudimentary kit at the back of one of the drawers. If Laiya could get the bleeding to stop, she would see about getting the Banshee medic to sew her up. There was no way she was going to subject herself to the backwoods doctors on Tyndall. Most of them were more accustomed to practicing on animals than they were on humans.

"So," she said to Neal, sitting on a chair across from him and holding a bandage to her side. "What the hell is going on here?"

"It wasn't my fault, Torrin." Neal dry-washed his hands and avoided her gaze. "They offered me twice what you usually pay me to give you the scoop on that job. And they said they'd cut off my hands and feet and dump me in a ravine out of town if I told you anything about the payoff. With that and what you paid me, I made a huge profit and I didn't get killed. How can you expect a businessman to pass that deal by?"

"So you sold me out for a few measly credits? Do you have any idea what almost happened to me?"

"I'm sorry, Torrin, I really am. But the job was legit, wasn't it? Those Orthodoxans made good on their deal, right? Obviously you got out of there, so there's no harm done."

"Oh yeah, they were fantastic hosts. Don't you try going there. So now I know why you sold me out. But who put you up to it?"

Neal swallowed visibly, his Adam's apple bobbing sickly in his scrawny neck.

"I know you're scared of them." Torrin pressed him further. "They were nervous enough about me talking to you at the bar. Do you really think they would have let you live once they were done with me?"

Neal stubbornly kept his silence. Beads of sweat broke out on his forehead and one tracked slowly down the side of his face. Frustrated, Torrin stood up and fetched another bandage from the kit. If she didn't staunch the blood soon, she was going to have some major problems with blood loss. The cut along the ribs was a lot longer and required both of her hands. Finally Neal stood up and came over to her. Holding the gauze over the wound on her side, he wrapped it deftly with a length of cloth.

"Thanks, but don't think that's going to get you off the hook. I still need to know who put you up to all of this. If need be, I can protect you." That statement was going to cost her back home. She would have to use the network the Nadierzda women had put in place to protect women. It had never been considered for use by men, but she knew that the situation was dire enough that she needed to pull out the stops if it would get this man to talk.

"His name is Monton," Neal finally volunteered. "He runs a ranch up in the hills. At least that's what he says he does. Truth is he has his fingers in all sorts of pies, none of them legal. The ranch is mostly a front."

"Monton. I've never heard of him. Why could he possibly want me dead?"

Her only response was an uncomfortable shrug from Neal.

"I guess I'm going to have to go ask him myself then."

"I wouldn't if I were you. From what people say, his ranch is huge and he has a ton of men on it. He'll kill you."

Torrin smiled. "I have a few tricks up my sleeve. You let me worry about it."

CHAPTER TWENTY-TWO

Jak followed Tanith from one updraft to another as they swooped their way through Nadi's skies. They were high enough that it was difficult to make out landmarks on the ground. For a brief moment, Sector 27's maps sprang to mind and she shook her head slightly to clear it. It was getting harder to avoid those flashes. She would have to trust that Tanith knew the area well enough to get them where they needed to go.

That wasn't going to be easy. Try as she might, she couldn't quite relax around Tanith. The woman was warm and open, constantly doing everything she could to coax Jak out of her shell, but there were times when it was too much. Torrin was just as outgoing as Tanith and seemed to have at least as many friends, but she also knew when to back off. She understood that Jak was the way she was. While Torrin had tried to introduce her to others on Nadi, when she'd been around, she hadn't pushed. She'd cajoled and wheedled, but Jak felt like she'd always had the option to say no.

Maybe it was the difference in their ranks, but Jak hadn't missed the way Tanith's eyes tightened whenever she'd turned down one of her many offers to go out after they'd gotten off duty. There was something calculating in Tanith's friendship, or so she often felt. Of course, it wasn't at all fair to compare Tanith and Torrin. For one thing, she would never be involved with Tanith the same way she'd been involved with Torrin. Her chest tightened at the thought. She missed Torrin's closeness most of all. The quiet minutes after lovemaking when they would talk without reservations were the times she felt most like they were connecting on a deeper level. Now that was gone also. There was no one who could see into her soul and accept her for everything she found there.

The exhilaration of flight helped calm her mind for the upcoming hunt, though it also let her mind wander in directions she would prefer it didn't. She needed to be completely focused for this run. It would be vastly different from her recent hunting excursions. Those had been for fun and to clear her head. This was closer to the assignments she'd been given back on Haefen. There was an excitement to hunting prey that could hunt you back, and anticipation crackled along her nerve endings.

Tanith started a lazy downward spiral that Jak followed until she could make out a small building in the distance. Their first stops were going to be at some of the farms to interview the occupants who'd seen the Sinosian tiger firsthand. As they got closer to the ground, the faint tracks of a mostly overgrown dirt road eventually became visible. They truly were at the edges of Nadierzda's civilization. Apparently, most of the settled areas were set up like this one. There was one central town with small settlements—barely even villages—radiating outward. Beyond those villages were large farms, and beyond them were smaller farms. The population grew sparser as they got further from that region's hub town. Eventually, there was nothing but crater walls and kilometers of shifting sand and blowing dust. That is until the next viable crater system came along and the cycle was repeated.

Most of the crater systems weren't connected. For the minority of those that were, the routes between were extremely treacherous and narrow. Most people traveled between them by air. Jak had heard there were grumblings in other areas from those who thought it was unfair that the spaceport was attached to Landing. She'd thought the setup was strange when she discovered that there were more settlements outside of Landing's crater system. An orbiting space station would have made much more sense, though it would also be more difficult to defend from the surface.

Tanith landed on a flat patch of grass, and Jak nosed in behind her. Now that they were on the ground, the weight of her backpack was much more noticeable. She shrugged it off and looked around.

The farm looked idyllic. With the little farmhouse and barn behind it, she thought she had stepped into an old holophoto. There were animals she recognized by the barn, a few old Earth milk cows and some swine.

"Nice landing," Tanith said, coming up behind her. Jak casually turned at exactly the right time to avoid being swatted familiarly on the behind.

"Thanks."

"Are you all they sent to deal with that tiger?" a voice called. Jak looked over her shoulder toward a woman who had emerged from the barn and was walking up the slight incline toward them. She was dressed in dirty coveralls and a wide-brimmed hat. She pushed the wide brim of her hat back a bit so she could observe them. Creases by her eyes and mouth spoke to a long life spent out of doors in the sun and the wind. Her skin was tanned dark, and light gray eyes watched them closely from under the hat's brim.

"We are," Tanith replied. "Major Tanith Merriam and Captain Jak Stowell from the planetary militia."

"Where's the rest of your crew?" The woman peered at the sky as if expecting more women to materialize. When they didn't, she pursed her lips in disapproval.

"It's only us, ma'am," Jak said. "And you are?"

"I'm Kaylin Mueller. This is my farm. That animal has killed three of my cows in the past month. How are you going to take it out without a hell of a lot more firepower?"

"We have all the firepower we need, Kaylin," Tanith hastened to assure her. "Captain Stowell here can shoot the wings off a gnat at twelve hundred meters. We don't need a lot of firepower when we have her accuracy."

"If you say so." Jak could tell that Tanith's words of praise had been less than effective in convincing the farmer, but she seemed content to let it go. Her attitude said the fools could do what they want, and she wouldn't lose any sleep if it got them killed.

"Is there somewhere we can talk?" Tanith asked. "I'd like to ask you some questions to see if there's anything you can tell us that will help us with our hunt."

"We can go inside. My wife will put on a kettle." Kaylin turned and walked toward the house. Tanith followed but stopped when Jak touched her on the elbow.

"You go ahead. I'm going to take a look around, see what physical signs I can find."

Tanith nodded and followed the farmer into the house. Jak started over toward the barn. If the tiger had taken three cows, it made sense to start with the cow enclosure. A quick circuit of the pen didn't turn up anything unusual. The barn was another matter. Large paw prints littered the ground by the barn's far wall. The prints were bigger across than her hand, even at its fullest extension. Deep gouges in front of the pads spoke to enormous claws. Even though it was called a tiger, she could tell by those claw gouges that it didn't share at least one aspect with the felines she knew. Its claws were not retractable.

There was something strange about the tracks. By their placement, it meant the animal wasn't killing the cows outside, as she'd assumed. It looked instead like it was making its way into the barn and killing the cows there. She looked up the side of the barn and noticed a window about seven or eight meters up the wall. There were more gouges on the wall below the window and unless she was mistaken, there were gouges on the windowsill as well. Not only was the tiger incredibly powerful to jump that high, but it was smart enough to figure out how to get in. She shivered a bit. There was going to be more to the hunt than she'd thought. Haefen had its share of dangerous predators, but from what she could tell, none of them matched the intelligence and power of the Sinosian tiger. This was going to be a challenge, one she hoped she was up to.

She followed the tracks away from the barn and toward a wooded area or as wooded an area as she was going to find on Nadierzda. The trees still looked stunted to her eyes, and it seemed strange that they all canted to one side as a result of the constant wind. Proper trees would have grown majestically up, but these curled unappealingly to one side and were short to boot. As sparse as the woods were, she decided not to enter them. There was no point in making herself a target for the tiger if it was around. From what Tanith had said, the beasts were mostly nocturnal, but she couldn't be sure if she walked right past its resting place for the day that it wouldn't attack her. The tracks looked like they were at least four or five days old, so it had probably moved on to another part of its range, but she hadn't made it this far without having learned when caution was warranted. After a final look toward the woods, she made her way back to the farmhouse.

She rapped sharply on the door and let herself in. Before she had gone more than a couple of paces, she was stopped by a raised voice from the kitchen.

"Make sure you're wiping your boots on the mat, young lady." The holler wasn't from Kaylin, but she walked back to the doormat and made a show of wiping her feet on it. When she joined Tanith and the two farmers in the kitchen, the older one gave her a dirty look.

"Ma'am," she said, nodding.

"Jak, this is Yasmeen, Kaylin's wife. They've been filling me in on what's been going on with the tiger."

Jak nodded again. "We have a problem. It's getting—"

"—into the barn, I know. Kaylin was just saying."

"The window's almost eight meters off the ground. That means that it can jump at least that high. That significantly increases its range and den options, I'm thinking."

Tanith looked thoughtful.

"I don't know that it can jump much higher than that," Kaylin broke in. "It tried to take a whole cow back out the way it came in, but I don't think it could get that high with that much weight. In the end it settled for a haunch. But it's been back two more times. I boarded up the window, but it tears through it like there's nothing there."

"You've never seen which way it came from or was going?" Tanith asked.

"No." Yasmeen shook her head emphatically. "We know when it's around, the animals go crazy with fear. But there's no way I'm letting my sweetie go out there when that thing's about. The last thing we need is a Sinosian tiger with a taste for human flesh."

"I think we've gotten everything we need," Tanith said, standing up from the table and putting down a surprisingly delicate teacup. "Thank you, ladies. We need to move on and talk to some of the other settlements out here."

Kaylin stood and stuck out her hand. Tanith accepted it and shook it heartily. Jak was surprised when Kaylin repeated the handshake with her. The farmer's hands were strong and callused. She must have noticed the same thing about Jak because she gave her an approving look and nodded slightly to herself.

"You might try the Martinas down the road," Yasmeen offered. "I know the beast has hit them a couple of times also. They have small girls, so I'm sure they'll be reassured to know you're out here looking into things."

"Sounds like a plan, thanks." Tanith took Jak by the elbow and guided her out of the house. They walked over to where their aircraft were secured. "So what else did you find?" Tanith asked on their walk.

Jak reclaimed her elbow without being too obvious about it, she hoped. The constant touches from Tanith made her feel like she was a skittish animal that was being domesticated. She cleared her throat self-consciously before answering. "Nothing else really. The tracks go off that way, but I wasn't about to follow them into the woods by myself."

"I should hope not. Do you want to follow them now?"

"There's no point. The tracks are at least a few days old. Besides, I have no desire to run into that thing now that I've seen what it's capable of. I think our best bet is to track it to its den and then wait for it to come out. From a distance. A very great distance."

"How prudent of you." Tanith grinned and squeezed Jak's shoulder. "I guess we need to find that den." She walked off and readied the ultralight for takeoff while Jak hooked the glider to the back of Tanith's ultralight, then strapped herself in and waited for Tanith to tow her into the air.

* * *

"This is crazy, how the hell are you going to get to Monton in the middle of his own ranch?" Laiya stood in the middle of her small living room, arms folded over her chest, eyes flashing. Neal, standing to one side of the room and as far away from the two women as possible, nodded in agreement. Tate stood in front of the windows, watching the street below with her plasma rifle in hand. The other Banshees were on the first floor, covering the store.

"I have a few tricks up my sleeve," Torrin said dismissively. "And we have one huge weapon that Monton doesn't know about." She smiled wolfishly and Tate turned her head to share her grin. "We have a Banshee unit. He won't know what hit him."

Torrin watched Neal closely. They were going to have to keep him on a short leash. He seemed contrite enough now, but there was no guarantee that he wouldn't try to sell the information to Monton to try to get back into his good graces. Apparently Monton really was a certifiable psychopath. Enough so that Laiya was aware of him, even though she'd never seen him in town. If it was illegal and unsavory, Monton had both hands in it, up to the elbows.

"That's fine, but I'm not letting you leave me here. I'm coming with you." Laiya simmered with barely contained anger. Her dark eyes snapped from beneath frowning brows. "I owe those bastards as much trouble as they've given me."

"You can't come. I need you to keep an eye on Neal here."

"Set a couple of Banshees on him, he won't be going anywhere."

"That makes no sense. You don't have the kind of training they do. There's no way I'm going to allow you to put yourself in harm's way for no good reason."

"You're not leaving me behind." Laiya set her jaw and stared at her boss, arms crossed.

Torrin looked Laiya in the eyes for a few moments before sighing. It was clear that she wasn't going to win this argument. "Fine," she said, conceding defeat with ill grace. "We'll stash Neal on the *Calamity Jane*. Tien can ride herd on him well enough, I suppose."

When Laiya grinned in triumph, Torrin forestalled her with a raised hand. "But you're not getting near any combat. You'll be creating a diversion for our diversion. The Banshees will keep most of Monton's men pinned down, and I'll sneak in with a handful of Banshees while they're otherwise occupied."

Gracious in victory, Laiya smiled sweetly. "I can do that. As long as I can make them sweat a bit and maybe pick off a few, I'll be happy."

"Then if there's nothing else to be done, I need to take this paragon of humanity back to my ship. We still need to pin down exactly where the ranch is. Will you be all right here by yourself tonight?"

"I'll be fine. I've been managing so far. Besides with the sleep I got yesterday, I feel like a new woman. Having the Banshees holding down the fort downstairs helps a lot too."

"All right. But let me know if anything happens and I'll be right back."

"Got it, boss."

Laiya laughed when Torrin shook a finger at her. Now that she'd won the argument, Laiya was perfectly willing to admit that Torrin was the boss. Torrin stood up and gestured to Neal.

"Come on, it's time to go."

"I need to stop by my place for my things," Neal said. Petulance lined his voice and was visible in the stiff lines of his body.

"I don't think so," Torrin replied emphatically. "Monton's men could be waiting for you. You're going to have to get by without whatever you have there."

"But all my money! You'd make me leave without a centicred to my name?"

"Which would you rather have? Your credits or your life?"

When it was put that way Neal had no choice but to grumble under his breath and glare at her.

"I'll be back in the morning," Torrin called over her shoulder as she shooed Neal in front of her and down the stairs.

She blinked in the sun as she and Neal emerged from the back of the store. The sun wasn't bright, but it was at an angle just short of setting and its rays pierced into her eyes. They didn't have a whole lot of time before dark and she wanted Neal out of town before then. Tate appeared behind her and flowed down the stairs.

"I'll accompany you to the ship, Torrin."

"Do you really think that's necessary?" Torrin glanced up and down the street. There was no sign of Monton's men and she heaved a mental sigh of relief.

"Since you showed up from collecting this one with all the signs of coming out second-best in a barroom brawl, yeah, I'd say it's necessary."

"We need to be fast and inconspicuous. The larger our group, the worse our chances of getting through undetected."

"And if you do get detected?" Tate's eyes were impassive, holding Torrin's gaze for a long moment.

For the second time that day, Torrin sighed and gave in. It was becoming a disturbing trend. "Suit yourself," she grumbled and activated the transmitter behind her ear. "Tien, do you read me?"

"I am picking you up loud and clear, Torrin."

"Good. I need you to pick three of us up ASAP. There's a meadow to the north of Dowson. Meet us there as soon as you can." She estimated it would take Tien about ten minutes to descend from orbit and land. Hopefully they wouldn't run into any delays on their way out of town. They had a little over a kilometer to travel on foot. She knew she was up to it, but she had serious reservations about Neal's condition. It had been a few hours since his last drink and his hands were already starting to tremble.

"Very good, Torrin. I will meet you there. Tien out."

"Come on, Neal." Torrin pushed him to the north. "We have a bit of a hike ahead of us."

The three of them made their way steadily out of town. Torrin insisted on sticking to side streets and alleys. It was a calculated risk. There were fewer people there and if Monton's men were to come upon them, they would have no reason not to attack. However, the people of Tyndall were so insular and clannish that there was a good chance they would ignore an offworlder being attacked in the street, so there was very little safety in numbers. At least on deserted side streets, they could see people coming and prepare for the possibility of attack.

Since she didn't know the layout of the town very well, she relied on Neal's directions. Their route grew circuitous and an uneasy suspicion tickled the back of her brain. They had ducked into still another dingy alley when she pulled him back between two houses.

"Neal, where the hell are we?" Torrin asked through clenched teeth.

"We're sneaking out of town, why?" he whined loudly, and she clapped a hand over his mouth.

"I recognized one of Monton's men from the tavern, that's why. What is he doing hanging around one of the alleyways we so coincidentally happened to come down."

The blood drained from his face, and he went from looking sickly to looking three days dead. She hadn't thought that he could get any paler, but in his panic, he proved her wrong.

"I thought we could stop by my apartment quick on our way out of town," he whispered hoarsely. "It's close to the northern edge of Dowson."

"Didn't I say that was a bad idea? And for exactly this reason. Get it through your skull. You're not going back home."

"Can't you..." His voice trailed off under Torrin's hard stare and he looked away.

"We're going over a few streets and then we're heading straight out of here before they realize we're over here."

"Too late," a familiar voice said from behind her. "It's so nice to see you again, Neal. And your little lady friend. I've missed her."

A glance over her shoulder revealed the trench-coated tough from the tavern. This time he was taking no chances with her. In his left hand, he held an ugly snub-nosed pistol that she didn't recognize. The muzzle was huge. If he hit them with a shot from that, whatever kind of shot it was, one of them would have a very large hole in them. With his right hand he beckoned them peremptorily.

"Come on out. I know someone who'd really like to meet you." He grinned nastily and ran his tongue over yellow teeth.

"Okay, okay. Don't shoot, we're coming out." *Where the hell is Tate?* She eased the plasma pistol partway from its holster. With her back to the gunman, she hoped he wouldn't recognize the movement. She looked into Neal's terrified eyes.

"When I turn around, you drop to the ground," she whispered to him.

There was no way to confirm that Neal understood without tipping off Monton's man. She backed toward him slowly, then whipped around, snatching the pistol the rest of the way from the holster and firing in one motion. She fired the first bolt of plasma from the hip and continued to fire as she raised the pistol to a more traditional firing position. Her shots went wide, though one plasma burst was close enough to crease the top of the gunman's left arm and his return shot went wide of both of them. There was a muffled thump and splinters from the nearby house rained down on them.

Great. His weapon has explosive charges.

With a surprised look on his face, he pitched forward. Smoke rose from his back and Torrin was overwhelmed by the stench of charred flesh. He clawed weakly at the dirt before all movement ceased and he lay there. She hoped he was dead.

Neal lay on the ground, hands wrapped around his head, eyes squeezed shut. Torrin scooped him up by the collar, and he swatted at her, eyes still closed.

A shadow darkened the opening between the houses, and Torrin raised her pistol, then lowered it when she saw who it was.

"It's about time," Torrin said. "Where were you?"

"I thought someone was following us. I held up a little bit to check, then you guys ducked in here, but I didn't see where you'd gone at first. Still, I took care of the problem."

"Next time, let me know."

"Of course." Tate's voice was as soft as ever, and her nod gave no indication that she had any issue with the abruptness of Torrin's tone.

Neal lay on the ground between them, looking back and forth during the tense exchange.

"We need to get out of here." Torrin hauled Neal to his feet. A gunfight had been exactly the kind of thing she'd been hoping to avoid. It would attract all of the wrong kind of attention, Monton's men or the sheriff, either one would be equally bad. She was well convinced that the sheriff was in league with Monton.

Neal scrambled forward through the narrow space between houses with Torrin and Tate hard on his heels. They burst out onto a side street. He pointed north and took off running. She was content to run behind him, her head on a swivel watching for trouble. As she'd suspected, he was in terrible shape and couldn't keep up the sprint for long. She stayed at a lope and pulled him along with her. He stumbled often, and she had to work to keep him upright. Tate pounded along beside her, watching their surroundings while Torrin dragged Neal on. The situation reminded her of her flight from the Orthodoxan compound the night Jak had rescued her. She chuckled and yanked Neal further down the road. At least this time she could be certain there was no way she was going to end up in bed with the person she was fleeing with.

The rest of their flight out of Dowson was thankfully uneventful. The sun had slipped below the horizon when they finally arrived at the meadow. She whistled in relief when she saw the beautiful outline of the *Calamity Jane* waiting for them.

"Open a hatch, Tien," Torrin ordered as they came running up on the ship. She didn't want to wait for the cargo bay doors to lower and raise before they could get out of there. A hatch popped opened halfway up the side of the vessel. Torrin jogged over and gave Neal a boost. Neal grabbed the lowest of the ladder rungs that ran up the hull to the open hatch, pulling himself up. She was right on his heels and almost caught the sole of a shoe in the face for her troubles. Torrin glanced down and confirmed that Tate was right behind her.

"Take us up," she said to the AI when she saw that Neal had disappeared into the vessel. She grasped the ladder rungs tighter when the ship started to vibrate in response. With a few lunges, she scaled the ladder two rungs at a time and threw herself into the ship just as it started to lift off. Tate piled in on top of her.

Neal was propped against the corridor's wall, gasping from their exertions.

"Do you mind?"

Tate grunted in return and rolled off her. She bounced to her feet and glanced around the small hallway junction. Torrin stayed down, catching her breath.

"Get up," she said to Neal after a few moments. "We have work to do."

She levered herself off the floor of the ship and hauled Neal up by the scruff of his neck. He grumbled to himself as she maneuvered him down the corridor and to the second set of sleeping quarters. The room was only barely appointed. It almost never had an occupant. Torrin had taken to storing extra supplies in the room. Nothing in there was worth stealing, but she made a mental note to search him before she let him back out.

"Stay here," she said, pushing him through the door. He turned to say something to her. "Tien, lock the door please." The door slid shut on top of whatever Neal was trying to say.

"The door is locked, Torrin." Tien's slightly mechanical tones rang through the cabin.

"Good." Torrin caught Tate's eye and headed down the hall to the bridge with her following. "Bring up all the maps you have of this area." Maps of Tyndall took up the main viewscreen when she entered the bridge. All she knew about Monton's ranch was that it wasn't too far from Dowson, but not much more than that.

"Tien, can you isolate all the ranches within a day's ride of Dowson?" The maps dimmed momentarily, then steadied with blinking patches of color. There were a large number of them. "Do you know if any of them belong to a man named Monton?"

"I'm sorry, Torrin. None of them are publicly registered under that name."

"Damn." She stood there and stared at the screen. The last thing she wanted was to bring Neal in, not right after she'd locked him in the spare bedroom. There didn't seem to be anything for it. There were too many options to choose from.

"Tien, unlock the spare living quarters." She looked over at the Banshee. "Do you mind getting Neal from the other room for me?"

A raised eyebrow was Tate's only response to the request. Torrin thought she looked faintly amused but couldn't quite tell. Without answering, the captain turned and left the bridge, returning a short time later, hauling Neal along with her.

"I don't know that I really feel like helping too much right now." Neal rather ostentatiously rubbed his arm where Tate had grabbed it. "You've shown me only the best hospitality so far. I mean would it be too much to get some food? And a drink. A stiff one."

Torrin closed her eyes. Neal was starting to grind on her. He almost got her killed with a faulty tip, then he led them back to the one place they could be sure Monton's men would be sure to be waiting. Opening her eyes, she pinned him with a glacial stare. Neal stepped back half a pace and bumped into Tate's solid form behind him.

"I could always drop you off in front of your house," Torrin said sweetly. "I'm sure Monton's men will treat you much better than I have."

His eyes widened and he opened and closed his mouth twice. "You wouldn't." His voice cracked and he swallowed hard.

She stalked toward him slowly and watched with some satisfaction as he cringed away from her and into Tate again. Without changing her expression, the Banshee took him by the upper arms and held him immobile. Torrin stuck her face in his, their noses separated by only a few centimeters.

"Try me," she said and smiled. It was little more than a baring of teeth and he flinched.

"O-okay."

Torrin backed up and met Tate's eyes. She let Neal's arms go and he looked over his shoulder at her before looking back at Torrin.

"What do you want me to do?"

"Show me which ranch is Monton's, if you would." She took him by the shoulder and propelled him toward the main viewscreen.

Neal stopped in front of the map; the look he shot at them over his shoulder was of pure terror. "I've never been there. I have no idea where it is. I got my instructions from one of his men."

"You must have some idea where it is."

"It's to the east, about half a day's ride. But that's all I know, I swear."

"Tien, isolate the ranches out that way."

The screen dimmed and shifted, zooming in on the area east of Dowson. There were still too many ranches, but at least there were many fewer than before.

"That's not right," Neal said. "Half of those are way too far. I meant half a day's ride by horse, not truck."

Once again the screen changed, zooming in even further. The number of ranches narrowed to three.

"Do you know anything else about Monton's ranch?" Torrin pressed further.

"He raises cattle," Neal offered.

"Who doesn't on Dowson?" On the screen one of the ranches blinked out leaving only two.

"One of the ranches raises only emu, Torrin," Tien informed her.

"What can you tell me about the two that are left, Tien?"

"One ranch is called the Flying V, the other is the Double M."

Torrin chewed her lower lip a moment, looking back and forth between the two properties. "I bet it's the second one. From what I've heard, there's no way Monton would go about not naming his ranch after himself in some way."

Neal nodded in agreement. "It's true, he thinks he's a bull among steers."

"Tien, I need you to take us into orbit over the ranch. We'll do a sweep of the area and see what's waiting for us down there."

CHAPTER TWENTY-THREE

Jak and Tanith's fact-finding mission had been very successful. In some ways, maybe too much so. After interviewing all the farmers who had been hit, they had plenty of data but little discernible pattern. All the farmers had lost multiple heads of livestock, but the timing was all over the place. One farmer had been hit four nights running but hadn't lost any animals since then. There were a few farms where the tiger seemed particularly at home. It had returned to those farms many times since it appeared in the area.

"I think it has to be in the area of the farms it's hit the most," Jak said as she gnawed on a strip of dried meat. She and Tanith were sharing a simple meal under the stars. Tanith had been insistent on not depending on the locals for supplies or shelter. Jak didn't understand her resolve. On Haefen, she'd rarely had the opportunity to operate in friendly territory. Not to take advantage of the resources that were being freely offered seemed counterproductive to her. However, Tanith was her superior officer, so she would abide by her decisions for the time being.

The time she spent with her on an active mission had driven home the fact that Tanith, although she was the head of ground forces for Nadierzda, had little to no actual combat experience. Eventually, she would probably be an adequate commander, but Jak didn't want to be one of her soldiers if she were ever in a real combat situation. Tanith had some devious ideas and was quick on her feet mentally, but she also displayed an alarming willingness to sacrifice her soldiers to obtain an objective, at least in the abstract. Jak had served under commanders like her on occasion. They hadn't lasted long in the Devonite army and had ended up being shuffled quietly into desk jobs. What really concerned her was that very few women on Nadi would know any better.

"What makes you say that?" Tanith asked distractedly, her attention on the campfire.

"It puts them at the middle of the tiger's range. It hits those the most, then ranges out to the other farms."

"What about the one that it hit so many times at the beginning but then never bothered again?"

"I'm willing to bet that the tiger came into the area close to there. I'm sure if we search, we'll find some way that it passed through from another area. If I remember correctly, there was a small canyon not far from there that led to one of the smaller craters. If I were a betting woman, I would say it came here from there."

Tanith nodded with absent interest. "That seems reasonable. I don't see much point in tracking where it came from. I'm more interested in where it is now."

"That makes sense. I think we should do a flyover of the most heavily visited area tomorrow and see if we can narrow down possible den sites."

"I'm afraid that's going to have to wait a day. We need to head back to the base at Landing tomorrow. There are some things I need to catch up on."

"Are you sure?" Jak was surprised to hear Tanith backing off on the hunt. She'd been very gung ho until then, insisting that the locals needed the predator dealt with as soon as possible. After having seen firsthand what damage a Sinosian tiger could wreak on a large herbivore, Jak wholeheartedly agreed with the sentiment.

"I can stick around and do a flyover if you're going to be busy."

"No, I'm not comfortable with you doing that. Your piloting skills have definitely improved, but the air currents along the edges of the crater are tricky. Very unpredictable. They get even worse where the canyons and smaller crater systems meet the larger crater. No, you'll need to come with me. Besides, I'm sure you'll be happy to get a shower and sleep in a real bed."

Jak made a noncommittal sound at the back of her throat that Tanith took for agreement. The conditions out here were no worse than what she'd had to endure on some of her long-range assignments on Haefen; for the most part they were far better. Nadierzda's climate was much drier that Haefen's and they were rarely rained upon. The few times it had rained, the temperature had been so warm that the rain had brought a welcome coolness that was actually very soothing. As far as she was concerned, there was no good reason to go back to the base quite yet, but Tanith seemed adamant, and she wasn't sure enough of her position to push back on the matter.

The next day, a flight of a few hours put them back at base. Tanith had been preoccupied since their discussion the night before, and Jak was happy to be parted from her for the day. As soon as they landed, Tanith secured the ultralight with the anchor and headed toward her house.

"Meet me tomorrow morning at 0800 hours," Tanith tossed over her shoulder as she walked briskly away. "I should be ready to go by then."

It was only as she was stowing her own aircraft that Jak wondered exactly where she was supposed to meet Tanith. The major hadn't said. After mulling it over, Jak decided she would simply have to meet her at Tanith's house a little early. That way Tanith wouldn't be waiting on her at the planes if she hadn't meant to meet at the house. Satisfied with her reasoning, Jak finished securing the sailplane and headed over to the barracks.

To her surprise, she was greeted often on her way over. The women seemed genuinely happy to see her, which was a little disconcerting. She hadn't realized she knew this many of the women on base, let alone that she'd made a big enough impact to be missed. The feeling was a new one, and she decided she liked it. Overall, she was starting to feel a little more like she belonged. The sensation of belonging was a warm one and she hugged it to herself.

On her return to her barracks, she took Tanith's advice and took a shower and a nap. It did feel good to be clean once more, though she slept as well under the stars as she did in a bed. Refreshed, she went looking for more supplies. She loaded up her remaining ammunition and wondered how she'd get more when this ran out. Still, if things went badly, having extra rounds could make all the difference. She also stocked up on rations. The tiger had already proved more elusive than she had anticipated, and she had no real idea how much longer they would continue tracking it. She could always supplement the rations with hunting as she had many times before, but experience had taught her that preparation trumped luck. Her recent cross-country trip with Torrin had taught her as much.

Thinking of Torrin brought the usual flash of pain and anger. Torrin's betrayal was still beyond her comprehension, but there was a new emotion in there also. She missed Torrin terribly. It was weird, she thought. The person who had caused her so much pain was also the one who could best take the pain away. What was she going to do without her? Angry at herself for dwelling on Torrin again when she'd promised herself that she was over the woman, Jak rammed the extra rations and ammo into her backpack.

There were still a few hours before lights out, so she headed over to the shooting range. There hadn't been many opportunities for practice when they'd been out in the field. The most practice she and Tanith had put in had been in spotting. Tanith was especially eager to learn more about spotting and had requested training every evening while they'd had enough remaining daylight. She'd even talked Jak into working with her a bit at night. While Tanith had a lot of good instincts for spotting, Jak was unconvinced that she had the proper focus. When they were finished with the mission, Jak was going to tell Tanith that she should concentrate more on shooting and find a partner that she could trust to spot for her. There was no point in telling her beforehand, since Jak was certainly not going to trust Tanith with the shot at the tiger. And since a spotter was a welcome addition, especially on an assignment like theirs, she would keep her mouth shut for the time being.

It felt good to be taking some time with the targets. She worked out at the end of the range, taking shots that were as far away as she could manage there. Originally, the range hadn't gone back that far, but after Jak had started training, the base commander had seen fit to expand it. Now Jak could work up to two thousand meters away from the targets. That wasn't near the outside of her range, but it had been as much room as they could safely arrange for her. When she needed to work out at further distances, she went hunting.

"Ho, Captain Stowell!" A familiar greeting rang out across the range. She looked up and saw a couple of the Banshees she'd recommended for additional training crossing the range toward her. They were staying well clear of her line of sight. Both of them carried the closest thing to sniper rifles she'd been able to find. They were plasma rifles and so would never match the range of her rifle, but they were adequate.

"Perez, Hamilton." She greeted them absently and continued lining up her shot. The wind was blowing a fair clip from west to east, but there were eddies along the two kilometers to her target. She scanned the range's periphery, checking for cues on changes to the wind's direction and speed, almost without realizing it. She dropped a bead and over, then gently squeezed the trigger. With a roar, the rifle went off. Tongue between her teeth she watched as the bullet crossed the two thousand meters and buried itself in the faraway target. It was a hand's width from the center and she frowned in irritation.

"Nice shot, Captain," Perez offered. From where they stood, it would be impossible for her to tell how the shot had ended up. From here, the

Banshees wouldn't even be able to tell if Jak had hit the target. They just assumed she'd hit a bull's-eye every time.

"It was all right," she grunted. She eyed them out of the corner of her eye as she chambered another round. "What can I do for the two of you?"

"We were coming out to practice," Hamilton said. "Saw you here and thought we'd say hello."

"Maybe see if you wanted to give us some more pointers," Perez added quickly.

"If it's no bother." Hamilton sighed, shooting Perez a dirty look.

"It's no bother at all," Jak said as she lined up her next shot. This time she paid closer attention to anything she could find that would tell her what the wind was doing. After double and triple checking to make sure her shot was lined up correctly, she squeezed off another shot.

"Wow," was all Hamilton said. She'd been watching the bullet's trajectory through her scope. It looked like it had landed less than a centimeter away from the center of the target.

"Much better," Jak said. She pushed herself up. It was good to know she could still tune distractions out and focus to get the shot off. "Let's move up to a range where your rifles actually have a chance of hitting the targets."

"Do you think you could train us on your rifle sometime?" Perez asked as they walked down the range.

"We'd need to see about procuring some more rifles like mine. All you guys have are plasma weapons."

"If you need someone to ask Torrin about getting some more, I could do it." Perez was looking at her with something akin to pity and Jak didn't like it.

"I'm perfectly capable of talking to her if I need to," Jak snapped.

"I only thought—" Perez cut off when Hamilton accidentally trod on her foot. "Hey, what'd you do that for?" Hamilton jabbed her in the side and Perez looked down and caught the look on Jak's face. "Uh, never mind."

"It's fine," she grated from between clenched teeth.

"You know, Captain, you've been really good about training us on this. Maybe we can return the favor? How would you like some hand-to-hand combat training?" Hamilton sounded like she was desperately trying to change the subject. The idea was a good one though. Jak had seen Torrin tossing around men who outweighed her by a good margin. Her skills in close-quarters combat were adequate—hand-to-hand combat was a skill that anyone who spent any time in the trenches needed to know—but being able to do it with the same facility as Torrin couldn't hurt.

"Actually, I'd really appreciate that. I know enough to take care of myself against men who haven't been overly well-trained. Nothing like what you guys can do, though. Can you give me my first lesson today?"

"Sure." Hamilton looked a little surprised. "So soon?"

"We're heading back out tomorrow morning and I don't know when I'll be back next. And since you don't know if you'll be around when we get back, we might as well strike while the iron is hot."

"You're going to be really stiff," Perez warned, a concerned look on her face.

"Perez really wants you to be around when that happens so she can offer you a massage." Hamilton's stage whisper brought an indignant look to Perez's face.

"Hey, that's not true," Perez defended herself. "Well, not totally. I mean, I'm sure the captain would enjoy a massage for stiff muscles, and if she needed one I would offer."

Jak shot her a look, her cheeks flaming.

"I'm joking! Unless you're okay with it, in which case I'm completely serious."

Hamilton broke out into peals of laughter and Perez grinned over at her. It was clear that the two of them had been engaging in this kind of banter for years. Jak wondered what it would be like to share that kind of bond with someone. Of course, that someone would have to actually stick around, which seemed to be a problem. Maybe she was some sort of jinx. She shook her head to dispel the nagging thought and focused on the Banshees.

"Well, I'm serious about training you to become decent snipers. So you'd better get prone if you want my help."

The two women dropped to the grass and laid out.

"Not a word, Perez," Jak warned her. Wisely, the private kept her mouth shut and smiled beatifically instead. Against her better judgment, Jak smiled and shook her head. "These targets aren't going to shoot themselves, Banshees. Show me what you got, and I hope for your sakes that you've been practicing since the last time I worked with you."

"Yes, sir," they replied in unison. Jak smiled again. So this was what it felt like to belong somewhere.

* * *

Not for the first time, Torrin wished she had ocular implants like Jak's. Being able to see in the dark would have been very useful right about now. When the implants were finally moved to the production stage, she would be among the first to get one. There were perks to being the boss, after all. She squinted across a field at a series of long, low buildings on the other side of a wooden fence. They were lit up with torches and floodlights, or she wouldn't have been able to make them out at all. Both of Tyndall's moons were out, and there was a decent amount of light, but not quite enough for the naked eye.

Back in the *Calamity Jane* with Tate and Neal, she'd scanned the Double M Ranch, then perused the satellite imagery. The ranch was extensive, with over a dozen buildings. Some of them were much too small for a man like Monton to live in, and others were much too large and likely housed livestock. They'd finally settled on three buildings. Neal had thought it unlikely that Monton was bunking with his men and was adamant that he was set up in the smallest building. It was a little smaller than the other buildings. From where Torrin watched, crouched under the trees, she could see that it was the only two-story building on the premises. It seemed that Neal might have been right after all.

She checked her chrono. Two minutes until the main group of Banshees would start the diversion. Shortly after that, Tien and her counterpart on the *Oleander* would join in from above. If all went well, Torrin's little group would be able to waltz in and have a little chat with the man who threatened her interests on the planet. She fiddled idly with the cloaking collar, remembering the only other time she'd used it, back when Jak still believed in her. The sniper had placed her life in Torrin's hands, then had covered her as they made their way off the planet. It was an apt metaphor for their relationship, Torrin decided. They were at their strongest when they leaned on each other. Together they were more than the sum of their parts. It was too bad their bond had broken so easily.

A dull thud echoed through the night and after only a few moments, the ranch boiled with activity. With the speed of the response, it was clear to Torrin that the men at the Double M Ranch were no strangers to violence. Their response was surprisingly organized. She hoped the Banshees would be able to hold their attention. If they didn't, the men running toward the explosion were going to find her little infiltration group easy prey.

Uncertainty and lack of control over what the others involved in a plan were doing were two of the reasons she hadn't stayed long in the Banshees. She'd fretted over what the others were doing, if they'd been caught or injured. The ones who hadn't made it back weighed especially heavily on her. When she quit the Banshees she'd been a sergeant, one of the youngest ever. She had a talent for leadership, but the responsibility over life and death that came with the territory had been more than she could cope with. After one mission went very wrong and resulted in the death of two of her soldiers and half the women they'd been sent to rescue, she'd had enough. She, along with her good friend from the unit, Audra, had quit and moved on to getting their fledgling business off the ground. Audra had recruited Mac to run the books. It had been evident very quickly that Mac had much more to offer than simply bookkeeping. They'd brought her on as a full partner and Troika Corp. had been born.

Torrin's talent for leadership had worked out very well for her, and she'd rapidly turned into the public face of the company. Best of all, the responsibility had been much different and she'd never had to put her employees directly in the middle of a military operation. Until now, that was.

Overhead, the high-pitched whine of engines sliced through the night. The *Calamity Jane* came in hard above her, then banked away to the north where it hovered, sending shot after shot down toward the compound. A few seconds later, the *Oleander* swept overhead, bristling with weapons that opened up on the men below. Between the cacophony of explosions, Torrin could hear small arms fire as the men reacted to the ships. Tien was under strict instructions to be careful and not to endanger the ship. The AI had solemnly agreed, but Torrin thought she'd detected a note of glee over her assignment. Something was warping her AI into some serious risk-taking behavior. If this continued much longer, Torrin was going to have to overhaul her personality module.

The diversion certainly looked serious enough and appeared to be fulfilling its purpose. Torrin's approach appeared clear and she glanced to either side of her position. Four Banshees crouched with her in full-power armor. No exposed flesh showed except for the chins under the visors of their helmets. They'd engaged their active camouflage and were hard to make out, the armor's edges melting into the scenery. Nodding, Torrin clasped the cloak's end around her neck and twisted the leads. Looking down, she could no longer see her feet. Satisfied that she was invisible, she set off across the field. The Banshees overtook her easily, running with mechanical ease. She could hear the faint creak and hum of the armor's motorized joints.

This field had been allowed to grow over and was an unruly mass of scrub and grasses. The other fields around the ranch had either been cultivated or were barely more than sandy lots. The plot overgrowth gave them the best chance of evading discovery.

Even though she knew she was invisible to the naked eye, the jog across the empty field was nerve-wracking. It felt like every eye was upon them, but they made it across without taking any fire.

Monton's ranch looked like a bee's nest that had been used as a piñata. Men ran back and forth. They lined the sides of buildings and took shots off into the dark. Tien and the *Oleander* had the attention of the majority of the men, but every now and again a knot of people would dash off toward the side where the Banshees still launched their distraction.

Carefully, Torrin followed the Banshees as they skirted around the edge of the compound's buildings. The two-story house that was their target was at the other end of the compound. She knew no one would see her, but the Banshees were definitely visible. They were hard to see, but not impossible. Eventually, the odds that someone would see the shadowy forms rippling through the dark would catch up with them. They picked their way from one structure to the next to minimize their chances of discovery.

Finally, they peered at the front of the house from behind a small building. From the look of it, Torrin thought it was probably a chicken coop or had been at one time. There was no sign of chickens now and none of the stomach-turning aroma that usually accompanied the birds. To her chagrin, the commotion had failed to draw off the two heavily armed and very competent-looking sentries. The door into the house was closed, and there was no way they could get in without alerting them. As they watched from behind the coop, a man in a duster appeared at a run and pounded up to the stairs. This was their chance. Taking the chance that the attention of the sentries was fixed on the approaching messenger, Torrin took off after him. On her way past Tate, Torrin pounded her on the shoulder. She had to sprint to catch up with the man and she slipped in right behind him. He took the steps two at a time and approached the sentries. Torrin was right on his heels.

"Report for Monton," he barked, and the sentries nodded.

"What the hell are you doing?" Tate's voice rang through her transmitter. A decided edge had erased the usual softness of the Banshee's voice. Torrin ignored her. Answering Tate's question through her subdermal transmitter would give her away.

The runner pushed past the sentries and Torrin slipped after him. The doors swung wildly in his wake as he pushed his way through them. Torrin pivoted quietly toward the right-hand sentry. She pulled her vibroknife out of the sheath on her thigh, making sure she didn't give away her position. Unsheathing the knife was harder than she'd expected, since she couldn't see it. She had to rely on feel alone and for long moments, she stood, poised on the balls of her feet until she finally fumbled open the sheath's clasp. The knife in hand, she reversed it and rushed the last few steps to the first sentry and brought the pommel of the knife down behind his ear. The sentry collapsed and his partner whirled toward Torrin. She froze, knife held in front of her, knowing he couldn't see her, but not quite believing it.

"What the…" The sentry squinted at her as a ripple ran through the knife and Torrin let loose a torrent of invectives in her head. This must be the glitch Jak had talked about. Torrin shifted to her left, as the sentry raised his rifle. Her stomach clenched as he sighted on the space where she'd been. A shape detached itself from the shadows behind him. An armored arm snaked around his neck, pulling him backward and squeezing. Another form swooped in and yanked the rifle from his grip before the hapless sentry could squeeze off a burst and give away their presence.

Two more blurred forms leaped onto the porch. One planted a hand in Torrin's shoulder and shoved her against the wood siding of the front of the house. For a moment she wondered how she'd been seen, then she remembered the thermal setting on the Banshees' visors. That was inconvenient. She hoped none of the men they were going up against had equipment of similar quality. It was worth remembering that the cloaks only worked on the visible spectrum of light.

"Don't you ever pull a stunt like that again." Torrin couldn't read Tate's expression, but the frozen edge in her voice impressed upon her exactly how angry the Banshee captain was.

"I saw an opening and exploited it." Torrin tried to shrug off Tate's hand. It didn't budge, and she struggled angrily for a moment. "If you don't mind, our opening is closing rapidly."

"Fine." Tate withdrew her hand. "But you and I are going to have a little chat once this is through."

How exactly had the captain expected her to communicate what her plans were, Torrin wondered. She wasn't visible and speaking had been too great a risk. Muffled thuds of plasma bursts made her look over. The Banshees stepped away from the downed sentries, plasma pistols smoking. Twin tendrils of smoke rose from the sentries' temples where they'd been permanently removed as threats.

She didn't dwell on the savagery, but a long-dormant disquiet lurked in the back of her mind. Instead, she pushed her way through the swinging doors. Banshees followed on her heels. They stood in an elegant foyer and looked around.

The house's interior was surprisingly quiet. The thud of explosions and near-constant crackle of small arms fire did little to penetrate through to the silent interior. The decor was not what she'd expected from the outside. The home's rustic exterior masked an elegantly furnished interior. Torrin might not like Monton's methods or designs on her business, but she couldn't fault his taste. The understated opulence screamed money far louder than Hutchinson's gross overindulgence ever had.

The sound of men talking floated down the stairs toward them. Two Banshees ghosted up the steps with Torrin behind them while the remaining two took up the rear. Tate had her hand on Torrin's shoulder. French doors stood immediately opposite the top of the stairs. A long hallway stretched to either side. The voices seemed to be coming from behind the double doors. Tate let go of Torrin and gestured to the two Banshees coming up the top of the stairs, telling them to stand guard. She held up three fingers, then two. On one, two Banshees burst through the doors, Torrin in their wake.

A man who could have only been Monton sat behind the large desk situated in front of a bay window that took up most of the wall. Torrin could barely make out his profile as he watched the chaos unfolding outside. She couldn't help but think that Jak would have had a field day with him. In front of those large windows, he would have been appallingly easy to eliminate from the outside.

The runner wheeled around at their sudden entrance. This close, he was much younger than Torrin thought, still a boy. He couldn't have been more than sixteen. Torrin doubted he had even started shaving yet.

Monton swiveled in his chair and regarded them. His eyes were a brilliant green as dead as chips of stone. In his eyes, Torrin could see that he didn't care about the life or death of anyone around him. She'd thought Jak's eyes reflected death. They merely reflected Jak's indifference to her own life, not a monumental indifference to anyone else's continued existence. He wasn't unattractive and was older than she'd anticipated. A full head of silvered hair framed a face with incongruous laugh lines. Torrin couldn't imagine this man smiling, let alone laughing.

Monton steepled his fingers. "Well, this is a surprise."

"What the devil—" the runner blurted as he was disarmed and shoved to the ground by one of the Banshees. The woman stood above him, aiming her plasma rifle at him while he trembled on the ground. Torrin stepped past them and deactivated the cloaking device at her neck.

"Hello, Monton," Torrin greeted the man at his desk. Those dead eyes followed her as she moved toward him. "You and I have some things to discuss."

"I can see that. It seems my initial assessment was somewhat inaccurate. I thought we were being attacked so we couldn't get out. You were holding us here so you could get in. And you are?"

"I'm sure you're familiar with my work. You've been doing your best to dismantle it."

Monton smiled suddenly, revealing startlingly white teeth. The lines on his face creased deeply. "Torrin Ivanov. I was told you'd be a tough nut to crack, but she didn't say anything at all about you being this aggressive."

"She? Who is that? You have a partner?"

The smile on his face sly, Monton spread his hands but said nothing.

At a nod from Tate, the Banshee jerked the runner to his feet and pushed him forward to stand next to Torrin, who pulled out her pistol and dug it in below the terrified boy's jaw.

"You should really reconsider your silence. Your man will greatly appreciate your cooperation."

"I'm sorry, Torrin. May I call you Torrin?" Monton's face creased again when she emphatically shook her head to the negative. "Torrin, you're laboring under a bit of a misconception. I see absolutely no reason to bargain with you. If you think that a gun to the head of my subordinate will convince me to tell you all my deepest secrets, then you're sadly mistaken."

For all of his smiles, the man was as serious as a shipboard plague. He was calling her bluff. She had no desire to kill the man standing next to her, and somehow he knew that. The man grinning at her from across the desk was a different story. Suddenly, her fingers itched to put a bolt of plasma through those too-white teeth.

CHAPTER TWENTY-FOUR

With an uncharacteristic bounce to her step, Jak made her way down the road toward Tanith's home. Little girls chased each other through tidy yards, giggling and shouting. This area of the base had a group of single-family homes. They were reserved for the highest ranking officers and for lower- and mid-rank officers who had wives and children. Fortunately, it wasn't a complicated layout, as Jak was still having problems with the neural artifacts of the last upload she'd received on Haefen. If she didn't concentrate, she had a tendency to start orienting herself based upon the maps of Hutchinson's sector.

She'd spent a pleasant afternoon in the company of the two Banshees, Hamilton and Perez. While they'd mostly trained at the range, the easy camaraderie the two women showed her had bolstered her typically sour mood. Since she'd arrived on Nadierzda, no one had been hostile to her, but the newer trainees treated her with a kind of relentless hero worship that was exhausting to deal with day in and day out. The Banshees didn't look at her as some kind of demigod; they treated her at face value and as one of their own. It was a bond she'd never been able to share with anybody and she was really enjoying it. She'd gotten glimpses of this type of closeness with the Devonite troops but had never been able to relax her guard enough to take advantage of it.

True to their claims, she was stiff from the hand-to-hand combat training she'd gotten after finishing with sniper training. They'd thrown her around with galling ease, but she had learned a thing or two. The experience was good for her, she thought. It was easy to feel superior because she was so much better than they were at sharpshooting. She needed to remember that they had their own skills, and they were easily as good at theirs as she was at hers.

The stiffness in her muscles and joints was complemented by the pain in her head. After training was over, the two Banshees had corralled a handful of women from their unit and they'd headed out to the bar. Jak had drunk more than was wise. It was more than she'd ever indulged before, and she was paying the price. Various pains aside, though, at that point the only thing that would have made her happier would have been to turn back the clock on Torrin's cheating.

Her rucksack slipped off her shoulder and she stopped a moment to swing it around and hitch it back up into place. When she looked back up, she caught a glimpse of blond hair on a woman who was just leaving the door to Tanith's house. The woman looked familiar, and when Jak zoomed in on her face, she recognized the blond bitch she'd last seen in Torrin's lap.

What on earth is she doing at Tanith's house?

She didn't have to wonder long as Breena turned around and was pulled back and wrapped up in a passionate embrace by none other than Tanith Merriam.

Jak stood, rooted to the spot, as she considered the implications of what she was witnessing. If Breena was so hot for Torrin, why was she in Tanith's arms? She knew Torrin was still offworld. Maybe Breena was so unfaithful that as soon as Torrin had left, she'd jumped into the arms of the next available woman. Something about the whole thing bothered her. Something about the situation bored its way into her brain. She couldn't put her finger on it. She did know one thing, though. There was no way she wanted those two to know that she'd seen them. Watching them still kissing, she slid to one side of the street and crouched down by a hedge.

Breena and Tanith continued kissing for quite some time, long enough for Jak to get uncomfortable. Finally, their lips parted. Tanith said something that Jak couldn't make out and Breena laughed. As they disengaged, Tanith swatted Breena's behind. Jak rolled her eyes. That was one behavior of Tanith's that she really couldn't stand and it suddenly had a whole new context for her.

Breena gave Tanith a small wave before sliding behind the wheel of the small car parked on the street. She blew Tanith a final kiss and drove away, passing Jak without any sign that she'd noticed the sniper crouched behind the bush. After allowing a few more minutes to pass, Jak resumed her trek to Tanith's house. She took her time. She wanted to arrive at such a time that it would be clear that she couldn't possibly have seen Breena. The scene she'd witnessed was going to be her little secret until she could figure out what it was about it that bothered her so much. One thing she did know, she would need to be on her guard around Tanith.

The little house was identical to the others around it. It was built low to the ground with heavily frosted windows. Many of the homes in the city had force fields instead of windows, but that was an extravagance that someone had apparently decided wasn't necessary for the military women of Nadi.

Jak knocked crisply at the door.

"I'm coming," Tanith called from inside the house. "What did you forget—" She swallowed her words when she opened the door and discovered Jak on her doorstep.

Jak put on a mildly confused frown. "I'm pretty sure I've got everything."

"What are you doing here? I thought we were going to meet at the hangar."

"You didn't specify, so I thought I'd meet you here early to make sure you didn't have to wait on me if I went to the wrong place."

"Good thinking, I guess," Tanith said. "I'm almost ready. You might as well come in while I get the rest of what I need together."

Jak followed her into the house and stood awkwardly in the living room as Tanith puttered around, wandering in and out of the small rooms at the back of the house. True to her word, she was mostly packed; all that seemed left to do was tracking down a few last-minute details.

The living room was very nice. A large console took up the majority of one wall, picture paused, a woman caught leaning in toward the camera. The furniture looked plush and comfortable. The room smelled faintly of sex, and Jak blushed when she identified the smell. She decided not to sit on the couch.

A large machine took up one corner of the room. It looked out of place. The rest of the living room was made for comfort and leisure, but the machinery didn't go with the decor. Jak wandered over to it and inspected it idly. There was no way to tell what it was for and she soon grew bored and ambled across the room to take a look at the vids Tanith had loaded in her console. They were mostly pornography, and Jak blushed again at some of the thumbnails on the screen.

"I see you found my little collection," Tanith said from behind her. Jak whirled, the thumbnails still up on the screen. "There are some good ones. If you ever want to borrow one, let me know."

"Uh, no thanks. I don't think it's the best thing to be watching in the barracks. Not good for discipline."

"I'm sure you're right. Well, if you decide you're interested, you could always watch it here."

"Oh, okay. I'll let you know." To Jak, the answer was fairly noncommittal, but the light in Tanith's eyes led her to suspect the major had other ideas.

"What's that?" Jak pointed at the large machine in the corner. She wasn't really that interested, but she wanted to head off Tanith's errant thoughts. Whatever Breena's status, it was clear that Tanith didn't consider herself bound to her in any meaningful way.

"Oh, that." Tanith flipped a hand at it dismissively. "I track down equipment for the militia, so I need a comm system. Messages come in at all times of day or night, so it makes more sense for me to have one here, that way I can head out when I get a good tip." She grinned widely. "I have my own ship too. It simplifies things for me. I don't need anyone else to make runs to pick up new gear."

"You don't go through Troika for that?" How could Tanith afford her own ship? *Majors must be paid a lot more than captains, if she can afford that.*

Tanith shot her an incredulous look. "Would you? No, I can procure my own gear, thanks. Relying on Torrin usually isn't a good idea."

"So are you ready to get back to the hunt?" Jak asked quickly. She didn't need any more reminders about Torrin, not when she was finally in a decent mood.

"That I am." Tanith shouldered her own rucksack and allowed Jak to precede her out of the house. "We can take my bike."

Jak was silent on the way over to the hangars and Tanith didn't prod her too much for conversation.

Their return flight to the southern end of the crater was uneventful. As previously agreed upon, they scouted the area around the three farms by air. The flight and scouting helped Jak regain some of her cheerful frame of mind. If she could have returned to Haefen's majestic woods, her day would have been perfect. At least on Nadierzda, no one was trying to kill her.

As they were scouting, Jak caught a glimpse of a long crack in the sheer face of the crater. She angled her sailplane for a better look. Sure enough, the crack looked like a narrow canyon.

"I think I found something," Jak radioed to Tanith. She still didn't have an implant, but true to her word, General Lethe had procured a transmitter for her. It fit securely around her neck, with a small piece that fit securely in her ear canal. Jak had set it to voice activate, allowing her to keep both hands free for flying.

"Where is it?" Tanith came back. It was disconcerting to hear a voice that clearly with little static or distortion. It felt a little bit like Tanith was leaning in to speak directly into her ear.

"Check your three o'clock. There's a fissure in the crater wall."

"Got it. Let's go down to take a look."

"Are you sure that's a good idea? If we're right, the tiger could be in the area."

"We should be all right, it's daytime after all. Tigers are predominantly nocturnal. I want confirmation that we're staking out the right place."

After a little more flying, they found a spot where they'd be able to land and Tanith would be able to tow Jak back into the air without too much difficulty. Her landing was perfect and Jak congratulated herself mentally. She was really getting the hang of the sailplane.

"Looks like you'll be ready for an ultralight soon," Tanith observed as she was gathering her gear. Jak noticed that contrary to her words of encouragement about the tiger, Tanith was arming herself to the teeth. Prudently, she made sure all of her weapons were close at hand. Most important were the sidearm and knife. If they happened upon the tiger accidentally, the rifle would be almost useless at close range.

"I'd like that," Jak said.

"I bet you would. I'll make sure it happens as soon as we get back." Tanith swung her pack onto her back and set off toward the canyon. Jak couldn't trust her direction sense so she was happy to let Tanith take point. Normally, she would have chafed at not breaking the path, but there was no telling where they would end up if she led. The terrain wasn't exactly difficult, especially not compared to the mountains in Haefen that she and Torrin had traveled over. It was funny, but that all seemed so long ago, and yet it had only been a few months. Her life had changed so much in that short time. She wondered if she was even the same person. It was so hard to tell.

Rolling hills were sparsely populated with low trees and more heavily with boulders of varying sizes. This close to the crater wall, it looked like some of the larger chunks of rock had tumbled from the crater's top. Jak looked up a trifle nervously to see if there were other boulders perched precariously at the crater's edge. The top of the crater was too far away to see. Even when she activated her implant's zoom feature, she still couldn't make out the edge clearly. Tanith seemed unconcerned and she tried to mimic the major's laissez-faire attitude.

Twenty minutes of walking put them right near where the crater walls sloped up at an acute angle. They followed the wall for another ten minutes until they came to an old rockslide. A stream, barely more than a trickle, had carved a small channel through the mass of tumbled rocks. The canyon started about five meters up the sheer wall, and the stream was fed by a small waterfall. The water dyed the canyon walls a brilliant orange. With the sunlight sparkling off the water, it was one of the prettiest sights Jak had seen on the planet. She'd been convinced that Nadierzda was all shades of brown and tan with the occasional splash of green. Until now, she'd found the landscape rather dull.

"Is that what I think it is?" Tanith asked, pointing to a disturbed patch of mud alongside the stream.

"It sure is," Jak replied, looking at the all-too-recent paw print in the mud. She crouched next to the print and reached out her hand. The print was bigger than her outstretched hand; the claws dug deep furrows into the ground.

"That's all the confirmation I need," Tanith said. "Let's get out of here."

"There's something else," Jak said and pointed.

"Shit!" Tanith swore fervently. In the muck a meter or so away were more paw prints, much smaller than the ones Jak had just inspected.

"There's a cub. At least one, anyway."

"What the hell do we do with a cub?" Tanith asked.

"I don't know. I really don't like the idea of killing young. But we can't leave it if we kill the mother either. Can Sinosian tigers even be domesticated?"

Tanith stood to one side of the stream, arms crossed under her breasts and frustration tightening her features. "I don't know. I'm going to need to touch base with Lethe."

"Can it wait until we've gotten out of here? Having a mother out there is making me really nervous. You can never predict how they'll react to intruders."

Tanith looked nervously up the side of the rock fall at the canyon's opening. "Excellent point. Let's go and I'll call in on our way."

* * *

Torrin stared at the silver-haired psychopath. Indecision held her immobile. The boy in her grip wasn't the direct threat, the man in the chair before her was the issue. If he wasn't around, pulling the strings, who knew what the runner would be up to? She wasn't sure what to do and was doing her best not to let her indecision show through. Some of it must have been apparent and Monton stood.

"Let me help you out with that," he said, standing and reaching into a desk drawer. The Banshees snapped into action, raising their rifles at the same time as Monton pulled a sleek-looking pistol out of his desk and fired three shots into the hapless runner. The sound of the concussions was deafening and shocked Torrin out of her hesitation.

The Banshees moved forward as one and Torrin was grabbed and pushed down behind the desk. There was one more report and a high-pitched crack and a projectile went winging off into the wall. Torrin struggled against the arm holding her down. The commotion from the other side of the desk came to a sudden conclusion.

"We need him alive," Torrin yelled. "Don't kill him!"

"You heard her," Tate said from behind her. She sat back on her heels and Torrin pushed herself up. Behind the desk, Monton was facedown on the floor, a Banshee kneeling in the middle of his back, her foot securing his arm. She kept him immobile while he struggled against the heel on his forearm. The pistol lay barely beyond his reach and the Banshee casually lifted her foot to kick it further away. Monton grunted in agony as her unsupported weight bore down on his back.

The door was unsecured and Torrin glanced back at it. Following her gaze, Tate gestured to the third Banshee who nodded and took up a position by the door. A stand lamp stood to one side of the door and the Banshee lifted it off the ground and dashed its top on the floor. The handles on the door were a needless affectation, but they worked nicely to hold the lamp in the door as a makeshift bar. Torrin nodded in approval at the woman's quick thinking. They would have some time to make an escape if anyone came looking for Monton.

The Banshees righted the desk chair and muscled Monton into it. Ropes from the drapes sufficed to secure him to the chair. Torrin double-checked the knots to ensure the bonds were tight, not particularly caring that they would be extremely uncomfortable. His cavalier attitude toward others had really hacked her off. Torrin glanced over at the runner, his feet barely visible around the corner of the desk. There was an outside chance that he was still alive and she moved around the desk to check his pulse. The boy was definitely dead and she drew her fingertips down over his eyelids, shutting eyes that still stared blankly in shock. She patted the dead kid's shoulder in commiseration, then stood back up, glaring at Monton. She unsheathed the vibroknife and moved toward him.

"So let's talk," she said and he raised his head and looked into her eyes. His own eyes were still dead, without any betrayal of emotion.

"Look at you," Monton said, a slight sneer playing around his lips. A livid bruise was rising from the side of his temple and a trickle of blood ran from a cut in the middle of the bruise. Somewhere in the scuffle, he'd been bashed in the head by a rifle butt. "You're painfully softhearted. She did say you wouldn't be able to do what needs to be done."

"She?" This was the second time he'd alluded to a woman. "Who is she?"

Monton chuckled hollowly. "I'm not supposed to tell you. She'll castrate me if I do."

"But she knows me? What the hell is going on here? Why are you targeting my people?"

"One question at a time, if you please. It will make it easier to ignore them. My head is splitting, or I'd be able to ignore all of your questions at once."

Torrin grabbed Monton by the collar and pulled him toward her, the chair rolling quietly across the room's plush carpeting. "Cut the crap, and answer my questions. Things will go a lot better for you if you talk to me."

Monton actually yawned in her face. "You don't have the stomach for it," he said lazily. "I heard you tell them that you need me alive. Talk about showing your cards. Hasn't anyone ever told you that negotiation involves keeping things back until the time is right to reveal them?"

The vibroknife in her hand pulsed menacingly as she brought it up to the side of his face. "I am prepared to use this if I need to. I'd rather not, but I've done things I haven't wanted to before. So answer the question. Why are you doing this?"

"All right, all right," Monton said with an air of being put upon. "I'm going after your business because she's paying me extremely well to do so. She wants you out of the way and when you didn't have the grace to get killed on that backwater planet, she had me create a diversion to bring you back out here. You're getting too close and a little ahead of schedule. You weren't supposed to get here until your little shopkeeper had been killed and your store torched."

"Yeah, well, I'm sorry to disappoint. Trying to find out who tried to have me killed piqued my interest."

"It's really too bad. I had quite the welcome party planned, and now you've ruined it."

"So who is she?"

"Back to that are we?" Monton frowned slightly. "You're so tedious. I won't tell you. No one frightens me, but she comes close. She's even more ruthless than I am. She'll kill me when she finds out that I told you."

"If you don't tell me…"

"You'll what, kill me? We already covered this. You don't have the stones and you need me."

Torrin smiled thinly. She could feel her mouth stretching unnaturally and knew that nothing in her smile touched her eyes.

"Oh no, Monton. I won't kill you. I'm going to maim you instead. You'd be surprised what you can live through."

"You don't have the guts," he said. Despite his bluster, Torrin saw the first sign of emotion in his eyes. Monton was definitely worried.

Hating herself, Torrin looked into the visor of the Banshee standing to Monton's right. "Pull out his hand." The woman reached over and worked at one of his hands in the bonds holding him in place. "Try me," she said to Monton.

"You won't," he insisted, even as the Banshee pulled his hand out and laid it palm-down on the desk.

"Last chance," she said. She hoped that he would take it. Monton glared at her. The vibroknife hummed steadily as she raised it. At the top of her reach she paused and looked down at him. He stared mutely back at her, jaw set. Torrin brought the knife down, plunging it into the back of his hand. The knife passed through his hand and the desk with equal ease. It only stopped when the hilt guard couldn't go any further.

Monton screamed and writhed in his chair, his shriek piercing her head, and she steeled her face not to betray her unhappiness with her actions while her stomach roiled violently. Blood pooled rapidly under his hand and dripped down the front of his desk.

"You bitch!" he howled.

"Answer my question, and I won't start on your fingers. Do you still doubt that I'm capable?" She hoped he wouldn't answer that. Her stomach surged again, and she swallowed hard to keep her gorge down.

His only answer was to whimper and writhe in his seat, paying more attention to his pain than to her. She wiggled the knife where it was still embedded, vibrating in his hand. The screams the movement wrenched from his throat were raw and visceral. Blood dripped crimson down his chin where he'd bitten through his lip.

"I asked you a question," Torrin reminded him and pulled the knife out. She spread his fingers and held the knife over his thumb menacingly. "Who is she?"

"Fuck you." Monton writhed in his chair enough that the Banshee directly behind him put both hands on his shoulders to hold him in place so he didn't loosen his bonds.

"You know I'm capable of it, so save yourself more pain and tell me what I want to know." She was giving him every chance to end the torture. She didn't like causing pain, but he wasn't giving her any choice. There was no way this scum would get away with targeting her people. If he hadn't targeted them along with her, she might have let him slide. They could have gone somewhere and duked it out until one of them came out victorious, but if he had information that would ensure her people's safety, she would do whatever it took, no matter how much anguish it caused her. She had no doubts that this scene would haunt her dreams that night and for many nights to come.

When he still refused to talk, she pressed the knife through the large joint on his thumb. He howled again and blood spurted from the wound where his thumb had been barely a moment before. His eyes bulged from his head as he stared in disbelief at the digit lying next to his hand.

Monton sobbed in agony, making his words hard to understand. "Okay, okay, but don't take any more of my fingers. Her name is Merriam, Tanith Merriam."

"What did you say?" Numb, Torrin wasn't sure she'd understood. Behind Monton, Tate and the other Banshee shared glances through their visors, then looked over at Torrin who'd inadvertently stepped forward at his words.

"Tanith Merriam."

Torrin dropped back a step, shocked to the core. Blood roared in her ears and the room dipped to one side. She felt like she'd been slapped in the face. Tanith had been her best friend when they'd been growing up until they'd had their falling out. It had been years since they'd seen eye to eye or could even stand to be in the same room together. She knew Tanith didn't like her, but she had never dreamed that she would go to such lengths to get rid of her.

"And she hates you," Monton continued maliciously. "She hates everything you stand for. I can see why."

"Listen, you misbegotten sack of goat swallop. You're going to leave my people alone. You're going to leave me alone. You're going to cut off all contact with Tanith. Do you understand?"

Monton stared at her, face flat and unreadable. "Absolutely. You'll never hear from me again."

Torrin regarded him levelly. He was lying through his teeth. "You try anything at all, and you'll be answering to these ladies, and they aren't nearly as restrained as I am. If that's what you want, then by all means, come after us. But when they catch up with you, they're going to carve you into the smallest pieces possible while still leaving you alive."

His eyes flinched and skittered from one side to another, not resting on her. It made Torrin sick to think that she could scare a psychopath that badly. For all of his fear, he still had no intention of leaving her alone, she would have bet money on it. There was only one way to end this and acid roiled in her stomach. She looked up and met Tate's eyes. The Banshee nodded approvingly at what she saw there.

Torrin lifted her pistol to the side of Monton's head. His eyes widened. Apparently he finally believed that she was capable of doing what needed to be done. Killing him was necessary. There was no way he would leave her people alone. Before she could think it over too closely, Torrin pulled the trigger. His head jerked, then sagged to the side. The stench of burning flesh and hair filled the room.

Torrin stared at the body that slumped in the chair, smoke rising from the burned crater on the side of his head. She willed herself not to care. This was not how she liked to operate. Violence should have been a measure of last resort, not something to be entered into in cold blood.

It was too close to the calculated way Jak approached her work. As far as she was concerned, self-defense was the only viable excuse for this kind of work. She seized upon that idea and drew herself up to her full height. It would have been them or him. When it came down to it, she would always do what needed to be done. *That doesn't mean I'll ever be comfortable with it.* She wiped hands damp with cold sweat on the front of her pants and looked up at Tate.

"Someone's going to take his place." There was no tremor in her voice. "All we did was slow things down."

"Maybe, but we've also bought you time. Time to reinforce your store, and time for us to go ask Major Merriam what the hell is going on."

Tanith's name made her too sick to her stomach to answer right away. Torrin turned away from Tate when she heard someone try the door. When the doors didn't open, they were yanked back. The stand lamp held up under the abuse, but Torrin could see it bending from the strain.

"Boss," a rough voice hollered from the hall. "Boss! Are you all right in there?"

"Looks like that's our cue." Torrin glanced at Tate. "Time to make ourselves scarce."

"You did what needed to be done to keep our people safe. If he really knew Tanith, then she could have compromised Nadi's location at any time."

"I know that." Torrin didn't need Tate to rationalize her actions. She knew what she'd done was necessary. "Let's get out of here." Torrin glanced back at the door quivering under the force of the blows of the men trying to get in. They didn't have much time and all she wanted was out of this room that smelled of blood and death. She reached up and activated her subdermal transmitter. "Tien, pick me up at the rendezvous point. Let the others know that it's time to break things off."

Without waiting for a response, Torrin hurried to the bay window behind the desk. She picked up a small table and hurled it at the window. It bounced off without leaving a dent. The window was made of shatterproof glass. No wonder Monton hadn't been worried about sniper bullets. With a flick of her wrist, the vibroknife hummed back to life. She was able to force the blade through the glass, but not without serious effort on her part. It was slow going.

A crack at the door drew her attention. An ax's large blade protruded through the wood. Fortunately for them, Monton had paid for nice doors made of sturdy wood. As she watched, the blade was pulled back and she could see an eye peering through the hole. The Banshee fired her plasma rifle at the hole, and the eye was obliterated by the plasma bolt. Shouts went up on the other side of the door and the rhythmic thudding on the door redoubled in intensity.

"Hold that door," Tate yelled. The two Banshees joined their compatriot at the door and Tate joined Torrin. Following Torrin's lead, she pulled out her own vibroknife and plunged it into the glass.

As the sound of plasma fire rose behind them, Torrin swore internally. She put her back into working the vibroknife through the glass. She'd made some headway when she remembered Monton's pistol. After a quick glance to locate it on the floor by the wall, Torrin picked it up and gestured Tate out of the way before firing the gun point-blank at the cracks they'd made. Finally the window gave out under the strain and little squares of glass rained down on her.

Shouts of triumph announced that the door had finally given out. She glanced back to see the Banshees backing methodically across the room toward them as they picked off anyone foolish enough to step into range of their rifles. Torrin threw herself through the empty window, trusting they would do the same. They were only one story up and she did her best to tuck and roll when she hit the ground. Evidently, she was rusty at taking those kinds of falls. Her ankle turned with a sickening pop that reverberated in her bones.

Short of breath and hurting, she pushed herself to her feet and ran as best she could into the night. Each step on her right ankle sent pain shooting through it and up her leg. She heard the Banshees hit the ground behind her. It sounded like they'd done so with more grace than she'd mustered. Two of them rapidly overtook her and pulled her arms over their shoulders and slid an arm under her rump, carrying her with no visible effort. Behind them, the night lit up with muzzle flashes, and bullets kicked up the ground around the Banshees' feet. The men were shooting blindly and none of them came close to hitting them. Torrin held on tightly as she was carried toward the rendezvous point.

The two Banshees were running in step and each double footfall was like a drumbeat on her soul, driving her forward. Jak. She'd been getting awfully chummy with Tanith before Torrin had left Nadierzda. What would Tanith do to Jak to get back at Torrin? The thought was a constant refrain as they pounded through the night toward their waiting ships.

CHAPTER TWENTY-FIVE

Their vantage point was a good one. Jak had found some narrow space atop a cliff about a kilometer and a half from the canyon where they'd found the troubling paw prints. There had been barely enough room to land their planes, which were collapsed down as much as possible and pushed off to one side. Tanith had secured them as well as she could. Otherwise it wouldn't have taken much more than a gust of wind to knock the aircraft over the edge.

A river ran below the cliff. Even up here, a dozen meters from the water's surface, Jak could hear the booming rush of water. She'd looked over the edge when they'd first arrived. The water was almost completely white. The rapids didn't go on for very long. If she turned her head to the left, she could see where they calmed down to a flat expanse of blue.

Their position wasn't perfect. There was only one way out, by plane. Two if she counted going over the cliff and into the river. The chances that she would survive that exit were pretty slim. Her sniper's sensibilities were on edge over the lack of escape routes. She tried to calm herself by reminding herself that they weren't in hostile territory. There might be a major predator down there, but it didn't have troops of men trying to kill her.

Jak leaned her head to the side and peered through the scope again. She'd been laid out in a prone position for hours now. This was something she was used to, hours on a stalk, waiting for her enemy to put his head out. There was something comforting about being back at it again, this time in defense of women she liked and whose safety she valued more than her own.

To her left, Tanith shifted her weight and Jak closed her eyes in irritation. The woman had no experience with this kind of work. The practice they'd done back at the base had been for short periods of time. It seemed Tanith wasn't responding well to the reality of the sniper's life. Worse, her shifts in position and attempts at conversation were preventing Jak from entering her semimeditative trance. As a result, time was passing very slowly.

"How do you keep from going completely stir crazy?" Tanith asked, unaware she was mirroring Jak's thoughts.

Jak took another look through the scope to make sure the Sinosian tiger hadn't made an appearance. After thoroughly surveying the area, she considered Tanith's question.

"Keep an eye out and let time wash over you," she finally said.

"That's very mystical of you." Tanith propped herself up on her elbows and trained her spotting scope on the distant canyon. "So that's all there is to it?"

"Not really. It took me a long time to learn it. It's like meditating. You kind of go away inside your head. Your eyes are searching, but you let go with your mind. When something changes, your mind snaps back into place."

Tanith groaned and rolled over onto her back. She stretched out her legs, shaking them to improve the circulation. "Ugh, then how do you deal with the constant immobility?"

"It's a lot easier to get the proper motivation when you know you're being hunted at the same time as you're hunting. The possibility of getting killed is an excellent motivator. All it takes is letting down your guard for a moment for everything to go badly wrong."

"It can't be that easy," Tanith scoffed. She rolled back onto her belly and raised the scope again.

Jak gritted her teeth in anger. "Easier. I've lost more people than I care to think about through a moment of stupid inattention. Starting with my brother."

"Oh geez, I'm sorry." Tanith was the picture of repentance. "I forgot about your brother."

"Yeah, well, it's not something I like to think about. It takes me to a place I don't like to go." Jak tensed when she felt Tanith's hand on the small of her back. When she didn't immediately say anything, Tanith started rubbing in small circles. "Please don't do that. We need to be focused on the tiger, not on me."

Tanith withdrew her hand in reproachful silence. Quietly, she went back to watching the cliffs by the waterfall. Jak rolled her eyes. There was simply no dealing with the woman. Tanith took every opportunity she had to try to bond with Jak, and when she was rebuffed, she got all silent and moody. It felt like she was trying to make Jak feel guilty. Manipulation was the one thing that pissed Jak off above all others. She had no time for games, and manipulative little maneuvers like that were the biggest time waster of all.

"Just keep an eye on that canyon. The tiger has to come out eventually." Silence greeted her suggestion. With an inward sigh, she decided to throw Tanith a bit of a bone. "Try tensing then relaxing each muscle group when they start to feel like you need to move them."

"Got it" was Tanith's only response to her advice. That was fine with Jak. She went back to watching for the tiger's appearance. She grinned suddenly when it occurred to her that Tanith had no idea what she was going to have to do when she needed to go to the bathroom. That would be entertaining.

They stayed there at the top of the cliff for the rest of the day. Tanith tried to engage her in conversation a few times, but Jak gently rebuffed her attempts. She wanted to be already in the zone when the tiger made its appearance. Talk brought her out of that, and she was sure their window of opportunity was going to be small.

The lengthening shadows concerned Jak. It was more difficult to judge distances when some areas were in shadow and others in light. The rocks around the canyon mouth made for plenty of shadows. She watched as shadows from the crater's edge started creeping toward them as the sun began to sink behind the crater's edge. Shadows had just engulfed the canyon mouth when Tanith grabbed her arm.

"I see movement!" she hissed in excitement.

Jak trained the scope on the canyon mouth, but she didn't see anything. The shadows were making it more difficult to see, but it was still too light to engage her night vision.

"Talk me over to it," she instructed.

"It's at seven o'clock from the canyon mouth. Down a ways, by the top of the rock fall."

A quick glance through the scope was enough to locate the tiger. The animal's raw power and easy movement sent a shiver through her. For a moment it looked up and appeared to be staring right at her through the scope, then it put its head back down and resumed drinking from the stream at the top of the waterfall. From their vantage, the animal was a mass of bunched muscle and bony ridges. Vertical marks striped its body from head to tail in shades of dark green and light tan. She was the perfect animal to disappear into the grasslands of Nadierzda's craters. They were lucky the tiger had made her den in the canyon. If they'd been going up against her in the grasslands, they would never have seen her.

Carefully, Jak lined up the shot. She carefully checked the wind's trajectory and speed. There were two places where the wind seemed to be changing direction and speed. She lined up the shot to account for the change in wind speed, the distance and their elevated position.

"What are you waiting for?" Tanith hissed. "Take the shot."

"I'm working on it. I don't have a good angle on the eye." The prominent bones of the large cat's face did a good job of protecting its eyes. With the tiger's head at that angle, if she took a shot, there was next to no chance that she would hit it in the eye. The chances were already vanishingly small. It would take all her skill to pull off the feat and she wasn't going to spoil her opportunity by rushing the shot. She tracked as the tiger turned to look behind her.

"There's the cub," Tanith announced, her eyes glued to the scope. "It's leaving the safety of the canyon now."

"What are our orders for the cub?"

"We're to leave it alone. Once we notify the general that we've dispatched its mother, they're going to come in to pick it up. The soft touches on the Ruling Council didn't approve of killing a baby, even a baby that will grow up to become a natural killer."

The news relieved Jak. Tanith might be contemptuous of those on the council who felt compassion at the cub's plight, but Jak shared their concern.

Below them, the tiger had its back to them as she tracked her cub's slow progress out of the canyon and down to the rock fall. It was visible through her scope now. To her admittedly inexpert eyes, it looked very young. It was uncoordinated and its head was big for its body, feet comically large. The tiger reached over and picked up the cub by the scruff of its neck, then jumped down the rock fall in one smooth motion. Jak muttered a curse as she moved quickly to track the animals.

"Keep your eyes on them," she ordered. "If they make it to the grass, we're going to have a hell of a time tracking them." Tanith's only answer was a grunt of assent.

The tiger wasn't going very far. She merely leaped down to the bottom of the rock fall and carefully deposited the cub, who rolled over onto its back and swatted playfully at its mother's shaggy head. The tiger used her nose to nudge the cub to one side, where it rolled to its feet and pounced again. It got a big chunk of impressive ruff that lined its mother's jawline. The tiger shook her head to dislodge the cub, then gave it a playful swat with one large paw.

The animals' hijinks weren't making things any easier for Jak. She had the shot lined up but still wasn't getting quite the right angle on the tiger's eye. Their movement meant she had to keep shifting to follow them and had to keep readjusting the crosshairs so they compensated for the wind and distance. The two animals at play also made it harder for her to see the tiger as a killing machine that needed to be taken out for all their sakes.

"Looks like you've got a clear shot," Tanith commented. "What are you waiting for?"

"Do we really need to kill it? Can't it be captured instead?"

"Don't tell me you're having second thoughts. You saw what it did to the livestock at the farms. You haven't seen what it can do to humans, but I have. It's not pretty. There is exactly one way this ends if we don't take it out now, and that's with the deaths of people you've met on their farms. Take the shot, soldier!"

Jak closed her eyes quickly, then reopened them. She drew a couple of steadying breaths. The tiger looked up toward them once again, the cub playing at her feet. Without thinking, Jak exhaled slowly and squeezed the trigger, holding the tip of her tongue between her teeth. She held her breath as the bullet leaped out toward its target. It was far enough away that there was a lag before the bullet found its target, but even before it hit, she knew it had flown true. It struck the tiger squarely in the left eye and the animal slumped to the ground. Jak leaned her forehead on the scope.

"You got it!" Tanith rose to her knees exultantly. "I can't believe it, you dropped one of those things with only one shot. That was beautiful." She leaned down and engulfed Jak in an exuberant hug. Jak made no effort to extricate herself from Tanith's embrace. Her heart bled for the beautiful animal she'd just killed and physical contact with someone else, even Tanith, made her feel a little better.

Tanith laid herself along Jak's body. She tilted Jak's head toward her and pulled her in for a long kiss. Shocked surprise froze her in Tanith's arms. Tanith took the opportunity to slide an insistent tongue into Jak's mouth. Finally, Jak managed to pull herself away from the other woman.

"What are you doing?" she demanded.

"Celebrating! Come on, you know it felt good. Let yourself go, ride the moment."

"Tanith, I can't do that. I'm sorry, you're great, but—"

Tanith's face clouded with anger. The change on her face was so quick that Jak scooted back a few centimeters. Gone was the affable woman Jak had gotten used to having around. In her place was someone with anger enough to set the planet on fire.

"But what?" Tanith asked quietly. "I'm great, but you're still in love with Torrin?"

"Well—"

"What the hell does it take to get you to make a clean break with her? With her past, you wouldn't think it would've been that hard to set her up, but she was so sickeningly devoted to you that I had to make something up out of the whole cloth."

"Wait, you did what?" Jak surged to her feet and stood over Tanith. "Why would you do that to me? To us?"

Tanith laughed wildly, with an edge that made Jak's skin crawl. "Grow up, Jak. I didn't do anything to you but try to do you a favor. She's not worth it. I could tell you stories from when we grew up." Tanith clambered to her feet.

"Bitch!" Jak swung her hand at Tanith's face. Tanith intercepted her hand and caught it at the wrist, squeezing. With a wordless yell, Jak dropped her rifle and slapped Tanith with her free hand. She put everything she had behind it and Tanith's head snapped back. When she turned back to look at Jak, the imprint of her hand was already welting up on Tanith's cheek. She grabbed Jak's other hand and twisted it viciously. Jak was forced up on her toes to try to alleviate the sudden pressure on her wrist.

"Why do you all stand by her so stubbornly?" Tanith shoved her face into Jak's. "Ever since before Galya picked her over me, it's been like that. She wouldn't leave Torrin either, and I had to take care of her, which is what I'm going to have to do now. Again." Jak couldn't tell if she was angrier at the rejection or at the inconvenience of taking Jak out.

"Took care of her? What are you talking about?"

"You wanted to know about Torrin's first girlfriend? 'Boo hoo, Torrin won't talk to me about her long-lost love, I'm so lonely.'" Her voice rose in a cruel mockery of Jak's frustrated tones. "Well, here's the whole story, and not even your precious girlfriend knows it. Torrin thinks her first love left Nadierzda rather than be with her." Tanith chuckled quietly. "Truth is, she had no plans to leave Torrin, so I helped things along by marooning her and her sailplane in the sands on the surface. I doubt she lived more than a day out there. No one ever thought to look for her, not when she'd left a note saying she was leaving, then disappeared onto a transport. By now, she's been torn apart by a sand dune. No one will ever find her."

Jak struggled in earnest. Tanith was clearly insane. Her hatred for Torrin burned brightly in her eyes, turning them into glittering stones. This was the canker Jak had been looking for, the proof that Nadierzda couldn't possibly be as perfect as it seemed. She'd found it all right, and it was going to kill her. Jak had no desire to end up dead on Nadierzda's surface, but it was no use, Tanith had a strong grip on her. Her knowledge of close-quarters combat was superior to Jak's. She barely even seemed to notice that Jak was trying to escape.

"It's too bad, really," the crazy woman mused as Jak thrashed in her grip. "You're awfully cute, talented too. What I could do with your talent at my disposal....You're like a weapon that just needs to be pointed in the right direction. Still, you've done well in your training. I'm sure that one of the trainees could do almost as well. Shellin, for example. She's gotten quite proficient and she doesn't have nearly the independent streak that you do."

Struck by Tanith's words, Jak did the only thing she could think of to throw her off. She leaned forward and covered Tanith's lips with her own. The other woman froze, then shifted her weight, pulling Jak against her. Her lips ravaged Jak's, tongue plunging insistently into her mouth, taking and claiming her. She dropped Jak's left wrist and wound her fingers through Jak's collar, pulling her closer still and cutting off her air. Jak stealthily dropped her hand to her leg and slowly unsheathed her combat knife from its leg sheath.

"Don't think I don't know what you're trying to do," Tanith gasped when she finally relinquished Jak's lips. "Throwing yourself on my mercy isn't going to change your fate." She chuckled throatily. "Though I could be convinced to postpone it a little longer."

Tanith leaned back in for a kiss, and Jak was unable to control her disgust. She turned her head before she could stop herself. A spasm of rage crossed Tanith's face, and she shoved Jak away from her. Jak staggered back and a rock rolled under her heel, her ankle suddenly folding over. She tumbled to the ground. Tanith stalked toward her. She had a pistol in her hand, and it was trained unwaveringly at Jak's head.

"Now would be a good time to start begging if you're so inclined," Tanith said, barely controlled rage seething in her voice.

Jak scuttled backward on her hands, one leg dragging. The pain was so intense that even the smallest pressure on the foot sent tears of pain flooding into her eyes. Fingers encountered empty air and she stopped. She looked up and encountered the ugliest smile she'd ever seen on Tanith's face. How had she ever thought of the major as a cheerful, friendly person?

"You could do me a favor and go over the edge."

At that moment, the option didn't seem like such a bad one. In a choice between Tanith and the river, the rapids didn't seem so daunting. She might actually survive entry into the water; it was the rocks and the force of the water that really concerned her.

Tanith took another step closer and Jak seized her opportunity. Like the Banshees had taught her, she swept her leg out and took Tanith's feet out from under her. With a muffled oath, Tanith went down in a heap. Sadly, she didn't topple over the edge. As Jak pushed herself to all fours and went scrabbling along the cliff edge, she considered that it would have solved all of her problems. She moved as quickly as she could, but she wasn't fast enough. A hand grabbed her bad ankle and twisted viciously. Jak screamed as pain seared through her damaged leg. The rifle was just out of her reach and she stretched to grab it. Her fingers grazed the stock, but before she could close her hand around it she was hauled back.

Tanith kept hauling her back toward her until Jak was once again in her arms. In a cruel mockery of her previous embrace, Tanith wrapped an arm around Jak's neck. With a hand behind her head, Tanith squeezed hard. Jak pulled at her arm and twisted desperately in her grasp. Nothing worked to dislodge Tanith's iron grip. As the edges of her vision collapsed in on her, she remembered the knife. Panic was setting in, and it took her precious seconds to fumble the knife out of the sheath. She was only going to get one shot at this. Forcing herself to concentrate she gripped the knife's handle and brought it down next to her leg, into Tanith's.

A blood-curdling scream and the slackening of the arm around her neck told her she'd succeeded in hitting something. She tore herself away from the madwoman and crawled toward the dubious shelter of the tethered planes. A glance behind her told her that she'd hit Tanith, but not seriously. She sat there, one hand clasped to the gash in her leg, the other reaching for her pistol.

Jak only had one option left. Without thinking, she slithered under the body of her sail plane. A whoosh and a thud by her ear set her ducking to avoid the shot even though she knew it was too late. How many times had she watched someone duck too late and there she was doing it herself. The edge of the cliff met her questing fingers. She wrapped her fingertips around the edge and pulled with all her might, sending her body tumbling into the void.

* * *

It was all taking too long and Torrin chafed at the delay. Tien was running the autodoc on her leg. Apparently she had a lower leg sprain. It was nothing she needed to worry about too much as long as she didn't need to move around a lot.

"You need to be careful, maybe go to ground for a few days," she said to Laiya. "Monton's death should slow them down a bit."

"Or it'll piss them off and they'll come in here guns blazing," Tate said in her soft, measured tones.

"There's no way I'm going to leave the store unattended," Laiya said. "Those goons will take it out if no one's there."

Torrin shook her head. "It's not what they'll do when there's no one there that I'm worried about. It's what they'll do if they find you."

"The Banshees are staying, aren't they? And besides, they aren't going to try anything tonight."

"They're staying," Torrin confirmed. "But if those guys decide some revenge is in order, it's going to get uncomfortable in a hurry."

"I need to get out of here." Neal's face was a sickly shade of gray as he broke in on their conversation. He'd been sitting quietly in the corner of the med-bay listening to them argue for the past fifteen minutes. "Some of those animals saw me talking to you. I'm going to be first on their list when they come looking for payback. And they will."

"You did help us out." Torrin eyed him consideringly. He really had burned all his bridges. She supposed she should have felt bad about that, but considering the grief his actions had put her through, it was no more than he deserved. "You have a couple of options. I can take you and drop you on a different world." She raised her hand to forestall him when he opened his mouth. "It's going to be the nearest inhabited world, and we'd be leaving right from here. I don't have time to collect your credits. I have to get home."

Neal closed his mouth with a snap and set his jaw while glaring at her. "What's my other option?" he finally said.

"You stay here and work with Laiya until the problems die down. The Banshees will be sticking around for the near future. They may even escort you to your home to pick up some of your things and your precious credits."

"That's not fair!" Neal's voice rose in whiny protest. "You said you'd take care of me, keep me safe."

"The Banshees are far better equipped to keep you safe than I am." Torrin could feel her nostrils flaring as she fought to keep her composure. "You want to talk about fair? What about the part where you sold me out for a few credits?"

"Torrin, maybe you should just take him." Laiya was unhappy, her lips pursed. Torrin guessed that she didn't want to be saddled with Neal.

"Make your choice," Torrin said, ignoring Laiya's protest. She glared at Neal, who had the grace to look somewhat abashed. He stood there, hands in his pockets and gazing back at her.

"I'll stay here," he said. Credits had obviously trumped his safety; Torrin wasn't in the least bit surprised.

"That's great," Laiya muttered. Neal blushed, his face an angry scarlet when he overheard her derisive voice.

"Good." Torrin craned her torso to catch Tate's eye. "Take care of both of them. I have more support for Laiya on the way, but you and your people will probably want to stick around until things die down."

"We won't let anything happen to them. I'm under orders to stick around until the situation is secure and no Troika employees are in danger."

"Good, and thanks. If there's anything or anybody you want me to send along after I get home, let me know before we take off."

Tate nodded, looking thoughtful, and Torrin turned back to Laiya.

"There, you have all the support I can get for you. Try not to get yourselves killed. And if you have to make a choice between your lives and the store, don't be stupid. The store's replaceable. Now get out of here. I have to get back to Troika yesterday."

"Aye, aye, ma'am!" Laiya turned on her heel and grabbed Neal's collar, pulling him along behind her. Tate followed them closely.

"Don't forget to check in regularly," Torrin called after their retreating footsteps.

"I know," Laiya's response floated back to her down the hallway.

"Tien, how much longer is this going to take?"

"It will be another thirty minutes, Torrin. Muscle and sinew take longer to mend than bone or skin."

"I don't have time for this. Once everyone has debarked, plot a course for Nadi. I'm going to put together a burst packet and I need you to send that along to the Ruling Council. We need to warn them about Tanith. If Tate communicates any requests to us before we go into peripheral space, add that to the burst."

"As you say, Torrin."

"Oh, and Tien, I need you to shave as much time as possible off our trip home. Well, as much time as you can save without compromising Nadierzda's location."

"Yes, Torrin."

She knew it was probably her imagination. Tien's tone hadn't changed at all. The AI's tone never altered, but Torrin was reading a feeling of exasperation from her. She supposed she really shouldn't be telling the AI how to manage her business, but she had to get home before something happened to Jak. Something was going to go terribly wrong, if it hadn't already. Dread hung over her in an almost perceptible pall.

As she sat there fretting, she heard the distant metallic clang of the cargo bay ramp being lowered. Mentally, she wished Laiya and the Banshees luck. She couldn't include Neal in that group. While it would have been much better if they'd been willing to go to ground for a few days to see if Monton's men tried any kind of retaliation, she understood their need to stand up for themselves.

Too much time passed before she heard the cargo ramp slam back into its closed position. Almost simultaneously, the *Calamity Jane*'s engines roared to life. They throbbed insistently for a few moments before she felt the vessel lift into the air. She glared at her leg in the autodoc and willed it to work faster. Right now she was what was slowing them down. They weren't going to be able to jump to FTL until she was in cryostasis.

Finally the contraption popped open. Torrin pulled her leg free and ran down the corridor to the cryochamber, trying to ignore the subtle weakness of rebuilt muscle. As she ran, she shed her clothing and practically threw herself into the open cryopod.

"Put me under, Tien," she shouted. "Now." She steeled herself as the large-bore needles slithered out and stabbed into her arms and thighs. The price she paid for speed was in sharp pain that was followed quickly by numbness and then by nothing.

CHAPTER TWENTY-SIX

The first sensation she awoke to was a gentle rocking. Something was lifting her gently, then letting her slide again. Slowly she became aware of wetness under her cheek, wetness and grit. She turned her head and was rewarded by shards of pain burrowing their way into her skull. Where was she? The river? Then where was Torrin?

She pushed herself up on her hands. They sank into the soft sand of the river's bank. With great effort she managed to pull herself up the bank onto firmer ground. Pain shot through her head with every movement. There had been some large rocks in the river. She must have smashed her head into one of them after she threw herself in to…To what?

A vague feeling of danger kept her moving. It was a faint but insistent nag. There were some trees a short way off. She would be safe there. She was always safer in the trees.

Agony greeted her first step. Her ankle couldn't bear any weight, which she discovered when she toppled back over into the mud on the river's edge. She pushed herself up to her hands and knees and half-crawled, half-tumbled to the shelter of the small stand. *Maybe that's where Torrin went.* Fractured images of watching Torrin slip under the water's surface filled her mind. It wasn't quite right. There had been sheer rock walls where Torrin had gone under; sandy banks were all there were here. Her head was fuzzy, and she was having trouble concentrating.

Jak grimaced sourly. Of course she was having trouble concentrating. She'd managed to crack her head open. A concussion was a very real possibility, but her first priority had to be finding Torrin before heading back toward the fence. There was no way the Orthodoxans were going to be able to track her now. The unanticipated dip in the river would throw them off for sure.

Her strength gave out right as she reached the edge of the trees. She collapsed against the trunk of the nearest tree and rested her face against the smooth bark. All she needed was to rest for a little while. As she laid there, half-propped up, she lost track of time. Nothing really mattered; she floated along in a daze. Pain and disorientation skimmed across the surface of her uncaring mind.

What was that shape in the sky, she wondered. It was too big to be a bird. She stared at it quizzically. The vague unease at the back of her mind built to screaming intensity until her mind shrieked at her to get out of there, to hide, to fight back. It crested into full-blown fright when she realized that whatever it was had to be man-made. Had the Orthodoxans come up with a new weapon? No, it was something else, something her mind shied away from touching. She needed to get further away from the edge of the wooded stand.

On all fours now, she crawled further into the trees. When she was satisfied that she couldn't be seen from the air, she stopped again. This time as she lay on the ground her mind stayed focused. She needed a plan. Wandering aimlessly in the wilderness was a recipe for getting herself killed. Worst of all, Torrin was out there alone. She had no woods skills to speak of and didn't know the Haefonian wilds. Pushing herself into a sitting position, Jak went through her pockets. She had food or at least she thought it was food. The packages weren't familiar to her. A couple were labeled as beef, one as veggie. Veggie? Since when was that an option? At least she had her pocketknife. No combat knife, though she had the sheath still strapped to her thigh. The knife must have come out in the river. The only other items she had were a firestarter and a canteen. She bemoaned the loss of her rifle. Its absence, more than anything else, had her feeling naked and exposed.

A plan. She needed a plan. She would wait until she was sure that flying contraption had cleared the area, then she would search the river for signs of Torrin. The idea that Torrin might be dead filled her with panic. Her chest tightened and she wheezed, trying to catch her breath. She hadn't known Torrin for even a day, but losing the smuggler felt like it would kill her. The reaction was extreme and she wondered at it. Her thoughts raced, churning, going nowhere. Finally she forced herself to think past the worry of losing Torrin. If she couldn't find her, she would have to carry on back to the border.

Satisfied that she had some direction at least, she leaned back against the nearest tree. She would wait for a little bit and then go check for the mysterious flyer.

* * *

Jak woke with a start. Her neck was stiff, her ankle throbbed and her head felt like it was ready to split open. She raised a hand to her temple and encountered a crusted mess. What had happened? Where was she? Something had happened. There had been a river and Torrin. No, Tanith. Or was it Torrin? *Who's Tanith?*

The small stand of trees stood around her. She could have sworn she'd been in the forest, but this didn't look like Haefen's woods at all. The trees were miniscule and scrubby compared to the majestic giants she had grown up with. If she wasn't on Haefen, then she must be...where? She sneezed at the dry air and pain erupted in her head. All she could smell was hot sand. Something was very wrong. It seemed like she should know what had happened, but the answer kept sliding from her grasp.

With deliberate care, she pushed herself away from the base of the small tree. She must have been lying there for some time; the pattern of the bark had been pressed into the side of her face. Small pieces of bark had adhered to her skin and she brushed them away impatiently.

She wracked her memories for what had happened, but she could bring up only bits and pieces, like shards of a mirror, but each showing a different reflection. Together, none of them made any sense. All she could do was work with what she could remember most clearly.

What was that even? she wondered. She knew who she was, but beyond that there wasn't a whole lot she was sure of. *Torrin.* That was a name that stuck out in her memory. The emotions that she felt were almost equal parts pleasure and pain. If Torrin had been in front of her right then, she wasn't sure if she would have punched the woman or kissed her.

Tanith. Anger seared through her, leaving her almost breathless at the intensity of the emotion. There was no question how she felt when she considered that name. She could bring to mind a mental image of a smiling woman with short, wavy hair. The feelings were out of all congruity with the image, however. If Tanith had been in front of her, she would have shot her. If she'd had a gun, that was.

"What do I even have?" Jak wondered aloud. Even as she asked it, she knew. Some food, a firestarter, a pocketknife and her canteen.

First things first, then. She needed to fill the canteen and get moving. The reason for needing to move on eluded her at the moment, but the urge was unmistakable and undeniable. There was a large branch in arm's reach. It was straight enough, and it wasn't like she had a whole lot of options. She pulled the branch toward her and used it to lever herself off the ground. It acted well as a makeshift crutch and with it she was able to move without agonizing pain from her ankle. The ankle still didn't feel good, but keeping her weight off it helped.

Slowly, she crutched her way out of the trees toward the river. It didn't take long to fill the canteen. As she bent forward, something bound around her neck. Reaching her hand up, she encountered a small piece of technology. It looked vaguely familiar and definitely wasn't Haefonian in origin. Turning it in her hands didn't reveal any secrets as to its origin or function. Finally, she discarded it. If it wasn't going to help her, she didn't need it.

Turning away from the river, she struggled to orient herself. If the river was at her back, and the bend was there, then she needed to head west and north. The terrain was unknown to her and familiar at the same time. The decided lack of blue to the landscape should have been jarring, but it wasn't. She had no reason to believe that safety lay in any direction, but something drew her to the northwest. At least it was away from the cliffs. Those didn't feel good at all.

Slowly she crossed past the small stand of trees and toward the rolling grasslands of this other world. It really was very strange, she thought. She was all alone and completely lost somewhere that definitely wasn't her home. She was worried, but she wasn't feeling the terror she knew she ought to be.

Torrin. Maybe she could explain things. The first thing she was going to do when she saw her was to kiss her, Jak decided. Then she would punch her. That sounded like a good plan, and it lifted her spirits as she slowly made her way along. As she walked, she watched the skies. Something told her to keep her head up and to stay away from any flying machines she should happen across.

The idea of a flying machine was vaguely ridiculous to her. There had been none of those in Haefen for decades. The only flying machine she'd seen had been…Torrin's spaceship. That was right, Torrin had come from offworld. Maybe it was Torrin that she was trying to get away from? That didn't seem quite right either, but if she saw anything in the sky that wasn't bird or insect, she would go right to ground. Years of caution and hypervigilance had taught her to heed her instincts, and her instincts were screaming at her about threats from the skies.

* * *

The sun's rays stabbed into her eyes. It was low on the horizon and at exactly the right angle to shine directly into her face. From the amount of pain the light was causing her, she had one more confirmation that she was battling a concussion, on top of everything else. As if she needed the extra confirmation. The vomiting had confirmed that, as had the chunks of time she kept losing.

Finally, she had to turn her back on the sun to dull the pain and regain her bearings. There were some farmhouses close by. She could head that way, steal some food and maybe bunk down in a barn for the night. It was tempting, but she knew better than to involve civilians. Orthodoxan farmers were so beaten down by the military that they would turn her in if they found her. Also, she was missing her breastbinder. It was likely that they would discover her gender and do worse things to her before they turned her over, if they didn't decide to keep her for breeding purposes. Better to give the farms a wide berth.

A nearby cow regarded her curiously, then went back to grazing. Jak blinked in surprise. She hadn't noticed that she'd blundered into some farmer's pasture. The cows looked strange. They were white with large brown patches and short horns. She hadn't seen too many cows, but the ones she was used to were always a soft brown, with wide noses and no horns to speak of.

She looked west, shading her eyes with both hands, crutch secured in her armpit. She could skirt the farms quickly if she headed that way, then she could swing back north again. The sound of an engine caught her attention and she looked up sharply. To the east was one of those aircraft. It looked like a spaceship. Where had that thought come from? She'd never seen a spaceship in her life, so how could she recognize it as such?

The craft was headed in her direction. There was no way she could let it find her. It'll have heat-sensing capabilities, her mind whispered. She needed to find something that could camouflage her body heat.

A cow went plodding by her, followed by another, making their way purposefully down to one of the barns. More and more cows were joining them. Jak hesitated for a moment, then hobbled in among the cows. She kept to the densest concentration of the bovines. She had to move constantly to avoid being stepped upon, and their large bodies jostled into her. Keeping steady footing wasn't easy since she was still relying on the branch to help keep most of her weight off her injured ankle. Every jostle threatened to send her sprawling. She had a feeling that if she went down among all these hooves, she might not get up again.

This better work. In theory, the mass of bodies would camouflage her heat signature.

The ship passed by above her, shiny and black, the setting sun glinting off its hull. When she saw it more closely, she was glad she'd decided to hide. The ship looked lethal and its hull had multiple mountings of what she could only imagine were some very nasty weapons. The back ramp was open and someone stood in the opening. Jak had to engage her implant to zoom in on the figure. Sure enough, he scanned the ground, one hand holding himself steady, the other holding a scope up to his eyes. Jak had no doubt that he was looking for her. The uniform was odd; it looked nothing like the Orthodoxan uniforms she was used to. Maybe this was a new kind of unit. If that was the case, she definitely had to get back to Camp Abbott to let them know.

The cows had brought her over to the side of one of the barns. They milled by the fence. There was no sign of the farmer yet, but it was likely he would turn up soon. The cows definitely knew it was feeding time and they lowed intermittently but insistently. The ship disappeared behind the barn, and Jak crawled and shimmied her way out of the herd. She moved carefully and deliberately. There was no telling if there were any farmhands about, and she didn't want to give herself away. The people who worked the farm were now a bigger threat than the ship. Unless the ship doubled back around, she was clear for the time being.

Fortunately, those who worked the farm were otherwise occupied, and she was able to slip away without alerting anyone to her presence. She heaved a sigh of relief when she finally put some distance between her and the farms. She stooped to turn over a rock the size of her fist. It was all part of the trail she'd been leaving since the river. She hoped it would be subtle enough that the Orthodoxans wouldn't notice it.

"Ha," Jak said aloud. The Orthodoxans wouldn't have noticed her trail if she'd left phosphorescent footprints behind.

The trail was for Torrin. She'd spent as much time as she'd dared looking for her at the river. Finally, she'd decided it was time to move on. It was a long shot, but she hoped that by leaving a trail, Torrin would stumble upon it and follow it to her. If she was even still alive. Mentally, Jak shied away from the thought. It still brought her more pain than it should have.

It was the best she could do, she consoled herself. Torrin had seen her following the markings of her backtrail. Hopefully she would recognize them if she saw them again.

The sun was no longer in her eyes. It had slipped down behind the extremely tall cliffs ahead of her. Even from this distance, she could see that they were enormous. It didn't make sense. The escarpment wasn't close enough to see from here. She pulled up her mental map and swore. The only sectors she could access were the ones that she'd requisitioned for the mission. She had others that had been committed to memory, the old-fashioned way, but Sector 27 and surrounds were the only ones she could bring to mind. When she tried to remember other maps, the Sector 27 ones stayed firmly in her mind's eye. It was like trying to read a page that had another page glued overtop. She knew the other page was underneath, but she couldn't access it. And in this case, there was no way that she could peel away the intervening layer.

She knew the warning signs. Every Devonite schoolchild on Haefen did. The map download was acting as if she hadn't purged it quickly enough. The data was becoming corrupt and was overriding her natural memories. Since it was stronger and more coherent than a natural memory, it was the first thing to rise to the top when she tried to remember the lay of the land. How could that be? She'd only gotten the download four days ago. No, it was definitely more than four days ago. But how long was it?

Jak became aware that she was sitting with her head in her hands. The pain in her head wasn't getting better. If anything, it was getting worse. She felt like things were slipping away from her. There were so many holes in her memories, so many things that didn't add up. When she tried to examine the inconsistencies, her head throbbed.

At this point she didn't know much, but she knew she needed to find shelter for the night. She wasn't doing herself any favors by pushing herself like this. Shaking her head, she grabbed the branch and pushed herself off the ground.

* * *

Jak awoke with a start. She was cold and damp; morning dew glistened on her skin. A small deadfall had provided her with a little shelter through the night, but the exposure hadn't done much for her various injuries.

The ankle was starting to concern her. The pain wasn't improving. While she could move fairly well with the help of her makeshift crutch, she still couldn't put any weight on it. Not for the first time, she wished she had her first aid kit. That was back at the top of the cliff where she and Torrin had bunked down. She hoped none of the Orthodoxans would stumble across her stash. Maybe she'd go back and get it after she got back to camp.

She patted the ground beside her and sat up when she didn't feel Torrin. The sudden movement set her head to pounding again. As she massaged her temples, she remembered that they'd been separated at the river. That felt wrong. There was something else there, but like everything else lately, it dissipated when she turned her mind to examine it. So many times on this journey she'd had an unshakeable feeling of déjà vu. It was so familiar. Even the landscape was familiar, though she didn't know it. Jak worried that she was going crazy.

Maybe Bron's death had finally driven her over the edge. The men in her unit whispered that she was insane. She didn't feel insane, but she'd heard that crazy people never did. Surely it must be the concussion. Even to her, it sounded like flimsy rationalization.

Crazy or not, she still had a duty to make it back to camp. Someone had to warn them about those new Orthodoxan vessels. There was nobody but her. She laughed out loud. For so long, all she'd wanted was to be left alone. Here she was, all alone, and all she wanted to do was find Torrin.

She washed down a quick breakfast with the last of the water in her canteen. She ate less than half the meal in the pouch. She only had one left after this one, and there was still a lot of ground to cover before she made it back to the fence. If she'd had her rifle, she could have hunted to supplement her food rations. Just like she had the last time… There was that sense of déjà vu again.

Casting the thought and the specter of madness from her mind, she pulled herself up on an exposed root and emerged slowly into the light of day. It was already warm and the wind was like air from a warm furnace. Jak coughed and spat, clearing her mouth and lungs of sand. It got into everything. The sand could be exceptionally fine. When the wind blew like this, it ended up coating every available inch of flesh.

The cough turned into another and another. Before she knew it, Jak was on hands and knees as paroxysm after paroxysm of hacking wracked her body. She scrabbled for the canteen and between hacks tried to empty liquid into her mouth. A couple of drops from the bottle were all she could get out and they did nothing to moisten her throat.

It was quite some time before the fit passed. By the time she was aware of anything other than trying to breathe, the sun had risen well above the horizon.

Her breath hitched and it was difficult to return it to a reasonable rhythm. She was having problems filling her lungs. Breathing deeply threatened to bring on another coughing fit. Determined not to break out into more coughing, she slowed her breathing. Shallow breathing didn't seem to aggravate her lungs as badly.

Eventually, she was recovered enough to venture out of her shelter. The sun peeked through the constant haze that seemed to cover this place. She looked around for any indication of water. That was her first priority. There was no point in trying to access her maps to get a fix on her location. The only place that came to mind was Sector 27, and she'd had more than enough of that place to last a lifetime.

There was a glint of sunlight to the east. It looked like it might be sun shining off water. Sun off metal or glass didn't react the same way. Slowly, careful not to push herself, she headed off for a drink.

CHAPTER TWENTY-SEVEN

A constant whine drilled into her skull and Torrin became aware of the unpleasant sensations of being thawed out from cryosleep. Nausea rolled over her. She didn't always feel the need to vomit while being thawed, but apparently this was going to be a hard one.

She braced her hands on the inside of the pod while she retched helplessly. Nothing came up and her abdomen ached from the abuse. All fluids were removed during the cryo process. She'd seen firsthand what happened if not all fluids were removed. True, Jak's situation had been unusual, but the extreme dehydration kicked Torrin's ass every single time.

"Are you recovered, Torrin?" the AI asked when Torrin finally stopped heaving.

"More or less." Torrin groaned and pulled herself out of the cryopod. She snagged her jumpsuit out of a nearby locker and donned it while walking down the hall to the bridge.

"Torrin, I have queried the buoys for the correct path through the asteroid field."

"Good. What channel is space traffic control?"

"Channel foxtrot whiskey niner one."

"Thanks." Torrin huddled over the console and brought up the *Calamity Jane*'s communications module and input the current channel. "This is the *Calamity Jane* requesting entry vector. Do you read?"

There was a long pause before she received a response. She cocked an ear to listen carefully, their distance from Nadierzda making the reception poor. Static popped. She could hear a voice, but couldn't quite make out what it was saying.

"Tien, clean up the transmission and replay it if you would."

"Yes, Torrin." Static played through the cabin's speakers before resolving into recognizable words.

"*Calamity Jane*, thank the gods! Stand by for entry vector and for Lieutenant Krikorian."

Olesya? Why were they getting Olesya to talk to her? Something was wrong. She hoped Tanith hadn't done anything foolish when she'd been taken into custody.

"Ummm, understood. *Calamity Jane* standing by." She sat back in her seat as Tien started their maneuvers through the asteroid field. The wait was tortuous. Idly, she chewed at the edge of a fingernail, then grimaced ruefully when she realized what she was doing. Gnawing at her nails was a nervous habit she thought she'd broken as a teenager and one that only came back under extremely stressful situations.

Finally the comm crackled to life again.

"Torrin, are you there?"

"Olesya! I'm here. What's been going on down there? Did Tanith give you more trouble than you could handle?" She'd meant the gibe to be lighthearted and cringed when she realized how anxious it sounded.

"No, it's not that." Olesya hesitated. It was unlike her to pass up the opportunity to give Torrin a hard time, and the display of anxiety would normally have been good for a whole lot of good-natured ribbing. Torrin could hear Olesya take a steadying breath through the comm. Dread enfolded her. "It's Jak. She and Tanith went out days ago and that was the last we've heard of them."

Torrin gripped the console's edges with both hands, its sharp edges digging into her palms. She breathed raggedly, dragging air into her lungs in a vain attempt to steady herself.

"You haven't heard from either of them in days? I sent word about what Tanith was up to. Why wasn't she picked up?" The edge in her voice grated at her, and she took a couple more deep breaths through her nostrils.

"She's dead, Torrin. We found the remains of her ultralight in the sands. The windshield was busted out and had blood on it. It looks like she went through it when she crashed. The two of them were on a mission to take out a Sinosian tiger that's been terrorizing the countryside. We think something went down between the two of them."

"But no body?"

Olesya shook her head. "No, but that isn't unusual. I don't think we recover a body even in half the wrecks that happen up there. You know how quickly dunes can shift and pull a corpse into them, often in as little as a few hours. There's no way to know how far down she is by now."

"What about Jak?"

Olesya's hesitation stretched far too long. "There was something. We found her sailplane." She spoke haltingly. "It was at the bottom of a cliff and had plasma burns on the outside. Her rifle was at the cliff's top."

Torrin looked down when she felt a sharp pain in a knuckle on her left hand. Without being aware of it, she'd bitten down on the first knuckle of her index finger. There was no blood, but the indentations left by her teeth were already an ugly purple.

"Was there a…" She couldn't finish the question and let it trail off. It sat there waiting.

"A body? No. We scoured the river that ran under the cliff and found tracks that indicate she washed up downriver from where she went in. But that was four days ago and we haven't been able to find any sign of her since."

The laugh that was ripped from Torrin's throat took her aback. By the extended silence that came through the comm, it also surprised Olesya.

"I'll believe Jak is dead when I see her body. She's harder to kill than anyone else I know. Her training puts all of ours to shame. If she doesn't want to be found, she won't be."

"Normally, I'd agree with you. Thing is, she's been a little off recently. I mean more off than could be explained by you and her." Olesya's voice trailed off awkwardly.

"How do you mean then?"

"Her direction sense is off. I know she's been getting lost."

"That's odd. I'd swear the woman has a compass in her brain. I've never known her to get lost, not even when I was first taking her around Landing. Take her somewhere once and she can get back to it from wherever she is."

"That's why I'm worried. That and she knows she can trust us. Why is she avoiding the search parties? I'm worried that the direction thing is a symptom of something larger."

"Look, no offense, but I know her better than any of you. Get your unit together and anyone else who's been working on the search. You're going to debrief me as soon as I land and then we're going to go find her."

"Torrin, you know you have no authority over me or the Banshees."

"I don't care. I'm going to find my girlfriend. Anything that stands in my way is going to get run over. I will not let anything or anyone slow me down."

"I hear you. I'll talk to the captain."

"You do that. If anyone of a higher rank tries to interfere, make sure you ask them how Tanith was able to get away with selling me out and endangering the safety of everyone on our planet in the process. I'll go to the Ruling Council if I have to."

"I believe it. Here's your landing solution. They've routed all other traffic out of your way. You have top priority right now, which should tell you how concerned the brass is with Jak's disappearance."

Numbers and vectors crawled across Torrin's console. "I've got them, and thanks."

"You got it. See you soon, Torrin." Olesya terminated their transmission, and Torrin's fingers flew across the console as she input the landing coordinates. She reached over and swiped flight controls to her board. Tien was more than capable of getting them down in one piece. Since Torrin had authorized the AI to have full flight and propulsion access, she'd been pleasantly surprised. The AI was an excellent flyer, but she had similar tendencies to a lot of AIs. Specifically, she lacked imagination. It was one reason why Torrin always checked her FTL solutions. She also had too much tendency not to push the safety restraints far enough. Torrin hadn't gone so far as to authorize the ship to push the systems past the safety limits, but she could do so herself on manual control.

A swipe of her right hand across the console sent their speed up well past the safety limits. A red warning light blinked insistently in the console's corner. The ship's proximity alarms were going insane as she whipped them through the asteroid field at a decidedly dangerous speed. Torrin ignored it. She knew how much the *Jane* could take and for how long. The short trip to the surface wouldn't tax her too badly.

She gritted her teeth and steered past the last few asteroids in the field, then punched it. The engines throbbed below her feet; she could feel them through the deck.

"Tien, keep an eye on the readouts. I'm going to take her in as hot as I can."

"Understood, Torrin."

Torrin took the yoke with one hand and guided the *Calamity Jane* in on the provided vector. Her other hand danced across the console, making tweaks to instruments and working to keep her readings as close to the red line as possible. Before long the bridge was a discordant symphony of warning tones. She kept a running monologue with the ship's AI, instructing her on the changes she needed when she couldn't make them fast enough.

A few times, Torrin deviated slightly from the vector in order to shave a little more time off her entry. The ship was buffeted wildly as it hit the winds of Nadierzda's atmosphere. The upper levels of the atmosphere were unusually active on this day and Torrin gritted her teeth as she did her best to knife her way through the disturbances. Extreme turbulence gripped the ship, and she white-knuckled the steering column. Restraints had snaked around her at the first sign of atmospheric disturbance, and she mentally thanked Tien for keeping her from being thrown across the bridge.

Both hands occupied with keeping them on course, Torrin had no recourse but to shout orders to Tien. The hull was heating up quickly, and they were rapidly approaching the upper levels of heat tolerance.

"Slow us down a touch," Torrin yelled. Internally she cursed the delay. Every second counted. With Tanith dead under unknown circumstances and Jak missing, who knew what had happened. Worst-case scenarios started to unfold in her mind. They started with Jak lying injured in a ditch and went downhill from there. The scenario where Jak was bamboozled into running offworld with a faceless woman convinced Torrin that she really needed to concentrate on their entry.

The ship slowed enough that the hull's heat readings backed off to something reasonable. The level of turbulence dropped significantly and Torrin was able to steer much more easily. As soon as they dropped below the top levels of the atmosphere and the hull temperature was back to normal, she punched the speed back up.

As they went screaming over the southern edge of the crater, there was a loud boom. The Ruling Council wasn't going to be happy with that. They frowned on pilots breaking the sound barrier over populated areas.

Landing sped toward her on the horizon. At the last possible moment she cut their acceleration. The *Calamity Jane* bucked and yawed crazily, and Torrin spun her around and dropped her toward the space that had been cleared at the spaceport. As they were about to hit the ground, she kicked in the antigrav and the *Calamity Jane* came to a soft stop a few meters above the ground.

Torrin clawed at the safety restraint and pushed herself away from the seat as soon as she was able.

"Tien, bring her in for tethering and line up the boarding tube." She threw the words over her shoulder as she sped down the hallway from the bridge. The boarding tube was only partially extended when Torrin opened the exterior hatch. She waited impatiently and was trotting through the tube before it had been completely secured.

Olesya sprinted up as Torrin exited the tube into the spaceport proper.

"You made good time," Olesya panted. "I had to run from the control tower to meet you. The others are waiting in the *Nightshade*. It's on the other side of the port." She took a couple of deep breaths, then went loping off in the opposite direction. Olesya set a punishing pace and Torrin had to stretch her legs to keep from being left behind. It was gratifying to know Olesya was treating the situation with as much seriousness as she was.

"What did the Ruling Council say?" she asked as they sprinted through the concourse. Women threw themselves out of their way and stared as the two sprinted by.

"For once they're as concerned as we are," Olesya said grimly. "They understand how much of an imminent threat Tanith's exploits are to Nadierzda. I think they have designs on Jak helping to foil whatever plans Tanith might have put into motion. At the very least, I think they're hoping that Jak might know some of what she was up to."

"She was up to being a crazy bitch," Torrin said heatedly. "What I've found out is enough to make you cringe. I can only imagine what they'll uncover at her home."

"Her home was pretty much empty when planet militia got there. Aside from some heavy communications equipment, everything else was scrubbed clean. Interestingly enough, Breena, your ex, is nowhere to be found and neither is Tanith's ship."

"I'm not surprised. I've suspected that it was Breena who helped set me up with the Orthodoxans. Someone input faulty information on Haefen into Tien's memory banks, and Breena was the last tech to work on the AI."

"In that case, she probably took off in Tanith's ship when she heard we were after her. It's likely that she's the one who wiped all the computers at Tanith's home. She certainly has the chops to have pulled off a complete system wipe."

They sprinted through the civilian concourses. Women watched wide-eyed as they dashed by. A jumble of featureless hallways separated the civilian and the military parts of the spaceport. As the two of them pounded down the long, blank hallway, a sentry saw them coming. She threw open the gate. Torrin nodded in appreciation as she tore through the opening on Olesya's heels.

The military section was very spartan compared to the civilian areas. Drab paint and hard floors dominated. It had been years since Torrin had been on this side, but it had changed very little since her stint with the Banshees.

"Where is everyone?" Torrin shouted to Olesya.

"They're out looking for Jak and Tanith. No one thinks there's much hope for Tanith—there was way too much blood in the ultralight. But if there's a chance she survived, she needs to answer for her actions. As for Jak, we should be able to track her down before it's too late, but that isn't going as well as we expected. The Ruling Council didn't want to panic the population, but they authorized full mobilization of ground and air forces."

"Wow." Torrin was amazed. She hadn't thought the council would take the issue quite this seriously. She was heartened to find out about the depth of the response.

The port's military section was much smaller than the civilian one and before long she and Olesya were dashing through the boarding tube to the *Nightshade*. Torrin wasn't familiar with the layout of the ship. It was a newer class than the one she'd served on. From the little she was able to see as they darted through narrow corridors to a small briefing room, the designers had rectified a number of flaws in the original design. She had to duck at the last moment to avoid bashing her forehead on a low pipe. Clearly, they had not addressed all of the flaws.

The briefing room was small. It had been designed to hold the unit's full complement of officers and noncoms. Now, however, every member of the unit was apparently crammed into the room. They clustered around the table and stood against the wall. A woman with a face like a hatchet saw them enter. She rose and pushed her way through the throng of women toward Torrin.

"Torrin Ivanov, I'm Captain Axe Yozhin." Her hand swallowed Torrin's in a powerful grip. "We're ready to get things rolling now that you're here. Everyone here has the utmost respect for Jak. We're hoping you'll be able to help us bring her home."

"So what do you have so far?" Torrin asked.

Captain Yozhin walked back through the crowd toward the large table. Women melted out of her way. There was barely enough room for Torrin and the captain at the table. Torrin glanced back at Olesya.

"I've already seen it," her friend called. She was backing out of the room. "I'm going to make sure the engines are hot so we can take off as soon as you're up to speed."

Torrin nodded gratefully and turned back to the captain. The table was also a large console, and it shimmered to life as Torrin watched. Axe's hands flew along the edge of the table. Strands of light grew out of the table's surface toward the room's low ceiling. As she watched, a three-dimensional model of the crater was sculpted from light before her eyes.

"We found where they were stalking the tiger. From the body we found, it looks like Jak got it. From the decomposition of the animal's corpse, we know she was alive four days ago."

"How do you know it was Jak?"

"It was killed from a bullet through the eye from almost two kilometers away. No one else on this planet could have made that. Your woman's a damn good shot."

It was a good explanation and Torrin nodded again, Jak could definitely have made the shot. The model zoomed in on a narrow cliff part of the way down the crater's extreme southern edge. A river ran under the cliff face.

"At some point she went into the water." The model zoomed in further. A broken sailplane was fetched up among some rocks at the river's verge. Even from the hologram, Torrin could tell that the river's course was fast and rough.

"How could she survive that?" she wondered aloud.

Axe shook her head. "We have no idea. There was also evidence of plasma fire on the plane's fuselage." She zoomed the hologram all the way in until Torrin could see pits marking the plane's side. "We found more plasma fire on the fuselage of the ultralight that we recovered from the sands."

"It's possible she was injured," one of the Banshees piped up. "That would explain some of the tracks we found downriver."

"Ivanov, meet Perez. She did most of the preliminary scouting. Found Stowell's trail on the riverbank." The holographic image spun with nauseating speed. As the view was pulled back from the close-up of the sailplane, it shifted and spun, flying over terrain to stop over a much different stretch of river.

The river here was wide and smooth. Torrin had gotten the impression that they'd covered a lot of distance, but it was difficult to tell. A gentle loop in the riverbank had been responsible for the formation of a sandy beach. It was narrow, but wide enough that she could see imprints of feet and hands.

"The tracks get muddied here. It looks like this is where she washed up. She left the bank but returned at some point and left again."

"This is where it gets strange," Perez broke in. "It looks like she crawls away originally. That makes sense for someone who's half-drowned. When she comes back, she's on her two feet." Axe zoomed in on a set of tracks on the bank. "Or rather, one and a half feet. From the tracks there, it looks like she made herself a crutch. She's definitely favoring one leg."

"So she can't be moving that quickly. Why hasn't anyone been able to find her?"

Axe zoomed out of the close view of the riverbank and returned the display to a two-dimensional format. She highlighted a wide swath between the bend in the river and Landing.

"She should be somewhere along this path. We've been going over it with a fine-toothed comb, but we can't find anything else." Frustration laced the captain's tone. She rhythmically opened and closed her right hand into a fist. It looked like she was hoping to find a part of the problem that she could hit. Torrin sympathized with the urge.

"Have you looked anywhere not along that path?"

"Of course we have," Axe snapped. "We haven't hit those areas as heavily, but I wasn't going to rule them out completely."

Torrin stared at the map on the console. Something about that bend in the river tickled the back of her mind. She couldn't put her finger on it. It was like an itch between her shoulder blades that she couldn't quite reach, no matter how hard she tried.

"You need to get me out there, ASAP," she said finally.

"I was hoping you'd say that. You know Jak better than any of us here. If anyone'll have some insight into her actions in this situation, it's you." She looked around the table, managing to meet the eye of every Banshee gathered there. "You heard the woman, we'll be taking off shortly. Get to your stations."

She cleared the room and directed Torrin to follow her. This time Torrin remembered to duck to avoid coshing her head on the pipe. Axe led her quickly to the bridge. It was significantly bigger than the one she had on the *Calamity Jane*. Olesya greeted them as they entered.

"She's hot and ready to go when you are, Captain."

"Good." Axe settled herself at a central console. Two more consoles sat ahead of her, right under the forward viewscreens. Olesya sat at one, a soldier Torrin didn't recognize except to know that she'd seen her at the briefing was taking her place at the other. The equipment was as sleek and shiny as the ship's hull. The *Calamity Jane* was Torrin's pride and joy, but she couldn't help but feel a small tinge of envy over Axe's *Nightshade*. The Banshee ship had been commissioned and built less than five years before. For the Fringes, it had cutting edge technology. It wouldn't stand in a ship-to-ship battle against the League's newer vessels, but Torrin wouldn't have bet against it in a fray with one of the older vessels. Her thoughts churned. There had to be a way that Haefonian cybernetic implant tech could be used to give them an edge with their military vessels.

"Go ahead and strap in over there." Axe pointed to a row of three bench seats. Torrin hastened over and cranked herself in. As soon as her restraints were secured, Olesya flipped a switch above her head. The overhead lights took an amber cast. The ship would be taking off soon. Torrin remembered the protocols the lights represented. Amber meant the ship was going to be engaging in activities that required the occupants be strapped in. It was usually used for breaking or entering orbit, for taking off or for entering areas of high enough turbulence that the ship's artificial gravity might cut out.

A red light meant battle stations. There was little chance of that code being necessary on this mission. No color to the light meant that people could move about the ship normally.

The engines had been barely perceptible, a throaty hum that was barely loud enough to vibrate the floor panels. Now they opened up into a basso-profundo roar. Yes, this ship was definitely many times over the better of her own vessel. She marveled at the power the *Nightshade* held. The last Banshee vessel she'd been on had been a bucket of bolts compared to this one. Then again, it had been a bucket of bolts compared to the *Calamity Jane*.

The engines really opened up and she was pressed back into her seat by the acceleration.

"The Ruling Council has allowed us to clear the airspace in our search grid." Olesya's voice came in through her implant. "It allows us to get in and out in a hurry. We'll be at the site soon. Just sit tight."

CHAPTER TWENTY-EIGHT

Torrin knelt in the shallow water and looked up the riverbank. This was approximately where Jak had washed up. Her tracks had long since been washed away by the river's course, but the tracks she'd left further up the bank were still there. This side of the bank was sheltered from the prevailing winds, and the tracks hadn't blown away. It hadn't rained in the past week, which had also helped preserve traces of Jak's passage. From her vantage, she could see the small stand of trees not too far away.

"I bet she took shelter in the trees," Torrin called out to Axe and Olesya, standing further up the bank. "I assume you checked there?"

"We did," Axe confirmed. "It looks like she spent some time there, probably holed up for the night, then struck out in the morning."

"I'll want to see that also," Torrin said. She pushed off the sandy bank. As she put her weight on her right hand it came into contact with something hard. A little digging uncovered a small transmitter.

"What did you find?" Olesya asked excitedly.

"It's a transmitter. I guess this rules out us being able to track her down by triangulating the signal." It was no surprise that the Banshees hadn't been able to locate Jak by pinging back her transmitter. It had been in the water and sand for a while. It was never going to work again. She looked up at the sky in frustration. She couldn't tell if Jak was purposely blurring her trail, but at this point, it was beginning to look like she really didn't want to be found.

That niggling feeling returned as she surveyed the area one final time. There was a sense of familiarity to the circumstances.

"You know…" Torrin trailed off thoughtfully, chewing on her lower lip as she realized why this seemed like something she'd done before.

"Know what?" Axe asked.

"This reminds me a bit of something that happened after Jak and I escaped from the Orthodoxan colonel's compound. I went over a cliff and ended up in a river. Jak jumped in after me. The current swept us down the river and over the rapids. The beach we ended up on wasn't so different from this one. The trees are even in sort of the right direction for where we ended up after she pulled me out of the river."

"How is that important?" Axe asked.

"I'm not sure yet. But it's worth remembering." She pushed herself up and tossed the ruined transmitter over to Olesya. A useless swipe at the knees of her jumpsuit let her know the clinging sand wasn't going anywhere for a while. That wasn't important. Finding Jak and getting her to shelter and medical attention before she had to spend another night in the open, that was important.

Torrin strode over to the trees, Olesya and Axe at her side. The rest of the Banshees were in the *Nightshade* a little ways downriver. They hadn't wanted to risk ruining the tracks.

"There's what Perez noticed," Olesya said, indicating a set of tracks. There was a third indentation in addition to those left by Jak's feet. One foot had barely made any impression at all, and at times there was no evidence that the foot had touched the ground.

"Even I can read that," Torrin said, "and my trail craft wasn't particularly good, even back when I actually had to use it." The evidence that Jak was hurting made her heart twinge. There was nothing she could do about Jak's pain, but she would have given anything to take it away.

The interior of the small stand bore some evidence of Jak's passage. Torrin could point out the tree where she'd spent some time by the disturbed leaves at its base. She gently trailed a hand over the dry leaves. It was fanciful, she knew, but she imagined she could still feel Jak's presence.

"Do you know why she would have gone back to the river?" Olesya asked.

"If I know Jak, it was probably to fill a canteen. She's a fanatic when it comes to survival. She knows exactly what to do to give herself the best possible chance."

"I can show you where we picked up the last of her tracks," Axe offered.

"Let's follow her footsteps exactly. I'd rather make sure we aren't missing something." The crutch mark made Jak's trail laughably easy to follow. As they walked past the last of the trees, following Jak's footprints, Torrin noticed something. She squatted down to consider a rock.

"So it's a rock, what of it?" Olesya asked, coming up to stand next to her.

"It's been turned over." Torrin picked up the rock in question and turned it over. It had been in the ground for quite some time before being dug out. The top was rounded and had been scoured smooth from years of exposure to Nadi's constant winds. The bottom was jagged.

"She probably hit it with the crutch accidentally and popped it out."

"I don't think so. Look at the crutch mark. It's on the opposite side. She had to stop and dig this out to turn it over. I saw her do this before, on Haefen." Torrin stood, smiling, the rock clenched in her hand. "Do you know what this means?"

"She wants to be found," Axe said, an answering smile spreading across her face.

Torrin looked up from the tree's base and noticed a barely noticeable chunk cut out of the tree's bark.

"Here," she said and pointed to the small notch. "She's leaving us a trail this way also. I bet if we start following the trail as far as you guys have gotten, that you'll see these."

"Olesya, get more Banshees down here," Axe ordered. She followed Torrin to the river's edge as the lieutenant called in reinforcements. Torrin searched the ground near where Jak must have filled her canteen and found another overturned rock.

"We've got another one!"

"Great." Axe came and stood next to Torrin. "Landing is that way." She pointed north and slightly east.

"You'd think that would be the way she was most likely to go," Olesya added as she rejoined the two of them. "Instead we found the last set of tracks over that direction." She pointed almost directly northwest.

That was completely counterintuitive. Jak should have taken the shortest path to safety, but she hadn't. Maybe Jak had swung the other way to throw pursuers off her trail. There was no sign that Tanith or anybody else had stopped here, but they could have had their own air transportation. There would have been no need to land to track Jak if a visual had been established. In that case, Jak's trail marking could work against her.

"Let's go to her last known location. Now that we know how she's marking her trail, we should be able to pick her up fairly easily."

Olesya led her and Axe to a patch of sandy terrain a few hundred meters to the northwest. Away from the riverbank, the ground firmed up. It was less sandy and didn't show Jak's tracks nearly as well. She knew Jak could have tracked a light breeze that was a week old over even harder packed terrain, but this was far beyond her skills. On their way there, though, they found another overturned rock and a shrub with a notch cut from the trunk.

The tracks turned out to be in an odd sandy patch of ground. It wasn't very large and Torrin stared at it. These tracks didn't appear to have been left purposely, unlike the rocks and notches. It looked more like Jak had wandered through the softer ground without noticing. Maybe Olesya had been on to something when she'd mentioned that Jak had seemed a little off lately. It would have been no big thing for Jak to avoid that patch, and yet she'd blundered right through it.

As she mulled over the troubling development, a group of Banshees arrived on antigrav sleds. It looked like Olesya had called in half the unit. Axe approached them and started filling them in. Two women got off their sleds and climbed on behind a couple of the other women. The rest of the Banshees had been riding pillion. They listened quietly, then dispersed on the sleds.

"They know what to look for," Axe said as she rejoined Torrin. "We should have some more information to go on soon."

"Look at this," Torrin said. "She could easily have avoided this area. I'm worried that something's wrong. Olesya said she'd been acting a little strange."

"It's possible that she received a blow to the head in the river," Axe said thoughtfully. "If that's the case, she could be experiencing some profound disorientation."

"Captain, Torrin!" Olesya joined them at a run. "I received a transmission. One of the Banshees has found more tracks."

"Good, let's get over there. Torrin, you can ride behind the lieutenant."

"Or I can drive the sled and you two can ride together."

"I'm afraid not. You're not a member of the militia any longer. If one of the sleds gets totaled and the brass finds out I let a civilian drive, I'll get my ass handed to me."

"There's no way I'm going to ride on the back!"

"Then you won't ride at all." Axe met her mutinous stare with a level gaze of her own.

Olesya chortled softly. "Come on, Torrin. I'll drive carefully for you."

Torrin shot her a deadly look that only made her laugh louder. She climbed on behind the lieutenant.

"If you tell anyone about this, I'll kick your ass."

"You mean you'll try to kick my ass."

"I bet I can still beat you three out of four falls."

"You're on," Olesya crowed. "When we get Jak back to Landing, I'll be happy to take your credits."

She opened the throttle and they leaped away over the terrain. The antigrav gave them a smooth ride over the low hills. It was a nicer ride than wheels would have given, but Torrin would stick with wheels any day. It was impossible to feel the road on the antigrav sleds; wheeled bikes were far more responsive. Shortly, they met up with the Banshees who'd found more signs of Jak's passage. In the distance, Torrin could see more sleds converging on their location.

Before the sled had come to a full stop, Torrin was already jumping down. Axe and Olesya stayed on their sleds and watched as she approached the Banshees. One of them tossed her a fist-sized stone.

"We found it right here," the burly woman said, indicating a spot of ground with a large divot out of it. "It was lying right next to the hole."

"That's another one, all right," Torrin confirmed. She looked back. The river was barely visible in the distance. "What's the angle from the river?"

"It's on a northwesterly trajectory, ma'am," the soldier replied.

"Good job, Hamilton," Axe said. "Let's spread out and find another one."

Torrin walked back over to Olesya and swung her leg over the back of the sled. "Head northwest, and keep the speed down. I'll look for more traces."

"You think she's going to keep heading away from Landing?"

"I think so. When you said she was a little off, how did you mean?"

Olesya skewed the sled around, then took off to the northwest. She was going slowly enough that Torrin could scan the ground.

"She got lost on the way back to base one night. Took a wrong turn, she claimed. But it seemed to me that she had to really pay attention to navigate her way back. I'm not sure what would account for that, but then I'm not a doctor."

There was another small group of trees coming up and Torrin pointed it out to Olesya.

"Take us over there. Jak is most comfortable among trees."

Obligingly, the lieutenant turned toward the stand. They were not particularly impressive. To Jak's eyes they would have been little more than shrubs, but for this area of the Nadierzdan wilderness, they were as close as they were going to find to a forest.

Once again, Torrin jumped down before the sled had completely stopped. She jogged in among the trees. The notched mark jumped out at her.

"I've got another one," she called back to Olesya. "Tell Axe to meet us here. We need to figure out our best way of operating here."

"Got it," Olesya replied. While she was talking to the captain, Torrin ran her fingertips over the mark. This was as close as she'd been to Jak in weeks. Despite, or more likely because of, the physical and emotional distance they'd had between them, Torrin still missed her. Time should have softened some of the pain at her absence, but it was only making it worse. None of her normal pastimes had mitigated the pain either. She wasn't used to the void in her life that another's absence caused. She was the one who did the leaving; women didn't leave her.

"She'll be right over," Olesya said from behind her. Torrin jumped; she hadn't heard the lieutenant approach. She'd been so mired in her own thoughts that she'd been oblivious to anyone else around her.

Olesya grasped her shoulder and squeezed comfortingly. "She misses you too, you know."

"How do you know?"

"She was full of questions about you. Does that sound like somebody who's written you off completely?"

"Not so much. Maybe she'll be ready to listen this time. She was so mad before and Tanith was there whispering bullshit about me in her ear."

"To be fair, Tanith didn't really have to make up too much. You are a bit of a player."

"No, I'm not, not really. I was only ever with one lover at a time. Well, except when she brought a friend."

"Yeah, it's that kind of reputation that makes it easy for a woman to wonder about you. Especially a woman who's in her first relationship and whose lover is constantly working. You didn't exactly create the best set of circumstances."

"Don't you think I know that?" Torrin asked, frustrated. "But what else was I supposed to do? Nadierzda's future rested on the work I was doing."

"I know that, and I don't think you made the wrong decision." Olesya spread both hands, hastening to reassure Torrin. "All I'm saying is look at it from Jak's perspective. She had nothing to compare your relationship to except the nasty bits of gossip that have been floating around here. You know there are plenty of people who wouldn't hesitate to tar you with that kind of brush."

"I guess."

"Besides, something tells me that she won't be giving what Tanith told her nearly as much credence as she had been."

"That's something at least."

"So cheer up, will you? I'm sure things will be fine once we finally catch up to her."

Torrin didn't say anything, but she tried to take solace from Olesya's words. At least her statements assumed they would find Jak. They moved on to the next sign and kept moving to the one after that and beyond. Their progress was fitful and Torrin chafed against the slow headway they made. Even though Jak was heading steadily in a northwesterly direction, they had to move from one marker to the next. There was no telling when Jak would change directions. At least they were moving more quickly than Jak was able. Every now and again they would come across Jak's actual tracks beyond the trail she was carefully leaving for them. She was still using the crutch and putting next to no weight on the one foot.

Midway through the afternoon, the signs dried up. They had been following the overturned rocks and notches when without any warning, there weren't any more.

"Axe, we have a problem," Torrin reported through her transmitter.

"Still no sign?"

"Yes. We've had no sign of her for about forty-five minutes now." That was troubling in itself. The longest they'd gone without finding any trace of her had been fifteen minutes.

Torrin stood on the sled's rear pegs and looked around the landscape. The land had transformed into rolling hills and signs of cultivation were appearing. There was a clump of farms back a little way from where they'd come.

"Do you think she holed up in one of the farms?" Olesya asked.

"I don't know. It's possible, I guess."

"You don't sound convinced."

"It's not like her. She doesn't like to bring other people into her problems. Also, she doesn't trust easily, especially not strangers. Still, I think it's worth a look, especially since we seem to be out of options."

"Captain," Olesya radioed Axe, "I suggest we check out the farms. Maybe Jak's holed up there."

"Affirmative. In the meantime, I'll have the Banshees start a spiral search pattern from the last mark we found."

"Got it. We'll meet you by the farms." Olesya turned the sled and gunned it in the direction of the small farming community. As they got closer, Torrin could see that it wasn't even a village. It was three, maybe four family farms grouped together. It wasn't an uncommon arrangement in Nadierzda. The farms would start up around a water source, usually a spring or a creek. The water would serve as the hub for the farms and each farmer would farm out from that source, like spokes on a wheel. If they were particularly successful, eventually more women would be attracted to the area and a village would form. This settlement was definitely in previllage stage.

Milk cattle roamed the rolling pastures around them. They observed the women with dull interest, then went back to chewing on grass. Torrin had no use for cows. She appreciated the milk, meat and leather the animals provided, but she had no interest in getting any closer to them than the products that were made from them.

Moving Nadierzda's goods across the galaxy's fringes gave her another appreciation for the cows. The smuggling aspect was something she liked to keep her hand in, and it occasionally led to some exciting opportunities. The opportunity that Haefen had offered was unusual. Hopefully she would be able to retire from smuggling completely at some point. When Nadierzda was stable, she would be able to work as a respectable merchant. All she needed was somebody to settle down with.

Jak was the one; she knew it, felt it deep in her core. Here was somebody who could keep her on her toes, who had her own distinct skill set and who would challenge her. She loved Jak. It was the first time she'd been able to say those words, even to herself. She settled further into the seat of the sled. Love. It was something she'd scorned for a long time. Something that would weaken her, an overly sentimental emotion that would only keep her from having fun. Except it didn't feel that way with Jak. It felt right. They belonged together, they had fun together. The most mundane activities were exciting again because she shared them with the woman she loved. If Jak felt in any way like that about her, then there was no way she had to be worried about other women. There was no doubt that Jak cared for her. Had cared for her, before Torrin screwed things up with her jealousy, her lack of attention and playing into Tanith's manipulation. When it came right down to it, she had no one but herself to blame for the entire situation. It was amazing things between them hadn't gone sideways sooner. She should have told Jak how she felt, instead of covering it up with work and sex. If only she had said something.

She was so wrapped up in self-recrimination that she hadn't even realized they'd arrived. Olesya killed the power on the sled and it settled slowly to the ground. Axe slid to a stop nearby and joined them.

"Zakaria, our pilot," Axe said to Torrin, "says we flew over this area a couple days ago. It was while we were running some routine sweeps out of our designated search area. There was no sign of Jak on any of the scans. She's convinced that there's no way that Jak was here."

"If anyone can avoid the scans, it's Jak. I think it's worth looking into."

"Fair enough." Axe trotted over to the nearest barn. From the outside, there was no sign of anybody, but the captain disappeared into the barn anyway. From her own farming experience, Torrin knew the farmer could be almost anywhere on her property. At this time of day, her cows would be grazing and they wouldn't be coming in for feed and milking for two to three hours yet. If the farmer wasn't in the barn, then she could be off fixing fences or any one of the numerous chores that farming required.

A short time later, Axe exited the building with a smiling woman. They were chatting, the farmer flipping her multitude of blond braids animatedly.

"Yozhin conquers another," Olesya chuckled.

"Really? She has a face like a tomahawk."

"Oh yeah. The best part is that she hardly ever realizes it. She thinks people are just being nice. I've seen women practically throw themselves at Axe's feet and she never noticed. Her wife is a lucky woman. Well, except that she's gone so much."

"This is Ranya," Axe said as they joined them. "She owns this farm and is as close to a village head as they have here."

"Hello." Ranya smiled at them warmly, dimples flashing. "Welcome to Roost."

"Roost?" Torrin asked, extending a hand toward the farmer.

Ranya took her hand and shook it emphatically. The calluses on her fingers and palms reminded Torrin of Jak.

"Yes. We're on a bit of a high spot in the area, so Roost."

"I see. Did Captain Yozhin tell you what we're doing out here?"

"She did. I also heard the news over the wideband transmission that was sent out. A soldier named Jak Stowell is missing? Do you really think she could have made it out this far?"

"We lost her trail not too far from here. Does this mean you haven't seen her?"

"No, I'm sorry. The only thing I saw was a ship. We don't get too many flybys out here; we're a little removed from the flight path. It was flying low and slow."

"That was us," Axe said. "We were flying a bit of a grid search outside of our main search area."

"Your flight put my cows out a bit. You came by right before milking."

"Something bothered your cows?" Torrin seized on the information. Her mother's goats had never seemed overly bothered by spaceships, but goats were, well, different. Her mother's goats had been more than a little skittish—she'd spent many nights trying to track one of the little bastards down after it had gotten spooked and skittered off—but ships had never bothered them at all.

"They're not used to ships passing over."

"Do you mind if we take a look around?"

"No problem. If anyone asks what you're doing, you let 'em know that I'm okay with it."

"Thanks." Torrin turned to Axe and Olesya. "Take a look and pay attention to anywhere that would take a track. There's plenty of mud in the area, lots of opportunities for Jak to accidentally leave a trace."

"I still think we're wasting our time," Axe said.

"Do you have any better ideas, Captain?" Olesya asked.

"You know I don't," Axe replied testily. "This is as good as anything while the Banshees look to reestablish the trail. At least we've got some shade out here."

She stomped off. Olesya sighed.

"She's frustrated. We were making good progress and now that things have ground to a halt again, she's getting antsy. I think she's getting really worried that we won't find Jak. Or that if we do…"

"It'll be too late," Torrin said. "I know how she's feeling. It's been a long time since she went missing. If it were anybody else, I'd be freaking out right now, but if anyone can pull this out, it's Jak."

"Ivanov! Krikorian!" Axe's shout was excited. "I found something!"

CHAPTER TWENTY-NINE

Her head hurt so badly she could barely see straight. The memory corruption was advancing, and Jak knew that pain was a part of it. Other memories were being compromised by the Sector 27 charts. When she tried to remember what she was doing in this strange place, all she could think of was the layout of the sector. Her continued trek to the northwest was the only thing she could think of to do. She didn't even know why anymore.

There was a bridge coming up. She knew that she was going to have to get past it. It wasn't going to be easy. It certainly hadn't been the first time. First time? This was her first time going this way. Something had happened, and she and Torrin had ended up off course. Only she couldn't remember why Torrin wasn't with her anymore. Her absence didn't seem right at all. She had to be nearby.

Jak stirred from the hollow that had been her only shelter overnight. It had been too much effort to try and find more adequate refuge. As soon as she'd found something that would keep the wind off of her, she'd taken it. The pain in her head and ankle kept her from truly restful sleep, but it had felt so good to stop moving. The inexorable urge to keep going forward, to get back on the other side of the fence had allowed her to pause for only a few hours.

She looked around. No sign of Torrin. She was confused. Had Torrin gone for food? They were out. She'd run out last night. Or had it been the night before?

There was a ridge to the east a ways. Beyond that ridge was an old Orthodoxan logging road. What? No. That was no help at all. Besides that, the charts in her head weren't corresponding very well to the actual terrain. Most of that she chalked up to her concussion and the disabling effects of memory corruption.

Her canteen was almost empty again. She would have to refill it as soon as she could. The contents were less than a complete mouthful and she swallowed it all down.

With a heave and help from her crutch she was able to gain her feet. Blood roared in her ears and her vision dimmed. She held herself stock-still until the spell passed.

There was still no sign of Torrin. A small rock poked out of the dirt at the edge of the hollow and she pulled it out of the ground and turned it over. For some reason, her mind clung to that activity. It was almost as much a compulsion as her trek north and west was. Whatever the compulsion's root, she felt a little better for having fulfilled it.

She made her way slowly out of the hollow. The gentle rise and fall of the terrain wasn't the easiest thing to navigate on only one good leg. It was better than the ravines and ridges around Hutchinson's compound.

The lack of rain was troubling. It was as unnatural as the constant wind and warm tones of this place. The only blue she saw in the landscape was the muted blue of the sky. Even that was more of a tan from the constant wind and sand.

She hoped she would have more answers when she got back on the other side of the fence. For now, the only option she had was to continue moving forward.

* * *

"Over here, by the barn," Axe called. Torrin and Olesya hastened to join her. Sure enough, the churned-up muck by the barn held the clear imprint of Jak's crutch. Ranya ran over to join them.

"Well, would you look at that," Ranya said. "How did we miss that?"

"Why would you have thought to look for it?" Torrin asked bitterly. "Even I thought it was a long shot, and I'm supposed to know her better than anyone else." Olesya patted her comfortingly on the back.

"Captain, we flew over here in the early evening, right?" Olesya asked.

"That's right." Ranya nodded her confirmation from the other side.

"I wonder if Jak didn't sneak in among the herd so she could avoid detection."

"That sounds like something Jak would do," Torrin said. "Bloody dangerous though, especially with a bum leg."

"She should have recognized the *Nightshade*. Why did she hide from us?"

Why had she indeed? With Tanith's betrayal and attempted murder of Jak, she should have been ready to come out at the first sign of friendlies. Unless she didn't know they were friendlies.

"Oh, shit!" The three women looked askance at Torrin over her sudden outburst.

"What's the matter, Torrin?" Axe asked.

"I think I know why she's avoiding everyone. Axe, I need to get back to your ship. Now!"

With an annoyed look at Torrin's commanding tone, Axe radioed the ship.

"It'll be here right away. It's going to land in the south pasture."

Torrin took off at a full-out sprint, followed by the Banshees. As she ran, she radioed her own ship.

"Tien, I need you to transmit maps of Haefen to the *Nightshade*. Send over everything Jak and I passed through on our way out of Orthodoxan territory." Jak's strange trajectory made perfect sense to her now.

The *Nightshade* landed a few minutes later, the back hatch already open. Torrin pounded up the ramp, accompanied by Olesya and Axe.

"I need the briefing room," she said to Axe. Wordlessly, the captain took the lead. This time, Torrin was so preoccupied with her sudden epiphany that she did bang her head on the pipe.

"Bring up the maps that Tien sent over." Torrin instructed Axe. A few swipes and a couple of seconds longer, the maps of Haefen and the Orthodoxan's western-most territories were on the screen. Torrin leaned over them. She pointed out Hutchinson's compound and traced a line west to a ridgeline overlooking a river.

"That's where I went into the river. Can you zoom in on that area for me please?" Axe complied and the area expanded. Torrin followed the river's course a short way with her fingertip before pointing exultantly to a shallow bend in the river.

"There's where Jak dragged my ass out of the river. Does it look familiar?"

"It does a bit," Olesya said slowly. "It kind of looks like the stretch of river where Jak washed up. But the terrain's completely different. There are no mountains in that area."

"Are you saying that she thinks she's back on her home planet?" Axe did not sound convinced at all.

"How about this?" Torrin went back to the console and traced out the trek that she and Jak had undertaken through the Haefonian wilderness.

A steady path in a general northwesterly direction developed beneath her fingers. "Now overlay that track over Jak's on the maps of this area and adjust the scale so it's the same."

Wrinkles creased Axe's forehead as she complied with Torrin's instructions. A few moments later, she looked up from the console.

"Well, I'll be." Jak's trail matched the journey she and Torrin had taken those many months ago. Step for step, it was almost the same as that long overland trek.

"She must have gotten disoriented by a hit to the head," Torrin said. "If she has a concussion and some associated memory loss, then she might think she's back on Haefen."

"Is that even possible?" Axe asked.

"If it isn't, then you explain how the trails match up so well." Torrin stepped in next to Axe and took over the console's controls. Deftly, she brought the maps of Haefen back up but kept the two routes visible. Jak's second route ended where they stood. Torrin swiped over until she got to the bridge.

"We need to find her before she gets here," Torrin said, indicating bridge.

"Why is that?" Olesya asked.

"Because we had to kill eight men to cross it. If she's reliving our journey, then there's no telling what she'll do when she gets here. We already know she didn't recognize your ship. I think she's convinced she's still behind enemy lines. If I'm right, then she's a danger to anyone she meets."

"I guess we should be glad she doesn't have her rifle," Axe commented.

"Yes, we should be. But we know she still has a knife. She's very good with it, and no one's going to see her coming until too late."

"There's no guarantee that she'll stick to this route. Maybe she won't get that far."

"We can't afford to assume she won't. I say we head over to whatever point matches up to this on our maps and work our way back."

"Tell you what we'll do," Axe said. "We're going to have the Banshees that are already out there continue the search from here. Now that we have her trail again, they can follow it from this end. Since we're already in the ship, we'll take it to the place you're worried about. We'll follow the trail back and hopefully intercept her. If you're right, then we'll make sure she doesn't hurt anyone. If I'm right, then we won't lose the trail again."

"That works for me," Torrin conceded.

"Zakaria, I'm sending you a map and route." Axe had her hand up to her left ear as she started for the hallway. Olesya took her place at the console and busily worked her way through the appropriate charts. "Set a course based on the route you're being sent."

Torrin followed closely on Axe's heels as she strode to the bridge. The pilot was already inputting the course when they entered, and Torrin quickly took her place in one of the observation seats. The amber light flickered on in the compartment. This was going to work. It had to. As much as she wanted to get Jak back, it was as important that they manage it before Jak hurt someone. If Jak was as disoriented as she suspected, whatever might go wrong wouldn't be her fault. But Torrin also knew there was no way she would be able to convince Jak of that. The sniper would never forgive herself if she hurt one of Nadierzda's women.

"Take us to that point with all possible speed," Axe instructed from her chair.

"Captain, we won't be able to perform any scans at that speed," the pilot said cautiously, glancing back at Axe.

"Once we get there, we'll work our way back along the course you set. It's important that Captain Stowell doesn't get that far."

"Acknowledged, Captain. Ready to proceed on your mark."

Olesya moved into the bridge and took her seat at Axe's right hand. The captain watched as she restrained herself.

"You may proceed," Axe said as soon as the lieutenant had engaged the safety harness.

The ship's engines opened up and it leaped into the air, hovering for a second. The pilot was good, better than good. She pushed them forward as soon as they stopped their vertical movement. Torrin was pushed back into the yielding softness of the seat's back, which was made of a gel-like substance that helped prevent the friction sores that could be caused by the constant vibration from the ship's powerful engines. There were circumstances when the crew had to spend hours at a time in the chairs, and the Banshees had to be in fighting shape when the engines cut out. Torrin had outfitted her chair with the same gel even though she didn't have nearly as much occasion to be spending those kinds of hours in the chair.

As they sliced through Nadierzda's sky toward their destination, Torrin was unaccountably nervous. More than anything, she wanted to see Jak again, but she worried about what they would find. Would Jak be all right? How far gone was she? Would she still be angry about what she'd walked in on with Breena? The vibration of the engines served only to heighten her anxiety. She closed her eyes and concentrated on her breathing and tried to calm her racing heart.

Scant minutes later, the ship slammed to a stop with enough force that Torrin was pushed forward in her harness. With her crew strapped in place, there was no need for the pilot to think of niceties such as a gentle deceleration, Torrin supposed. The ship hovered in place and the main viewscreen flickered to reveal a view of the outside. Smaller screens to either side held Jak's likely path and a map of the local terrain.

Torrin disengaged the harness and moved forward to peruse the local map. As she watched, points of color started blooming on the map's surface. The Banshees had started scanning the immediate area. To her disappointment, there was nothing that resembled human life on the scan. There were plenty of small animals, but nothing big enough to be a person. It had been stupid to hope that Jak would be right there waiting for them, but unconsciously she had been wishing for exactly that.

"No sign of Captain Stowell," the pilot announced.

"I was afraid of that," Axe replied.

"Captain, we don't know whether or not she beat us here," Olesya said. "If we go back along the trail and she's already further ahead, then we run the risk of losing her."

"This is exactly why I didn't want to split our resources," Axe grumbled.

"Why don't you send the ship back on Jak's path?" Torrin said. "I can take one of the sleds and keep going forward. Once you've made sure she's not along the trail, you can come pick me up."

"It'll have to do. Olesya, you're with Ivanov."

"Got it, Captain." The lieutenant slipped her harness, gathered Torrin and hustled the two of them out of the bridge.

"Come on, before Axe decides on something else," Olesya breathed in Torrin's ear as they left the compartment. "She's on edge and sometimes she gets a little…"

"Imperious?"

"Something like that."

They stopped for some rations and water from the ship's stores, then continued on to the aft cargo bay. The bay door raised on a view of green grasses on rolling hills.

Olesya limbered up one of the antigrav sleds secured along one wall. She threw her leg over the machine and gestured for Torrin to climb on behind her. Having to ride on the back still irked Torrin to no end, but she knew better than to give Axe an excuse to change her mind. She mounted the sled behind the lieutenant and waited for the pilot to bring the ship the rest of the way to the ground. Olesya revved the engine and Torrin barely had a split second to throw her arms around the lieutenant's waist as she gunned the sled through the opening.

They landed more smoothly than Torrin would have imagined, but she still squeezed Olesya tightly as they came to a stop. The torso she had her arms wrapped around with a death grip shook with laughter at her reaction.

"Asshole," she said with heated emphasis.

Olesya only laughed harder and moved the sled forward as the ship above them swiveled and moved away slowly.

"There was something on the map I think we should check out," Torrin said, leaning forward to shout into Olesya's war. "After we clear that we can start looking for tracks."

"Sounds good. Where are we headed?"

"There's a grain elevator to the north and west a ways. It's close enough to where the bridge was on Haefen. Hopefully Jak won't head that way, but we need to check it to be sure."

* * *

The sun beat down on her head. She was so tired of all the sun. Jak closed her eyes to try to relieve the glare that drilled into her. She thought they must be in the middle of a record-breaking heat wave. She couldn't remember the last time they'd had so many consecutive sunny days. The heat showed no signs of letting up. There was no sign of rain either, which was doubly puzzling. It rained every day, almost without fail, but since she'd woken up on the riverbank, there hadn't been a drop out of the sky.

For the past day, she'd felt like somebody was watching her, and she kept her head on a swivel, taking care never to be silhouetted against the sky. She was so on edge, waiting for whatever it was to happen. Her feeling of dread had only increased as she continued further along her path, and yet, she could barely even stop for sleep. Something still goaded her on, ever forward. All she wanted was to lie down, but she couldn't manage it for more than a few hours without needing to keep going. Staying put caused her physical pain, and her only relief came from continuing her evermore arduous trek.

Her ankle was still a mess and the crutch was becoming its own problem. Her shoulder was an aching mass of muscle. Constant use had caused large, painful blisters to open on her hand and she was developing a sore in her armpit. If she didn't make it back to the fence soon, she was going to die out there.

Not being able to see Torrin again was her biggest regret. The previous day, she'd come to the painful conclusion that Torrin had probably died in that river. In all likelihood, she'd been washed away and drowned. Jak's other regret was not getting the chance to kill the sniper who took Bron from her. For a second she saw the boy with the rifle. He was right in front of her. She stumbled and fell, sprawling full length into the grasses. The fall sent pain coursing through her entire body. The litany of injuries made themselves known to her in a cascade of pain and she lay on the ground moaning.

When she could gather herself enough to look around, the boy with the rifle was gone. *Fool*, she cursed herself mentally. He'd never been there. She was jumping at shadows from her own messed-up mind.

"I'm going crazy for sure," Jak mumbled and shook her head, surprised to hear her own voice. It was rough with disuse and coughing. Even though she'd found water and had refilled her canteen, the cough was back. She did her best to keep her throat wet, but that was only partially successful in keeping the constant hacking at bay.

Inexorably, the pressure to get moving mounted as she lay prone on the ground. Unable to withstand it any further, she pushed herself up to hands and knees, located her crutch and pushed on.

According to her map there should have been a bridge coming up soon. She needed that bridge to get across the river.

"What river?" Jak asked herself out loud, startling herself once again with the sound of her voice. The map clearly showed a river, a damn big one. She needed to get across to make it to the coast so she could get around the end of the fence. Without the river, there was no bridge, and without the bridge she wouldn't be able to get home.

Nausea gripped her belly as the pain in her head intensified. Things were so wrong, but she couldn't stop. Nothing made sense, and every time she tried to pick through the confusion, the pain in her head only got worse. Panting with the effort of holding her headache at bay while she tried to piece together all the inconsistencies, she stopped dead in the middle of calf-high grass.

When she finally looked up, she saw a raised structure cutting across the landscape. It didn't look like anything she was familiar with. If it was a wall, it wouldn't have man-high cutouts along its entire length. Something metallic glinted all along the very top of the structure. For the life of her, she couldn't figure out what the structure could be used for. The Orthodoxans were full of surprises lately. It stretched as far as she could see to the east. To the west it met up with a tall building.

She pulled up the map again and it snapped into focus in her mind with almost no effort. The tall, unfamiliar building was in roughly the same location as the bridge was supposed to be. The long, low structure followed a similar path to the river that was supposed to be there. Maybe the mapmakers hadn't known what to make of those structures either, so they'd substituted the closest geographic markers they could come up with.

Her logic was off, she knew that, but she didn't have a better explanation. When she got back to camp, she would have a long chat with the quartermaster about the slipshod quality of his maps.

Even though it wasn't the bridge she'd been expecting, the tall building was her next destination. It was close enough that she was able to satisfy the urge that drove her forward.

A couple of hours of halting movement brought her close enough to the tall building that she could watch it from the crest of a low hill. It seemed right, spying on the occupants, like she'd done it before. For a moment she missed Torrin so badly that the pain felt tangible. Her breath caught, and she quickly took a drink, making sure to breathe shallowly and quickly to stave off another paroxysm of coughing.

The low structure went through the middle of the small compound of buildings. Now that she was closer, she could see that the tall building wasn't the only one in the area. A couple of smaller structures, including what looked like a tiny house, were clustered together. Behind the house, Jak could see what looked like a large garden, full of vegetables and fruits. Her stomach growled loudly. It had been a while since her last real meal. She tried to think how long, but couldn't remember.

If she could get down to the garden and help herself to some vegetables, then sneak past the structure that split the landscape, she'd have a clear run to the coast. If she could gather enough vegetables, then she would be in good shape to keep up her flagging energy for a little longer.

Carefully, she surveyed the area. There had to be people around. After all, someone was keeping the tall structure operational, and the garden certainly looked well-tended. She hoped there were civilians in the area and not Orthodoxan soldiers. She should be able to overwhelm civilians if caught, even in her weakened condition. Soldiers, even piss-poor ones like the Orthodoxans, would definitely overpower her. For a moment she was very conscious of the absence of her breastbinder. Whatever had possessed her not to wear it out on a mission was beyond her. Unfortunately, her breasts, when not bound down, were very noticeable. She'd often thought it ironic that someone like her who had no use for breasts had such a nice pair.

Somewhere in the pit of her stomach that unknown, yet familiar curl of desire unfolded. Her breasts were good for something, she knew, but couldn't remember what.

Groaning, she dropped her head into her folded arms. Of all the times to be thinking of sex, on surveillance before a raid was the worst. Just when she could least afford to be distracted, she was. She needed to focus. Food would help. Once her blood sugar was back up to an acceptable level, she would be able to concentrate more clearly.

She needed to get some food soon, and she went back to watching and planning.

CHAPTER THIRTY

Jak hadn't spent enough time planning the garden raid. She knew it, but the lure of all that food had been too overwhelming to resist. There were at least two people down there. At least one of them was female, to her relief. Women meant civilians, especially if they were walking around. Whoever she was, her man must be somewhere around there. Orthodoxan women were never unaccompanied. Jak thought wistfully that he must be good to her, if she was allowed to roam the area on her own. Where would the woman even go out here? a dark corner of her mind asked. They were in the middle of nowhere. There was no point in restraining her. It wasn't like she could leave.

The woman had come out and picked some vegetables before disappearing back into the house. By the angle of the sun, Jak assumed she was getting food together for dinner. Her stomach growled loudly at the thought. How she would have loved to have joined the woman for a meal. Real food sounded so good, never mind that stopping in would be a death sentence. After she was turned over to the Orthodoxan authorities, she would die. On the spot, or slowly in one of the breeding pens. The only difference was the length of time and the amount of suffering. That wouldn't happen to her, she promised herself. As much as she hated the idea of hurting a woman, she would do what she needed to in order to survive.

Unable to deny herself the opportunity to eat some of the luscious bounty below, Jak slid over the hill's crest. There was another, lower hill between her vantage point and the garden. She skirted the hill's base so as not to expose herself to any watchful eyes. A large rock provided cover from which she could observe the house a little longer before moving again.

There was no further movement from the house so she moved forward cautiously. It was difficult to move stealthily with a crutch. A large part of success in stealth was the ability to move very slowly and smoothly. The crutch definitely threw that off, but she wasn't sure she could have crawled the entire way to the vegetable patch. Also, if she was caught without it, she would have no options for escape.

The patch was so close that the smell of tomatoes threatened to overwhelm her already tenuous self-control. The scent was strong enough that she knew they were ripe, and only the threat of discovery kept her from lurching forward. Jak tried to keep her movements slow, but hunger took over and she closed the distance between herself and the closest tomato plant with as much speed as she could muster.

With trembling hands, she plucked a tomato from the plant. It was bigger than the size of her fist and she stared at it for a second before taking a huge bite out of the side. With her other hand, she twisted off another tomato, even larger than the first. She had no bag. Where was she going to put the delicate fruit? After a moment, she created a pouch with the front of her shirt and dropped the beautiful red orb into it. Chewing busily, she skulked along the row of tomatoes. She thought she'd seen... Yes! Sweet peppers. These were her favorite. They weren't blue-green like she was used to, but rather a brilliant yellow. The shape was familiar, and they looked big enough to be ripe.

As she popped the last bite of tomato in her mouth, she pulled the nearest pepper off the vine. Bringing it up to her nose, she inhaled deeply. It had the slightly pungent smell she was used to, but with an additional layer of sweetness. Unable to help herself, she took a bite. This pepper truly was sweet. She'd always thought that sweet peppers were named so because they weren't the hot ones. This one definitely lived up to the name. She reached over to harvest a couple more and dropped them in the impromptu pouch of her shirt.

Further down, she caught sight of what could only be zucumbers. The hardy vegetables were ubiquitous where she'd grown up. They were one of the few vegetables hardy enough to withstand the growing conditions at a higher altitude. Truth be told, she wasn't overly fond of them, having had a multitude of them as a child. Right now, they were perfect. Her mouth watered at the sight, and they were hardy enough that she didn't have to transport them in her improvised pouch. Quickly, Jak set about filling her pockets with the long, green vegetables.

A loud banging caught her attention and she looked up, panicked. The house's back door had just swung shut and she could hear footsteps crunching up the gravel path to the garden. She froze for a second and then regretfully put aside her stash of vegetables. The only weapons she had were her knife and the crutch. If she went down, she would have more to worry about than her ankle. If she couldn't get a drop on the Orthodoxan woman and knock her out, she was probably going to have to kill her.

"Got it, babe, I'll get enough for all of us." Jak could barely make out what the woman said. Someone called something in return, but they were too far away for Jak to make out the words. She melted into the foliage as well as she could. Some of the plants were tall, but none of them were tall enough for her to disappear completely. She would have to do her best and hope for the woman's sake that she wasn't discovered.

* * *

The grain elevator was quiet when Torrin and Olesya pulled up on the antigrav sled. There were no farmers with their shipments of grain and no sign that a train had been by recently.

"There should be someone around," Olesya said. She killed the sled's power and it settled to the ground. "Let's see if we can find the owner or a worker."

Torrin followed along in the lieutenant's wake, eyes peeled for any sign of Jak. She shaded her eyes and peered at the surrounding hills. The area was nothing like the bridge where they'd killed those eight men, but she couldn't be sure of Jak's state of mind.

The gravel road beneath their feet crunched loudly in the silence. The entire scene was quiet and idyllic. The wind barely blew; it was the merest pleasant breeze. Without as much dust blowing around as normal, the sky shone a brilliant blue. Not as blue as the sky on Haefen, but close. Around them, the low, rolling hills were shades of green and gold. In the distance, she could see fields of wheat, only now starting to turn. The sun's rays barely caressed the tops of the hills. Before long, sunset would be upon them.

The road passed under the maglev rails. The rails were high enough that most cars could drive beneath without issue. There was a gate, and Torrin could see where the rails would detach and lift like a drawbridge. She assumed that was so bigger trucks could pass through. A small building was set to one side of the gate. It looked a little like the tollhouse at the bridge on Haefen, and Torrin shivered a bit at the memory. She had no desire to see the walls of that small house painted with the blood of her people in the same way she and Jak had done to the Orthodoxans.

Olesya knocked on the small building's door. After a moment a young woman opened the door and looked quizzically at them.

"You don't look like farmers," she said. She adjusted a billed cap to shade her eyes against the lowering sun. "Can I help you folks?" Her brown hair was short enough that it barely stuck out of the back and sides of the cap. Torrin looked her over carefully. Before she'd met Jak, this was exactly the kind of woman she'd been most attracted to, though come to think of it, Jak fit the same mold. Short-haired, boyish and competent. She loved a woman who looked like she could handle herself.

"Have you seen any sign of Captain Jak Stowell?" Olesya asked after giving Torrin an exasperated look. Torrin shrugged. She wasn't dead and she could appreciate a good-looking woman if she wanted to. The distraction was welcome and eased her anxiety for a moment. She noted a wedding band on the woman's ring finger.

"I heard a general announcement over wideband that she was missing." A puzzled frown creased the woman's brow. "Is she still missing? She's been gone a long time if she is."

"I'm afraid she is," Torrin answered. "We're out looking for her. I'm Torrin Ivanov, this is Lieutenant Olesya Krikorian."

"I'm Sean Boyle," the woman replied. "I know who you are. We sell our grain to your company. I met with one of your partners to negotiate the contract. Short woman, very charming."

"That would be Audra." Torrin grinned widely. "If you're not cursing her name, then she probably thought you were cute and took it easy on you during the negotiation."

"That sounds about right." Sean smiled back at her. Torrin could see how Audra would find the woman attractive. Her eyes crinkled appealingly at the corners when she smiled. "I don't know why you'd be looking for her all the way out here. We're in the middle of nowhere, not on the way for anything except grain to market."

"We have reason to believe that she may be coming this way," Olesya said.

"You can't miss her if you see her," Torrin added. Though their chances of seeing her were pretty slim, she admitted to herself. "She's way shorter even than Olesya, super short blond hair and the bluest eyes you've ever seen. We think she's injured." Torrin hesitated, not sure how much to tell Sean. She didn't want her to think Jak was an immediate danger, but the fact was that Jak could cause a lot of damage if she wasn't in her right mind.

"She's been gone for a while," Olesya said when Torrin's pause stretched on too long. "We think that might be because she received a blow to the head and has become disoriented. If you do see her, be extremely cautious."

"Oh, wow. I'll keep that in mind." Sean's eyes widened at the lieutenant's cautions.

"Do you mind if we look around, see if there's any sign of her?" Torrin asked.

"No problem," Sean replied. "I'm working up some payment paperwork that's a little behind, so I'd love to help you."

"Thanks for the offer, but it's probably best if we do the searching." Olesya tipped a finger at Sean. "We'll let you know if we find anything."

"I'd appreciate that. Good luck, ladies." Sean gave the two of them a small wave, then retreated back into the small office. They were blasted with cool air as she shut the door. Torrin could appreciate why she wouldn't want to leave the door open any longer than she had to. The heat of the Nadierzdan day could be oppressive, and when there wasn't as much dust in the air, the sun's rays beat down cruelly on the landscape.

"Where do you want to start?" Olesya asked.

"Let's do the near perimeter of this place. If we don't find anything, we should probably start working our way back toward the ship."

"Sounds good. I'll take the west side." The lieutenant walked away, leaving Torrin to look around on the eastern side. She walked among the buildings and inspected the area around the massive grain elevator, then on to the elevated rails. There was no sign of Jak. Disappointment and elation warred together in her. Disappointment because she desperately wanted to know that Jak was all right. Finding her tracks would have let her know the she was still alive at least. She was elated because it meant Jak wasn't on a collision course with hurting someone.

Torrin carefully worked her way back around to the office building, checking again for any sign of her lover. She had barely gotten back before Olesya showed up. A shake of the head let her know that the lieutenant had also come up empty.

Their thorough searches had taken up a lot of time, and the sun balanced on the hills. The light was getting dimmer as oranges and reds lit up the western sky.

"Still nothing," Torrin said. Olesya shook her head again.

Sean answered the door to Torrin's knock.

"It looks like you'll be all right," she said. "We haven't seen any sign of Jak."

"Good," Sean said. The look on her face said beyond words, exactly how relieved Sean was. "Say, it's getting late and I bet you've been working hard all day. Why don't you join my wife and me for dinner?"

"Oh, we really shouldn't," Torrin demurred. If Jak wasn't there, she wanted to continue looking. "We ought to be moving along."

"Actually," Olesya said, "I wouldn't mind some food." Torrin shot her a look, which she ignored. "It's going to be too dark for us to continue our search soon anyway. We've been working hard, and a little time out for food isn't going to kill anybody. Besides, it's been a while since I had a home-cooked meal."

Sean grinned. "Excellent. Keelie will be so happy. We don't get a whole lot of visitors out here. She's way more social than me, and I think she misses people sometimes. Let me close up and we can go over to the house." She disappeared into her office and reappeared moments later.

"So how did you end up with a grain elevator?" Torrin asked as they walked toward the small house. The pretty little home had been on Olesya's side. It wasn't large, but it was obvious that the women who lived there loved it very much. Like most other Nadierzdan buildings, it was one story. It seemed to be built around a central courtyard, and Torrin couldn't see any exterior windows, which made sense. It reminded her of her mother's house, but much homier with little landscaping touches Irenya would have thought too frivolous.

"Bought it from my aunt," Sean said. "I didn't want to take up farming like my mom. I have three sisters who are more than happy to do that. I wanted to do something where I could make a little more profit, but all I really know is grain. This seemed like a good fit when she was ready to retire."

"Makes sense." Torrin stopped as Sean opened the front door and went in, holding the door for them.

"Honey, we have company for dinner," she called as Olesya and Torrin filed in behind her.

A lovely woman with a thick, waist-length blond braid appeared from around a corner. Torrin could smell food cooking and her stomach growled. Olesya elbowed her in the ribs.

"Sean, babe. I'm happy to see guests, but I could have used a little more notice," she chided gently.

Sean walked over to her and embraced her, kissing the side of her neck hungrily. "I'm sorry, hon. But they just kind of showed up, and I know how much you miss seeing your friends from town. I thought you'd like some company for dinner."

Keelie smiled and turned her head to meet Sean's lips. They shared a quick smooch. "I'm not saying I'm unhappy, but I'm going to need to get some more food since we're having guests."

"I don't mind waiting, ma'am," Olesya said. "It smells amazing in here."

The dimples Keelie flashed their way gave Torrin a pretty good idea what had first attracted Sean to her lady love.

"I'm Torrin Ivanov," Torrin said. "This is Lieutenant Olesya Krikorian."

"It's good to meet you two. I'm Keelie. I'm going to let my wayward wife entertain you while I head out to the vegetable patch to supplement dinner." She gave Sean another kiss, longer this time, then disengaged herself. Sean made a show of reluctance at being forced to relinquish her hold. As Keelie disappeared back into the house, Sean led them through a door into the interior courtyard.

It was surprisingly cool for all the heat they'd had that day. The roof had enough of an overhang that it shaded the interior area for most of the day. A small pool with a fountain burbled quietly in one corner. Plants covered every horizontal surface.

"She's lovely," Torrin said. "Have you two been together long?"

"We've been married less than a year." Sean filled with pride at the compliment. "Before that we were together for about a year and a half. Not living together, not until I could support us. But we dated."

"You have a really nice home," Olesya said.

"Thanks. Keelie does most of the work. She's a total witch with plants. She's been working on cultivating different varieties of flowers. Wants to see about selling them in town when her hybrids start breeding true. In fact, she's been working on an edible tulip that's absolutely amazing. I'll have her bring some in for dessert." Sean jumped up and jogged to a door on the opposite side of the courtyard.

"Young love, no wonder they're so into each other," Olesya said, a small smile on her face. Her smile widened and she leaned over to smack Torrin on the arm. "Are you and Jak that nauseating?"

Torrin's smile was pained. She missed Jak terribly and in private they'd been even worse than Keelie and Sean. In public, Jak could be very antsy. They'd had very little opportunity for affection when others were around.

The look on her face must have said volumes, and Olesya cringed. "Sorry, Torrin. You know I don't always think before I open my yap."

"Nothing's changed then, I take it?"

"Not really, no."

Sean's voice called out to Keelie from the back of the house, and her wife answered.

Torrin smiled wistfully. "One day, maybe we'll be like this. Of course we have to find Jak first."

A bloodcurdling scream raised the hair along Torrin's arms. The women glanced at each other, then bolted through the door Sean had exited through. They came pelting out the back door to a scene out of Torrin's recent nightmares.

Sean stood with her back to them. Beyond her was Keelie, face slack with animal terror. Wild-eyed and not really seeing, Jak's face gazed at them from over Keelie's right shoulder, but what really got Torrin's attention was the knife Jak held to Keelie's neck.

"Shit, Torrin. Looks like you got your wish." Olesya took in the situation with a glance, then started moving slowly away from her.

"Let go of my wife," Sean yelled, face pale, stepping toward Jak and Keelie.

"Come any closer and I will slit her throat," Jak growled. Torrin's heart sank even further. She recognized that raspy tone. Jak was back in disguise as a man.

Breathing deeply, Torrin moved out from behind Sean so Jak could see her more clearly. Jak's eyes flicked to her, then back to Sean. There was no sign of recognition.

"Jak, honey," Torrin called out. "It's me."

Another glance from Jak, she blinked and looked again, then a third time. There was definitely something wrong with her. Even from where she was standing, Torrin could see the yellowing remnants of an ugly bruise that spread across half of Jak's temple.

"Torrin." Jak's voice was hesitant and went up in register. She shook her head, and cleared her throat. "Are you all right? I thought you were killed? I saw you go in, but I couldn't find you." Her voice had roughened again, this time Torrin thought that maybe it was emotion. Her confusion was palpable and she licked her lips nervously.

"You need to get her away from Keelie," Sean said hotly, taking another step toward her.

Jak backed up a step, face set back in hard lines. "Don't move. I don't know what's going on here, but I can't let you report me."

"No one's going to report anyone," Torrin soothed. "I've been so worried about you. I've been looking for you."

"You found the trail I left you?" Jak's eyes were hopeful.

"I did. It was very helpful."

"But why are you with him?" Jak injected layers of venom into the pronoun. "He's one of them. Keeping his woman like a slave. Worse than a slave, like an object. A thing!"

"I would never," Sean protested. "I love her!"

"Sean, I need you to go inside," Torrin said in a low voice. "She's confused and you're not helping right now."

"No way in hell. I'm staying right here until we get Keelie back."

"Sean!" Keelie cried out. The quaver in her voice betrayed her fear and Torrin winced. There was no way she was going to get Sean out of there. She thought maybe she could talk Jak down, but if Jak thought Sean was an Orthodoxan then she wasn't likely to let Keelie go.

At Keelie's cry, Sean took another half step forward. Jak pulled the knife up to Keelie's neck and pressed the tip in. Torrin could see the flesh of her neck indenting slightly. If the knife had been any sharper, Jak would have drawn blood. With a frustrated groan, Sean stopped. She stared helplessly at her wife and Jak then back at Torrin.

"Do something," she implored.

"Jak, you need to let that woman go," Torrin said. "You're among friends. No one here wants to hurt you."

"That's not true. I need to get you back on the other side of the fence. We're not safe here."

Her worst fears confirmed, Torrin wondered how to convince her delusional lover that they weren't on Haefen. If Jak's trip through rural Nadierzda hadn't convinced her of that, Torrin wondered what she could say that would change her mind. It didn't matter, she decided. For Jak's sake and for Keelie's, she had to try.

"Jak, honey. We're not on Haefen anymore. We're on my home planet. This is Nadierzda."

Confusion crossed Jak's face again, chased by a look of agony.

"That's not possible," Jak panted. Whatever pain she was in clearly affected her strongly. She groaned and swayed a little bit, grabbing Keelie's shoulder with her free hand for support.

"But it is possible," Torrin said. She was going to need all of her powers of persuasion for this one. "I know what you're expecting, and it's not here. If we're on Haefen, where's the river? Remember the river that was so wide we couldn't cross it except by that bridge. You thought the bridge would be here, didn't you?"

"Yes, but it's not." Jak looked so confused and lost that Torrin's heart went out to her. She moved forward toward her. "I thought it was a mapping error."

"It isn't, Jak. You aren't on your home planet, you're on mine. Try to remember."

Jak's face screwed up as she tried to follow Torrin's directions. She closed her eyes and furrows creased her brows. She tilted her head as she fought with pain so intense that Torrin could see it written in every tense line of her body.

Movement from behind Jak caught her eye. Olesya was approaching Jak from behind, her pistol raised. Torrin caught her eye and shook her head warningly. She knew she could talk Jak down. Olesya's first priority lay in getting the civilian out of danger. She wouldn't want to, but she would take Jak out if she felt she had no other option.

The lieutenant returned Torrin's look. She held up a hand and waggled it from side to side. Torrin nodded reluctantly. It was a Banshee hand signal. It meant to kill only if necessary.

Torrin took another step closer to Jak.

"Remember, honey. You were so sick when we first got here. You spent a long time in the hospital. Then you finally got sick of lying around and you snuck out with my sister. I was so mad at both of you. You scared the crap out of me."

Jak swayed again. "I can't remember," she said through gritted teeth. "I feel like I've done this before. Like everything I've been doing since I woke up on the riverbank is something I've done before, but I can't remember what comes next."

Clearly describing how she'd gotten to Nadierzda wasn't getting through to Jak. Maybe she needed something more visceral, a memory attached more to sensation.

She took another step forward. She was close enough that if she'd reached out, she would have been able to graze Jak's arm. It was so tempting but she didn't want to startle her.

"How about this? Do you remember the first night we made love?"

Jak's eyes shot open and met hers. "We did what?" She sounded appalled and intrigued. "But you don't know—"

"That you're a woman?" Torrin grinned widely. "Jak, I know that under those clothes you are every centimeter a woman. In fact, I know every millimeter intimately."

Jak's nostrils flared and her eyes darkened, not with pain but with arousal. "How can that be?"

"McCullock tried to attack me and you burst into the room like my very own holovid hero. You threatened to kill him, and I accidentally saw your naked chest. Can you imagine my surprise when the rough man who'd taken me across Haefen turned out not to be a man at all, but an incredibly desirable woman?" Torrin stopped to lick her lips, not with nervousness, but with her own remembered arousal.

"I can't remember," Jak whispered, devastation in her eyes.

"That's too bad. You were hot as hell. We made love, and I brought you to your first orgasm."

"I can't remember," Jak groaned, closing her eyes.

Torrin closed the gap between them and put her hand on top of Jak's. She could feel the handle of the knife between Jak's fingers. Keelie's eyes rolled, trying to see the knife. Jak's hand shook and a thin trickle of blood dripped down Keelie's neck.

"Let go of the knife, Jak," Torrin said quietly.

Jak opened her eyes and stared dumbly into Torrin's. Taking a wild chance, Torrin leaned forward and pressed her lips to Jak's. For a moment there was no reaction, and then Jak's tongue trailed across the tip of hers, then nothing. Torrin pulled back in time for Jak's eyes to roll back into her head. She started to topple. Torrin held onto the hand with the knife and steered it clear of Keelie.

Sean leaped forward as Keelie ripped herself free of Jak's unconscious hold. The dead weight dragged on Torrin's arm, and she pulled her unconscious lover to her as she lowered her to the ground.

She caressed Jak's cheek lightly, tracing the pattern of the bruise. Now that she was close enough, she clearly saw the jagged wound at her hairline. It had started to heal, but the new skin was angry looking. Jak had lost weight and Torrin could hear the tortured wheezing of breath into and out of her lungs. Her eyes filled with tears as she stroked Jak's face, trying to convince herself that it was real. This had all the earmarks of a terrible nightmare, except that she couldn't wake up.

A hand landed comfortingly on her shoulder. She looked up to see Olesya standing over her.

"Good job, Torrin. Axe is on her way with the *Nightshade*. We'll get her home soon."

At her words Torrin burst into tears and pulled Jak closer to her. She'd thought that everything would be better when she found Jak. Everything was far from okay. Her worse fears had been realized. She was never leaving Jak's side again.

CHAPTER THIRTY-ONE

Jak opened her eyes gingerly. After so many days of pain, she had no reason to expect today to be any different, but when the light hit her eyes there wasn't even the faintest hint of an ache. That was unexpected and she sat bolt upright. The room was familiar; she'd been here before. The woman sitting in a chair by the bed was also familiar. She regarded Jak with a hopeful look in her eyes.

"Your hair," Jak said. "It used to be longer."

Torrin looked startled, then laughed and touched the not quite chin-length curls self-consciously.

"You can thank your general for that, remember?" The sound of her voice thrilled Jak. It reached down into her and caressed parts of her body that she hadn't paid attention to for quite some time. Her face reddened at the rising arousal she was feeling. Her blush deepened further until she felt as though her face must be seconds from bursting into flame. Memories were coming to her, but not of her general. She closed her eyes as she remembered Torrin's fingers on her and in her in the most intimate way.

"Are you all right?" Torrin looked concerned and perched on the edge of the bed. She reached out a cool hand and caressed Jak's forehead. Her fingers did nothing to soothe the ache Jak was feeling. At her touch, a surge of arousal flooded through her belly and pooled between her thighs.

Confused, she pulled back from Torrin's distressing touch. "I'm okay. I think."

"You don't feel feverish."

"I was remembering." She caught Torrin's eyes and blushed again.

"Oh." Torrin caught her blush and grinned, her own face flushing, not with embarrassment but with her own arousal. "Oh!"

"I've been here before, but I can't remember what happened."

"It's okay. Kiera said your memory would be patchy. You had a major trauma to your head. She said there's something else going on, but she can't figure out what. It's like you have a partial brainwave or something. Somehow it's overlaid your regular thought patterns. She explained it better than that, but I didn't really understand." She shrugged.

"I think I know." When Jak closed her eyes, she saw the patterns of the Sector 27 map graven on the interior of her eyelids. When she tried to remember other things, the grid was what she saw. She knew the doctor, she remembered that, but when she tried to bring up a memory of her face, she could only think of the topographic contours of a ravine in Sector 27's southwestern section.

"You'll need to tell the doctor," Torrin said. "She says she managed to clear some of the extra fragments away and that healing your concussion should also help."

"It's one of the last downloads I got on Haefen, before I crossed the front lines for Hutchinson's compound. It never got cleared out and now I'm experiencing some side effects."

"What can we do about it?"

"I don't know. I might have to go back." The idea of going back made her head feel light. How did she really feel about it? There was fear there, but under that, the sharp edge of anticipation. "If the doctor can't fix it, it'll only get worse."

Torrin's face tightened at her words. She didn't look very happy, and Jak grasped at the fragments of memory that filled her in on Torrin's reluctance. More memory fragments came back to her, but they were sharp, as if they'd recently happened. Memories of wandering through an unfamiliar landscape. These made her head hurt, and she grimaced.

"What's wrong?"

"I'm remembering something, I think it just happened. Did I hurt someone?"

The look on Torrin's face told her everything she needed to know. Sorrow bound her chest, squeezing the breath out of her lungs. It had been bad, she could remember that much. She'd been so scared. They'd been out to get her and there had been so little that she could do. She'd had no weapons, no shelter, few supplies and Tanith was going to kill her. That or the Orthodoxans. Her breathing grew ever more labored as she struggled to remember what had happened, but it was a hopeless jumble. The pain in her head returned, and she tried to push it aside to figure out who she'd hurt and how badly.

A loud beeping startled her and the door opened. A tall, dark-skinned woman rushed into the room.

"What happened?" she demanded. Practically shoving Torrin out of the way, she took Jak's shoulders and gently but firmly pushed her back against the bed. A mask hung from a pole next to the bed; she unclipped it, then deftly slipped it around Jak's nose and mouth. "Breathe," she ordered Jak. "Slowly."

"I don't know, Kiera," Torrin said defensively. "She asked if she hurt anybody, then started freaking out."

Kiera's face softened slightly. "Jak, you didn't hurt anyone, at least not badly. You scared a couple of farmers, that's all."

From what she could see of Torrin's face, there was more to the story than Kiera was letting on.

"Baby, it really is okay," Torrin hastened to reassure her also. She reoccupied her spot on the edge of the bed and took Jak's nearest hand between both of hers. Jak's heart pounded at Torrin's touch, and Kiera turned to glance at the readout, then looked back at the two of them and rolled her eyes.

"Jak, we need to talk, but not until you've recovered a little more." Kiera looked down at her until she nodded. "You have a whole lot of people who want to talk to you, but I'm not going to let them in until I'm sure that you're in shape to handle it."

"Is it about Tanith?"

"Mostly," Torrin said. "A couple of other things, but mostly her."

Jak tried to sit back up when she remembered some of Tanith's last words to her. Kiera held her down with a hand on her shoulder. It was comically easy for the doctor to hold her down and Jak quit struggling.

"It was all her, Torrin," she said instead. "She did this to me. And what she did to you. And to us." To her horror, her eyes started to fill with tears. She tried to tamp down her emotions. She hadn't cried in front of anyone else since she'd been a little girl. She'd still been Jakellyn the last time that had happened. Torrin wrapped her in a comforting embrace, but instead of that calming her, Jak dissolved into loud, wracking sobs.

"It's okay," Torrin whispered in her ear, hand moving in a soothing pattern between her shoulder blades. "Let it all out. I've got you."

Determined to get her emotions under some semblance of control, Jak brought her hands up to disengage Torrin's soothing hug. As soon as her hands touched Torrin, she found herself pulling her lover closer to her and bawling into her neck. She was powerless to do anything except hold on to Torrin while she sobbed out years of pent-up anguish. The years of concealment, of constant terror of discovery and, more recently, of being bereft of her family, doing it all without anyone to support her. After all she'd been through, the point of light that was Torrin had been guiding her through to a place she could truly belong, and she'd tried to throw it all away. How could she have been so stupid as to believe that Torrin would betray her so?

Through it all, Torrin held her close and murmured low, nonsense words of encouragement. How long she cried, Jak didn't know, but finally her sobs subsided into sniffles until she hung limply from Torrin's embrace, clutching weakly at her shoulders.

"Better?" Torrin asked solicitously. She pushed herself back a bit and ran the pads of her thumbs under Jak's eyes. With a tenderness that threatened to undo Jak all over again, Torrin erased the tracks of years of tears.

"I think so," Jak replied, throat raspy. Embarrassed, she looked around for Kiera, but the doctor was nowhere to be found.

"She'll be back later," Torrin said. "I think she was trying to give us some privacy."

"Johvah, but she must think I'm a mess." Jak sniffled again. Torrin reached out an arm and handed her a box of tissues.

"I doubt that. You've been through enough trauma for three lifetimes, probably more."

"I'm sorry I didn't believe in you. In us."

Torrin shook her head. "It's not your fault. You were set up. We were set up."

"I know, Tanith told me. I think." Jak hesitated. Her memory was so patchy that she wasn't sure how much of what she remembered was reliable.

"What's the matter?"

"Tanith said something. About your old girlfriend. The one who left you without saying goodbye."

Confusion creased Torrin's brow. "You mean Galya? What about her?"

"Tanith killed her. She said something about dumping her in the sand dunes. I think she did it because Galya wouldn't leave you for her."

Shock and horror painted Torrin's face. She stared at Jak, mouth open in a silent O of surprise. She opened and shut her mouth a few times before she could muster anything to say.

"She killed her? But that was almost two decades ago!"

"I think it's what turned her against you. She couldn't accept that someone might choose you over her."

"She always was so damned competitive." Torrin's gaze turned inward for a moment as she searched through her memories. "When we were kids, it was fun, but it started getting really intense when we joined the militia. I usually won most of our contests, but it's not like Tanith always lost. She was always happy to rub it in my face when she got the upper hand in something. I wonder when that changed to resentment." She looked up at Jak, tears in her eyes. Now it was Jak's turn to embrace Torrin and to soothe her as she cried. Jak held her as her shoulders heaved in silent sobs. When she stopped, she pressed a kiss to the side of Jak's neck, then pulled away.

"It's a little funny, you know," Torrin said. "I loved Galya. She was my first love and when she walked out on me, it hurt so much that I decided I'd never let anyone get that close to me again. I mean, getting physically involved was okay, but I couldn't bear to become that emotionally involved with anyone ever again. Until I met you, that is." She gave Jak a watery smile, blinking away the last of her tears. "I love you, Jak. I think I've loved you since before I knew you weren't a man."

Joy so intense it was almost painful shot through Jak. For a moment she forgot to breathe, and all she could do was stare at Torrin. Tears threatened again while something loosened in her chest. For the first time in a long time, she felt like she was finally able to breathe. As she struggled with the intensity of her feelings, Torrin's eyes started clouding with worry. She turned away, agony in her eyes, and Jak still couldn't speak.

Jak reached out and grabbed her wrist before Torrin could stand. The stiffness of Torrin's body betrayed her hurt, and Jak hauled on her arm as hard as she could. She knew she was weak from her recent ordeal, so she put everything she had into it. Torrin collapsed across the bed with a surprised squeak and Jak ripped off her oxygen mask, snapping one of the bands in her haste. Before Torrin could move, Jak fastened her lips over Torrin's. She put every ounce of emotion into kissing Torrin, trying to show her with the passion of her response how deeply she felt.

Her tongue skimmed over Torrin's lip, then dipped hesitantly into her open mouth. Emboldened by the arms that came up to wrap around her neck, she deepened their kiss. She felt like sparks were shooting between the tips of their tongues. One hand gripped Torrin's hair; it was barely long enough for her to get a grip. She tightened her fingers until Torrin moaned into her mouth.

When they came up for air, Torrin stared up at her from where she lay across Jak's thighs.

"I love you too," Jak said in a rush. Joy filled Torrin's eyes. Jak giggled, then blushed at the unfamiliar noise that had come out of her. "I love you," she repeated, watching as joy lit Torrin's face again. The giggle didn't embarrass her at all when it resurfaced a moment later. She grabbed Torrin and crushed her against her chest. "I love you, I love you, I love you."

EPILOGUE

The last of the boxes had been unloaded from the cargo bay. Rudrani cracked open one of the crates and inspected the contents for damage. So far, this hadn't been exactly what Nat had expected to be doing when Torrin had finally unbent enough to allow her to do some work off planet. So far, in fact, this was all awfully, well, work. If she'd wanted to do that, she could have done it on Nadierzda and without the strange stares she and Rudrani got from the Devonites. That wasn't entirely fair. Most of the Devonites had gotten used to her already, but there were still a few who continued to pay them entirely too much mind. Rudrani claimed she would get used to them eventually. Eventually couldn't happen soon enough for her.

"Can you hand me that spanner?" Rudrani asked, hand out, not even looking.

Nat rolled her eyes and walked over to hand the tool to her. Honestly, it had been right there by her. Apparently, she was too lazy to even reach over and take it. She liked Rudrani just fine. More than just fine actually. The two of them had gotten to know each other very well since they'd landed on Haefen. Rudrani was an excellent and attentive lover. She had mentioned that Torrin had threatened her with physical harm if she slept with Nat. It was that as much as the fact that Rudrani was extremely attractive that had sealed the deal for Nat. After hearing that, she'd practically thrown herself at the other woman. Rudrani didn't seem to mind at all, quite the opposite actually. The only problem was that now she acted as if Nat was there solely for her convenience. It was going to take more than a few rolls in the sack to get her to wait on Rudrani hand and foot. If this kept up, she was going to have to cut her loose. There was no rush, however. She could wait until they got back home. The trip home would be very uncomfortable otherwise. And Rudrani really was an amazing lover, no point in letting that go to waste.

"Not that one, the other one," Rudrani said critically. Nat obligingly fetched it for her and calmly handed it over. "There's no need to pout."

"Pout?" Nat was aghast. "I'm not pouting. I'm helping you out."

"The life isn't all fun and games you know. There's a hell of a lot of hard work that goes into what we do. That's why we play so hard. Remember, it's work first, then play."

"I know it's work, believe me. Don't think I've watched my sister all these years to come away with a different idea." She knew Torrin worked hard, but she'd sort of hoped that had meant that she wouldn't have to also. It wasn't that she disliked hard work; it was that she didn't like it when it was boring.

"Glad to hear it." Rudrani had a twinkle in her eye like she didn't believe a word of what had come out of Nat's mouth. "Why don't you start breaking down that other box? The quicker we're done here, the faster we can get on to something more exciting." The heated glance left no doubt what she was implying.

"Consider it done," Nat said and headed to the nearest crate with alacrity. She pried it open with loud squeals and groans as the pseudo-wood resisted her attempts, futilely as it turned out. With a loud pop, the lid finally came off the crate. She stared at the machinery inside, wondering where the instruction manual for all of the wires and parts could be found. Another pop, louder than the one before, caught her attention.

"What was that?" she asked Rudrani. Nat turned and stared uncomprehendingly at the scene unfolding in front of her. Rudrani slumped to her knees, hands around her own throat as blood gushed from a gaping wound. Before Nat could do more than start moving to help her, Rudrani toppled over, eyes glassy and staring. Nat froze in her tracks for a moment, paralyzed. She shook off her paralysis, rushed to the prone woman's side and tried to feel for a pulse. Her neck was a shattered ruin; there was too little left to even check her pulse. Blood pooled from Rudrani's corpse, staining the knees of Nat's pants where she knelt.

That's going to stain, Nat thought fuzzily. *What am I doing?* The last thing she needed to be worried about was the state of her pants. She clamped her hand around Rudrani's neck, trying to stanch the flow of blood. *This can't be happening. What is going on here?*

A stinging pain to the back of her shoulder startled her out of her futile fumbling. She slapped a hand down on her shoulder, smearing Rudrani's blood on her jumpsuit. Her questing fingers encountered a small metal flechette. It stuck out of her flesh. She pulled it out with a grunt and more pain. The tip must have been slightly barbed because it hurt more coming out than it had going in. She stared at it blankly. What in the seven hells was that thing? Her vision blurred out for a moment and she shook her head to clear it. The movement turned into vertigo and she keeled over to land on her side. She tried desperately to push herself up, but her muscles wouldn't cooperate. They were starting to go numb. The paralysis spread quickly and before long she couldn't even blink. As her vision started to disappear into a long tunnel, a pair of boots walked toward her across the forest clearing.

"Yes, I think you'll do just fine." Nat could hear a low voice. It didn't sound like it knew she could hear him. In her head she was screaming, but out loud she couldn't so much as moan. "She'll have to come for you." She felt herself being picked up and had a quick glimpse of the forest floor and Rudrani's body before darkness swallowed her.

Bella Books, Inc.

Women. Books. Even Better Together.

P.O. Box 10543
Tallahassee, FL 32302

Phone: 800-729-4992
www.bellabooks.com

Printed in the USA
CPSIA information can be obtained
at www.ICGtesting.com
JSHW082151140824
68134JS00014B/172